"TOUCH ME," CLINT SAID SOFTLY,
"AND WE BOTH GO UP IN SMOKE."

But his words came too late. She had already touched him lightly on the sleeve. She found herself in his arms.

"I warned you," he murmured into her hair. "We both know what happens when we touch." Mourning shivered as she became intensely aware of each throbbing movement of his body against hers, every stroking caress of his fingers. Her obligatory resistance was going the way of a snowball in Hades.

His kiss was not the kiss of a gentleman, but a bold, insolent assault on her mouth that both intrigued and frightened her. Just for a moment they were two fiery people, the hotspur and the firebrand, hurled together by a ruling passionate hunger that conquered all reason.

MY ENEMY, MY LOVE

ELAINE COFFMAN

A DELL BOOK

Published by
Dell Publishing
a division of
Bantam Doubleday Dell
Publishing Group, Inc.
666 Fifth Avenue
New York, New York 10103

ISBN: 0-440-20284-1
Special Dell Edition

Printed in the United States of America
Published simultaneously in Canada

March 1989
10 9 8 7 6 5 4 3 2
KRI

With much love to my daughter, Lesley, who started it all

 # PROLOGUE

Fate leads the willing, and drags
along the reluctant.
Seneca, *Letters to Lucilius* (1st c.)

"Aunt Harriet, can you tell me how it is that a person can wait for something, forever it seems, without it ever coming to pass, and then, just about the time you've decided it won't ever happen, it does?"

Harriet Ragsdale held the wooden spoon aloft, as if to emphasize the point she was about to make, and then opened her mouth. She promptly closed it. She didn't, she quickly discovered, have an answer for that particular question . . . just as she rarely had an answer for any of the questions her niece, Mourning Howard, put before her.

Harriet looked at her niece, her golden head bent over the letter she had read and reread, for what must be the umpteenth time since it had been delivered last week. "Land's sake, do you sleep with that wee scrap of paper? It seems that it's become permanently affixed to your body since the day your Uncle Francis handed it to you. I don't know why you bother to re-read it. With your faculties, it was committed to memory by the second reading, or I miss my guess."

"I just can't figure it out," Mourning said, folding the letter and tucking it away in the pocket of her apron. "Why didn't Mama come for me herself?"

Staring at Mourning had long been a favorite pastime of Harriet's—not because she was beautiful, for she was, and not because the things she said were terribly clever, and they were. No, it was simply because the girl was a paradox—all frailty and strength, sense and nonsense, mixed with a gentle sort of wildness. She was different, not seeing things as others did, going at life with the dedicated seriousness of a child at play.

Harriet smiled as she studied her niece. There she sat, her dress immaculate, her apron without a blemish, her person delicately perched on the kitchen stool, her chin cradled in her hands, a puzzled expression on her face. Nothing wrong there, but Harriet knew Mourning's exterior was wont to suffer, at times, the consequences of her wild and willful spirit. By dusk Mourning would be as disheveled as that pair of Francis's long johns left on the clothesline during that storm last spring—the one that sent the Mississippi on a flooding rampage.

"I just don't understand it," Mourning said again, and Harriet could tell by the glazed expression on her face that Mourning's mind was miles away—possibly as far away as Texas. As Harriet considered her niece, she felt a swelling of affection for this daughter of her only sister. Allowing her own mind to drift a few miles off course, Harriet ventured to put herself in Caroline's place, but even then she was unable to find an explanation. Why didn't Caroline come for Mourning, instead of sending John's son?

Of course Caroline wrote all that nonsense about the son's going to St. Louis on business, and how convenient it would be for him to stop in Memphis the last week in April—on his way back to Texas—but Harriet wasn't convinced. Caroline should have come herself. It wasn't as if Texas was a hard trip, coming or going—not that she'd ever taken the trip, of course. Heavens! Texas couldn't be more than a short float on the Mississippi, a quick paddle in the Gulf, and a fast hop to San Antonio. Any fool knew the difficult thing about Texas wasn't getting there . . . it was living there.

"I simply can't believe she expects me to go all the way to Texas with a total stranger," Mourning was saying. A vision of the stranger leaped to the front of her mind, dreadful and quite foreboding, like the outrider of gloom. Just how many intimidating adjectives could she rightfully apply to this unknown person? The possibilities were endless. She sighed impatiently, growing tired of her gallows humor.

When Harriet detected the morose air that had settled over Mourning like a dusting of too much talcum powder, laughter threatened to get the better of her, but she did some fast thinking and said, "Perhaps she doesn't see him as a *total stranger.*"

"Not to her maybe, but I've never laid eyes on the man. I scarcely remember John Kincaid. The last time I saw him was four years ago, when he married Mama."

"Caroline did mention a chaperone, Mourning . . . and you know your Uncle Francis has been looking. He'll find someone, I'm sure. Don't fret. It will all work out tolerably. You're worrying about things before they happen."

"What's the point in worrying about something after it happens?"

Harriet opened her mouth and closed it again. She did that a lot around this young relative of hers. Mourning was just too clever for her own good. "You've got to remember . . ."

". . . That there isn't any point in scratching where it doesn't itch," Mourning finished. "Aunt Harriet, do you think it was a mistake for Mama to leave me here?"

"Certainly not!" Harriet answered, without having to think upon it. "What other choice did she have? You still had some schooling to finish, and God only knows where you'd find an education in a jumping-off place like Texas . . . backward as they come . . . full of savages and misfits. Back then it hadn't been a state long enough to get a spot on the map—still hasn't if you ask me. Besides, you were just too young."

"I wasn't exactly a lap baby. I'd been off sugar tits for years."

"Like I said, you were a gawky fourteen. . . . Why, it's just been the last year or two that you've feathered out some, much to my relief. You were always way too thin."

"Mama said I get that from Papa. He was tall and slim, wasn't he? And good-looking to boot?"

Harriet smiled. Since Mourning was knee-high to a grasshopper, she had taken every opportunity to steer conversations toward the physical attributes of Clay Howard. Poor little mite, deprived of a papa like she was. If Clay Howard wasn't already dead, Harriet would've considered throttling the man. "He wasn't body-modest if that's what you mean. . . . Oh, you've heard all that before," Harriet said with a wave of her hand, as if dismissing the subject. But then she saw the impish grin on Mourning's face, and Harriet sighed. "Yes, Clay Howard was tall as a reed and willow-slim, and better-looking than a body had a right to be. But I've told you before and I'll say it again: He was a damn fool, going and getting himself killed like that, with your poor mama expecting you like she was."

Mourning wanted to ask Aunt Harriet if she meant to imply that it would have been all right for her papa to go and get himself killed, so long as he did it after she was born; but she knew if she got Aunt Harriet all riled up, she would never get answers to the questions she had.

"His dying like that almost killed Caroline," Harriet went on. "I never thought you'd be born to draw a breath, but you had something else to say about that, I guess. And now, here you are, all grown up, out of school, and getting ready to leave your family."

"That's what I was talking about, Aunt Harriet. That's what I don't understand. When Mama first left I was so lonesome for her . . . I thought the time for me to join her would never come. But the last year or so I've been having second thoughts. *This* is my home. I love it here. I love all of you. You're my family. I don't want to leave. Of course I want to see Mama, but I'm not so sure I want to live in Texas. I'm not sure why anyone would want to."

Harriet certainly saw the wisdom behind those words, but she knew it was her duty to encourage Mourning. Caroline depended upon it. "It was decided a long time ago that you would go . . . before Caroline accepted John's proposal and made the decision to live with him in Texas. She loved John, but she wouldn't have married him if she wasn't confident the two of you would be back together in a few years. It was as hard for her to leave you as it was for her to accept Clay's death. Your refusing to go would break your mama's heart. She's waited for this moment a long time."

"I know, but . . . Oh, I don't know what's wrong with me. I guess I'm just nervous about going to a strange place with a strange man and living with strange people."

"Didn't you say you remembered John Kincaid?"

"Of course I do. I remember him, but I don't *know* him. I remember I liked him very much . . . more than anyone else that came courting Mama."

Harriet snorted. "Maybe that's because he *was* the only one. At least the only one Caroline let hang around long enough to be introduced. All the others she chased off with a broom."

"Did Mama ever mention anything about John's son in any of her letters?"

"Just that he had two sons. I think it's the older one that's coming for you."

"I know," Mourning said with a glum tone.

Harriet's face illuminated with sudden understanding. "Is that why you're so apprehensive?"

"I don't know. I feel like I'm sitting on the anxious bench. I'm just uneasy. I wish this wasn't happening to me. I don't know why."

"Try looking at it as a wonderful new experience."

Mourning tried, but that made her more fidgety. How many times had Uncle Francis said, *Experience is bought with trouble*? And how many times had he said, *Mourning Kathleen, your middle name is trouble . . . Trouble with a capital T*?

Seeing her words were not very persuasive, Harriet tried another approach. "Just remember, being uneasy for no reason is no more than the little end of nothing whittled down to a fine point. It's the unknown that's making you so troubled."

There's that word again. Trouble. Another nail driven into her coffin.

Harriet laughed at the glum-faced girl. "Honest to goodness, Mourning, stop looking for scorpions under every rock. I'm sure John's son is just as delightful and charming as his father, and once he arrives you'll see there was no need for you to be so concerned. No reason at all."

PART
ONE

The young are permanently in a
state resembling intoxication; for
youth is sweet and they are growing.
Aristotle, *Nicomachean Ethics*

**April 1860
Memphis, Tennessee**

He was out cold.

She could tell by the way he lay sprawled on his face in the hay. He was no threat now . . . this devil dressed in black. Whatever he was going to steal was safe.

He had come down off the ridge from the south, out of a whirlwind that carried the smell of rain, riding a stud the color of the darker side of the sun.

Panic was an emotion new to the girl who stood watching, shadowed by the dark screen of trees at the edge of the wood. For what seemed an endless stretch of time she could not move, startled into immobility by the dark shape that appeared like temptation, from out of nowhere. So much in tune were they—horse and rider—that it was difficult to tell where one stopped and the other began. A shiver ran down her spine as a man as beautiful as sin dismounted before the barn. She felt as if she had been touched by the serpent. Now she understood the lure of the apple. *How art thou fallen from heaven, O Lucifer, son of the morning . . .*

Her heart began to pound furiously, her alarm turning to anger. He led his horse into the dimness of the barn.

Dropping her basket, the girl followed him. The pale light at dusk cast long shadows and she waited for her eyes to adjust. Without moving, she listened until the soft hollow sound of hooves stepping lightly on the moist humus floor ceased. It came then, the creak of leather, the jingle of a cinch buckle, the sudden grunt of someone carrying a burden. He was removing his saddle. He intended to steal a fresh horse!

She moved along the row of stalls, quick and silent, past the soft breathing of horses, slipping into deeper shadows. She could see him now, faint and gray in the failing light some five feet away. His chestnut stallion snorted and tossed his head, his headstall gleaming in the dimness as if studded with silver. He led the stallion into a stall, removed the bridle, and turned, shutting the door behind him with a click.

The stranger slung the bridle over his shoulder, moving with stalking sureness until he stopped at the stall of Pegasus, the pride of Windy Hill. "Well, now, you're a fine one, aren't you?" he said with a compelling voice. He scratched the blood bay stallion and laughed when Pegasus tried to pull something from his pocket. "No you don't. This is my last pouch of tobacco," he said as he reached for the latch on the stall. "Let's have a better look at you —with those legs I bet you can run like the very devil."

A black shadow seemed to pass overhead, like the portentous croak of a raven, filling her with a fierce and eager will to protect. She could not let him steal Pegasus. There was no finer-bred stud in the state of Tennessee. Feeling panic rising inside her, she did not hesitate a moment longer, but began to search for something— anything—to use as a weapon. Her eyes lingered for a moment on a pitchfork abandoned in a rick of hay, then moved on . . . not even a thief deserved that. Her gaze drifted around the barn—over the crescent blade of a scythe, past the curved iron plate of a moldboard plow, ignoring the jagged teeth of a crosscut saw, passing quickly over the handle of a pickax. She paused, her eyes backtracking for a moment; then her small unsteady hand closed over the broken handle of the ax.

She kept her eye on the back of the stranger's dark head as she stepped noiselessly behind him, bringing the handle down with all her might. A sickening crack. A muffled groan. His body slumped, then fell. The stallion beside him reared and stomped nervously, tossing his head, his delicate nostrils flaring, eyes rolling wildly. But he was safe. Whoever the stranger was, he would not ride Pegasus this day.

The girl was small, slender, and golden-haired with eyes the color of a lazy, moss-filled pond in late summer, but she wielded an ax handle with the dexterity of someone much larger. Her dainty appearance was suggestive of a fragile porcelain figurine, all magnolia blossoms and ecru lace, spiced with the scent of potpourri. There was nothing about the small angelic beauty that would suggest the wild spirit of a peregrine falcon and the mischievous nature of a ring-tailed coon, both of which she embodied. Earlier in the day her hair had been bound neatly on top of her head, and her dress pressed and clean, but the tortoiseshell combs had long since disappeared, and her dress was now smudged and wrinkled.

It was this imperfect image of southern femininity that stood staring down at the stranger. The thief was still overpowering, even while unconscious. An uneasiness gripped her and she glanced at the body before her. He lay unnaturally still. Had she killed him?

The gray light of late afternoon began to fade, and shadows inside the barn grew long and thin. Within her, curiosity and some strange unnamable emotion struggled with the desire to run and hide.

A chilling gust of wind rattled across the rafters overhead; the herald of a spring rainstorm. It would be dark soon and she was alone, here, with this man . . . this thief . . . or worse.

He had not moved, this darkly clad stranger with hair as black as pitch. Even in repose he looked deadly. She lit a nearby lantern, more to chase out the gloom than to give light. The blush of amber flame cast a golden luster across a chiseled profile that was already heavily bronzed.

"What kind of thief are you?" she said, knowing he couldn't hear, but needing the sound of a human voice, even if it was her own.

He wasn't an ordinary thief, she could tell that much—not dressed the way he was. A black broadcloth frock coat and tight black trousers hugged the contours of his muscled torso and long, well-defined legs. His boots were of supple leather and fitted him to perfection. He was a powerfully built man, tall and perfectly proportioned. Black hair, black clothes, black boots; the epitome of darkness and evil. A shiver passed over her. All too aware of what she had just done, she considered her options.

She could tie him up. . . . But what if he woke up while she was tying him? Besides, she really couldn't bring herself to touch him anyway—he was far too sinister. Perhaps she should go to the house for a gun. . . . But what if he came to, surprising her when she returned? No. It was best to stay right here and guard him until help arrived, and she fervently prayed that would be soon.

She heard a faint moan, then the crackle and snap of newly cured hay. The man stirred. Her thoughts vanished as panic covered her like perspiration. It came again, the rustle of dry hay, the hissing vigor of labored breathing. A garbled sound tore from the stranger's throat, then faded. A fearful silence hung like an icy chill to the heart, a nightmare to the soul. With the sluggish movement of one roused from profound sleep, the man strained to lift his head, quickly checked the impulse, and fell back, lying unnaturally still. Minutes passed in silence.

She stood alone, just behind him, bathed in purple shadows and pale light, watching in a witless sort of way. His long-shanked body looked hard and aggressively masculine against his bed of sun-bleached hay. She felt her limbs stiffen with expectancy as her eyes collected particulars: the dark, glossy hair that curled in a manner a woman would covet, the lean hardness of muscle, the perfect symmetry of elongated bone, the startling contrast between broadness of blade and slimness of flank. Who was he?

Her heart thumped madly as she imagined what could happen if he were to wake before help arrived. *Thank you, Lord, that he is unconscious, and please keep him that way,* she thought, praying her blow had been strong enough to keep him out . . . just in case God was too busy to intervene.

But God was occupied at the moment, so the long form sprawled before her stirred once more. With painful deliberation he lifted his dark head. The logjam in her brain cleared and with it came sudden realization. He would soon be on his feet—injured, angry, and dangerous. Like a long-tailed cat in a roomful of rocking chairs, she was nervous.

A moan, mixed with slurred syllables and garbled words. Then the body before her shifted as if it would rise. "Christ! What the hell hit me?"

They say the simplest words convey the greatest message, and she was having no difficulty receiving the one he sent. Choking tendrils of fear crept over her, and she found herself dissolving in regret—not so much in remorse for what she'd done, but more in fear of what he'd do when he found out. Somehow, in solving one problem by clobbering him, she had created a new one of even greater proportions. What *does* one do with a man one has just knocked senseless? With acute foreboding she remembered her grandmother's words: *It is indeed a bold mouse that breeds in the cat's ear.*

Her thoughts were all going in circles. Something had to be done, and quickly. But what? *Oh, why is thinking such hard work?* She didn't have an answer for that, but fondness for sleeping in a whole skin prompted her to action. *Run!* But before the message could be put to action an outrageous quantity of excitatory secretions surged into her blood. She froze.

A shudder traversed the stranger's body and he shook his head as if to clear his jumbled thoughts. Feeling the searing pressure of panic, she raised the ax handle higher, preparing to deliver another blow.

It never came.

Her feet were jerked from under her, hurling her backward. An instant later a solid weight made painful contact with her body, driving the air from her lungs as the weight rode her down, slamming her into the hay with unbelievable force. She went wild beneath him, arching, clawing, striking out in pain and fear, futilely trying to dislodge him. Desperate to protect herself, she sank her teeth into human flesh. She heard a muffled curse. Then she was thrust away from him. Hard fingers dug into her soft arms, and a hand clamped over her face, muffling her screams and halting the flow of air. Panic driving her, she fought against his suffocating hand, desperate to breathe. As she felt consciousness slipping away from her, a harsh voice laced with pain ordered: "Hold still, damn you."

Her self-preserving instinct seizing control, she yielded to the greater force. The constricting bands around her were immediately loosened. Long and raspy, her indrawn breath was broken by spasms of coughing as she inhaled deeply. Rough bits of straw scraped against her face as she lay beneath his crushing weight, panting, trembling, and frightened. She no longer had any thoughts of escape.

"Good Godamighty . . . a woman." The moment his hand brushed against something resilient and soft he knew he had a woman under him—and a damn fine feeling one at that. There were some things about a woman you could identify by touch, and the ample breast beneath his hand was one helluva way to do just that. It was one thing to be knocked out colder than a cucumber, and quite another to wake up with a big warm breast beneath your fingers. And it *was* a breast. There was no denying that. He glanced down, trying to see if she looked as good as she felt, but her face was covered with a snarled mass of yellow hair mixed with hay.

The girl lay rigid and unyielding beneath him. With the return of her reason came the knowledge that lying perfectly still was her only assurance against sure suffocation by the hand that held her tighter than rabbitskin glue.

In obvious pain, and compassionate as the monarch of hell, the man smiled sardonically. "It's the habit of the snared," he said, in a coldly savage voice, "to fossilize when the predator is near. Lying there quaking like a one-winged moth won't save you now. Tell me, girl, why did you crack my skull?"

Whatever clarity remained in her brain began to dissipate as fear advanced with the taste of bittern. Seconds ticked by and she awaited her fate at the bottom of the carnivores' food chain. She looked into cold gray eyes as her warm tears ran in meandering little streams into the wilds of her hair.

The man returned her stare, without pity or even understanding, while the lamplight played about his face.

"Tears," he said in a dangerous tone, "are the ape of virtue and a poor substitute for valor. I'll ask you just once more for the reason behind the clubbing." Viselike hands dug into her arms and he shook her hard. "Well?"

She blinked, then stared with fright, into a pair of seething silver eyes surrounded by a sun-darkened face that looked more than capable of murder. Her galloping heart bolted, seeking refuge behind her chicken-liver as she continued to cry.

Indifferently, he studied her. He spoke with a rapier-sharp edge to his voice. "A good philosophy: When all else fails, cry. Tell me, angel, do you have any other resources available? Speech perhaps?" His eyes drifted from her face to a point that, if not her bosom, was uncomfortably close. With the sensuous move of a stretching jungle cat his eyes traveled slowly back to her face.

Humiliation laced with embarrassment tinged her pale, flawless skin with the faintest kiss of color. Where was the spirit and spunk of the girl who, moments before, had cold-cocked this horse thief? And why would she, the daredevil of Shelby County, suddenly turn chicken? One glance at his hard face answered that readily enough.

Recognizing a pickle when she was in one, she realized that her immediate problem was not saving the pride of Windy Hill, but taking charge of her fate and extricating herself, painlessly if possible, from this scoundrel's clutches. A somewhat nervous evaluation of her situation produced one revelation: Recognizing a problem is one thing, solving it is a horse of a different color. *You stupid, stupid girl,* she told herself. *What are you going to do?* Unhappily, she didn't have an idea at the moment, but prayed one would be coming along any minute now. Desperate, she covered her face with small trembling hands.

"Another clever move," he said. "Am I supposed to run and hide while you count to ten?" He pried her hands away from her face. "You must have a speech problem, angel," he said coldly, "or could it be your hearing?" In the space of an instant he let her know he would tolerate no more silence. "Whatever the problem, you'd better have it corrected by the time I repeat myself. Why?"

It wasn't much of a question, as far as questions go, but packed into that one word was more well-phrased content than what lay between the covers of Encyclopaedia Britannica.

Infusing her gelatinous backbone with starch, she spoke hastily before the look from those hot eyes melted her resolve faster than a candle in a firebed. "I thought you were going to steal Pegasus," she said.

"Who the hell is Pegasus?" he asked, his words erupting like a volley of cannon fire. He kept his eyes locked with hers. "Don't try to divert me by saying something cute either . . . I *know* mythology."

There was a discreet silence. Then, "He's the stallion you were looking at when I hit you." She felt herself cringe at having to bring that up again. "What were you doing here in the barn if you weren't going to steal something?"

Contemptuous eyes swept over her, one arrogant brow rose. "I'll ask the questions."

With his black hair spiked with hay, he still possessed one of those arresting faces she would have to describe as beautiful—wholly masculine, but beautiful nonetheless. She swallowed hard.

"Why the lamentable look, sweetheart? Don't you have an answer?" Judging from the way she stood her ground, the girl could not know just how absurd she looked with her false bravado. All puffed up like a blowfish with a penitent spirit. "I suppose your sudden remorse is to be expected," he said with a hint of amusement. "All criminals turn preacher when faced with the firing squad."

At the mention of a firing squad, she made a small, terrified whimper and wondered how she could have been so foolish as to actually think she could sidetrack the devil.

On his face, lying flat in the hay, he had been formidable. Looming above her like an approaching avalanche, he was a thing of epic proportions. A trembling quiver of fear shivered down her backbone at the same instant a stabbing coil of attraction wrenched her insides. From a face like his, legends were born—as well as a few indecent thoughts. If she were going to put a face and body on the archangel Gabriel, this man possessed it. Just thinking about that steamed up everything from her brain cells to her toes.

"The weapon," he rapped sharply, "the one you used . . . what was it . . . a wagon tongue?"

Dare I tell him? she asked herself. *Dare you not?* came the reply. "An ax handle," she answered, her eyes drifting to the ax handle lying where she'd dropped it. His eyes tracked hers, lingered for a moment, then returned to her face, impaling her with an icy stare. If he was looking for a successful way to intimidate her, he'd found it. Feeling the urgent press of a few things other than justification, she said quickly, "Will you get off me?"

"Will you answer my question?"

"If you stop mashing me to a pulp. I can't breathe. How can you expect me to talk?"

"Your mouth's been flapping like laundry for the past five minutes. Why the sudden change?"

"Are you going to let me up, or not?"

"Be quiet, angel, or I'll find a reason to keep you here." Something flickered in his gray eyes and she knew then, he was not going to let her up.

It came as a surprise when he released her, rolling his weight from her body. "You move, and you're flat on your back again," he said, knowing that was all the threat he needed to hold her.

"May I sit up?" He waved his hand as if saying *be my guest.* She sat up quickly, pulling bits of hay and hair from her face.

"What? No answers? Ah, sweetheart, if you miss our close companionship, I'll be glad to rectify my mistake immediately."

His voice was soft and detached, the way she imagined he

would sound if giving instructions on how to skin a polecat. She wanted to take that soft, detached voice and beat him over the head with it, but he looked about two shakes away from pouncing. "I thought you were a horse thief."

He considered her for a moment. "I'm no thief," he said, "and suspicion is no reason to kill a man."

She reminded him that he was still breathing, and he gave her an inclined look that poured over her like drawn butter.

"We don't take too kindly to thieves or nosy drifters around here," she said, her eyes on him. *What madness ever possessed me to wish for a strong man I couldn't control?* If she got out of this scrape with her hide intact, she would be forever devoted to weak-minded men.

He was sitting, at the most, two feet away from her; and feeling safe from this distance, she glanced at his dark face, forgetting that lightning can strike from very far away. His expression was intent, powerful, and oh so readable. There, behind the soft seduction of those eyes bathing her in a sunny warmth lay the promise of sweet beguiling answers to every erotic question unimaginable—and mysteries unbelievable, unthinkable, and more than likely unperformable. She'd be willing to bet he knew the why and wherefore of things she couldn't entertain a conjecture of if she lived till shrimps learned to whistle. Feeling like one who has leaped into the lake but doesn't know how to swim, she shuddered involuntarily, her eyes squeezing shut, her head dropping to her chest.

"You're too damn stubborn to swoon, so don't think you can play me for a fool," he warned.

Her head came up, her eyes were wide and searching his steadily. "You may be right to call me stubborn, and you're not the first to do so, but in saying I play you for a fool, you err. I may be stubborn, but I'm not stupid."

"I've seen no proof of that," he said.

"What you consider stupidity is only . . ."

He waited, the moment spinning longer and longer, yet she remained silent. "Your stupidity is only what?"

"Fear," she said, seeing the shock of surprise spread across his face.

≈ 2

Wondering if perhaps he was at the wrong place, the stranger asked, "This *is* the Ragsdale Plantation?"

"Yes."

"Do you live here?"

"Yes."

"Where's your master?"

She blinked at him. "My master?"

"Your master, my sweet simpleton, would be the person who owns this plantation and pays your salary."

She blinked again in confusion. "My salary?" Had the blow she'd delivered to his head addled his wits?

"Hellfire! This conversation is going nowhere fast. One round of questions with you goes in more damn circles than a spinning top." He scowled at her, his head still making a few revolutions. "You do know what a top is, don't you—that cute conical device that spins on a steel-shod point?"

He was staring at her with an intensity that made her feel a few points below stupid. She hesitated, then her irritation, as it usually did, got the better of her common sense. "I am familiar with the *toy* you speak of. Have you lost yours?"

She had an inkling that restraint did not come easily to this man, for his entire body screamed irritation, his hands clenching in a manner suggesting a powerful desire to be placed around her neck. Having acquired a pretty fair grasp of the somewhat monstrous if not twisted complexity of his mind, she decided to jump before she was pushed. "I don't work here," she said, her throat closing with the involuntary gulp that comes after being force-fed castor oil.

She wasn't convinced that he wasn't a thief, but she knew one thing—unequivocally, he was a breed of man she was unaccustomed to. There was no decorous behavior, no soft and lilting speech, no glorious and dignified respect for her gender. Not one drop of the milk of human kindness flowed through his veins. He was everything a well-bred man was not: a resolute barbarian, wholly uncivilized, offensive, and basely crude. His language was atrocious and unfit for a lady's ears, his manners despicable—belonging in a barnyard—and his bearing bordered on debauchery. Any woman would be a fool to give him a second glance. She looked at him again.

His eyes traveled across her face, not with cold indifference, but lingering on each detail with the heated devotion of a man with an appreciative eye for feminine flesh. The hot weight of his eyes on her mouth . . . *Lord! Is this what it's like to be kissed?* she wondered. *Only better?* She watched him across the short space that separated them, feeling her senses peppered by diversions, as if she could still feel the gentle caress of his breath stirring more than the soft curls on her face. It was frightening, this new realm of perception, these new emotions not guided by reason. The onslaught left her uncertain and beguiled, unable to respond normally.

"You may not work here, but it's apparent you're not the lady of the house. Who are you?" he said. "Some poor orphaned relative?"

"Poor orphaned relative?" she repeated, her brow creasing in puzzlement.

"Damn! My brains have been addled by a half-wit! I'll see if I can phrase it simple enough for even your inadequate mind. If you don't work here . . . and it's obvious you aren't the lady of the house . . . what the hell are you doing patrolling the premises like some three-headed dragon?" Immediately his face lit up with understanding. "Of course," he said with new insight, "you're here for the amusement and companionship of one Francis Ragsdale. You're his mistress, is that it?"

It was the last straw, an insult past tolerating. He had thrown her to the hay, crushed the life out of her, cursed like a fieldhand,

and now had the unmitigated gall to call her a mistress. Eyes shimmering with tears, she stammered, "What kind of monster are you to even suggest such a thing? I would never . . ."

He saw the horrified expression in her eyes and interpreted it correctly. "Spare me your incessant chatter expounding your virtue," he said. She started to speak, but he cut her off. "I know, I know, I've shredded your reputation and defiled your honorable name. Tell me, angel, have you ever bedded a man?"

She spoke with that puzzled softness compounded of confusion and distraction. "Not by myself, but I helped my aunt once."

"Hellfire and damnation . . . I didn't know it could be a family undertaking." He smiled then, looking at her with an expression that wavered between tolerance and disbelief. "I have a very lurid imagination, but the vast possibilities of what you've just suggested escapes even my creative powers." He considered her a moment, humor playing about the corners of his mouth. "So . . . you helped your aunt bed a man, did you?" He gave her a lazy smile of admiration, considerably warmer than its predecessor. "Tell me, sweet . . . how, exactly, did you manage to do that?"

She looked at him as if she were convinced fools grew without watering. "It was quite simple," she said in that breathless little way she had, thinking surely no one could be so dense. "My aunt's cousin, who happens to be a man, was kicked by a horse and I helped her put him to bed."

His entire body relaxed, and one corner of his mouth tilted up in a rather charming, lopsided manner. Then a smile that would have knocked the most celebrated beauty in Memphis flat on her bustle spread across his face. "You," he said honestly, "are either functioning with half a brain or you're undeniably innocent. Tell me, angel, which is it?" Seeing her blank face, he added, "What I want to know is . . . have you ever done anything with a man that could make you pregnant? You do know where babies come from, don't you?"

She felt sick. Her usual headlong lack of caution had once again put her in a vulnerable position. "I didn't just get off the boat," she said, glaring at him. *Please, dear God, don't let him ask me that again.*

"Well? Have you ever been on a belly ride?"

She tried her best to form a mental picture of that, her eyes almost crossing from the effort. But it was no use. Mental pictures didn't seem to be forming. She directed an angry glare toward heaven. *Thanks,* she mumbled under her breath. *What fool said, If God doesn't give what we want, he gives what we need? I need this?* For the first time in her eighteen years she questioned the workings of divinity.

"Don't answer," he said. "I have other ways of finding out."

They say the heart's letter is read in the eyes . . . and he was sending her a billet-doux that would scorch the paper it was written on. She was green as gourds, as far as men were concerned, but a plastered wall could read the intent in those hot eyes.

"You have the morals of a jar of slop," she said. "I'd rather die than have you touch me." She rose to her knees, forgetting his threat and the consequences if she moved.

It happened so fast, she had no time to react. A hand shot out, clamping her wrist, yanking her around and jerking her into his arms. It was at this point she realized that, for the second time that day, a body was pressing her back against the hay.

Feeling the sting of tears, she moved her hands to push against his chest. Beneath her fingers she could feel the restraining wall of muscle that surrounded a heart beating with irritation.

"Dammit! Hold still!"

Scorched but not defeated, she was gaining momentum like a rolling snowball. What had transpired between them, instead of making her submit, made her more stalwart in revolt. Every intolerable insult she had suffered made her anger more instant and furious. Like her prideful South, convinced she was right, she was determined to the last drop of her blood to defend her honorable person, regardless of the opposition. She was one angry, defiant woman.

She bucked again, hoping she jarred his arrogant brains. She had, and the face before her loomed ominous and dark. "I'm warning you . . ."

Apparently unaware that a woman and glass are ever in danger, she replied, "What else can you do besides curse and make threats? You better guess again if you think your words are going to frighten me." Spitefully, she wiggled again.

He contemplated showing her just what other things he could do. His head pounding, his patience tried, he looked down for a moment at the snarled ball of yellow fluff with the sizzling green eyes that were shooting daggers through him. For some perverse reason he found what he saw enchanting, and that irritated him. Then he made another startling discovery: The man who desires a woman that irritates the living hell out of him is supremely frustrated. And that made him speak with more anger than he actually felt. "For your benefit," he said succinctly, "I will repeat myself once, and only once." He paused, and then phrased the words with great care: "Keep . . . your . . . lily . . . white . . . ass . . . still!"

Her mouth dropped faster than ripened fruit. They eyed each other, each one looking for a place to drive the fatal shot. His head was splitting and he wanted answers to some questions. Her nerves were frazzled and she wished she'd hit him harder. They were like two cats thrown over a fence with their tails tied together. Every time one moved it caused the other discomfort. Lamentable though it was, she was too angry to see the flash of compassionate admiration in his eyes for what it was. Honest.

A disturbing smile curled across his lips. "What's the matter, sweetheart? You afraid I'm going to toss your skirts?"

Her heart, which had been pounding furiously, crashed to her feet. She was too nervous, too frightened, and too inexperienced to artfully evade the bluntness of this brute with any finesse. "Toss my skirts?" she repeated, thinking surely he didn't mean literally.

"Rape," he said, feeling as deranged as she was from the thrill he received in scaring the overstarched drawers off her.

She gave him a sour look. "It crossed my mind."

"A short trip, obviously."

Her flayed skin burned under the prick of his amusement, while her bewildered constitution considered another alternative. Feeling the stinging swell of tears behind her eyes, she discovered how hopelessly embarrassing it felt to be bested by a man.

The stranger studied the delicate face, the tightly held mouth that tried in vain to quell its own trembling. The thought that he could have pushed her too far lingered like the afterburn of a slap. Intuition told him that overriding her fear was a spirit that would push her to fight to the finish. Any other time he would have given her a run for her money, but right now his head was hurting like a son of a bitch. "Don't worry," he said, "I'm not going to rape you . . . at least I don't think I am."

The darkening shadows within the barn lent sharp outline to the beauty of her face, but it was her hair that held his attention.

He had never seen hair so fair, or so curly. This woman's hair had not been crimped; it crinkled and curled as tightly as the wool on a newborn lamb, and of its own accord. He lifted his hand to rub the back of his knuckles across the fresh texture of her cheek. Her eyes, as they watched him, held the soft impatience of a little creature nuzzling for its milk. *Little mouse, if that look was meant to distract me, it's doing the trick, but I'm not too sure you want my thoughts headed in the direction they seem to be taking.* He closed his eyes, sorry that he was putting her through this cat-and-mouse routine—ready to wring her neck one minute, wanting to feel her body respond with passion the next. He opened his eyes slowly, making no attempt to hide the sleepy, heavy-lidded look. "No," he said, his words gently spoken against fragrant curls, "I'm not going to rape you. . . . Perhaps I'd settle for a kiss."

"Either way I lose."

His face darkened with annoyance, but his voice still maintained that tone of mocking sarcasm that made her want to slap his arrogant face. "You sound like a woman lacking experience in either."

The look she gave him declared her innocence, but she was too beautiful to be that. "Innocence or guile?" he said, then paused. "I wonder if it's possible?" He closed his eyes, unable to distinguish if it was due to the dull throb in his head or his overriding impulses. When he opened them, he focused on her face, as if considering something for a moment, then he answered his own question. "No," he said, "not innocence. Not with a face like that." A tapered finger trailed from the point of her temple to follow the curve of her lips. "Poor buttercup. It doesn't matter anyway." He laughed a low, husky chuckle. "No, don't look like a skinned rabbit. You're safe for now. Thanks to this rumbling in my head."

The heat of his body was burning a hole through her and she squirmed beneath him. A blue flame flared in his eyes. "Have a care, girl, I'm no eunuch."

She endured his dissecting gaze because she was afraid if she said anything he would put her in a more uncomfortable position than the one she was already in—an absurd idea, really, for as far as uncomfortable positions went, this one was in a league all by itself.

She cast an eye up at him, and what she saw made her draw in a sharp breath. A fool could see what he was thinking, what he intended to do. He was going to kiss her!

It wasn't the idea of a kiss that worried her. She had been kissed before—sloppy youthful pecks on the mouth, chaste kisses on her cheek, even a fairly long, inexperienced kiss from a childhood beau who pressed his tight dry lips against hers until they both collapsed with laughter. But this was no laughing matter. This was no callow youth experimenting behind the smokehouse. This was Adam *after* the apple, all full of knowledge and information. And that frightened her. *Apples . . . temptation . . . sin . . .* She knew what happened to Eve, skipping around Eden buck-naked.

"You don't have to look like a scalded cat. It's been years since I throttled my last woman," he said with a deepening smile.

"Why are you doing this?" The words croaked from her dry throat as she pushed against unsympathetic chest muscles. What little energy she possessed was spent on that tiny protest. Not a thimbleful of resistance remained. "I'm sorry I hit you. It was an honest mistake. If you had any feelings at all, you'd let me up."

"Oh, I have feelings," he said, his gaze following the velvet line of throat to the rise and fall of generous breasts, "and they are functioning perfectly."

He did something quite delicious with his hips as he spoke, and that was the spark that revived her. Suddenly finding the spunk she was famous for, she said hotly, "If you value that homespun hide of yours, you'll let me up."

Showing no surprise, he said, "My, my, now we're cutting our teeth on threats. Should I consider that an advancement in stupidity, or a retreat in logic?" He had planned to say more, but the tempting little filly beneath him bucked like her first saddling, sending fragmented shards of glassy pain shooting through the top of his skull. "Damn your eyes! Be still!"

She stared up at him, wide-eyed. His furious grimace struck fearful defiance to her very soul. He spoke under his breath, saying what he'd like to do to her. Thankfully she was unable to understand that indistinct garble of words. He cursed again, and roughly jerked both of her hands above her head, locking them in one clenched fist as he clamped his other hand upon her overproductive mouth. It tasted like sweat, leather, and horse. She squirmed and mumbled against his hand, trying to expel it along with a few salty words.

The flecked green eyes glaring at him were dilated with anger. "Hellfire, you stupid woman. Don't you know what I could do to you?"

It really mattered little if she knew or not. What mattered here was whether *he* knew. The immediate press of her panic button came from lying prostrate beneath a body that not only knew, but knew plenty. That made her squirm again and repeat salty, muffled words against his hand.

"Holding you," he said, shifting his weight to immobilize her, "is about as easy as tying a bell around a wildcat's neck. Don't you have any fear? I'm going to move my hand, but you open that mouth of yours again and so help me God, I'll clamp it shut . . . permanently." He read defiance in her eyes as he lifted his hand. "Don't you dare say another word. You're in no position to argue."

"That's pretty obvious," she said. "Naturally, you're the strongest."

He gave her a look that could boil water with the leftover heat. "I also happen," he said softly, "to be on top." The slow movement of hipbone against hipbone, although commonly flagrant, was a pretty lame trick. But quite effective.

She felt the first stirrings of a sweet response that she was unprepared for—a slow awakening of desire, a naked awareness of intimacy that beckoned like curled fingers calling her to follow—then leaving her trembling at the precipice of a whole new world that yawned before her like a smoldering abyss. Out of the blur, a face took form above her. She had been right to think him the old serpent, the tempter; for surely he dangled before her like Eve's apple. One bite . . . just one succulent bite. *No! No!* . . . her mind was screaming, fearing the loss of Eden, the regions of sorrow and torture without end. She was frightened, bold, shy, reckless—afraid of him now for softer reasons—and that made her harsh. "Get off me, you oaf! Why don't you go blow up a train or something?"

He had the audacity to look amused. "Tough little baggage . . . I'll hand you that. Are you always this entertaining?"

"Do you always take this kind of pleasure with helpless women?"

A smile seemed to loiter about his sensuous mouth. "I take

extreme pleasure," he said, lowering his head and brushing his lips
across hers, "with helpless women. I also give it."

Another surge of breathless desire ran through her with such
suddenness, she accepted, as the absolute gospel, every word he
spoke.

Unable to think of anything clever to say, and with some
primeval female instinct telling her that resistance would only
serve to— She snapped her eyes together, but it was no use. Even
with her eyes closed, her cheeks continued to burn beneath the
gentle pressure of his kiss.

Warm and dry, his hands moved across the wisps of hair along
her nape to rest on each side of her face. Talented fingers traced the
outline of her ear, stroking the sensitive lobe, and then slipping
around to the back of her head while his thumbs stroked the pulsing softness of her throat.

She gave a tiny, strangled whimper, and he kissed her forehead reassuringly. "Don't be afraid, little buttercup," he whispered, then lowered his mouth to press against the black silk of her
lashes. "I won't hurt you." His tone was strangely gentle, soothing.
He was beginning to draw her into his powerful control with the
innocent reassurance of his kiss and the gentle stroke of warm,
strong hands.

By kissing her, he had taken the upper hand, dissolving her
defiant anger. Suddenly she was in way over her head. This man
had outgeneraled and outfought her at every turn. And now they
were on his home ground, grappling in an area he possessed an
inordinate amount of experience in—and, she'd be willing to bet,
even more creative inventiveness. Muscle, maleness, and magnetism shrieked his expertise with a thousand tongues. Every movement of his lithe-limbed body declared promise, delight, and delivery. As that distressing fact glared like a red flag, her body
weakened. It collapsed completely when she saw through a tear-
shimmering blur that the monster was laughing at her. Laughing!
He obviously knew the knowledge she possessed about sensual
pleasure could be expressed in one word: nothing.

Shaking, she was filled with remorse. Nothing in her gentle
southern breeding or education had prepared her for this. It was
humiliating enough to find herself two blinks away from crying,
and now her self-reproach was sharpened by one glaring fact: She

was at his mercy and she knew it. To make matters worse, he knew it.

She listened to the soft tapping of rain on the roof and the sound of a bird nesting in the rafters, which made her wish she could sprout wings and fly away. It just wasn't her day. Everything from hairdo to resolve was collapsing around her. With a sickening sense of dread, she dared wonder what was next.

She didn't have to wait long. Once again, his mouth came hungering, but instead of a deep, satisfying kiss, he brushed his lips across hers: once, twice. Three times he faintly touched his warm mouth to hers, saturating her with unfulfilled promise. Something about this was immensely frustrating. Was it the gentle subtlety, or because of it? If she had possessed any strength at all, she should have used it to push him away. As it was, every ounce of strength was used to clamp her mouth shut while something deep within her said "don't."

He lifted his dark head, the gray eyes giving her a puzzled look. As if finding what he sought, he lowered his mouth to hers once more. The man smell of him was terrifying, yet his touch carried reassurance. His lips were warm, dry, and smooth— pressed against hers softly, as if giving her time to adjust to the strange feeling, like a new colt being broken to bridle. Her fear receded and the pressure increased, bringing with it the subtle touch of his tongue.

Without breaking the kiss, he brought his practiced fingers to her lips and with subdued pressure parted them. His hands moved across her, one following the line of her throat, the other nestled in the downy soft hair just below her ear. She never thought a kiss between a man and a woman would be like this. It was addictive, carrying both promise and fulfillment, settling around her like a sweet drugging cloud of opium smoke.

A head swimming with emotion is mindless with lack of control. Thoughts, as soon as they entered her head, rolled right out her mouth, with no regard for consequence. Confusion permeated every limb, leaving her weak-kneed and out of focus. It was the effect of this dreamlike state that prompted her to whisper, her mouth moving against his, like a seduction. "I feel as limp as a dishrag . . . a scarecrow with no stuffings."

He laughed, of half a mind to tell her she didn't have a thing to be concerned about. The soft feminine swell of flesh beneath him said she was stuffed with something that felt mighty damn good. He smiled down at the angelic honesty lying prone beneath him. "I'd be happy to fill you," he said in husky tones, "but not with straw." His mouth came seeking, driving all thought of meaning from her mind, while his was filled with images of what it would be like to bury himself within this whimsical creature with the apple-green eyes.

He raised his head. "I haven't had a kiss like that since I learned to dress myself," he said. A smile spread in teasing mockery. "That was a kiss, wasn't it?"

Her eyes flashed. "You tell me. You're the one with all the experience. What would you call it?"

He raised a brow; a wicked smile curved his mouth. "Well, if I was blindfolded, my first guess would be, I'd had too much to drink and woke up with my tongue stuck to the pillow."

What kind of satyr was she up against? The man had a face that belonged on a gold coin, the body of a Roman gladiator, the discernment of a wizard, and the disposition of a jackass. Blushing violently, she said, "Do you know what you are? Disgusting." She had a few more choice selections to deliver to him but he placed two fingers over her lips to silence her.

"That," he said gently, "is one of your problems, angel. You talk too much. Now be quiet, and let's try again."

"Again? Why, I'd sooner—"

Rude though it was, he had a way of interrupting that was really quite pleasant. It was a few minutes before she found the necessary air to say, "Instead of ravishing me, why don't you just steal what you came for and leave?"

He studied her, allowing his curiosity to move over her exquisite face. "I hate to disappoint you, buttercup, but this is *not* ravishment, and I didn't come here to steal anything. This will probably chaff you all the way down to those little pink toes, but I'm an invited guest."

The perfectly shaped mouth he had been admiring dropped open like a dew-filled tulip. "Oh." She looked at him with disbelief. Then her eyes narrowed suspiciously. "I've never seen you around here before."

"I have the perfect explanation for that," he said. "I've never been here before." Then, with a soft muttered oath, he released her wrists and sat up, propping himself against the wall. Gingerly, he touched the back of his head with a handkerchief that he'd removed from his pocket.

She scrambled to a sitting position, rubbing her wrists as she watched him dip the bloody handkerchief in a water bucket. "You're bleeding," she said.

He cocked a brow at her. "That's what generally follows a head cleaving. Don't tell me drawing blood wasn't your idea. It sure as hell wasn't mine."

With a groan he closed his eyes and dropped his head, his wrists resting over his knees, which were bent before him. She glanced in the direction of the barn door, which was rattling gently against the force of wind-driven rain.

"Don't even think about it," he said. "Do you think you could outrun me? I wouldn't advise you to try. Even with my head busted, it would be a miserable match. You'd never make it."

Her frustrated gaze flicked back to his face. There wasn't a sliver of emotion in those cool eyes regarding her. He settled himself more comfortably against the stall, lanky legs crossed, arms folded across his chest.

"Where is everyone?" he asked.

"They've gone to a Church Basket Meeting . . . a picnic," she answered, and then thought that wasn't too clever of her to reveal that. "But they're due back soon . . . any minute now . . . before dark."

Gray eyes glanced toward the barn door, passing over long shadows of late evening creeping across the floor. "They better get a move on. It's almost dark," he observed. "Is it their habit to take everyone with them and leave you here alone . . . *unprotected*?"

That last word went across her like a rasp. "I'm not completely helpless."

Touching his head, he curved his mouth into a smile that left her a witless lump, boneless as a jellyfish. "No, you're not helpless. I've proof of that," he said rather good-humoredly.

Fighting back a smile, she said, "We've had an outbreak of fever in the slave quarters, so the household help is down there. Today was my day to oversee. That's why I'm not at the picnic. I was just coming back to the house for more quinine when I saw you."

"So . . . we're all alone?"

The humor drained, like blood, from her face. She shifted,

feeling the strain all of this was placing on her nerves. She spoke in a desperate voice: "I've already told you they will be returning shortly."

Amused, he watched her. "Smooth recovery. You know, you're a very clever girl. Beautiful. Intelligent. Clever. You even cover your mistakes with finesse. I like that. You don't often see that quality in a girl as young as you."

"I'm not that young," she said with irritation. "You make me sound like a . . ." She immediately conjured up all kinds of fun he could have with the rest of that and snapped her mouth shut.

"Child . . . innocent child . . . inexperienced child," he offered, before another one of those gut-twisting smiles spread across his face. Then he said, "No," and giving her the once-over, added, "you're no child, innocent or otherwise."

The rain passed, leaving as quickly as it had come, taking with it the welcome chill. The air was heavy now, saturated with moisture, the stillness interrupted by the steady drip of rain off the eaves and the croaking chords of bullfrogs in the distance. Everything was so still . . . she could almost hear the evening mist as it rolled up from the river.

"How old are you?" he asked.

The sound of his voice after a moment's lapse startled her, and her voice was like a bark. "Eighteen." Then, speaking more softly, she said, "How old are you?"

"Twenty-eight."

So many conflicting emotions were doing flip-flops within her, she was beginning to feel deranged. Her insides were playing leapfrog, jumping from fear to anger. Next came anxiety, and embarrassment, followed by humor, and now she was on the verge of liking the man.

He was still watching her silently. She looked at him, met his stare, and looked quickly away, as though he might be able to learn something about her, some secret she was hiding. She was an interesting combination, mouse and tiger. Two opposites he would never have expected to see living in harmony within a body that should, by all rights, be captured on canvas and hung over a gentlemen's bar. There was a tenseness in her tightly drawn mouth with its perfect shape and rose-petal blush.

"Who are you?" he asked.

"No one you'd be interested in knowing."

Oh, but he would, he would. It was unlike him, but he checked himself, keeping his thoughts to himself. "Do you know Mourning Howard?"

She looked at him as if he had insulted her. "I might, why?" She made a move to get up, but discovered her skirts were pinned beneath the sharp points of the rowels on his spurs.

"Would you move your feet? My skirts are caught." She tugged at the fabric, but he made no move to lift his feet. He was certainly different from the men she was accustomed to. He did not treat a lady like a lady. Of course, she didn't exactly look like a lady, wearing her oldest dress, her skirts rumpled, her hair going in more directions than a road map.

"I asked if you knew Mourning Howard. Do you want to answer my question, or does this stubborn streak mean you'd rather kiss?"

If the devil can't come, he will send someone, and she was convinced this man was the replacement. "I *know* Mourning Howard, but I don't know you or why you want her."

"Just tell me where I can find her."

"Not until I know why."

"You're a daring little saucebox, aren't you?" His look was direct. "It's perfectly honorable, I assure you. She's the reason I'm here."

Her head flew up, her eyes widened. Her heart threatened to fly right out of her chest. Panic. Alarm. A swiftly spreading sense of dread. Emotions crowded along nerve passages all at once, not one of them getting through, leaving her blank. "What—" It came out as a croak. She tried again. "What are you going to do with her?"

Amusement glittered in his eyes. "Do? Why, nothing. Not in the sense you mean, anyway." She was even more alluring when she blushed. "Her mother is married to my father. I've come to take her back to Texas with me."

All the color he had admired in her lovely face vanished. Instantly. *"You've* come?" she managed to squeak. "You've come to take her with *you?"* It was obvious he wasn't going to help her make a fool of herself, merely giving her a look that said she was giving a gilt-edged exhibition all by herself.

The grooves on either side of his mouth deepened. "As an escort, nothing more. I've just come from St. Louis, so it wasn't out of my way to stop here in Memphis." Seeing the shocked look on her face, he added, "At her mother's request."

She was deathly pale. "You can't be," she said. "There must be some mistake. All the way to Texas with you? But you're . . ."

As if reading her thoughts, he said, "Listen, my little paragon, I don't seduce family members if that's what you're thinking. Even I had a mother. And, believe it or not, unlike you, I have a name."

"I know who you are, Clint Kincaid."

He stared at her with an expression that was startled, but difficult to read. "Who the hell are you?" he asked.

"Mourning Howard."

"Oh, shit."

It was her turn to smile. He eyed her with amused astonishment and then threw back his head in laughter, but only momentarily. As soon as the skull-splitting pain ricocheted from temple to temple, Clint groaned. "I guess I deserved that," he said.

"Yes . . . you did." The look he was giving her made her uneasy. Mourning bristled, then changed the subject. "You're early. We didn't expect you until next week."

"Finished my business in St. Louis a little ahead of schedule," he said. Eyes gray as goosedown considered her. So this was Caroline's daughter. Too bad. She was a real eyeful, but she was family. That made a difference. A *big* difference.

"Why in God's name didn't you tell me who you were?"

"I just did."

"I mean earlier."

"You didn't ask."

"Christ! Now we've regressed to platitudes. I don't think I deserve that," he said flatly.

Mourning smiled, thinking he deserved anything she decided to throw at him, including the cast-iron skillet and the rolling pin.

Clint's face darkened. "Are you packed and ready to go?"

A flash of irritation came and went. "I'm packed and ready . . . but I'm not sure I want to go—at least not all the way to Texas with you."

"Why is that?" he asked in a blandly curious tone.

"Because I have decided I don't like you."

"Don't tempt me," he said, "or I might take the time to find out just how true that statement is."

"You lay one hand on my person again and I'll . . ." Mourning couldn't think of a warning foul enough to threaten him with. Any fool knew the devil wasn't afraid of anything—except God—and He had been avoiding her a lot lately. She looked around for something to throw.

Clint laughed.

And that made Mourning furious. She jerked her skirt, which gave with a loud rip, and scrambled to her feet.

For an injured man he moved surprisingly fast as he grabbed her wrist. "Don't be in such a hurry," he said softly. "I know you hate to leave such a romantic setting, but do you suppose you could see to my head? I think I'm in need of a stitch or two."

"Come into the kitchen," she said sharply, then yanked her arm free. She turned and hurried from the barn. She stepped lightly across the barnyard to avoid soaking her slippers in the mud. She did not wait for him, the *ching, ching, ching* of his spurs telling her that Clint Kincaid was following close behind.

3

Gabriel Clinton Kincaid sat back in his chair, resting the heel of his boot on the rung of the chair next to him. He picked up the small tin of blue ointment and dropped the lid to the table, bringing the container to his nose. Satisfied it smelled as bad as it looked, he replaced the lid and pushed the tin back to join the assortment of carafes, cruets, ewers, and vials Mourning had placed on the table.

She dared a look at him, drawn by the curious way his face possessed an element of lightfastness. Clint, in the dark, groping shadows of the barn, had been a handsome devil. Now, his features illuminated from several kitchen lamps, his dark brand of handsomeness resisted change, the sharp curves and harsh angles neither surrendering their masculinity nor fading in power. He was still a handsome devil.

This man puzzled her and she didn't know why. It wasn't because of his handsomeness, or even his aggressive masculinity. And credit could not go to the heady sense of earthy awareness she felt around him. No, it was more subtle and consciously hidden, something that ran deep—a close cousin to loneliness—a hollow thump of sadness.

The whole idea of aloneness and separateness stuck in her craw. Of all the things about this man of mystery, it was this one undefinable aspect of his complex personality that pierced her heart and held her motionless. She found it somewhat curious that the first time she found herself seduced and intrigued by a man it wasn't because of looks, words, or even deeds, but by a sense of melancholy. There was a grief in him, and she didn't know why. Lost in her thoughts as she was, Mourning was not conscious of the direction of her gaze, which unfortunately rested somewhere in the area of the junction of his thighs.

"Keep on staring," he said, "and I may begin to grow on you."

There was probably a lot more depth and meaning to this remark than she was picking up, and there was something about his lazy eyes that made her think that she had saved herself a great deal of embarrassment by missing it. She caught the glimmer of amusement in his eyes, the sensual smoothness of his voice, not knowing these were not the kind of things one would expect from a man who spent the first six years of his life incarcerated.

Clint Kincaid was born on the left side of life, one foot in the grave, his finger on the trigger. From his lonely beginning he had learned to depend upon no one but himself. He was a loner. That's what the Texans called him, and they left him alone. To the Mexicans he was *Lobo Solitario,* Lone Wolf, and they respected him. To the Kiowas and the Comanches he was *Wolf-Who-Stalks-the-Lonely-Moon,* and they understood him.

Destiny had dealt him a hand from the bottom of the deck. He was shaped and molded by a quirk of fate that wrenched him from the warm cocoon of motherly love and thrust him into a world of darkness—a distorted existence full of imbalance and irregularity.

Because his life had been so lightly given he had little regard for it. Life or death, it made no difference to him. The *tejanos* said he was wild, the Mexicans said he was *muy valeroso,* and the Indians said he walked with death. They were all correct. He was wild in his defiance of his own life, he was brave in his fearlessness, and because of these he constantly flirted with death. His utter and complete disregard for himself made him a dangerous man. He did not love. He did not know how.

There was no memory of a mother's warm caress or soft lulling voice. There had been no one to kiss his fevered brow or lovingly tend his scraped knee, or remember his birthday. There were only dark and sinister dreams filled with vague and twisted memories of a small dark cell where the sun slanted through a narrow slitted window wedged in the thick wall, allowing only a sliver of light to pool on the floor.

The wounds were old now—old, but not forgotten. How does the child in the man forget his beginning, his formative years, the first six years of his life spent in a religious cloister high in the mountains of Spain? Where do you hide the memory of once-a-week outings and sunlight so brilliant against eyes that were accustomed to darkness? How does a man overcome the savage brutality of repeated whippings, the bread, cheese, and water diet, the hours spent on a stool reciting scripture until he could not sit up?

It was in a convent under the care of Sister Domenica that the life of darkness and pain began. His first memories carried no softness and warmth, only pain, grief, and hatred. How old had he been then? Three? Four? A shaggy-haired waif, thin and sullen, no mother, no father, no home. Even now, he could see the light of the candle as it flickered across the nun's harsh features, catching in her black eyes and the rosary that hung in the thick folds of her woolen robe. There was no sound but the hiss and sputter of the candle, the crack of a fire, and the rapid breathing of Sister Domenica. Although she beat him unmercifully, he would not cry. He had learned long ago that crying bought him a three-day fast.

Sister Domenica. He would never forget the last day he stood before her, her voice raspy as she spoke.

What do you have in your bundle, boy?

A piece of cheese, Sister.

Where did you get it?

From the kitchen, Sister.

Stolen from the kitchen?

I was hungry.

It would seem your past punishments have not been sufficient to prevent you from stealing. I am weary of trying with you, so I have something else in mind.

He could never find the memory of leaving the convent, or traveling to the monastery, though he strained his mind to the breaking point, searching the inner confines of his consciousness for some small recollection. It was hidden, repressed, deep in a tangled web of things too awful, too painful, to bring forth.

Crowded in his mind among the memories of grief and pain were snatches of the monastery—a Moorish-looking bower and gray stone floor that stretched below a fan-vaulted cloister, the sun shining through a mullioned window to dance across scrolls of parchment and leather-bound books. And Brother Thomas. Mad Monk Thomas.

He could still hear the crunching sound of feet walking down the darkened stone corridor, the jingle of keys on the robe of the monk as he unlocked the cell door. *You know what* limpideza de sangre *is, boy? It's purity of blood. PURE BLOOD, BOY. The chosen ones have it. You are half-caste, a mixed breed. A bastard. Your blood is impure. You must suffer in order to redeem yourself. Repeat after me . . . The Godly must drink from the chalice of bitterness. . . .*

Even after the crazy thrust of irregularity and pain had been put behind him, it was many years before he was able to grasp what had happened, how his grandfather, Don Orlando Santiago Mendoza de la Garza, was responsible. The echo of his father's words was still so clear in his mind.

You have to understand the European sense of tradition, the pride of those old Spanish Land Grant families, Clint. Your mother was young and beautiful, and she was betrothed to the son of another landed Spaniard. A betrothal was binding and legal, and her family's honor stood behind it. Doña Isabel had no choice. But unfortunately, she fell in love with me . . . a small rancher by their terms, a tejano, *and* Americano. *And I was married. The honor of his ancestors, his own haughty pride, demanded Don Orlando take action. Isabel was sent to relatives in Spain . . . gone before I knew her father had found out about us, before I knew she carried my child.*

Why didn't he want me to be with my mother? Why did he take me away from her?

It wasn't you, or even him, but his breeding, his Spanish character. Such adherence to traditional roles. Such a grand historical perspective—the noblest sense of loyalty, patriotism, courage, gravity, and honor. The culture of your mother dominates the West to this very day . . . from here to California. They prefer their native Spanish, observe Spanish law and tradition, and worship in their Catholic churches founded by Spanish priests. They were here first. They discovered this country, and were the first to explore, to build missions, to bring us the horse. They gave us much and got so little in return. They shared their architecture, their food, their music, their horsemanship. They gave us the names of states, rivers, and mountain ranges. They built an empire and then we took it from them. They were sensitive over losing the war for Texas independence. It was a bitter defeat for a culture with a long epic past. Three centuries of glory in which they ruled, masterful and proud, only to find themselves ignominiously stripped at the end. You were born at a time when Don Orlando's world was crumbling beneath him and he was trying to hold on to a heritage that had already been replaced.

In Spain, Doña Isabel gave birth to a son. "I want him named for his mixed heritage," she said. "Gabriel for his Spanish blood, Clinton for his American father." Her insistence that he be christened was her last kindness to her infant son. At Don Orlando's insistence, the tiny baby boy was secretly removed by relatives and placed in a convent. His mother was told he died, but Isabel refused to believe that.

A year later, John Kincaid's sickly wife was dead and he went to Spain to find Isabel—and he did, learning too late that she had borne him a son who could not be located. He married Isabel and searched for his son for a year, but when they learned Isabel was expecting another child, they gave up the search and returned to the ranch, where their second son, Cad, was born. Doña Isabel died shortly after Cad's birth. Her last words were in regard to her firstborn. "I know our son is alive, John. Find him. Promise me you'll find him."

For three years John searched. He made trips to Spain and searched relentlessly, and because of his dedication and the grief he bore, a relative came forward. "I am Doña Elena Carlotta de la Garza," the old woman said. "I am your Isabel's great aunt. May Don Orlando forgive me. I will tell you where to find your son."

He was a painfully thin, sullen child when John found him. Awakening to a softness and warmth, the boy surveyed the strange room. A room flooded with sunlight and beauty. A room where the floor was covered with furs and rugs, and where brilliant tapestries covered the walls. A crackling fire bestowed its gift of warmth while filling the room with soft, glowing light, making the tiled floors shine like bricks of gold.

"Gold," the boy whispered. "Streets of gold . . . Is this heaven?"

John, understanding Spanish, drew his firstborn into his arms, feeling the fragile bones. "No," he said in a choked voice, tears rolling down his face, "but I can promise you will see no more of hell."

And then it began, Clint's life in Texas. And now, twenty-two years later, he was a man, gentled somewhat by the love of a brother and father, yet forever branded by the hideous horrors he had seen and endured.

He was educated, seeing much of the world and acquiring the knowledge of many languages. Yet when he was older he chose to leave home again, this time to wander, learning the ways of his Spanish heritage and earning the respect of the Comanches and Kiowas. Perhaps it was because the Indians understood him, this man who walked with death and stalked the lonely moon.

Clint seemed older than his twenty-eight years—older and more dangerous. Perhaps it was the indifference in his eyes or the scornful curve of his mouth that marked him as dangerous, someone to be reckoned with. Many an outlaw or gambler could attest to that—if they had lived. Men respected him and women were drawn to his handsomeness. Yet for the most part Clint preferred to be alone.

He had known many women. His kind always did. Yet he never met one he couldn't walk away from, and he always would . . . in the end. There was no feeling, no attachment. He knew the hungry gnawing of desire, the slow smoldering coal of lust, the quick flaring flame of passion, but it ended there. He mated like an animal. His experiences with women involved no friendship, no companionship, no lasting entanglement—nothing but the mutual satisfaction of a lingering itch to copulate. The flame was extinguished as rapidly as it flared. To him, a relationship with a woman was a matter of desire, consummation, and satisfaction. Not that he wasn't a generous and curiously potent lover, for he was. It was just that Clint Kincaid managed to keep the inner workings of his mind and heart detached from the pumping of his loins. His wide travels and varied experiences taught him what women liked. And he gave it to them. He never left a woman unsatisfied. He just left.

Clint's eye came back to the woman fate had saddled him with. The one woman he could not leave. He wasn't particularly happy about that. But there wasn't much he could do about it either. He had promised Caroline. And Caroline was a good enough soul—for a woman.

He lingered upon the sight of Caroline's daughter, slim and straight as a cattail, moving about the kitchen with dignified grace —very subdued, very proper, very efficient. Yet something about her screamed *touch me*. And by God, he wanted to. But he wouldn't.

He reflected on that decision. The wild corruptions of his life had never bent to ethical or moral codes, but seducing Caroline's daughter seemed beyond what even he was capable of.

"I'm almost ready," Mourning said. "You might as well make yourself comfortable."

"Yes, ma'am."

Hearing a spark of humor in his voice, she looked up, expecting something altogether different from his nebulous gaze. No trace of humor lingered on his handsome face. His eyes were harsh. A fierce tension strained the atmosphere, caused by the intense attraction that had flamed between them, only to be smothered in the light of their newly discovered relationship. After what had transpired in the barn, Mourning knew they could never be casual friends. Yet the family bond between them demanded it.

He focused on the pure lines of her face: the sculpted mouth, the seafoam eyes with their gold-flecked depths, the sensitive flare of nostrils, the proudly erect head. He continued to watch her, torn between anger and vexation at the sharp edge of uncertainty and shame he saw in her eyes. For a brief moment he shifted his line of thinking to speculate on why she would feel shame. *Surely not over a couple of kisses.*

She felt his eyes upon her and glanced up, sensing his growing speculation, his unwillingness to forget what had passed between them. Startled by his penetrating look, she lowered her eyes, hoping he would think it nothing but modesty. "I'll see to your head now."

"Yes, do."

The cool derisive tone and sudden lack of interest in his voice scraped across her like grit. Her eyes swept back to his, and he was staring. Hard. She caught the curt inclination of his head, the overall composure that spoke of contempt. She could only call his smile a little bit wicked, a sign that he took notice of her unease. She wished he would look away. Yet he continued to stare, as if waiting for her to do something stupid—which, if she were honest, probably wasn't such a ridiculous expectation. Doing something stupid seemed to be a favorite pastime of hers.

Something about his expression spoke of resignation. Apparently he had made his decision. It was written all over his face. Etched across his frozen features was no more of a regard than one would have for tinsel the day after Christmas. He had set the boundaries. She would die before she crossed them. He wanted indifference? Distance? She would see that he got it.

"All right, Mr. Kincaid. The sooner we get this over with, the better it will be for all of us," Mourning said, failing miserably to sound like Aunt Harriet.

Clint glanced around the room to see who the hell *us* was. Finding no one but the two of them, he snorted and leaned back in the chair, crossing his long, lanky limbs at the ankles.

Strange how the *ching, ching* of his spurs reminded her of his staggering brand of masculinity. She needed a diversion. She tried conversation. "Is it a common practice in Texas to wear your spurs in the house, Mr. Kincaid?"

Slow and lazy, a smile lurked around his mouth. "Only if you anticipate a ride, Miss Howard."

She laughed. "Surely, Mr. Kincaid, you haven't done any riding inside."

"Inside what, ma'am?"

"The house, Mr. Kincaid. I doubt that even in the wilds of Texas you do much riding in the house." She smiled, pleased that they could have a normal conversation for once.

"I've done my share."

A shiver rippled down her spine, but she ignored it. "I think you're making light of our conversation, Mr. Kincaid." She smiled knowingly. "I seriously doubt you've ever ridden a horse in the house, not if I know my mother."

"I never said I did."

The towel she was holding dropped to the table and she clapped her hands on her hips in a way that made her arms stick out like the handles on a sugar bowl. "What kind of game are you playing? You have implied, sir, that you have, on numerous occasions, ridden inside the house. Now, have you or have you not ridden a mount inside the house?"

"Not a four-legged one," he said.

Horrified and shaking, she felt such intense anger and hatred swelling inside her, she couldn't speak. Appalled and blushing, she vowed she would never allow this man to use her to his advantage again. This was war.

Smiling broadly, he crossed his arms. "Now, is there anything else you'd like to know about me?"

"Go to the devil," she said.

"Tut, tut, Miss Howard. Is that any way to treat a guest . . . an *injured* guest?"

"You're not half as injured as I'd like you to be."

Up went his brows. "Don't forget, you were the one asking all the questions—about my personal affairs."

She slammed her hand against the table. "I *did not* inquire after your personal affairs. I don't want to know anything about you—personal or otherwise. I know far too much already. I wish you would stop hounding me. What are you after? What must I do to convince you to leave me alone?"

She saw the immediate tensing of his body. Moments passed while he looked at her. She was beginning to wonder if he would speak at all when she heard him sigh. "Is that what you really want —me to leave you alone?"

"Yes," she shouted, clenching her fists at her sides. Then, more softly, she added, "Yes, Mr. Kincaid, it's what I want above all things."

With an affirmative nod, he settled himself more comfortably in the chair. With interest he watched her carefully pour carbolic acid into a pan of water. Seeing the doubt on his face, she said, "It's a disinfectant."

He scowled. "It's also dangerous as hell."

This was said with such a mordant tone, she clenched her teeth. By far he was not the first man she had treated, or even the only good-looking one, but he was holding the distinction of being the most difficult.

"I'm careful," she said. Why had her mother agreed to let *this* man take her to Texas? And what about the praises Caroline had heaped upon his head when she'd written the letter? This was the only man she would entrust with her daughter's life? *What about my virtue?* Caroline wasn't *that* old. And stupid she'd never been. No, Mourning couldn't understand Caroline's reasoning, but he was here and there was nothing to do but go with him—all the way to Texas. Glancing across the table, she saw his eyes were closed.

Another opportunity to admire him opened like the jaws of a steel trap.

The marvelous perfection of his powerful length was blatantly displayed before her, drenched with sensual appeal. *If this man can be trusted to keep his distance,* she thought, *I'll eat three helpings of Aunt Harriet's Liver Pudding.*

Her eyes dropped lower. A scattering of emotions twinkled like tiny constellations in the green depths of her eyes. It wasn't that his clothes were different from what any other man would have worn, but what unbelievable things his magnificent maleness did to simple cloth. No other man could have given it what Clint did, or put that exact amount of tension on mere fabric. His manners might be lacking and his language base, but his body with the smooth, rhythmical blend of tendon, muscle, and bone was faultless.

"I can be had," he said with a lazy drawl.

Stricken, she felt a heated blush that seemed to explode from within. Nerve endings gathered in tense little knots along the line of her shoulders. She knew she shouldn't look at him, but she did. The crystal grayness of his eyes lingered upon her, stripping her to bare, trembling flesh. Excitement rippled and sang along her nerve passages. It combined with self-chastisement for allowing her thoughts to suggest what her body wanted to experience: the feel of his weighted body against her once more.

For the next few minutes, Clint's attention was riveted on the young woman across the table. She was making a valiant effort to ignore him and, strangely, succeeding. For some reason, that irritated the ever living hell out of him. Watching the angry tilt of her head, the determined lift of her small chin . . . he could tell she was still chapped. Maybe he could get a real rise out of her.

Lifting one foot, he inched it under the table—and under a few petticoats as well—and nudged the side of her leg. Her head flew up. "How dare you touch my person. You put that foot over here again and you'll draw back a nub."

Black brows shot up as he watched her whirl and stomp to the cupboard. *Draw back a nub? Me?* Poor little buttercup. She had more grit than brains. Funny, he couldn't help but admire that.

She marched back to the table and slammed down a pair of scissors. He looked at the scissors. He looked at her. "If you think you're going to use those on *my* hair, guess again."

Seeing the trap that yawned, she stepped around it carefully. *"If* you want me to see to your injury, you'll have to turn your back," she said in a strained voice.

A mocking smile crept across his face. "In case you've forgotten," he said, "that's how I got in this mess in the first place."

If he possessed any manners at all, tact was not among them. "Fine," she said, tossing the cloth she was holding onto the table and whirling away, "I've other chores."

Clamping a powerful hand around her wrist, he propelled her back to the table. The look in his eyes was so murderous, panic spun across her mind. Her stomach in knots, her heart aflutter, she was hardly surprised when everything else inside her began to quiver like calf's-foot jelly. "See to my head," he said gruffly, and straddled the chair, resting his arms across the ladder back.

It was downright indecent, the way he straddled that chair, his pants tighter than last year's underwear and just as revealing. How was she supposed to concentrate on tending his wound when he sat there displayed like a plucked chicken in a butcher's window?

Color exploding on her face, her mind screaming for diversion, she hastily parted the blood-soaked hair on his scalp. She found a Y-shaped gash about three inches long and still oozing blood. She grimaced. No wonder his mood was foul. The poor man's skull was cracked—just as he'd said.

"What are you doing?" he said. "Drawing a map?" He shifted his legs. "Clean it up and be done with it."

"It will need stitching," she chirped, rather matter-of-factly. "Do you want me to stitch it?"

"Hell, no! I don't *want* your goddamn hands on me," he shouted, wanting nothing more than to find the peace and quiet that had been his a short while ago. What he needed was a good stiff drink and about five hundred miles between him and this woman.

Her back stiffened. "Suit yourself. It'll heal better and faster if it's stitched, but it's your head," she said.

"You're damn right it is." A stabbing pain shot through him and all he thought about was leaving here, and the quickest way to do that was to let her have her way. "Oh, hell," he said. "Stitch it."

She spun around and hurried toward the door.

"Where in the Sam Hill do you think you're going?" He leaned forward, piercing her with his diamond-hard glare.

"To the library to get you some spirits . . . unless you'd rather impress me with your raw courage." She interpreted his snarling growl for agreement and skipped from the room, a smile lighting her way.

Tapping his fingers on the table, Clint waited. At least he was going to have a good stiff drink. A few minutes later, she returned, placing a cut-glass decanter and matching glass on the table in front of him. He eyed the suspicious contents. "What is this?"

"Extinct hair-tonic, old dental powder, nux vomica, used bed-bug poison, silver polish, rabid-dog foam . . ."

"Clever." Clint ignored the glass, choosing instead to drink straight from the decanter. Bringing it to his lips, he tipped his head back and took a big swig. Immediately he exploded out of the chair, knocking it over while spewing a stream of curses and liquid out of his mouth, drenching everything within five feet.

"What the hell is this slop?" he screamed in tones violent enough to do damage to his liver. "It tastes worse than cow piss."

"Ratafia," she said stiffly, exercising the greatest control while dabbing with disgust at the stain spreading rapidly across her clothing.

"Ratafia," he yelled, "that piss is for old maids." He threw himself into another chair.

"And simple-minded morons," she added, "who find it necessary to throw temper tantrums—not to mention beef-witted clodhoppers lacking the ability to speak with anything but sacrilegious profanity. Since you fit perfectly both descriptions, *Missster* Kincaid, the drink must be for you." With that she upended the entire decanter down the front of his shirt.

4

Clint leaped from the chair, sending it sprawling in the process. As if that wasn't enough, he kicked it across the kitchen for good measure. It flew across the floor, hitting the wall with a clattering thud. His scowling countenance and threatening posture were so violent, even the teacups in the cupboard rattled.

"This time you've gone too far," he bellowed, refusing even to blot his drenched shirtfront.

"I've gone too far? *I've gone too far?*" she shrieked at a much higher pitch while standing on tiptoe for added emphasis. "You come in here bugling like a bull moose, using language a gutter would refuse, and have the unmitigated gall to tell me *I've* gone too far! Insane. That's what you are, *Mr.* Kincaid. Hopelessly . . . irrevocably . . . insane."

They were squared off like Zeus and Hera, and the air between them snapped with electricity.

Clint gave her what she'd call a sullen look and sat down, in a different chair, leaving the two he'd knocked over where they were. With one brisk move, he shoved the empty decanter toward her. It stopped a hairbreadth away from crashing over the edge of the table. *"Ratafia,* my ass," he snorted. "This time, get me something fit for a man to drink."

She gave him the patronizing look she reserved for toddlers in the church orphanage and clamped her hands on her hips. Next came a smile so sweet, it would crystallize vinegar. "Would you happen to know where I could find a *man* to drink it? Your behavior, Mr. Kincaid, strongly indicates that you should be drinking *milk.*"

"I'm warning you," he growled, the veins jutting out along his neck. "You've gone far beyond the limits of my patience, woman. *Get the goddamn bourbon, and get it now.*" He clenched his fist and pounded the table with each word.

Whirling, she shot from the kitchen like an arrow from an overstretched bow. Returning moments later with a bottle, she slammed it down in front of him.

"Thank you." His voice was barely civil.

"You're most welcome," she said, her tones falling a tad shy of barely civil.

He took several healthy swigs from the bottle before recapping it. "That should be enough to deaden the pain of even your gouging and poking," he said.

Without a word she moved behind him, carefully parting the blood-matted hair. Holding it back with one hand, she leaned forward to pull the basin of water closer. Her arm brushed his neck and the soft bounce of her breast pressed warmly against his ear.

"Hellfire," he groaned, wiping his perspiring hands on his pants while holding his breath. Anything to ignore the feel of her comforting breast nuzzled against his ear. This was ridiculous. She was pushing those soft breasts against his cheek and all he could think about was turning his face full against them. He clenched his fists. *Jesus H. Christ. I'm no saint. Just how much abuse can a man stand? It's a helluva life when a man can't even control his own body. It's not possible,* he thought. *I can't be having an erection for a woman I find this irritating.*

Carefully keeping her thoughts to herself, Mourning meticulously washed the wound with antiseptic water and then poured silver nitrate over it. The scalding pain fired him straight out of the chair, which tipped over with a loud *thwaaaack.*

For the second time in mere minutes he kicked a chair halfway across the kitchen and screamed at the top of his voice. "What are you putting on me? Hot coals?"

"I don't know why I didn't think of that," she said, her eye on the overturned chairs. *Only one more to go, then the cabbagehead can sit on the floor where he belongs.* "Tell me, Mr. Kincaid," she asked, with flawless enunciation, "do you have a strong dislike for these *particular* chairs . . . or is it all chairs in general?"

He glowered at her, his fist clenching and unclenching as he made a big to-do about dragging up the fourth and only remaining chair, refusing to right the three he'd kicked over.

She waited until he had settled himself. "I'm going to start sewing now," she said. "Yell if you like."

He cocked his head, staring at her as if he'd never before laid eyes upon her person, but he remained silent. She began to stitch his head and he sat unflinching. When she finished, she gave an exclamation of satisfaction and cleared the table without so much as a how-d'ye-do for his welfare. Clint gritted his teeth and leaned back in the chair, his eyes dark and brooding as he watched her.

The bourbon had reduced the pain in his head to an occasional dull thump, and had warmed his body considerably. He tried not to watch her, but she was just too damn good-looking for her own good. The way she moved set his teeth on edge and his red blood to boiling.

She filled the coffee grinder with coffee beans, cranking the handle with a few jerky moves before it settled into a smooth, rhythmic motion. But there were a lot of other things in motion right now that were putting him through nine kinds of hell. She had a body that would tempt a saint, and that was something no one had ever accused him of being. His attraction to her was putting him in a difficult position. Parts of him were already there. Mentally, he measured her hand-span waist before his eyes lowered to her pelvic area. Good hips. Moving up again, Clint's sharp eyes lingered on her breasts, the way they responded to the movement of her arm. He wanted her.

She moved out of eyesight, doing something behind him. He could hear drawers opening and a lid rolling to a stop. A few minutes passed in silence.

"Would you like some coffee?" she asked, studying the tiny beads of perspiration that dotted his brow.

"Please," he said.

Returning to the table, she sloshed coffee in his cup and daintily poured herself some. "Cream?"

He shook his head. "No sugar either."

The room was wrapped in soft, muted sounds while they drank coffee in silence—each one lost in his own thoughts. Nothing could be heard, save the distant bawling of a lost calf, and closer up, the steady *tic, tic, tic* of the hall clock.

Clint was down to the dregs of his coffee when Mourning broke the silence. "Mr. Kincaid . . ."

"Clint."

"Pardon?"

"Clint . . . call me Clint."

"Clint . . ." she said, pausing from the feeling of intimacy that swept through her when she said his name. Her face all rosy, she tried again. "Clint, I want to apologize for the reception you've received. I . . ." She paused, catching the uncomfortable look on his face.

She blinked her eyes a few times, then, refusing to let him deter her, she continued, "I just want you to know, I'm sorry about your injury. It was entirely my fault, and . . . well . . . I'm just sorry we've gotten off on the wrong foot, that's all."

His unease was spreading to her. Desperate for something to do, she reached for the coffeepot. Over the dented lid, their eyes met, and locked. Maintaining his silence, Clint placed a hand over his cup. In her agitated state Mourning failed to notice his declining gesture. Hot coffee sloshed over his hand.

"Hell's bells!" Clint jerked his hand away with another curse. Mourning slammed the pot down and grabbed a tea towel and wet it quickly before wrapping it around his scalded hand. Next, she poured camphor into a small bowl and soaked a clean linen napkin in it. She placed the napkin over the scalded portion of his hand. "There, I think that should feel much better."

"Goddammit."

"I was only trying to help."

"I didn't ask for your help."

"Shall I put more camphor on it?" she asked. "Does it still hurt?"

"If you're so damn interested, I'll tell you. Yes, it still hurts . . . it hurts like a son of a bitch."

"Don't you swear at me," she shouted.

"The hell you say. If you don't like the way I'm talking, you can always get your ass out of here. I don't need your feeble attempts at nursing . . . my body can't take much more of it!"

"Mr. Kincaid," she said with false calmness, "I realize that speaking in the vernacular with coarse, tasteless language and profanity is an indication of an inadequate vocabulary and below-average intelligence. I am also aware that you are obviously severely deficient in both departments. However, I would appreciate it, and I'm sure my mother would also, if you would refrain from cursing in my presence."

"Like hell I will," he roared. "You've given me more than enough reasons to curse, and I don't give a damn whether you like it or not. And the same goes for your mother."

He is obviously the result of a long series of misalliances known to produce idiocy in its offspring, she thought. *I wonder if he has twelve toes?* Hoping he couldn't read her thoughts, she glanced up.

He gave her a look that cut like a scythe.

And the same goes for your mother . . . How dare he! Everywhere she saw red. "You are a vile, uncouth madman," she said, with such spleen, he actually blinked. "You have barged in here bellowing like a wounded bull elephant, using the foulest of language for absolutely no reason—"

He cut her short. "For absolutely no reason?" he boomed. "Hellfire, woman. If you want reasons, I'll give you reasons aplenty. First you cave in my head because you're too damn stupid to ask me why I was here. Then you poison me with some pisspoor excuse for a drink, before you pour the foul-tasting slop all over me. And if that's not enough, you take perverse pleasure in trying to gouge out my brains, scald the hide off me with boiling coffee, and then have the gall to tell me I have no reason." Finding himself long on words and short of breath, he paused. "Miss Howard," he continued, exercising the severest of restraint and control, "you are enough to make the most staid preacher cuss. And if that offends you, so be it."

It wasn't an apology, but it was probably the closest to one she'd get. They eyed each other warily, both realizing they'd come together like two battling rams and neither had emerged the victor. Further confrontation would only result in larger headaches than they both possessed at the moment. Unable to win verbally, they had resorted to a staring contest. Not a single word was spoken as they watched each other for quite some time. By some silent agreement they were on the verge of a truce.

In the end, it was Mourning who broke the silence. "Would you like to try again on the coffee?"

He nodded and pushed his cup toward her. She crossed the room, stretching across him to pour the coffee. Clint stared at her, the whiteness of her throat above the neckline of her gown, and below, the gentle swell of firm, young breasts. It was an almost irresistible opportunity, and her effect on him was powerful. The urge to grab her was almost overpowering.

Carefully she set the pot on the trivet next to his cup. When she drew back, her breasts brushed faintly against his arm. This time the opportunity was positively irresistible.

Before she could turn away he yanked her onto his lap.

They flayed and flapped, all sharp elbows and flying legs like two mating storks. For a brief moment his grip slackened, giving her enough leverage to break loose, and she twisted away, bolting across the room. He was up in a flash, stalking her.

"Come here, you little firecat," he whispered huskily between breaths. The heat in his voice passed through her skin like liniment. She shook her head against the tender persuasion of his words and backed against the cupboard, her breath coming in short pants. He was looking at her in a manner that said a very clever rendition of what lay beneath her clothing was etching itself, detail by detail, across his brain.

"No," she said. "Don't you touch me."

"Damnation," he mumbled, and sprang. She made a dash for it, going as far as the table before he twisted around in midstride and pounced once more, grabbing her just as she skirted his chair. The sudden movement threw them both off balance and they came crashing into the chair like a felled tree. Instinctively she reached for support, grabbing hold of him.

Slow recognition dawned.

A horrified gasp. A shriek of dismay. Shakespeare himself could not have expressed, with all the grandiloquent words at his disposal, the burst of emotion that followed sudden realization: Just *where* her hand was touching and *what* it was clutching were clear as branch water. No human hand could fail to detect what sprang to sudden life beneath her fingers. Shape, length, and proximity screamed identification in six languages.

She jerked her hand away and looked down for a last sickening assurance that she was, indeed, as disgraced as she felt.

He chuckled. "You really get to the root of the matter, don't you, Miss Howard?" His suggestive smile and taunting words sizzled across her nerve network with more flaming fireworks than The Ancient Free and Accepted Masons' Fourth of July picnic. She jumped from his lap.

He chuckled low in his throat. "No, sweet, don't tuck your head. My, you are embarrassed, aren't you? You're redder than a flamefish," he said with a grin. "If I embarrassed that easily, Miss Howard, I wouldn't go around putting my hand where it was sure to get a rise out of a man."

Waiting for him to shut up was like waiting for the millennium. Her jaw clenched tightly, a result of the humiliated rage she felt. In fact, Mourning feared herself on the verge of hysterics. If her Aunt Harriet had taken so much as a brief glance at her face, she would have sent her straight to bed.

While Mourning tried to sort through her favorite comebacks that seemed hopelessly lost in a mud-puddle of confusion, Clint decided to call a truce. "If you'll direct me to some water, I'll try to clean up," he said, carrying his cup to the cabinet and righting the chairs.

An hour later Clint was sitting alone at the kitchen table. He was trying to draw mental pictures of Mourning cleaned up. Would she look like a lady, or just a laundered version of the same tangle-haired imp he'd encountered in the barn? No matter how she looked, she would still be the same adorable rattlehead. *Yes, I'm going to take you to your mother, angel. But first I want to teach you a few things about passion. To see that hopelessly lunatic expression of awe on your face once more . . . just before I show you.* A smile crossed his face as he remembered their last blistering exchange.

"It's time you learned some manners, Miss Howard."

"I have manners . . . I know I haven't shown you, but I have them. Oh, please! I don't know why this is happening to me. Let me go, you clumsy goat! You're squashing me like a bottle-fly."

"A fool asks much . . ."

"And you of all people should know about fools."

"So . . . we're back to our fiery little courtship, are we?"

"Courtship! You have the most perverted courting methods I've ever seen. Five minutes with you and I feel like I've been courted by a porcupine. You have the stranglehold of an octopus and the predatory inclinations of a wild pig."

"Keeps you interested, though."

"Interested? Ha! I find you about as inspiring as a clam!"

"Oh? Let's see if I can give you what you really want. Together, buttercup, we can make your body sing."

"Make my what? . . . Oh, no, I'm not stepping into any more

*of your well-laid traps. I may be all vines and no taters, but I'm not
stupid."*

"Perhaps not stupid exactly, but you're stubborn as a blue-
nosed mule. Do you always go around like this? Tail up and stinger
out?"

"Go ahead. Make fun of me. You've already insulted my character, ridiculed my manners, terrorized my sanity . . ."

"Abused your body?"

"I was just coming to that. And, you have frightened me with
your base . . . Oh, never mind."

"But I do mind. Tell me. My base what? . . . inclinations?
Poor buttercup, has it been so bad, then?"

"You know it has. And you wanted it that way. You meant for
me to suffer and suffer sublimely. But I'm stronger than you
think. . . ."

"Mourning . . . My inflammable little simpleton. You're close
to quoting Longfellow, and God knows that can be, at best, tedious.
You have nothing to worry about. I told you before, I'm not going to
bother you. Look. My hands are in my pockets. You're safe. I'm not
attracted to immaturity or youth."

"Ha! Don't try to fool me. You're attracted to anything female
. . . Anything. Nameless. Faceless. It doesn't matter. As long as
there's a body."

The same fear had been hovering in the back of Clint's mind
for some time, but it took hearing it aloud, and from the mouth of
someone young and unsullied, for him to feel the jaded implica-
tions of it. *Have I really sunk so low? Am I capable of seducing
someone so young and simple-hearted? Caroline's daughter? A
member of my family? Christ! Even I can't be that indifferent.*

Beyond him, the windows were dark, a reflection of the hour.
A lone lamp glowed softly, giving interesting play to the hollows
and planes of his face and weaving red and gold highlights into his
ebony hair.

She found him with his back to her when she returned. He
was standing in front of the kitchen window, his dark shape a
black silhouette against the flat gray of night that stretched beyond. The moon was visible over his left shoulder, a stingy thing,
thin and scant, frugal with its light.

He seemed so very lonely—lonely and alone—and something
about that reached out to her, drawing her to him magnetically.

The distance between them lessened. One step. And then another. She was close enough now to touch the jet fringe of hair that curled at his nape. *This is insane,* she thought. *Why am I here? Why am I doing this?*

He turned suddenly, and lifted his hand, their fingertips almost touching. He tried to analyze his bewilderment. This wash of tender emotion, alien and strong, was lodged, like a pain, in his chest. She was holding a small candle, the tiny flame dancing on the tip of the wick, illuminating her skin with a pearly luster. Gainsborough, with his sensitivity, his delicacy of expression, could have painted her thus. But only Rubens, bringing to life the vibrant quality of his lusty nudes, could have captured her essence. She belonged on a pedestal, enclosed in a niche, flanked by naked cupids in high relief.

But she seemed shaken and withdrawn. He found this puzzling, for it was he who was so obviously shaken. She was quite the loveliest thing he had ever seen. But she was still looking at him in that startled way, and he wondered if she was frightened, her wariness making her cautious. *If there's one thing you should be around me, sweetheart, it's cautious.*

"Are you afraid of me?" he asked.

She placed the candle on the table, but she didn't answer him.

"If I didn't throttle you in the barn, I won't hurt you now," he said.

"I'm not afraid of you in *that* way."

Clint smiled and then laughed. "Just how many ways are there?"

"There's the funny kind of fear that comes when Mattie catches me with my finger in the mashed potatoes. And the usual kind, like the time I was sick and thought I was going to die, and . . ."

He waited for her to finish, his eyes studying her. A moment later, he said, "And what else, Mourning? What other kind of fear is there?"

"There's this kind," she said, her fist knotting and pressing against her diaphragm.

"Describe it."

"I can't. It's something I can feel here in my stomach. And my heart pounds and I feel breathless, like I've just run up the stairs. But I can't describe it . . . because I've never felt that way before."

"Do you feel that way now?"

"A little."

"Let's see if we can increase it," he said, stepping closer, bringing his body against hers.

She had thought he would stop there, just curious to see if his closeness affected her—which it did—but then, before she could escape, his arms were around her, the unexpected hardness of a body that was all muscle pressing against her. She closed her eyes against the inner chaos—the conflict of emotions that struggled within her, wondering which would emerge the victor: tears of humiliation or breathless desire.

As quickly as he had come against her, he released her, pulling away, their bodies no longer touching, but mere inches apart. Yet she was still entranced, still a prisoner of arms that were no longer there. She opened her eyes, wanting to tell him how it was with her, how she felt when he was so near. But something she saw in his eyes told her that would be a mistake.

He watched her, seeing her eyes narrow and fill with anger, yet she said nothing. So he did. "How do you feel now?"

"Like a fool. Used." Turning away, she walked rapidly toward the table where the candle burned, her hands wrapped around her waist.

The moment he stepped between her and the candle, she stopped, throwing her head back and giving him a look that struck him like an open palm. "You have a very cruel way of amusing yourself. It's a pity you can't afford the luxury of compassion. If you're always like this, I'm surprised your mockery hasn't frightened away all of your game."

"Not brutal. Honest. And I wasn't amusing myself. I was showing you that a little private embarrassment is better than public humiliation. You go at life so spontaneously, as if you've had no experience."

Anger flared in her eyes. "We can't *all* be experienced. I may be spontaneous, but at least I'm not arrogant. I can't imagine your ever being a child."

"And I can't imagine your being anything else."

He watched her, knowing he had gotten his point across, but there was no pride in it for him. Somehow, he didn't see her as simply bested, but utterly shattered, by his ridicule. Something stirred within him and he knew he should have been more gentle with her. He had never dealt with a woman under circumstances like this, and he was unsure of how to proceed. Although his conscience was prodded, it wasn't pricked. There would be no apology, he told himself, and at that very moment she looked at him, her eyes huge and questioning. *Is there a way out of this that is acceptable to both of us, sweetheart? I know you want a full apology. . . . Would you settle for a diversion?*

"Do you have a beau?" he asked.

"Should I?"

"You're very pretty. Why should you not?"

No, he told himself. He was wrong. She wasn't pretty. He had thought her pretty, earlier, before she went upstairs to dress. But then she'd reappeared, her golden braids gleaming and tied with ribbon, the intense green of her eyes glinting with fire, the expression of awe on her face—urging him to kiss her into dazed insensibility. She was beautiful, breathtakingly so. And she was doing just that—taking his breath away. *And how do we explain this?* Lustful thoughts? Fascination with the impossible?

Her eyes met his, and the world fell silent and still around them. Against the simple green merino frock her ivory flesh, moist and blushing from a recent scrubbing, had the flawless texture of fresh strawberry cream. And lord! That face . . . the fragile bone structure. And her cheekbones were exquisite—set high in a heart-shaped face above a pert nose, and vibrant green eyes he could lose himself in. But it was her mouth that held him fascinated—rosy, with a slight pout. It was absolute kissing perfection, and having quite an impact on the rate of his heartbeat. He closed his eyes, still seeing all the colors of spun honey in her hair, and her huge, extraordinary eyes. Yet, even then, with his eyes closed, the image of her did not fade. His eyes opened and he looked at her, fighting the urge to close his hands around the golden braids looped on each side of her head and pull her against him. She was stunning in her simplicity, and he would have told her, but he was too busy wondering how he could have treated something this lovely as he had. He forgot completely the parts of him that throbbed magnificently because of her. The only thought that hammered at him now was the desire to go back to that breathless moment when she entered the room, to see her as he saw her then. To start over again. On the right foot this time.

"Where do we go from here?" he said.

"*I'm* going back to my room."

He sighed. "Do you always scamper back to your room and tuck your head under your pillow when things don't go in a way that pleases you? I thought you were of a sturdier constitution than that."

"Well, I'd certainly look like a fool lighting into you with both fists . . . wouldn't I."

"Is that what you'd like to do? Beat me to a bloody pulp?"

"There were a couple of times— What's the point in talking about all of this? What's done is gone, and there's no reason to discuss it. We can't go back."

"No, but we can start over again."

He waited a minute, watching how his comment hit her, waiting for her response. He could see her weighing his words. He knew above all things, she was fair. She would want to do what was right. And in her mind, mankind was basically good and deserved another chance. At least he was counting on that being her reaction.

He smiled when she said, "How do we do that? Go back, I mean."

"I'll show you." He walked back to the window, taking his place, the exact spot he had been standing in when she entered the room. Catching the spirit of things, she skipped back out the door, asking him if he was ready. She reentered the kitchen the moment he said he was.

He turned when he heard her approach. "So you're back," he said.

His words, husky, and spoken so softly, touched her like a warm hand, the caress she felt surprising her. She had expected to feel just a little silly doing this sort of thing with him, because she couldn't see him playing games of any sort . . . unless, of course, they were parlor kissing games. But his tone suggested sincerity, and a quick inspection of his face turned up no trace of mockery or humor. Feeling a little unsure of this whole undertaking, she said breathlessly, "I'm back." Her heart clanked in her ears louder than a tin pan dropped down a flight of wooden stairs. Surely he could hear.

But he was thinking, *so young . . . so small.* Something within him felt protective. He dismissed the feeling, choosing instead to lift his hand, tracing his finger lightly down the bridge of her upturned nose, stopping at her mouth. *If she bites me, I'll wring that lovely neck of hers,* he thought, knowing all the while he wouldn't harm a hair on her perfectly braided head.

She was a refined and polished lady now. Nothing of the tangle-haired imp here. And the belated sadness of that touched him. He found that feeling remarkable, and totally out of character. But a lot of things had been out of character since he had first tangled with her. Perhaps she was right. Maybe the blow *had* addled his wits.

She looked down, lowering her head and breaking the contact. He looked at the small head bowed before him and smiled. Her part was crooked. Oddly, he found that insignificant discovery enchanting. Like a willfully stubborn curl that refused to be subdued, the ragged waif was peeking beneath the ruffled hem of the lady. Yes, she was a lady . . . a lady of mischief. He smiled again, pressing a kiss to the center of that crooked part. He knew the exact moment she drew in her breath and tried to swallow away the swelling tightness in her throat.

He lifted her chin with the curve of his forefinger. Touching her shoulder where the snowy ruffling of lace edged her bodice, he followed the line of it across her throat to the other shoulder, then paused, lifting his eyes to hers. "Did anyone ever tell you you're quite lovely?"

His voice, husky and edged with desire, swirled around her like snowflakes, lighting on her lashes and settling in her hair, then melting and making her tremble. She shook her head. "No."

He was close. So close, the moist warmth of his breath curled against her cheek.

"Would you like some pie?" she asked, wondering what kind of heartless destiny brought her together with a man who provoked her to say such absurd things.

"No," he said. "I'm not hungry . . . for pie."

He lifted his other hand to torment the highly sensitized flesh of her neck, just below her ear. She jumped, forgetting about the pie. He leaned closer and she clamped her eyes together and pressed the back of her hand over her mouth. It was a strange feeling to be both excited to near frenzy and scared witless. What was he going to do? Kiss her? Squeezing her eyes tight, she waited.

Outside, the wind was coming up, howling around the gabled eaves and moaning with a drafty wail down the tall chimney. The hall clock was still ticking; the abandoned calf had found its mammy. All was quiet—except for the loud gush of blood rushing through miles of arteries to pound repeatedly against her ears. But nothing happened.

It would appear she had not only a talent for saying the ridiculous but for expecting it as well.

Mourning opened her eyes, giving him a seraphic smile. His probing visual caress sent a responsive eddy of pleasure rippling across her. It was wholly unnerving, the way memories of lying beneath this magnificent man came swirling around her like an opaque curtain, close and choking, making the world seem suddenly distant. Everything vital remembered the intense sensation of being held in his arms; the drugging weight of his body, the play of hard male musculature against her own feminine softness, the pressing length of tempered steel thighs, the intense heat burgeoning between them, the exquisite promise of his body, the refined cruelty of its denial. Even during the moments when she feared him most, there had been a faint feeling tugging at her. One that seemed to flourish beneath his feverish touch. *What's happening to me? I haven't felt this dizzy since I was hurled off the merry-go-round when I was eight.*

She watched as he poured another cup of coffee. "The name Morning," he said softly, "it's quite unusual. Was Caroline crazy about morning glories, or were you born early in the morning?"

"It's Mourning . . . with a *u*, like Mourning dove."

Mourning. Lady of Mourning. Lady of Mischief. How many facets are there to you, and how many of them will you show me, sweetheart? "Mourning," he said. "Unconventional and unexpected."

He placed his cup on the stove and gently removed the dishtowel that she had twisted, absently, into a rope with her trembling hands. He folded the cloth, tossing it to the table a few feet away. "There's a story here," he said, his right hand finding her throat and sliding up, leaving a trail of goose bumps in its wake. "And I intend to find it. Tell me, my satin-cheeked beauty, how you got your unusual name."

Her eyes dropped to her hands. "My father was killed in a duel while acting as a second to a friend. The other man panicked and fired early. The bullet struck my father in the heart. I was born three weeks later, during the mourning period. I suppose," she said, with a catch in her voice, "it seemed the natural thing to my mother—to name me Mourning."

"So you never knew your father," he said, the strange gentleness and understanding in his voice surprising him more than it did her.

"No," she said, in barely audible tones. "But I'm surprised you didn't know that already . . . that my mother didn't tell you."

"I didn't spend a great deal of time at home, not until the last few months. I suppose Caroline, in her infinite wisdom, saw reason to keep me in the dark about you."

"Why would she do that?"

"Perhaps she saw a morbid parallel. . . . Why are you asking me? I was suckled on a wolf teat. I know nothing of the workings of a mother's mind." He turned away from her, returning to the chair.

His words, of course, made little sense to her, but something in his voice spoke to her. Here was a man who knew all about suffering and pain. That made her reflective. She didn't want to think about Clay Howard, or remember how handsome he looked in the painting over Grandmother Howard's fireplace. Because that made her feel just a little sorry for herself and for him. For dying so young, and because he never knew his daughter, and because of the great sadness that lived in Caroline for so many years. Maybe that was one of the rules—there had to be a great deal of sadness in life. She remembered her early years on their plantation in Virginia—just her and Caroline. She remembered the loneliness, the lack of a sense of family, and her own childish inability to understand why Caroline couldn't get her some brothers and sisters. Was that what prompted Caroline to sell out and move to Tennessee so they could live with the Ragsdales and have a sense of family?

Mourning soon forgot about the sadness she sensed in Clint Kincaid, because she was filled with her own. His arrival had stirred up old memories that were painful and made her realize just how dearly she had missed her mother and how desperately she

wanted to be with her again. Was it this sense of loss—first her
father and then her mother—that made her such a wayward child
and now a rebellious young woman? Was she, like Clint Kincaid,
looking for something and striking out at the world because she
could not find it? She couldn't answer that. Not right now. There
was too much pain that came with thinking. She could only think
about her father when she was happy. Now she needed more cheerful thoughts . . . of happier times.

Now, why, for goodness sake, did that stupid tear pick this
very moment to slip down her cheek? She raised the back of her
hand and brushed it away, much as she would an errant strand of
hair, hoping he wouldn't notice.

But he did.

"Come here," he said with unbelievable softness.

She heard the chair scrape as he stood, and she knew she had
to get away before he touched her. Turning, she bolted from the
room, the sound of her feet on the stairs echoing through the silent
house.

"Well, well, what have we here?"

Clint stood up as a rosy-faced man with wiry side-whiskers
and a pumpkin stomach stepped into the kitchen, followed by two
girls about Mourning's age and a woman who bore a striking resemblance to Caroline.

Clint shook hands with the man. "I'm Clint Kincaid," he
said.

"We weren't expecting you until next week."

"I concluded my business in St. Louis earlier than I anticipated," Clint said.

"Heaven's to Betsy," the woman said. "Francis, where are
your manners?" The woman smiled and stepped forward, extending her hand. "I'm Harriet Ragsdale, Caroline's sister, and
this ill-mannered brute is my husband, Francis," Harriet said.
"And our daughters, Anna and Melly."

Clint greeted the girls as Harriet looked around the room.
"Have you seen Mourning?"

"She's upstairs," Clint said.

Anna turned to Harriet. "May we go upstairs, Mama?"

Harriet gave a nod, then a sigh, as both girls tried to go

through the door at the same time. Then they backed up and went at it again, in single file.

"I don't suppose you would consider taking all three?" Francis asked, with a hopeful look in Clint's direction. He patted his stomach.

Clint laughed, saying *most definitely not,* and then Harriet said whenever Francis patted his stomach it was a sure sign he was warming up for one of his sermonettes.

"I can tell you that children in my day did not behave like that," Francis said.

"It's a good thing, my love, that you didn't know Caroline and me at their age," Harriet said. Seeing her husband's expression, Harriet laughed and began to fuss with the pins in her hat. Removing it, she placed it at one end of the table and turned toward Clint. "Would you like some coffee, Mr. Kincaid?"

"No thank you, ma'am. Mourning filled me with too much coffee already," Clint said.

"My God," Francis exclaimed. "What happened to your head?" Then, noticing the burned hand, he added, "And your hand?"

"It seems your niece mistook me for a thief when I was putting my horse in the barn and she cold-cocked me."

"And the burn?"

"That's the result of a minor disagreement over a cup of coffee," Clint answered.

Francis groaned.

"Mourning?" Harriet asked with astonishment.

Francis looked at Clint. He looked at his wife. "Harriet, sometimes you amaze me. How can you act surprised after all the scrapes that girl is always getting into? I personally find it hard to believe that's all she did while we were gone." He looked at Clint. "Or is there more?"

Clint chuckled. "None that you'd believe," he said.

"Try me," Francis said.

5

The next afternoon Mourning curled up in her window seat, parted the ball-fringe curtains, and looked out. Below her window lay a velvet stretch of ground washed in splashes of sunlight. A fat little robin was busily employed in the soft troweled earth between a lovely pink mass of sweet peas and blue forget-me-nots. Each botanical mystery had once again emerged as springtime crept over every living thing like a gauzy green veil. Warming sunrays touched freshly clipped hedges, flower beds, and freshly turned earth, and created shimmering sparkles in the water bubbling from an old stone fountain.

It was a scene that moved her strongly and brought forth a gush of tender memories. Home. For all her years here, she had hardly given it a thought, and now it was pulling and tugging at her heart. Home. Beloved and dear. Haunted by the ghost of her childhood. She had been happy here. She did not want to leave. But fate was pulling her away and fashioning her future.

Hang the future, she thought. *It's the present that has me worried.* Nothing was going right. Gloom settled over her. Not even the penetrating warmth of the sun could reach her melancholy heart. Within her everything lay like stiff, naked woods and frozen brown meadows. Mourning remembered the coolly detached composure and the warm kiss of Clint Kincaid. A sick feeling of pessimism overwhelmed her, trapping her usual cheerfulness and locking it away. With her head sinking as low as her spirits, Mourning rested her elbows upon the windowsill and speculated upon the effects of a dramatic leap from the second-story window.

Her thoughts went back to the evening before—just minutes after her family had arrived from the Church Basket Meeting. She remembered Clint standing with his splendid legs spread in a Texas sprawl. That, Mourning had not minded so much, although it was quite distracting. What she had minded was the way he stood in the library with an aura of unholy magnificence, laughing with Aunt Harriet and Uncle Francis, who were completely entangled in his silky web. Even the subtle dishevelment from their encounter had only served to embellish his staggering masculinity.

"Bah!" she said, giving the ball fringe a thump. "What do I care what that ham-handed thick-wit looks like? As if I give a no nevermind. He doesn't turn my head—all dressed up in his fancy duds. No matter how you dress a dog, his tail will still stick out."

So, he doesn't appeal to you, does he? Liar! Why did you stand there gawking like a famished hogfish in a school of mudminnows?

Why? Mourning Kathleen, you know very well why. Every perfect inch of the man was devastating—from the metallic glint of lamplight on raven hair to the suggestion of a shapely booted leg. Riding on the heels of that thought came the bittersweet memory of a tantalizing face and erotic mouth that had kissed her with all the delicacy of a thunderbolt.

She lifted her hand to touch her lips. His kiss. That had been real—the tender sting of recalled passion too genuine to be otherwise. No matter how hard she tried to erase the memory, the thoroughly disturbing reality of it had remained with her all through dinner, expanding with heart-wrenching vividness by evening's end. In Clint Kincaid, she sensed a power, a violence of emotion that branded him different. Perhaps it was the disparity between his mental polish and the tough, almost gritty restlessness she saw in him.

Last evening she had been steeped in anger, listening to Clint's Byronic eloquence as he recounted the events and details of their encounter. Spellbound, and hanging on his every word, Aunt Harriet and Uncle Francis sat with Clint on the camelback sofa. While Mourning was abandoned upon the mammy bench, where she witnessed, incredulous, the way he smiled and bamboozled his way into the Ragsdales' good graces. Only to be rewarded with a glass of Uncle Francis's finest French brandy—brandy Uncle Francis refused to share with anyone. Mourning, on the other hand, was dismissed after she'd offered a few ill-fated comments such as *"Oh, no, that's not how it was at all,"* or *"I did not put my hand there,"* or *"How can you believe what he's saying? Can't you see? He's twisted everything to make himself come out smelling like a rose."*

In a very short time Uncle Francis and Clint were as thick as flies in August. Just thinking about it made her mad all over again, the way Uncle Francis laughed and slapped Clint fondly on the back and said, "A rose by any other name is still a rose, eh, my boy?"

Embroidered phrases aside, Mourning saw with bruising certainty that she was not only encouraged but assisted by her loved ones to make a humiliating spectacle of herself.

The man in the library last night was no more like the stony-eyed stranger who had run roughshod over her earlier, than a fig is like a partridge. He had scattered convincing words like chicken feed, and Mourning had only stared, dumbfounded, as Uncle Francis and Aunt Harriet gobbled every grain. Each time Mourning related an event, Clint countered with a more believable version. A man like that would pour water on a drowning mouse.

Mourning could think of only one thing in his favor. Clint had delivered the coup de grace swiftly. As the women were retiring from the room, Mourning overheard Uncle Francis speaking to Clint.

"Why do I have the feeling we've won the battle but lost the war?" he said. "Much as I hate to admit it, I'm afraid we haven't heard the last of this. It's not like Mourning to let a sleeping dog lie."

With tactical brilliance, Clint replied blandly, "Then your niece needs to learn, the more you tramp a turd, the broader it becomes."

The afterclap of Uncle Francis's overzealous laughter followed like gloom, down the hall and up the stairway. Humiliated and unable to fix her mind upon anything else, Mourning went to her room. Submerged in shame, a headache pounding, she found sleep a long time coming.

But that was last night. Today Mourning mustered her courage by reminding herself, church wasn't over until the singing was done. That hero of the hayloft might think he had her over a pickle barrel, but there was more than one way to skin a mule. There wasn't a man born that would get the best of her.

Pressing her nose to the window, Mourning smiled in a distracted way at the hound under the sycamore that was raising the dust with his tail. Clint Kincaid sauntered across the yard. In gentleman's dress, he conveyed a sense of style yet he remained a man of the saddle. The West was in his walk. The hound stopped the mad thumping of his tail and greeted Clint affectionately. The smile drained from her face. Even the dogs were hornswoggled.

Remembered shame and witnessed treason are painfully strong allies, and Mourning found she had not the strength nor discipline to withstand or fight. So she left the window and moved to her bed, flopped across the quilted counterpane, and considered herself betrayed. Her slippers dropped to the floor with a thump, and she wiggled her toes against the cool satin comforter that lay folded at the foot of the bed. She contemplated her dilemma. The crux of the matter was, it rankled most severely to think her family would entrust her, body and soul, to a man she wouldn't trust as far as she could throw a bull by the tail.

But what could she do? At this point her choices were, at best, grim: acceptance, suicide, or retreat. Acceptance had such a bitter aftertaste. Retreat was not in her vocabulary. And Mourning could think of only one favorable thing about suicide. It wouldn't become a habit.

Suddenly laughing at the lunatic inclination of her thoughts, Mourning peeled away gloom as a snake sheds its skin. Her damp but resilient spirits revived, she took off in full pursuit of the unknown. In the time it would take to examine a hot horseshoe, Mourning decided her next performance for Clint Kincaid would, by far, rival the previous one. She would go to Texas. But *not* with him.

A flash of doubt came in the form of Grandmother Howard's words: *Never meet trouble halfway. It's quite capable of making the entire trip alone.* But Mourning quickly ignored those words of caution.

Mourning was thinking she wasn't known throughout Shelby County, Tennessee, for nothing. *I'll think of something* . . . A slow smile of satisfaction curled across her face. As sure as the displacement of a little sand could change the course of a river, Clint Kincaid was about to find his course altered. Drastically.

The rest of the day passed more slowly than the seven-year itch. Giving the family members who thought Clint was so wonderful her share of his attention, Mourning excused herself from an evening in the parlor. As she walked from the room, Clint, talking to Francis over a map of the plantation, looked up.

"Are you retiring, Miss Howard?"

"Yes, Mr. Kincaid, I am."

"Conversation not to your liking?" he asked smoothly.

"Not particularly."

"Ahhh . . . the painful truth."

"It's not the truth I find painful," she said stiffly, "but the stretching of it."

A soft knock at her door two hours later turned out to be cousin Anna. Three months younger than Mourning, Anna Claire Ragsdale was just about that far behind her cousin in mischievous devilry.

Before Mourning could answer, the strawberry blonde with laughing brown eyes popped her head through the door. *"Pssst, Mourning, are you awake?"* Anna whispered in a tone loud enough to be heard in Chattanooga.

"Yes, but I won't be the only one if you don't shut up," Mourning answered, yanking Anna into the room and checking the hallway before closing the door.

Anna then said, "I would've been up earlier, but I was waiting until Mr. Kincaid and Papa retired to the library." Anna stumbled further into the room, heedless of her graceless feet, her mind on other matters. "Don't you think he's quite a sinfully handsome rogue?"

"Sinful, yes," Mourning said. But Anna didn't appear to be listening. *Beguiled by that snake already,* Mourning thought. There was little doubt now. . . . Clint Kincaid *was* Lucifer, hiding behind a beautiful face.

"I do wish *I* were going with Mr. Kincaid," Anna said with indecent fervor.

Mourning never doubted that for a minute. "Never mind all that," Mourning rushed. "I need your help."

"With what?"

"An escape."

"An escape?" Anna repeated. "From what?"

"Clint Kincaid."

Anna looked at Mourning as though her head were transparent and she hoped to find the reason written on the wall beyond. "You want to run away from him?" she said. Then, with a higher pitch, "Clint Kincaid?"

Mourning held up one hand and made a big X across her chest. "Cross my heart."

Anna frowned at Mourning with great concern and shook her head, disbelief clear in her words. "Hang it all, Mourning! No one in their right mind would run from a man that looks like he does. I'll wager half the women that pass him on the street end up with eye ruptures. His kind don't grow on trees, you know. If they did, I'd build a tree house and never come down . . . and you want to escape? I don't understand it. I really don't. *Escape?* Why?" Anna paused. She stared at Mourning. "Whatever is the matter with you? It must be the heat or . . . Mourning Kathleen Howard, is it your monthlies?"

"No," snapped Mourning, "it isn't. That's all I need to make this a perfectly sublime day."

Anna caught her own reflection in the mirror and began pinching her cheeks to restore the color that had drained away. Her face lost its serious look. Her lovely taffy-colored eyes dilated as she spoke to the mirror, a dreamy look of rapture on her face, her cheeks warmly flushed. "You know, a man like that . . . he had to be born beautiful."

"What has that got to do with anything? *All* babies are born beautiful," Mourning said, thinking Anna was acting as daft as the time she fell out of the willow tree and landed on her head. "Anna?"

But Anna was absently wrapping her hair ribbon around her finger, a silly smile on her face, her mind clearly out of control and running amok with sweet abandon. "You can bet your bottom dollar his mama didn't have to tie no lollipop around his neck to get the girls to play with him."

Mourning wanted to argue that point, but Anna looked in good enough form to last five rounds with Daniel Webster, so she decided to let things be. Anna, she decided, was the only person she knew who could appear intelligent by accident. Mourning gave a half-pathetic sigh. "I'm leaving tonight," she said. "Will you help me?"

"Tonight?" Anna said. "Why tonight? Mr. Kincaid told Papa he planned to leave day after tomorrow."

"I know, slackwit. That's why I want to leave now. I don't want to go with him. I'm going *alone*. Understand?" Mourning looked at Anna, unable to decide who irritated her more, Anna or Clint Kincaid.

Anna rambled on, as if someone had oiled her jaws. "You can't run away. You just can't. What about Texas? What about your mother? What will she think? Mourning, you simply cannot run away. Aunt Caroline is expecting you. How will we explain? We can't very well tell her we've misplaced you. Think, think! You absolutely, positively *have* to go to Texas."

"I *am* going to Texas," Mourning said. "I'm just not going with him."

"If you want my two cents' worth . . . *I* think you should reconsider."

"Anna, I said I needed your help, and I do. But not to make up my mind. I've already done that."

Anna didn't say anything. She could see Mourning had made up her mind. And Mourning was as obstinate as they came when she had her heels dug in like this. There was no changing her mind now—not even a two-by-four to the head would convince her. It was like Papa said: *Mourning would rather die than bend.* "All right," Anna said, giving in at last. "I'll help. But I swear if brains were dynamite, you wouldn't have enough to blow your nose." Then with a tone of sheer exasperation: "What do you want me to do?"

"Help me get out of the house."

"Now?"

"Right now."

"But you can't get out now."

"Why can't I?"

"Because Papa and Mr. Kincaid are still downstairs drinking brandy, and you *know* how long Papa can drink brandy. Besides, the door is open. It may be morning before you can leave."

"That's too late," Mourning said. "I'll just have to find another way."

"Want me to pack your valise?" Anna asked eagerly.

"No, it's packed," Mourning replied, thinking that once Anna got into the spirit of things she was all cooperation. "You wait here —by my window. Watch for my signal, then toss the bag down."

"That's simple enough," Anna said. "Now comes the hard part. Just *how* do you plan to get down there?"

"I'll go through the kitchen," Mourning said.

"But you'd have to pass the library to get to the kitchen. I told you, Papa and Mr. . . ."

"Oh, fiddle," Mourning said. "I've got to get out of here tonight."

"How about the window?"

"The lattice is too shaky. . . . I want to leave *town,* Anna, *not* the face of the earth."

"Right," Anna said, then giggled. "How about the attic? You'd have to be awfully careful."

Mourning usually didn't need help getting into trouble, but with Anna around, she always had it. "Of course," Mourning said. "Why didn't I think of that? I'll go upstairs to the attic and then across this wing to the kitchen wing, then down the back stairs."

"Mourning, you know how creepy that attic is even in broad daylight," Anna cautioned.

The stairway to the attic was narrow and steep, not to mention dark. Afraid to carry a candle, Mourning groped along the wall until she reached the newel post, and then began her ascent. This wasn't going too badly, so far, but the real test would be navigating the attic in the darkness. One thing knocked over could alert the entire household.

At the attic door she paused, and hearing nothing but silence, she stepped inside, closing the door softly behind her. An eerie silver light filtered through the dormer windows, casting long, shredded shadows across the accumulations of several generations of Ragsdales. She crept forward, skirting a wire dress-form and a brass bird-cage with ease, so much ease, in fact, she failed to notice Uncle Francis's snowshoes resting against an old trunk, and sent them sliding to the floor with a rumbling *thwack.* She hesitated, then hearing no sound, slowly inched forward, working her way through the cluttered maze at a snail's pace.

Voices. Faint and deep. She must be over the library. She paused, hearing the indistinct shuffle of feet and the tinkle of glasses blending with muffled voices. Hushed whispers. A laugh. Fading footsteps. Apparently they were retiring. A few more steps would have her over the kitchen wing. She passed another window —the moonlight, absorbing all the color from her face and clothing, leaving her bathed in light, pale and ghostly.

Mourning moved slowly, one step, and then another, creeping her way through the unbelievable assortment of mishmash that created nightmarish obstacles: dozens of unmatched gilt candlesticks, an old sled with a broken steering bar, a mahogany curveback chair, an old oaken tub with copper hoops, a spinning wheel, broken bellows, tarnished andirons. Now came the difficult part. There was an area, where the two wings of the house joined, where the attic was not floored. For some forty odd feet she would have to walk over narrow rafters until she reached the floored section that lay above the kitchen.

Balance was required for this crossing, but Mourning was not worried. Over the course of years, the three cousins had spent countless hours playing in the attic, one of their favorite pastimes being races across the rafters. Of the hundreds of times they'd raced, there had been no mistakes, save one.

Once, many years ago, Anna had snagged her petticoat on a splinter and gone crashing through the floor, which happened also to be the ceiling of the guest room below. The ornate plaster molding on the ceiling had been irreparably damaged and a furious Aunt Harriet declared the attic off-limits. Of course that didn't stop their visits to the attic; it merely made the girls more cautious.

With a twinge of apprehension, Mourning glanced up, her breath locking in her throat. Not fifteen feet away on a rafter running horizontal to hers was something furry, difficult to recognize because of the contrasting dark shadows and oblong pools of light. The creature moved into the light. Masked and luminous, its eyes studied her: a raccoon. For some unknown reason the raccoon turned sharply and ran toward her, with such speed, the creature was under her skirts before she knew it.

Mourning struggled valiantly to maintain her balance, but balancing on a narrow beam is difficult. With a raccoon up your skirts, it's nigh impossible. Her descent was fluid and smooth, like an angel falling from grace. On her way down she made two quick prayerful requests: one, that there be a bed below her, and two, that it be unoccupied.

After consuming far too much brandy, Clint had retired to his room and was sitting on the bed removing his boots. A thump and

squeal overhead drew his immediate attention. Before he could
glance up, a shower of flying plaster and debris crashed upon him.
As he cursed angrily, his hot eyes flashed upward, immediately
softening with amusement. Dangling above him was the most pro-
nouncedly curved and provocatively clad lower torso he'd seen
since he'd been in Paris. Swinging perilously like a poorly secured
chandelier, the well-formed legs thrashed and flailed with more
dramatic flair than a Shakespearean tragedy. Then, with a loud
crack the surrounding plaster gave way and the shapely legs were
hurled like a javelin.

Mourning's rapidly descending body came to an abrupt halt.
Next came a horrified squawk, followed by a corresponding exclamation of "Oaf." Bits of molding and plaster continued to rain
upon the unfortunate couple wreathed in billowing dust upon a
collapsed bed. A voice, hoarse and throbbing, emanated from close
by. "So glad you could drop in, Miss Howard."

Identification was immediate.

Her goose cooked, there was nothing to do but lie there until
the wild pounding of her heart subsided.

A trumpeting voice shattered the stillness. "For the love of
God, what harebrained madness are you about now? I've heard of
hitting below the belt . . . but in this, Miss Howard, you take the
cake."

Mourning dug ten panic-stricken fingers into the hard thighs
of Clint Kincaid. Waiting for an idea, she closed her eyes and
pretended she wasn't there. But *there* she was, little Mourning
Kathleen Howard, whose closest encounter with the male anatomy
had been when she was seven and caught Teddy Snodgrass making
a branch behind the henhouse with a little pink worm.

The irrepressible panic of finding her head resting heavily on
the inner thigh of this man, her body wedged between the legs of a
virile male whose . . . Well, nothing, absolutely *nothing,* about
this man would be little or pink. It was just one too many wagons
on the bridge.

Apprehensive as a frog on a busy road with a busted jumper,
she probed her brain for a way to get out of her dire situation. But
she came up with nothing. By now Mourning was desperate. She
tore her eyes away from him and looked down. She tried, in a rage
of consuming modesty, to cover her drawers. One more stick was
tossed on the fire when she found her skirts were trapped under six

feet, two inches of uncooperative male. She tried moving away from him, but with the hopeless tangle of limbs and bedding . . . it was not to be. Lifting the corner of a sheet over her head, Mourning was determined to rearrange and disengage herself as soon as possible.

"What are you doing under there," Clint asked, "looking for an excuse?"

"No," came a muffled voice. "Looking for a way out."

"It's a little late for that, isn't it? Have you ever heard of forethought? No? How about prudence? Surely to God you don't test the depth of a river with both feet. Oh? You do? That may be the key to all of this. Tell me, angel, what do you have in that adorable little head of yours? Fungus?"

"Just what I needed," she said, pulling her head out, "fresh wit." Clinging forlornly to the last remnant of her shredded pride, Mourning added, "If you were any kind of a gentleman, you'd help me out of this mess."

"This must be some kind of record," Clint said in a voice that traveled up her spine like a warm palm. "A woman who throws herself at a man, in his own bed, and then expects him to act like a gentleman."

"I did not throw myself at you!"

Clint's eyes lifted to the gaping hole in the ceiling and then back at her. "No?" he said. "Are we up to admitting we're falling for me, then?" Seeing her pained frown, the trembling mouth, he felt an instant gush of compassion. Desire came immediately after. With one slender brown finger he traced a path of erotic patterns across her cheek.

"Whatever pleases you, sweet. But I will tell you this. I've never had a woman go to this much trouble to get into my bed. And it's an absolute first to have one want to leave once she got there."

Hot water, Mourning thought, must be her natural element, because she spent a great deal of time in it. Her life was just one long process of getting weary. Wearied to the teeth, she turned her attention to her immediate problem.

Now, Clint enjoyed a physical conflict with a woman as much as any man, probably more, but he had never anticipated such an aggressive woman as Mourning suddenly became. It was a new discovery: A woman, when she regresses to a lower stage of evolution, has no qualms whatsoever about fighting dirty. All teeth and talons, she came at him with all primal forces operating. From the pounding, panting, yelling heap, Mourning emerged and struggled to her knees only to be yanked backward and thrown to her back with Clint's brooding face sitting in judgment above her.

"Care to explain what you were doing traipsing around in the attic this time of night?" he asked.

When she couldn't make the words come out, Clint kindly tendered helpful persuasion. He shook the answer out of her. "I'm going to Texas on my own, so I won't have to go with you," she said, her voice sounding rattled.

"Guess again," he said.

The struggle resumed primitive simplicity. Over and over again, Mourning struggled from the mayhem to her knees only to go down again, howling a wordless battle-cry. From the midst of the tangle of arms, legs, canopy, and petticoat came a hoarse assortment of words and phrases that placed grave doubts upon the legitimacy of Clint's birth.

At last, thoroughly disheveled, Mourning was subdued. Clint, in similar ruin, gave no heed to his condition, despite the swelling of his left eye. Knowing she owed him some explanation, and that she wouldn't be released until she gave it to him, Mourning stammered, "I know you won't believe this . . ."

It was the first time in his life that Clint Kincaid had a woman lying prone beneath him who wanted to talk. "Try me, Miss Howard," he said, panting between words. "For some strange reason I find I'm willing to believe almost *anything* that involves you."

"I knew you'd be mad," she said, wondering why the way out of trouble is never as simple as the way in.

Calm and no longer cursing, Clint was distracted by a wadded lump of bedding, twisting and thrashing frantically at the foot of the bed. With a nod in the lump's direction, he said, "Who's your friend?"

"A raccoon," Mourning answered, "it ran under my skirts. That's why I fell."

A mental picture of that drew a wide grin from him. The snarled bedclothes became untangled and a raccoon leaped out, hissed at Mourning, then hit the floor at a dead run before it vanished in the shadows.

That was it! Frazzled and trembling, Mourning went limp as

noodles against the starched fragrance of Clint's shoulder. Securely held in his arms, she buried her head further against him, her small arms clinging tighter than a lamprey.

"Hey," he said softly. "What's the matter?"

"I don't know," she cried between sniffs. "I just feel like crying. This hasn't . . . Oh, I don't know what I'm saying. I just feel like I'm being pressured."

He grinned. "Buttercup, you *are* being pressured . . . believe me."

Seeing the wicked gleam in his eye, she cuffed him lightly on the arm. "You have a one-track mind! I mean I'm feeling *really, really* pressured." She sniffed again, rubbing her nose against his shirt-sleeve.

"I know," he said charitably, "and it's building up steam by the minute. If I don't get you out from under me *fast,* we may both be sorry."

She had only enough energy to collapse. The tears, when they came, stung her eyes and choked her words. Here she was trying to choke back tears of frustration and embarrassment on the one hand, while all manner of involuntary feelings were erupting on the other. Weak as a day-old calf, she relaxed beneath him.

"Now I have you trembling and willing in my arms," he whispered through three inches of plaster dust to reach her ear. "Your timing, as usual, my madcap little friend, is perfect. No, angel, before you throw yourself at me again, I suggest you look up. We're not alone."

Through streaming locks and plaster-dusted lashes Mourning saw the slow assembling of a curious mob. The entire Ragsdale family joined the cook, three maids, and the butler at the foot of Clint's bed.

"Well, well, well. What's this?" Francis said, his eyes going from the ceiling to the rumpled bed, then to Mourning, where they rested. "Tell me truthfully," he urged, "is this a jump to conclusions, or a big letdown?"

Mourning didn't answer, but Clint gave it a go. "Would you believe I just caught an eavesdropper?"

Harriet, who had been standing in silent awe, finally said, "I can't believe this."

To which Francis replied, "I find that hard to believe, my

dear. The girl has a mind like a weathercock. What would you expect from a pig but a grunt?"

"Uncle Francis," Mourning said, wearily dragging herself from the bed, "you can get your point across without stabbing me with it."

Standing regally before her uncle, Mourning looked so coolly unaffected that Clint had to glance upward to reassure himself. Seeing the gaping hole, he crossed his arms behind his head and smiled, ready to wait this one out.

Francis, turning to Clint, said, "Have you any thoughts as to what I should do with my niece?"

Clint, who knew exactly what he'd *like* to do with her, gave the matter some thought.

Meanwhile, Mourning, praying the memory of this humiliating scene would be much kinder than the reality, shook the plaster dust from her skirts. Shoulders back, head held at a proud angle, Mourning walked toward the door, then paused. "Mr. Kincaid, your opinion isn't worth a pitcher of warm spit." And with that she walked out of his room.

6

At half past three the next afternoon, Clint stood before the wide sweep of windows overlooking the driveway of the Ragsdale plantation. He planted his feet wide apart, rocking on his heels as he gazed out. Beyond the windows, a tall row of well-manicured trees, dressed in the bright green foliage of spring, shimmered in a haze along the gravel drive. The hollow crunch of crushed rock rang under the shod hooves of matched chestnuts stamping with impatient anticipation. Warm April sun enriched the patina of the glorious curls bouncing beneath Mourning's bonnet as she was handed into the open carriage by Dr. Lance Prescott.

Clint studied her as she sat down, skirts methodically draped across the seat, displaying herself like the royal barge. Quite a change from the tangle-haired hoyden dangling through his ceiling last night. He wondered how fond she was of the fair-haired doctor everyone in the family found so handsome. Clint shook his head with bewilderment, unable to imagine how anyone in their right mind could find that anemic-looking pantywaist handsome. Clint had never cared for fair-haired men—an aversion that was fast moving to include blond women.

The image of *Dr. Lance* on the veranda this morning, plucking a caterpillar off Mourning's generous bosom and calling it a *woolly worm* was too vivid in Clint's mind for him to think of Lance as anything but a bonehead. He watched their carriage clatter down the tree-shaded drive, Mourning chatting and smiling as if she were on top of the world, when a few minutes ago she had frostily greeted him with a peculiar lift to her nose—as if she had just whiffed something most foul. He turned away at the sound of footsteps.

The library door opened and Francis Ragsdale stepped into the room. "Sorry I'm late. I've been down at the kennel delivering hounds," he said. "Peart near wore myself out too. That new bitch I bought last year just whelped eleven pups. Jumpin' jehosaphat! I think that makes five litters in two months. I've got pups coming out my ears." His eyes sparkled and he laughed mirthfully. "That's enough to harelip ole Thaddeus Hamilton for sure. I've a mind to traipse on over there now and spill the beans." He chuckled again, and shook his head. "Thad owned that bitch for five years and she never whelped a single pup and . . ." Laughter got the better of Francis. When it passed, Francis slapped his knee. "I got eleven pups on the first try. By damn! That calls for a drink." Francis stood, his stomach still twitching with laughter.

Francis went on talking as he walked to a table displaying an assortment of fine liquors in decanters that had to be Irish crystal. Clint relaxed in his chair, looking like someone had just tossed him into it, a slow, easy kind of smile on his face.

Clint liked Francis Ragsdale, his easygoing nature and good humor. Francis was one of those men who seemed to go through life seeing a heap of common stones not as a rockpile but as a cathedral. It was something he had in common with his niece, but in Francis Ragsdale, youthful exuberance had been tempered with wisdom—something Mourning had not acquired. Yes, he liked Francis. He was a man's man—easy to be around.

"Yes, sir, I'm as proud as a dog with two tails," Francis said, still chuckling. He poured himself a brandy and handed one to Clint. "How's that head of yours?"

"All right. A few headaches. Nothing more."

"That was some kind of blow you took . . . makes my old head throb just thinking about it. Did you up proper, didn't she? 'Course that gal's never done anything halfway." Francis dropped into his leather chair and leaned back, propping his feet on the desk. "You still planning on leaving tomorrow? Might be a good idea to wait around another day or two and let that head perk up a mite. I don't cotton to your taking off before you're back on your feet."

"I need to get back," Clint said. "Before my courage fails me."

"Don't I know it," Francis said. "A wise man would see the wisdom in that—leaving before Mourning can regroup and have another go at it." Smoke from his carved German pipe curled wreathlike around his head. He picked the pipe up, taking a couple of draws on it before putting it down again. "Only one problem I can see with your plan."

"What kind of problem?"

"The chaperone we hired is in New Orleans and not due back here for five days."

"Do you know where she's staying in New Orleans? Maybe we could make connections with her there?" Clint said.

Francis looked at Clint over the top of glasses that teetered perilously on the tip of his nose, apparently lost in thought. "Yes, by George, I do have it. Can't tell you what a relief that is. Harriet kept me awake half the night with her jawing about finding another chaperone," he said. "I swear that woman could talk the legs off a stove. I kept telling her we could trust you—you being family 'n' all, but that didn't sit too well with Harriet. No siree! When that woman's mad, she could tear up an anvil."

Francis took another drink and Clint was glad for the distraction. He wasn't sure how much longer he could keep a straight face.

"What it all boils down to—and I quote my lovely wife," Francis said, *"Lucifer was an angel and Judas was a disciple. Look where that got us. If you think for one minute, Jonathan Francis Ragsdale, that I'm going to let my niece travel with Mr. Kincaid, you're dumber than a doorknocker.* Now, don't take it personal. Harriet just took one look at you and refused to let Mourning go without another woman along." Francis scratched his chin. "Said she wouldn't trust a man that looked like you with an eighty-year-old nun."

"Of all the women in the world, your niece is safe with me," Clint said. "I plan to keep my distance—I value my hide too much. Anyway, I can't help thinking your niece can take care of herself."

"She sure can. Boy, you were some mess by the time we came home from church." Francis chuckled and dug around in his drawer. "Now, where in the hell did I put my makin's?"

Clint grinned. By damn if he didn't like Francis better and better.

"Ah, here it is," Francis said, pulling his tobacco pouch out of a drawer. "I know Mourning can be a handful—I'll grant you that much. There's never been a yardstick you could measure her by; she's as unpredictable as spring weather. I guess I've been partly responsible, never could bring myself to spank her—not that she didn't deserve it plenty."

"It's never too late."

"My boy, I'll pass that responsibility on to you."

"Thanks," Clint said dryly. "Tell me, was she always so . . ."

"Yep. I'm not lying when I say there wasn't a wilder-looking or worse-acting child to be found in the entire state of Tennessee when Caroline and Mourning came to live with us."

"When was that?"

"Let's see. Mourning couldn't have been more than five or six. Caroline stayed on the plantation in Virginia a few years after Clay died, but it was just too much for a woman to run, so I convinced her to sell out and come live with us. Those first two or three years they were here came close to being the undoing of me. That little mite had me a-comin' and a-goin'. Mourning was clever as a minx and sly as a fox, capable of being everywhere at once and guilty of nothing. She rebelled at everything you told her and went out of her way to do the exact opposite. In all my years I've never seen anyone as headstrong and stubborn."

"I see she hasn't changed."

"My boy, you've seen only one small grain of sand, I'm talking about the whole beach. That girl was downright dangerous. She accidentally set the milking barn on fire while trying to make her own firecrackers and chopped down half the boat dock when we told her a new tutor would be dropped off there. She has fallen out of trees, up the stairs, off the bridge, through the ceiling, from the roof, and out of a boat. She has broken her arm, cracked her head, been chased by cows, flogged by geese, kicked by horses, and run over by a wagon. There were times when we thought she would either break her own fool neck or blow up the entire house, taking all of us with it."

Clint laughed. "I have to keep reminding myself we're talking about a girl here," he said.

"And I'm only hitting the highlights." Francis grinned, as if remembering all the mischief making with fondness. "You know, it's a good thing this plantation has always been prosperous. That girl cost me a small fortune in medicine and medical bills alone. It was common knowledge that our bills at the apothecary were outstanding, and Dr. Henderson was called out here so much, he seriously considered moving in with us for a spell. Mourning was constantly being brought home half dead, but always miraculously bounced back from every mishap with more energy than before."

The library door flew open, crashing against the wall with a loud *thump* as Harriet and Anna entered.

"Anna," Francis said, standing to give his wife a peck on the cheek, "you've been slamming that door for fifteen of your eighteen years. Dare I hope there could be an end in sight?"

"Sorry, Papa," she said, giving him an affectionate kiss. "Mama and I are off to Aunt Prudie's for tea."

Francis's bushy brows lifted in surprise, and he looked at Harriet. "Prudie's?" he repeated.

Harriet laughed. "Yes, Aunt Prudie's housekeeper eloped last week—at the age of fifty-six if you can imagine—and poor Prudie is about to lose her mind."

"Really?" Francis said, "I didn't know she had one to lose."

"Oh, Francis, be nice," Harriet said. "She means well. I think she is basically a very loving person."

"An attribute she keeps well hidden," Francis said as he gave Clint a wink. A round of laughter filled the room. "Well, my dears, do have a pleasant afternoon," Francis said.

Two kisses and a swat to Harriet's backside later, Francis laughed and patted his stomach. "I think all this laughter is good for my indigestion, damned if I don't." He settled himself back in his chair, and seeing Clint rub his temples, asked if his head was bothering him.

"Just a throb now and then," Clint said.

"It probably won't make your head feel any better, but you're not the only man to suffer injury at Mourning's hands. I think those in-between years were the worst for both of us. . . . You know, no longer a child, but not yet a woman?"

Clint nodded. "Her growth seems to be stuck there."

"Well, I can tell you she's sent many a young man home with a black eye or a bloody nose when he made reference to her new womanly curves or tried to kiss her. I'm telling you, getting sweet on that girl was baitin' trouble. Not that it stopped any of the lads around here—lapped it up, they did. She always had more beaux than she could shake a stick at."

"What was the average life expectancy of one of them?" Clint asked, touching his own bruised eye.

Francis laughed. "Not long. They either retreated in shame when she continued to best them in every situation or she ran them off."

Of all the things he'd heard Francis say, Clint thought his last statement the most sage. He could well imagine just *how* Mourning ran them off. Two days with her and his own body was near ruin.

Francis refilled his snifter and turned to Clint. "More brandy?"

"Yes, thanks." Sipping on his brandy, Clint reclined further in his chair, wondering if there was the remotest possibility that Dr. Lance Pussyfoot could convince Mourning to marry him. Oh, to go to Texas alone, he thought. Yet, at the same time he was wishing she would stay behind, he was remembering a certain green-eyed imp with more energy than a steam-engine. How much of that exuberance was real, and how much of it was manufactured to hide the sadness he knew existed deep inside her? She was smart—and clever too. She did a good job of hiding her pain and sending out a message of wild-eyed defiance and mischief, but his questions to her about her father had touched something painful, something she didn't want him to share. He'd be willing to bet that inside the living core of that snarled ball of honey-colored curls lived a sad and lonely little girl who never had a sense of belonging. It was a feeling Clint knew well. But he also knew women.

Any man fool enough to pity Miss Mourning Kathleen Howard would find himself neatly tacked to the nearest fence post.

"Have you ever seen a drunk chicken?" Francis was asking.

"What?"

"Have you ever seen a drunk chicken?" he repeated.

"I can't say that I have," Clint replied.

"Well, I'm sorry you haven't, because it's a damn funny sight," Francis said. "When Mourning was thirteen she and Teddy Snodgrass soaked bread in bourbon and fed it to the chickens. Poor things staggered all over the place until Harriet took pity on them and locked them up in the henhouse until they were sober."

Clint threw back his head with a crack of laughter.

Francis's eyes reflected the fondness he felt for Mourning as he spoke. "I don't think there has been one rule of etiquette she hasn't broken, and it was beyond her to conform to rules of propriety. If you told her not to do it, she did it. If it was something only boys did, she had to be the first girl. If someone did something well, she had to do it better. I remember one summer the neighboring boys built a canoe. Know what she did?"

Clint, at this point, was afraid to speculate. "I couldn't begin to guess."

"She built a raft," Francis said. "Damn good one too. Launched the blasted thing right into the Mississippi. Caroline nearly fainted when Anna and Teddy came running home shouting that Mourning was being swept down the river to New Orleans—and damn near made it. The little chit had floated ten miles before we were able to catch her."

"She built it?" Clint asked. "By herself?"

"Yes, she did," Francis said. "She found a picture in a book and used it as a guide. Mourning was smart as a whip in school, and what she didn't know she could fake."

"What a little hellion," Clint said with all seriousness.

"Now, Clint, I don't want to give you the wrong impression. Mourning has learned to behave like a lady—she won't embarrass you on that account. Of course she does have that stubborn streak in her that's a mile wide and almost impossible to deal with, and then there's her rather unpredictable nature. But I'll tell you one thing: If you ever win her to your side, you've got a friend for life. She's as loving and loyal as they come, and quite a little scrapper when defending her loved ones. Never had to worry about Anna and Melly when Mourning was around."

"This is changing the subject," Clint said, "but it's pertinent. Does she speak Spanish?"

"Not that I'm aware of. She speaks fluent French, a little Italian, and can read Latin and Greek, with a smattering of Hebrew." As an afterthought Francis added, "Picked that up from some Jewish boy she used to play with."

"That won't do her much good in Texas."

"Oh, I don't doubt she'll pick up Spanish before you know it." Francis released a wreath of smoke and watched it rise and fade out of sight.

"Has she ever had any serious suitors?" Clint asked. "Or was that too dangerous?"

Francis laughed. "Oh, she's had several proposals—all of which she heartily refused."

"What about the doctor?"

"Lance? Oh, he'd like for it to be more. He even discussed an offer of marriage when he found out she was leaving, but Mourning turned him down flat. Didn't even have to think about it." Francis tapped his pipe and refilled it. "I'll tell you something else. I'm damn glad she did. Not that he's so ugly he'd turn a horse from his oats or anything . . . Well, I don't know how to say this, but he just isn't right for her. 'Course Mourning is smart enough to see that. She told me herself that Lance was as dull as a widder woman's ax. It will take a special kind of man to love her."

"Yes, a brave one," Clint agreed.

Once again the library door slammed against the wall, and Mourning rushed into the room, the lavender moiré ribbon from her capote hat untied and trailing. "Uncle Francis, I'm back," she said, peeling her Bismarck kids from her hands.

"I give up." Francis looked at Clint and shook his head. "No one ever comes through that door the normal way."

Clint laughed. "Doors and tables don't last much longer than suitors around here," he said as a small piecrust table teetered threateningly on its three legs as Mourning swept by. He watched the sweep of her crinolines rustling beneath a silk dress of lavender and gray plaid. A moment later a silver-framed picture crashed to the floor.

"Thank goodness it didn't break," Mourning said, stooping to replace the small oval frame on the table. Seeing Clint, she stopped suddenly. "Oh! I didn't realize you had company. I'm sorry, Uncle Francis." She made a move to leave when Francis stood.

"We were just finishing up here. How was your ride and Dr. Prescott?"

"They were both fine," she said, refusing to look in Clint's direction. "Oh, Uncle Francis"—her voice trembled with excitement—"Melly just told me about the pups. Are you going to see them? May I go with you?"

"Well, by all means, let's go," he said, taking Mourning's arm. Francis stopped at the door, glancing back at Clint. "Well, come on, my boy. You've got to see this litter of pups."

Mourning held tightly to her uncle's arm as they walked to the kennels. As they approached, an enormous hound bounded out of the brush, barreling down the road. Mourning stopped and held open her arms as the great beast ran toward her. Francis walked on ahead, stopping to talk to the kennelman.

Clint watched the wrinkled mass run right into Mourning, sending them both tumbling to the ground. Amid the tangled confusion that she was—all petticoat, hair, and great slobbering dog—was a most infectious giggle. "Pharaoh, you lumbering lummox. I ought to box your ears, and I would—if I didn't love you so much."

By the time Clint reached her she had righted herself and was kneeling with her arms around that gigantic monstrosity with an overabundance of skin, whose sole purpose in life seemed centered on giving her face a complete washing.

Clint couldn't help eyeing her with new insight. It struck him again how young she really was, watching her frolic in the middle of the path with a dog second in size only to a grizzly.

"Well," Clint said, feeling the irresistible urge to prod her, "I feel slighted indeed that I didn't receive the same welcome you see fit to bestow upon a dog."

"Mr. Kincaid," she said, calling the beast to follow, "you didn't look like a man who would be content to stop at licking my face."

Before the full impact of her words hit him, she was gone, running down the path, the dog loping beside her.

"Well, I'll be damned," Clint said with astonishment, and then again, "well, I'll be damned." Her words were still ringing in his ears, and suddenly he stopped and threw back his head and laughed. He glanced at her once again, catching the white flounce of a petticoat ruffle as she went through the fence and disappeared around a building. "You little devilkin," he said.

Clint leaned against the gate, thinking of all Francis had told him, trying to mesh that together with what he had witnessed firsthand about Miss Mourning Howard. Like a popping cork she had burst into his life—a toast to extol unrestrained pleasure. And he wasn't sure how to handle that. The essence of Mourning, like good champagne, was in the bubble, producing a light, tingling sensation that made people laugh. She was made to sparkle. With a shake of his head, he followed her.

There were eleven in all—fat, squirming, and blind, and Mourning adored them. Lined up in a row like plump little cabbages, the pups were snuggled against Cleopatra's warm body, nursing hungrily. Cute as they were, even Mourning couldn't sustain her exuberance—there not being much excitement in watching newborn pups nurse for a prolonged period. She was about to leave when Uncle Francis was called away by the kennelman, and Mourning was obliged—well, stronger than that—she was *told* to show Clint the litters of older pups.

Furry paws, bright eyes, and a wet tongue attached to a fat, fuzzy body that wobbled, licked, and sniffed; at six weeks, these pups were more to her liking. As Mourning cuddled a squirming pup, Clint came to stand at her side. Unease hovered beside her the moment he came near. She felt a mixture of pleasure and fear, much like the sensation experienced when hurling down the side of a snow-covered mountain in a runaway sled—exhilarating as long as you don't think about what lies at the bottom.

Pharaoh followed Clint, going around him to sit by Mourning. The dog was all feet, with a tongue that drooled magnificently, leaving a wet, sticky trail everywhere he went.

"Do you have dogs at the ranch in Texas?" she asked while pushing Pharaoh away from the pups.

"A few barn cats, but no dogs," he answered, staring at the back of her curl-tossed head. He stepped closer, noticing the sudden tenseness in the set of her shoulders, the tilt of her head. "Do you always recoil when anyone gets close, or is that reaction reserved for me alone?" he asked.

"I've never allowed that many people to get close, so I really can't say," she replied, and rose to her feet.

Clint frowned and ran his slender brown fingers through his glossy hair. "Then why are you allowing me to get this close?"

"Because I'm forced to," she answered honestly. "I have no say in the matter. It would never be my choice to go to Texas with you."

He lifted a finger and trailed it across her cheek, stopping at her chin, which he cupped in his hand and lifted, until her eyes met his. "Would it be so bad, then . . . to accompany me to Texas?"

"Is it so bad having to take me?" she countered, trying to sound as much in control as he did. The tightness around his tempting mouth relaxed as his hand left her chin, traveling across her throat. She could feel the heat of his body transfer immediately to hers. With practiced ease, his hand slipped under the heavy mass of hair and drew her closer. The moment shimmered brilliantly.

"A few simple alterations can transform the most difficult situation to one of extreme pleasure," he said with penetrating warmth. Then he lifted his other hand to her waist, his thumb stroking the ridge of rib, sending a shiver that skipped across her goose bumps.

"What alterations?" she hoarsely asked, suspiciously aware of the subtle betrayal of all her major body parts because of his golden smile.

"Oh—a reversal of your role, for instance. Say, adversary to accomplice." A smile lurked behind his brilliant eyes.

He was so devilishly handsome when he was amused. Caught off guard by this discovery, she was drawn into uninhibited intimacy with this forceful man, this stranger whose next few months had been linked to hers, by some vengeful fate or playful deity. Unthinking, she lifted her hand to flick a ladybug from his collar, and quite by accident, her fingers brushed against the smooth warmth of his neck.

He was as startled by this sudden contact of flesh as she was. The amused humor in his eyes vanished into the intense heat of his unfathomable gaze. Her name came forth in a rush of breath.

A strong shaft of afternoon light pierced the gloomy interior of the kennel and touched his back. Sunbeams highlighted his dark hair with platinum and increased the sharp clarity of his gray eyes, turning them to liquid silver.

His lips moved over hers slowly, tasting lightly at first. Then with brutal tenderness he lifted her to new levels of consciousness. His arms tightened around her, drawing her body against his with insistent pressure. It was like being drawn into a warm bath, and she felt as if she had stepped inside him, so surrounded was she by the drugging taste and feel and smell of him.

Her response was as intense as his. Only the flip of a coin could have decided who was more surprised by this. Elements, emotions, the universe, sanity—they all rushed outward.

He lifted his mouth from hers. The magic was broken, replaced by creeping tendrils of suspicious doubts and little niggling threads of shame. Every time they were alone together she ended up in his arms, and that was, she knew, a very foolish place to be.

Afraid of what might be lurking in the murky depths of his eyes, she lowered her head and pushed away from him. He allowed her to move a certain distance before his hands tightened on her arms, preventing her complete separation from him. They remained this way, the loud buzzing in her ears gradually fading, to be replaced by the soft-breathing animal sounds within the kennel, the occasional yelp of a pup.

"I think I should go," she said, and glanced into the vast gray sadness of his eyes and searched his face. He released her with such vigor, she felt useless and discarded, like one of a pair of old slippers.

"By all means," he said, "if you find my company that unpleasant." He looked as if he were going to say more, but a strange look came over his face. He lifted his hand to rub the back of his knuckles across her cheek. "Go, then."

He did not remove his hand, nor did he release her from the power of his eyes. Even under his spell, she knew she should not be here with him, alone. Aunt Harriet said being alone with a man encouraged him to *have his way with you*. Mourning wasn't even close to knowing exactly what *that way* was, but she did know it was *the way* to lose one's virtue.

"I didn't mean it as it sounded," she said. "What I meant to say was, I shouldn't be here with you—alone. It's very foolish of me."

"Yes, very foolish," he agreed.

"You are a man of experience."

"A great deal of experience."

"And I have none. I don't know your intentions."

"No, you don't."

"I really don't know you at all."

"True, but we could remedy that, couldn't we?"

"I—I would rather not."

He saw her tenseness, the flare of uncertainty in her eyes. "Are you afraid of me?" he asked.

"I think so. No, not really afraid," she added. "I'm not afraid of you, not in the sense that you will harm me, but I am afraid of . . . of something." She stood on one foot and then the other. She scratched her nose and trailed the edge of her slipper through the dirt. She smoothed her skirts and fussed with the kerchief in her pocket, wishing all the while she could evaporate and reappear somewhere else entirely.

His fingers lightly touched her throat, just below her chin—a light, simple stroke of the fingers, nothing more. "You feel something, then . . . when I touch you?" he asked. "Here?" His hand lightly outlined her sensitive earlobe.

"Yes." She stood quietly under his touch, knowing all the while she should not allow him to put his hands on her person.

"And here?" he stroked the satin-soft skin of her throat from one collarbone to the other.

"Yes," she whispered hoarsely.

"What about here?" His fingers lifted to play over her mouth, then softly parted her lips. Instinctively her tongue touched his finger and he rapidly released his breath before rubbing the moisture across her lower lip. "Foolish little rabbit," he said. "Ignorance of what we're about is no excuse. You should be more than afraid. You should be terrified that I might take you."

"Take me?" she said with a puzzled look. "I thought you were taking me . . . that's why you came, isn't it?"

There was laughter in his gaze. "You and I, buttercup, are probably not ready for sexual banter, so let's not start." Clint's hands threaded through her hair and brought her to her toes, lifting her mouth to his. The bubble of strange new emotions simmered within her. His mouth pressed over hers, increasing the pressure with the slow probe of willing lips. Whatever it was that had been simmering came to a rapid boil.

When he lifted his head Mourning clutched his sleeve as she staggered on legs as boneless as putty. "Don't move," she whispered, gripping him tightly, "or I'll be a fallen woman for sure."

His chuckle was subtle and pleasant. "Little beauty, you haven't the faintest inkling just how very close to the truth you've come. I don't really know why I'm doing this, but if you know what's good for you, you'll scamper out of here . . . *now!*"

She scampered.

7

"You what?" Clint shouted.

The thunderous report of Clint's words assailed Mourning's self-confidence. With acidic intensity, his eyes bored into the tumble of petticoats and birdnest hair standing timorously before him. If Mourning had been wearing boots, she would have been quaking in them.

"Well?" he said.

Feeling her nerves gather in tightly coiled knots, and a mustering of shivering prickles of skin along the back of her neck, Mourning took a quick peek at his face. Eyes dark as bootblack, and about as sympathetic, were regarding her. His face bore the same expression one would wear while trying to decide what to do about an epidemic of foot rot. Things weren't looking so good.

She stammered something quite inarticulate, gave a hasty curtsy, then bolted—her slippered feet skimming across the uneven planking of the narrow boat dock. One tiny foot had just stepped upon the grassy bank when the silence was broken by an ominous roar.

"Miss Howard, get your ass back here on the double."

His words, lacking good taste or tact, went beyond hopeless to end on a note that was quite terminal. She stopped. She turned around. She wished she hadn't.

Before she had time to think, her hand flew up and she gave him the hand-sign that Teddy Snodgrass had taught her to use *whenever you want to put somebody that's ass-chewin' mad in his place. It's even worse than layin' a slur on 'em.* When Mourning asked if it was worse than a *blessing out,* Teddy said, *Sure is. Makes 'em mad enough to tear up some cornrows.*

Clint looked mad enough to tear up something . . . but it wasn't cornrows. Feeling she had just created more problems than she could say grace over, Mourning knew she had pulled the wrong sow by the ear this time. She had stupidly flown into a rage and done something really stupid. She might as well prepare herself. Only a fool would insult an alligator before crossing the stream.

"Come here," he said.

As she came closer she saw his anger was gone. In fact, Clint was grinning like a barrel of possum heads. Tipping her tousled head to one side, she stared in dazed wonder. Seeing her confusion, he made a noise deep in his throat like he did sometimes when he was amused and didn't want you to know it. "Very effective," he drawled, "except that's the wrong finger. I think you just gave me the sign for coitus in Javanese."

His words were as slick as a smoothing iron. And he was so handsome when he was amused. But she should have known better than to allow herself to be distracted by that. She swallowed as he crossed his arms over his chest. She wasn't out of danger yet, so she decided to offer him some explanation. "I probably didn't express myself . . ."

"Oh? And here I thought you did. Obscene hand gestures from refined ladies have always been a favorite of mine."

Anything was better than the painful scrutiny he was subjecting her to. "I'm sorry about that. I've never done it before, but you made me so mad . . . I just didn't . . ."

He silenced her with a wave of his hand. "Please . . . you don't owe me any explanations. If you want to burn your ass, Miss Howard, it's punishment enough to sit on the blisters."

Mourning wouldn't have been able to move if someone had dusted her behind with gunpowder. To her horror, even her vocal cords were inoperable. His, of course, were functioning perfectly— a fact substantiated when he said sternly, "Come here. Closer."

She kept her eyes nailed to the planking as she walked back to him. Standing before him, uncomfortably conscious that she was the subject of his jarring dissection, she couldn't help wondering if he saw anything in her worthy of merit. She was inclined to think he did not.

"Have you ever heard of cause and effect, Miss Howard?"

"Yes." Of course she had, but never before did she put such meaning into three short words. He was the *cause* of all her most recent problems, and the *effect* of his powerful nearness was coming at her with everything from brain drain to heartburn. She looked at him and nodded.

"You have? Good. Then you understand just how complicated things can get? That's wonderful. You must also know how one thing can lead to another? My, we are making progress . . . so much, in fact, I think you're ready for the next level of understanding . . . *every why has a wherefore.* Correct? Ah, love, you do have something between those ears besides seafoam eyes, don't you?" His words might be gentle and understanding, but the tone of his voice told her he was not.

He was mad. Deep, seething mad. Fire-spitting, arm-waving, dish-throwing mad.

"Now," he went on smoothly, "we have seen the effect of anger . . . let's go back to the cause. Tell me again," he said even more firmly, "what you said, just before you hightailed it out of here in such an all-fired hurry."

"About the dog?" she whispered in a high pitch, then retreated to a safe distance.

"About the dog," he mimicked. "Hell yes, about the dog!"

His was definitely the face of a man who devoured helpless underlings while awaiting an equal. When he finally spoke, exaggerating the pronunciation of each word, Mourning had the sickening feeling that something awful was about to happen.

"I want you to repeat," he said, "exactly what you said . . . only this time . . . I want you to stand before me . . . and look me in the eye."

A twinge of apprehension told her she'd better tell him, but for the life of her she couldn't open her mouth.

"What's the matter, *Miss* Howard? No choice words to deliver? No harebrained, backwoods eloquence to insult me with?" he said. "That's a switch, isn't it? A minute ago you were all *piss and vinegar.*"

"I don't have to stand here and take your abuse and your filthy language," she said with a quiver.

"The hell you say! If you value that lily-white hide of yours, you'll answer me," he said, his words so loud, a flock of birds flapped out of a nearby tree.

She studied the taut cords of his neck and knew he was not mincing his words. Rattled now, she repeated the few pitiful words that had caused this foray into insanity. "I said, Uncle Francis has given me two pups to take to Texas with me."

"Over my dead body," he said. Even his nose, which was uncomfortably close, frightened her. "I might have been suckered into running a nursery, but that's where I draw the line. *I am not running a goddamn kennel.*" He noticed the way her eyes blinked with each word he shouted and he perversely got louder. "Just who in the hell gave you permission to appropriate two dogs for our trip?"

"I told you, Uncle Francis gave them to me."

"I don't care who gave them to you," he shouted. "I've heard of some harebrained capers, but *this* defies all predecessors." His voice changed suddenly, back to the deceptive velvet smoothness. "Do you know what you're going to do?"

She shook her head.

"You're going to give them back," he said smoothly. "That's exactly what you're going to do. Do you hear me? *You're going to give them back.*"

"They won't cause any trouble," she said.

He let out a long, exasperated sigh, then ran his fingers through his hair. "They're your pups, aren't they?"

She nodded.

"Then they'll cause trouble," he shouted.

She had never seen anyone so angry. "There is no need for you to scream at me," she said. "I'll thank you to speak more softly." But that only enraged him further.

At last, gaining control of himself, Clint spoke in normal tones. "Tell me something. Did it ever occur to you to *ask me* if we could take two pups? Did it? Of course not. I've seen your kind before, Miss *Makes all the Decisions.* It goes against your grain to consult a man, doesn't it? You and your female independence. You know what you are, Miss Howard? You are the worst kind of woman, a dominating bitch. Anything that puts you under a man's authority makes you shrivel on the vine, doesn't it? But when you find a man you can wind around your little finger, like that *milksop* doctor friend of yours, that really gets the juices flowing, doesn't it? Well, you've picked the wrong dog to pull by the tail this time."

He poked himself in the chest when he said, *"I'm* calling the shots on this trip, Miss Howard, not you." Again he pointed his finger and poked himself in the chest and said, *"I* make the decisions, with or without your knowledge or approval. All I want from you," he said, pointing the finger at her, "is strict adherence. Can you get that through those windmills you use for brains, or do I need to repeat it?"

He intended to go on, but his preoccupation with her breasts spread to his mind and he lost his train of thought. Looking down, he saw he still had his finger pointed and her eyes were locked upon it. With a sigh of exasperation, he lifted his pointing finger, looked at it, then at her. Her eyes were still frozen to his fingertip. "Miss Howard," he said irritably, "when a finger points at the moon, only an imbecile looks at the finger."

He threw up his arms in surrender. "What in the name of hell am I doing here?" he asked.

Her cheeks were crimson and tears shimmered in her eyes. He could tell she was as nervous as a . . . Oh, hell! He couldn't concentrate with her standing there like that—her cheeks flushed, the sun glinting with dazzling brilliance on her hair. Not to mention the way her breasts were bobbing with each shaky breath she took. What did she take him for? He was no saint. She was breathing on purpose, just to distract him, by God! He was ready for a fight and she wasn't giving him one. What the hell happened? The entire time he'd been around her she'd just been asking for someone to bring her down a peg or two, and just about the time he'd figured he was the man to do it, she decided to change horses in the middle of the stream. She was taking all the fun out of it. Who the hell received any pleasure from kicking a downed horse? He wanted her up and fighting, teeth bared, eyes flashing, maybe even a few of her caustic remarks. Hell! Even the finger gesture.

"If all you're going to do is torture me, I might as well lie down right now," she said.

As far as verbal stupidity went, this was an undisputed classic. Quickly realizing her blunder and knowing Clint's propensity for taking vulgar advantage, she knew he wouldn't let this one ride on by.

"Well, I'll be damned," he said.

"I'm sure you have been for quite some time, but there's no need to discuss your condemned future with curse-laden speech," she said eloquently, hoping above hope that she could turn aside the thoughts she knew he was thinking.

But he zeroed in on her empty-headed blunder like a homing pigeon. "You're right. I prefer to discuss your offer to lie down. What's your pleasure, angel? Here and now—or would you prefer to come to my room later?" His gray eyes twinkled pleasantly. "Miss Howard, do you have any idea what it's like to go hundreds of miles to Texas?" His new, softer tone assuaged some of the raw annoyance she'd felt earlier.

She glanced down at his legs, which were encased in a pair of elegant fawn-colored shepherd's-plaid pants—the kind she saw on gentlemen daily. Every bulging muscle in his thighs was delineated in vivid detail, much too graphic for a lady like herself to see, but Mourning wasn't having much luck with ladylike diversions. His dark-brown broadcloth coat and fine ruffled shirt looked peculiar on him—seemingly at odds with his lusty brand of maleness. He was a bawdy Texan camouflaged as a gentleman—a wolf in gentleman's clothing. He was all male any way you looked at it, and Mourning was trying desperately not to. Slowly his words began to penetrate her consciousness.

"We have to go by steamer to New Orleans, and from there we take a packet to Port Lavaca and then a wagon train to San Antonio. From there we go by coach to the ranch. Have you considered where those two pups of yours are going to be while we are doing all that traveling?"

"I have a basket and—"

"A basket," he roared. Then, in a lower tone, he continued, "Do you mean to stand there in your right mind and tell me you think two frisky young pups are going to ride all the way to Texas in a basket? You know what you are? *Looney!*"

"If I hold it . . ."

Clint clenched his fists at his side, afraid he might be tempted to slap her into the river. "You do that, Miss Howard. You just hold your cute little basket of pups all the way to Texas. You will not ask me . . . not once, do you hear, to help you with them. Is that clear?"

"Yes, clear."

"If I find just one of those pups, just once, somewhere besides in your basket, *I'll throw you all three overboard.* Do you comprehend that?"

"What if we're on dry land?"

The crackling veil of electric current jumped back and forth between them.

"I'm sorry I said anything to you," she said. "I see I was mistaken . . . thinking lower animal forms were the only creatures not endowed with reason. I will assuredly revise my thinking . . . to include all primates . . . particularly *men!* You'll just have to be patient with me. It will take me a while to get used to a man who wears blustering irritation strapped to his hip like a . . . a firearm."

"Revolver," he corrected.

"Revolver," she repeated.

He saw the challenge in her eyes, his humor mellowed a little by her daring. "Well, what did you expect on this labor of Sisyphus? Some mealymouthed orator?"

"Certainly not Diogenes . . . reviling everything in sight."

Silence. Clint scrutinized her for a moment. "Believe it or not," he said softly, "I'm not always an unreasonable brute. On occasion, I've even been accused of having feelings."

A smile threatened to break out on Mourning's face. Her annoyed irritation faded like lamplight at noontime. There was an answering vein of humor in the remarkable gray eyes that seemed to make tender amends in a manner that was both ardent and intimate. It was the first time she could ever remember having such cross words with someone and feeling as though she'd neither won nor lost.

Clint possessed a remarkable capacity for natural, unpretentious simplicity—his mind being unencumbered by the perplexities that plague lesser men. He could accept a woman on even terms. His self-esteem was secure enough to grant equality. His masculinity could share a woman's need for recognition and not suffer.

Literally stunned at this intense discovery, Mourning felt the immediate disintegration of a few more of her protestations concerning him. The look she fixed on him was one she normally turned upon saintly deities carved in marble.

Identifying that look, Clint knew it would serve no purpose to have her adoration getting in the way of things. "Look, angel, your seductive little hide's been granted a reprieve, not permanent immunity." He gave her a look of wide innocence. What he received in return was a cold green stare.

"Your eyes are very green," he said.

She frowned. He was changing the subject and that meant he was up to something. "Why are you telling me something I've known all my life? And why are you smiling like that?"

Clint nonchalantly disengaged a hopelessly entangled spider from her hair. "Did you know," he said offhandedly, "green is also the color of lovers?"

"Says who?"

He grinned. "Why, Shakespeare of course."

If she could have gotten her hands on a rolling pin, she'd have brought it down over his head. "No, I didn't know that, and it's quite indelicate of you to mention it."

Clint doubled over with laughter. "What a bewitching contrast you are, buttercup. Five minutes ago you were displaying a working knowledge of things only a waterfront whore would admit knowing, and now you simper and blush when I mention the word lovers." He cupped her chin with his hands, turning her head from side to side, to brush across his lips. The touch of his mouth upon hers was so very light, she wondered if it had really happened. "Tell me, angel, is this all the surprises I can expect from you, or dare I look for more?"

He chuckled at the vexed look on her face. Smooth as a baby's bottom, she ignored his teasing words.

"What do you mean, the color of lovers? Green? I thought green was the color of jealousy."

He grinned.

"What are you grinning at? You obviously know something I don't. Everything you say has some hidden meaning. It's like talking to an oracle." She put her hand to her head. "Oh, I don't even know what I'm saying," she said. "I'm beginning to feel puzzleheaded from all of this. All you know how to do is speak in riddles and kiss me till I'm weak as rainwater. Just what is it you want from me?" *Oh, stupid, foolish me, I've left him an opening big enough to drive a hay wagon through.* She whimpered distressingly.

She was just too openly adorable to resist. "Mourning . . ." The fading sunlight filtering through massive oaks touched her, blushing her cheeks like the velvet petal of a rose and sprinkling her soft skin with a dusting of gold. The look she favored him with was so pure and simple, it would dwell forever within his mind. It was not the type of thing he customarily found enchanting, and it might have escaped his notice had she not possessed such nonpareil beauty of spirit. It was remarkable, her exemption from awareness of her own physical attributes—and they were legion.

"What do I want from you, sweet Mourning? I'm a man," he said huskily, "no less responsive to captivating beguilement than any other." He tilted her head back, trying to see her face. Her eyes were huge and luminous, watching him with gentle trust. He lifted his hand, laying his rough fingers lightly against her cheek, trailing them along the pearly luster of her jaw to the sensitive shadow of her neck. "What I want from you, sweet Mourning, I have no right to claim, nor do you possess the charity to give it"— he dropped his hand and retreated a step— "for to do so would fill you with the pain of remembrance and the sorrow of regret."

"I'm not sure I understand . . ." She stretched her hand toward him.

"Touch me," he said softly, "and we both go up in smoke."

But his words came too late. She had already touched him lightly on the sleeve.

She found herself in his arms.

"I warned you," he murmured into her hair. "We both know what happens when we touch." His arms closed powerfully around her, and Mourning was hauled up against his body.

She shivered and her skin erupted with goose bumps as she became intensely aware of each throbbing movement of his body against hers, every stroking caress of his fingers. Her obligatory resistance was going the way of a snowball in Hades, and though it was untutored, her body was bent upon playing the traitor.

His kiss was not the kiss of a gentleman, but a bold, insolent assault on her mouth that both intrigued and frightened her. They were, just for a moment, two fiery people: the hotspur and the firebrand, hurled together by a ruling passionate hunger that conquered all reason—chafing one and humiliating the other. Both of them chasing rainbows neither expected to find.

Floating on the warm current of a kiss that was as swaggering as his walk, Mourning wanted nothing more than to be released from this binding subjection, and feared nothing more than to be granted her wish.

His deep voice penetrated the cloud she was floating upon.

"Tell me, my seductive little friend, are you as innocent as you seem?"

Mourning wasn't sure if that remark deserved a blushing smile or a scalding slap, but his overconfident smile made her want to forget the rolling pin and go for the nearest tree.

The pressure left Clint's grip, and she found herself thrust away from him. She managed to salvage a ragged remnant of a smile, which she used for cover while she searched for her voice. "You wouldn't know an innocent woman if you tripped over one . . . your expertise lies completely in the opposite direction."

His arched brows lifted. He disliked having to make the statements he had—statements that were sure to embarrass and infuriate her. Playing *big brother* to a woman he found as desirable as Mourning was both new and difficult, yet irrefutably required of him. It was a little theatrical, but he knew no other way to establish his control over her—wild and willful creature that she was.

"It would take me a *fast* two minutes to deflower you, angel. Then you'd be within *my* range of expertise . . . wouldn't you?"

She spun around and ran before he could call her back. It was her way of salvaging the minuscule drop of pride that remained.

He granted her that much.

Running across the stretch of lawn as if someone had switched her legs with a hazel stick, Mourning didn't stop until she reached her room.

For the next two hours and fifty-three minutes Mourning Kathleen Howard laboriously toiled at her desk over the first two chapters of a book she felt compelled to write. It was entitled *An Unbiased Account of a Lady's Encounter with an Overbearing Tyrant from the Lady's Point of View.*

The literary genius was distracted by a knock at her locked door. Papers were hastily stuffed into the desk drawer as she called out, "Coming."

"What have you been doing?" Anna said, stepping inside the room. "You're green as goose liver."

Anna always did have a way with words. "Don't ask," Mourning said. There was a short silence as Mourning took several military steps, then tucked herself into her chair with a thankful heart. Happily she was safe from any further encounters with *him,* here in her room, but that thought was not as comforting as she had hoped. Feeling quite as if she had just turned the corner from

Honeysuckle Lane onto Melancholy Drive, Mourning smiled wanly.

But it didn't fool her cousin. "You've been talking to Clint," Anna stated in a sympathetic voice.

Mourning leaned forward and rested her chin glumly upon her fists. "We did precious little talking," Mourning said pitifully, "mostly we just bantered harm words."

Anna expelled a sad sigh. "Oh, Mourning . . . he was so handsome too." She shook her head. "I don't know . . . I wonder why it is that you always manage to mess things up."

"That's what I love about you, Anna. You have such a way with words . . . almost poetic."

"I'm just repeating what Papa told Mr. Kincaid."

Mourning raised her head. "Which was?"

"He said you could mess up a rainstorm. But, never mind that. Tell me about your talk."

"There was a lot of shouting and a little mud slinging mixed in with a few barked orders, grave insults, impossible requests, stout refusals," she waved her arms. "Oh, I don't know . . . you name it, we did it."

Up went Anna's brows.

"Except that!" Mourning snapped, giving Anna a look that was as dark as a stack of black cats. "Anna, I swear, you're so dense, you couldn't see through a ladder."

"You may be right, but I can see through the cock-and-bull story you're feeding me. You might have had an argument, Mourning Kathleen, but unless I've misread the signs, you ended up kissing," said Anna with an expression as gay as the patchwork quilt on Mourning's bed. She picked up a book lying facedown on the bedside table. *"Cora, the Doctor's Wife?"*

"It's the one I told you about. You remember, the woman who had the mother-in-law who was cross and unfeeling? It's not too terribly interesting, but better than *Quackenboss's Grammar.*"

"Or *Greenleaf's Arithmetic,*" Anna added. Turning the book back over, she asked again, "You kissed him, didn't you?"

Mourning was afraid her face was rather like a glass of strawberry jelly, crimson and clear. "A little," she said reflectively, then added, "or rather he kissed me."

"What difference does that make? A man that looks like that . . . well, you take it any way you can get it. Oh, Mourning, close your eyes and see if you can remember it just as it was . . . then tell me," exclaimed Anna.

"I don't have to close my eyes," she said morosely. "I can describe it in a nutshell. You remember Josef Bergman, don't you?"

"The Jewish boy who lived with the Helmsleys?"

"Yes. He taught me a Hebrew proverb that describes Clint's kisses to the letter."

"Not, *If the camel gets his nose in the tent, his body will soon follow*?" Anna exclaimed in horror.

Mourning knew without a doubt that Anna was three pickles shy of a barrel. "That's not the one I was thinking of," she said.

"Well, I can't tell you what a relief that is," Anna said, rolling over and flinging her arms outward while staring in an overraptured manner into the canopy.

When Mourning didn't say anything, Anna said, "Well?" Sitting up, she said, "Mourning Kathleen, it is spitefully mean of you not to tell me. You know I would tell you."

"You're only saying that, Anna Claire Ragsdale, because you don't have anything to tell, and you know it."

"Will you take an I.O.U.?"

"Oh, all right! Old Hebrew proverb say: *When a rogue kisses you, count your teeth.*"

Anna folded with laughter and rolled across the bed. Mourning jumped up from her chair, and spinning across the room, fell down beside her. And there, upon the four-poster bed, as they had for years, the two cousins, close as sisters, lost themselves in secret discussions. On this particular occasion, they discussed everything they knew about men—which covered everything from *A* to *B* and took approximately one minute, then they dressed for dinner.

8

Dinner was a disaster.

Mourning was never sure, exactly, just why that was, because the meal itself was perfect. Even the blanc mange stood stiff, as it was supposed to, but by the time it arrived, the threat of disaster had chilled everything from conversation to consommé. Yes, things had taken a downturn long before the blanc mange put in an appearance—more precisely, it was between the sautéed onions and the glazed carrots julienne.

And Mourning had taken such care to dress for dinner, wearing an aqua silk dress she had never before worn because the neckline was far too daring, which was precisely why she chose it for tonight. Clint might think her a child, but before the night was over she would show him. Thinking about Clint's reaction and the strong disapproval her dress was sure to bring from Aunt Harriet and Uncle Francis, Mourning left her room in a hurry, slowing to a snail's pace when she glanced down and discovered the effect a hasty descent down the stairs had on her bosom.

She paused in front of the hall mirror to give herself a last-minute appraisal. Her eyes went immediately to her bosom, which, rising out of the dress like overproofed dough, looked nothing like what it had in her room. What had happened? A hasty accounting of events turned up the cause. The dress had not been fastened when Mourning stood before the mirror in her room. The culprit was the cut of the dress, high-waisted and excruciatingly tight above the waist, pushing everything below up. But there was no *up* to this dress. Absolutely nothing but cold, drafty air.

She let out a squeak of horror, and whirled, her hand open and spread over her breasts, her feet in a desperate hurry and heading for the stairs.

"There you are!" Aunt Harriet's voice came from behind her. "Hurry up, Mourning. Everyone is in the dining room. We are waiting dinner on you."

"I've got to change my dress, Aunt Harriet."

"Whatever for?"

"It's too low. It's indecent!"

"Turn around," Harriet said, coming up behind her. "Let me see." A smile crossed Harriet's face. "Why the dress is lovely on you, Mourning. And it *isn't* too low, and it *isn't* indecent. It's fashionable. Now come along. Francis is in a temper, and it won't improve until he's eaten."

"But, Aunt Harriet, I *can't* go in there like this."

"Nonsense. Come along, now. Hurry."

"I'm not hungry."

Harriet stopped and turned, her hands on her hips. "Mourning Kathleen Howard, march yourself into that dining room this very minute, or I'll have Francis *and* Mr. Kincaid drag you. From your room . . . half dressed, if necessary!"

Following her aunt, Mourning suddenly realized she couldn't possibly walk into that room and expose her exposed parts to the cold stares of a room full of blood relations and one arrogant semi-relation. She glanced at the skirted table next to the umbrella stand in the foyer, as she passed by. Mourning stopped, her eyes backing up to rest on the table, the *skirted* table with the silk shawl draped over it. Mourning looked at the fringed shawl. She looked at her bosom.

When Clint walked out of the dining room, he found Mourning curiously bent over a small table in the foyer, talking to herself as she wrestled with a lamp. Before he could speak, she swished the shawl off the table, leaving it looking rather naked on its four spindly legs, the lamp with its crooked chimney sitting on the floor.

"I'm sure there's a reason behind what you're doing, but at the moment it escapes me," said Clint.

She froze and did not move for a minute, then turned, clutching the shawl high under her throat. "What are you doing out here?"

"Looking for you. Your aunt offered my arm to escort you to dinner."

"Well, give it back to her with my thanks. I have two perfectly good legs that have been carrying me to dinner for years. Please. Just leave me alone. I don't need your arm—or anyone else's."

"Perhaps not, but it looks like you could use some help." Walking close enough to see the magnificent coloring of her eyes, he could also see the panic in them. "Rip something?"

"No."

He stepped closer, his hand reaching for the scarf. She scampered backward, coming up flat against the wall and holding the scarf tighter, using both hands. "Is there some problem with your dress?" he asked.

There was a reasonable silence. Then, "Yes!"

"Why don't you enlighten me and I'll see if I can help you. Otherwise your aunt is going to send someone looking for both of us."

She swallowed a big gulp of air. He was right, of course. Aunt Harriet would be wondering. Mourning realized she had no choice. She had to trust him. "The dress," she said painfully. "It's too low . . . Aunt Harriet won't let me change . . . Uncle Francis is in a temper . . . I'd rather die than make a spectacle of myself. . . ."

He swallowed a laugh, thinking it was too late to worry about that, but even while his eyes sparkled with amusement he found himself absorbed by her magnetic quality. "I assume the shawl is to wrap around your . . . upper body?"

Her nod was a bit frantic.

"Are you sure that's necessary?"

"Of course I'm sure," she snapped. "Do you think I'd be wearing a tablecloth if it wasn't?"

Clint had seen her do dumber things for less reason, but he simply said, "I was just wondering."

"Well, you can stop wondering and see for yourself!" Clint was the one person she *most* didn't want to see her like this, but desperation clouded her thought. She dropped the shawl.

He was so startled that at first he was completely taken by the lovely picture she made frowning down at herself in such a critical way. Then his eyes dropped lower. There was such a rush of extraordinary warmth that he was momentarily overpowered by it. "Beautiful" was all he said. Realizing what she'd done, Mourning quickly covered herself.

But Clint was already closing his eyes against the agony of strong desire. But even there, behind the darkness of his eyelids, the vision of the soft flesh of her breasts swelling above her bodice raced across him like a raging flame. When he opened his eyes, she was clutching the shawl to her throat, her face flaming with what he guessed was shame . . . or a sudden attack of acute modesty. But even then he wanted her. The vision of what lay beneath the soft shimmer of silk at her throat would live in his mind for some time.

"One of us," he said in a husky voice, "needs help."

Before she could pivot and run, she was caught and pulled against him, gently cradled in his arms. Her fists, clenching the square of silk, were trapped between their bodies. Sudden staccato gasps sent a wave of dizziness over her, while the burn of his hand caressing her throat was acutely sobering. His lips moved like whispered words over her cheek, and she thought he would kiss her. With his lips still soft against her cheek, his words came, soft and gentle against her flesh. "I should have my head examined, but if you'll stop holding that shawl in a death-grip, I'll help you cover yourself."

He released her and her mind went numb. Vaguely, she remembered his reaching for the shawl, instructing her to let him have it and put her hands down. From somewhere the sound of her own voice reached her . . . "You don't have to paw me, I'll *give* you the shawl. I *am* being still . . . you're the one who's moving. Why don't you use a pin? How tight are you going to tie it? Are you sure it won't come undone and fall in my soup?"

Mourning didn't realize he had finished until she felt his hand curve around her elbow, his words penetrating her daze. "We're going to dinner now, sweetheart, but I'm afraid you'll have to walk. It wouldn't look too good if I carried you in, slung over my shoulder, pirate-fashion. You do remember how to walk, don't you?"

"Stop treating me like a blithering idiot," she said in a cranky voice. After which she marched into the dining room, her head held at an imperial height, the silk shawl draped about her shoulders and knotted between her breasts, the fringe hanging past her elbows.

In a cluster around the dining table sat her family, Uncle Francis at one end of the table, Aunt Harriet at the other. Scattered between them were four chairs, two of them already occupied by Melly and Anna.

Across the room, Harriet's stupefied gaze slid from the top of Mourning's curled head to her slippered feet, then moved slowly upward, going as far as the silk shawl, where her gaze rested. At that point, Harriet, always the perfect hostess, should have greeted the latecomers, but she was momentarily distracted, trying to remember something. Her eyes locked on Mourning as Clint pulled out her chair. At that moment, Harriet suddenly realized just *where* she had seen that ridiculous-looking shawl her niece was wearing. With a horrified gasp, Harriet knocked over her water goblet.

While Harriet was busy dabbing at the spill with her napkin, Mourning hoped Clint was admiring the sophisticated figure she cut tonight at the dinner table. But when he took his seat across from her and she lifted her eyes to his, her confidence crumpled. His glance flicked over her indifferently, as if she were the same color as Aunt Harriet's imported puce wallpaper.

A branch of candles burned dimly in the center of the table, wax dripping down the polished silver to splash in a cloudy puddle upon the damask cloth. Across the table, the light glittered on the small diamonds set in simple gold studs in Clint's shirt. His eyes were hidden behind lowered lashes as his gaze rested on his fingers, which were stroking the stem of his goblet. He was listening to Francis's instructions about making connections with the chaperone he had hired.

"I received a telegram from Mrs. Colby today. You're to pick her up at her sister's. The address is in the pouch with the other papers I'm sending to Caroline. Can you think of anything else we need to discuss?"

"No," Clint said, "I think you've covered everything."

"I still can't believe it," Harriet put in. "You're leaving us tomorrow." She smiled across the table at Mourning. "Wish I had an adventure waiting for me, instead of that blasted garden that needs weeding." Harriet caught the gratitude in Mourning's eyes, realizing she had expected her to say something about the shawl.

"Saw the *Delta Belle* at the landing today," Francis said. "Didn't get a chance to talk to Captain Montgomery though."

"I did." Clint finished the last of his drink, not speaking until he returned the glass to the table. "Everything is set for tomorrow morning. We should be at the landing by ten." He went on to say the traveling time was good going downriver. "I should have our cabin assignments by then . . . which reminds me, I couldn't get a separate cabin for your servant. Will it suffice to have her in the same room with you, Mourning?"

"Sophie? Of course we can share a room. She's so excited about riding on a paddle wheel, she won't be able to sleep anyway."

Harriet added, "You should've seen her today, when we were packing your things. She kept asking me if I would swear on a stack of bibles that you would send her right back to Memphis as soon as you reached New Orleans. She is terrified you might change your mind and make her go to Texas with you."

"It's because Melly kept telling her all those horror stories about Indians and how they like to take scalps," Anna said. "She even drew pictures . . . blood and everything."

"Anna," Harriet said, "don't be talking like that at the dinner table."

"Well, it's true," Anna said in her own defense.

"Melly," Harriet said, "you shouldn't tell stories like that. You'll frighten Sophie unnecessarily, and the good Lord knows she is frightened enough as it is. Just mentioning the word Texas terrifies her. Besides, the Indians are nice in the part of Texas you live in, aren't they, Mr. Kincaid?"

"Even the *nice* ones will lift a scalp now and then. Especially if they like the color of your hair," Clint replied.

"They even scalp women?" Mourning asked.

"Especially the blond ones," Clint replied.

That slowed conversation for a while but then Clint proceeded to entertain the Ragsdales with tales of Texas, but not once did he give Mourning more than a passing glance.

Her sunny disposition at an all-time low, Mourning was on the verge of pleading a headache, preferring to be ignored in her room. But before she could, Aunt Harriet, the darling, noticed Mourning's discomfort.

"My dear Mourning, you look as if you've seen a ghost. Are

you feeling all right? You're as pale as rice flour, and I've noticed you haven't eaten enough to keep a bird alive."

A small sound of self-pity escaped Mourning's throat, but she managed a weak smile. "I wasn't very hungry. Just nervousness over leaving tomorrow . . . I'm sure that's all it is."

She would be leaving tomorrow. She did not want to think this might be the last time she would sit at this table, or dine with these beloved people. She tried to shut from her mind the memories of the years spent here, but they seeped through her resistance like tiny minnows swimming through a net.

Next to her, Anna and Melly had their heads together, plotting some mischief, while at one end of the table Uncle Francis was instructing the servant behind his chair to bring another bottle of his best French brandy. At the opposite end of the table, Aunt Harriet was laughing softly at something Clint said, then she rapped him across the knuckles with her folded fan. Left to her own enterprises, Mourning allowed her gaze to wander around the room, over the Turkish rug, the Watteau pastoral hanging over the sideboard, and finally resting on the dark windows framed by watered-silk draperies. Out there somewhere, in all that darkness, lay her future.

She was still lamenting her future when Aunt Harriet squeezed her hand. "Mourning, my dear, why don't you turn in early tonight. You have a big day tomorrow."

Mourning looked over at Clint, who was talking animatedly to Uncle Francis and simultaneously charming Anna and Melly. Still he continued to ignore her. A minute later, Mourning was on her way to her room, untying the silly shawl and draping it over her arm. She was just passing the parlor when she remembered she had not packed her piano books, so she stopped and went in.

The parlor was decidedly formal. Walls were daringly hung in a deep rose damask, while heavily draped windows of gold, cream, and rose watered-silk were gathered lavishly beneath intricately carved gold-leaf cornices. Rich carpets, paintings, and objets d'art gave the room the familiar warmth that Mourning loved and knew so well.

Music books clutched against her bosom, Mourning was leaving the room when something caught her eye. On a mahogany stand in front of the windows resided a large bronze statue of Pan, the son of Hermes. Pan, the god of flocks, had the torso and head of a man and the hindquarters and horns of a goat—like a few other men she knew—one in particular. A marvelously adept musician, Pan played the pipes and spent his leisure hours pursuing various nymphs—a pastime still favored by most men of Clint Kincaid's caliber. Unlike Kincaid, who had to beat women off with a stick, all of Pan's pursuits rejected him because of his ugliness.

Mourning had seen this particular statue not more than a million times over the past twelve years, but for some strange, almost mystical reason, when she looked at it tonight, she saw it in an unaccustomed light. She paused in front of the statue. Pan, she thought, playing his pipes and standing on his cloven hooves, was strikingly remindful of Clint Kincaid. As Mourning continued to stare, her imagination went on a rampage, and Pan's face began to alter, his hideous features softening until he was a handsome copy of Clint. While she stared, Pan dropped his pipes and began to chase an assortment of nymphs, catching one that Mourning thought bore a striking resemblance to herself. Pan pressed himself against her, forcing her back against a tree stump, and brought his mouth fully against hers. Mourning felt the kiss, the pressure and taste identical to the kiss Clint had given her earlier.

Her back to the door, she couldn't see it open, but she heard a hollow click as it closed. Turning to see who it was, Mourning found herself encountering the pearl-gray stare of a very real Clint Kincaid. Her fanciful interlude with Pan had been so real, she was momentarily stunned. Her face as expressionless as a wax doll's, she looked at him curiously, then glanced back at the statue.

His eyes tracked hers, then he grinned. "Which dryad are you, my lovely? Tree nymph?"

Her face was burning, her mind jammed with words, yet her mouth was as silent as a bell without a clapper. She blinked twice, trying to clear the blurred confusion dwelling in her mind.

"Hullo! Anyone there?" he said, stepping closer and tapping lightly on her head.

"What? Oh . . . yes . . . I mean . . . Of course someone's here," she snapped.

"Good," he said, leaning back against the sofa and crossing his legs in front of him.

Mourning clutched the piano books closer and glanced at the door, then at the long legs blocking her escape. "If you'll excuse me . . ."

"No."

"No?" she echoed.

"No," he said with a smile that was rather like Aunt Harriet's eclairs: rich and sweet.

His was a face that cleverly concealed inner thoughts. Mourning studied the rich black waves of hair layered around his collar and squeezed her eyes closed to block the endearing sight from her mind. One sense blocked, another rose to assume command. With her eyes closed, she was aware of the fresh-starched aroma of his fine linen shirt and the subtle play of lime-scented soap on his skin, and how they combined with the natural heat of his body to drug her.

She tried to hide her discomfort. It was a laudable effort, but she was simply too unsophisticated to conceal anything from him. A quick shift of her eyes in his direction told her he was anything but deceived. Before she could look away, he rose and leaned forward, his lips aiming for a kiss, but she looked away, intending to discourage him and succeeding in throwing his aim off. His kiss landed on her left eye.

Before she could say something she was gently encircled in warm, comforting arms. Her own arms, still clutching her music books, were trapped between their bodies. His chest was strong and his starched shirt smooth against her face. The heat of his breath was as warm and penetrating as a luscious massage with warm, fragrant oil.

His strategically placed hands at her back began to caress with a slow, escalating tempo, dropping lower. Warm palms cupped her buttocks and lifted her upward and inward. All the vital components of their respective bodies were lined up like a *corps d'élite* about to break ranks. With firm pressure he molded her against his perfect body and the ranks definitely broke. Through layers of clothing the expanding rigidity and shape of him was delineated in sharp, vivid detail against her belly. Frightened as she was, something within her said this was what she had waited for all her life.

The warm progress of Clint's breath approached fast and hard; she could feel his exploring lips searching for her mouth.

"Please. Let me go," she murmured weakly.

"Can't," was all he said before his lips found what they sought and moved over her cheek before closing hotly over her mouth.

"Mmmmff," was her last strangled attempt at speech. The

pressure on her mouth increased as he lightly taunted her into granting him entry. Sanity, judgment, common sense, reason— suddenly they were all empty words that held no meaning for her. All obstructions gone, she was a quivering mass of craving desire and aspiring hopes.

Pressing her more firmly against his hips, Clint groaned, a husky sound from deep within. "Sweet angel, if you are inexperienced, I'm likely to die from a more skilled representation. How'd you get so incredibly desirable?"

The unbelievable things he was doing with his hands and his mouth pushed her to the brink of insanity. She shifted against him and felt the immediate release of a warm current of air that wafted across her, stirring the soft wisps of hair along her neck—and a few other things as well. Slowly, with consummate ease, his very being began to surround her.

"Mourning . . . cherished angel . . . my ridiculous little angelet," he said with grating effort, his hands and words beguiling her. She could feel him reveling in her body's heated response. "Yes, darling girl . . . yes . . . Oh, yes . . ."

She felt herself move as he leaned back farther, spreading his legs, her body drawn intimately between. The jolting shock of it was quickly submerged under a lengthy, exalting kiss.

With trembling lips, she whispered, "Clint?"

"Hmmm?" he murmured, never stopping the feather touch of his lips across her cheek and along her throat. When she didn't respond, he lifted his head, his features heavy and drugged.

"What's happening? This is wrong. I shouldn't be in here with you . . . but I can't seem to help myself." She tilted her head and looked at him, then quickly ducked, her forehead pressing against his chest. "Does this always happen the first time . . . when a girl has never . . . if this feeling hasn't . . ."

He chuckled warmly against her neck. "No, angel, it doesn't happen to every girl . . . the first time . . . when she has never . . ."

"Then why is it happening to me?"

"It's no accident. Maybe destiny. Good luck. Fortune. Circumstance. Fate. Who knows?" His hands moved to cup her head, his lips brushing faintly across hers, again and again. "You have been kissed by the angels, smiled upon by the gods, exalted and raised to angelic heights."

"I know."

It was said with such an utterly childish honesty that it drew a deep rumbling laugh from him. Adorable green-eyed being that she was—he could press the issue and have her begging him to make love to her. The thought was the same one he usually found comfort in, yet he was finding anything but comfort now. It was out of character for him to desire a woman as much as he did her, while not wanting to destroy that which he found so perfect and complete. He wanted her. But something within him didn't want to lead her into commonplace promiscuity—to make her an object of sexual response. In spite of what her body said, she wasn't ready emotionally to handle a liaison like that. He found it displeasing to think of her on those terms. Yes. He wanted her. But there was a protective element involved, a desire to preserve her breathless innocence.

Clint Kincaid was guilty of many sins, yet he did not want Mourning to be just another one of his transgressions. In the end, what prevented him from seeing just how far she would go wasn't the thought of family ties, or even this new awareness of a compassionate and tender feeling toward her.

She chose that particular moment to grind her foolish little nose against his chest and that one innocent act probably saved her.

PART TWO

The flowers of life are but illusions.
How many fade away and leave no
trace; how few yield any fruit; and the
fruit itself, how rarely does it ripen!
Goethe, *The Sorrows of Young Werther*

9

**May 1860
Port Lavaca, Texas**

Mourning was standing on the deck of the packet thinking her departure from New Orleans was not the stirring experience her entrance had been a mere two days ago.

Tall masted ships riding low in the water and bearing exotic cargoes shimmered in the pink haze of dawn, which enveloped the harbor. Bobbing gently against their anchors, ships carrying adventurers from hundreds of different seaports crowded along the docks while fragments of conversations spoken in a dozen different dialects drifted up from bustling decks.

Clint, standing to one side, turned and gave Mourning an edifying smile before he took a few swift strides toward her. Immediately Mourning turned away, her small hands tensely gripping the railing of the passenger boat.

"Mourning . . ."

Silence.

"Mourning . . ."

Extended silence.

"Mourning, this is getting us nowhere."

"Good."

"Look, I know you're angry, but we can't continue this silent treatment all the way to the ranch."

She scowled. "Oh? Last night you couldn't wait to shut me up. Today you wish I'd talk. Who knows what tomorrow will bring?" She turned toward Clint, frowning earnestly against the bright glare of the sun's reflection on the water, and found herself temporarily blinded and his face out of focus. She lowered her eyes as his hand touched her arm solicitously. "Don't touch me," she snapped, trying to jerk her arm away. "I'm quite capable of standing on my own two feet."

He cocked a dubious brow, but said nothing. She felt the tightening band of his fingers close around her arm as he propelled her away from the bow of the packet. She was vaguely conscious of his comment to a group of inquisitive onlookers, something about a *new bride.*

Mourning saw the swelling assembly of passengers staring curiously. It hit her then. *New bride? Me?* Her jaw dropped with astonishment, then tightened with rage while she listened to him tell the gaping throng that she was upset because he had left his adorable little bride of two days napping while he slipped off to play a hand of cards. There were understanding smiles from overfed matrons, tittering giggles from young girls hiding behind parasols, and salty remarks from a rough-looking group of men who were several notches below the classification gentleman. She stared at him in disbelief, recognizing yet another perplexing twist to his phenomenal personality. Standing before her was a clever, urbane man who possessed an extraordinary sense of circumvention and dripped charm like hot candle wax.

"*Your bride?* How could you?" Mourning cried, horribly shamed by the elevated brows and whispered comments so critical of her.

"This barbarian is depriving me of my honor!" she shrieked to the astonished bystanders. "He is *forcing* me to accompany him without a chaperone."

He flashed a woman-leveling smile. "Now, darling, it's not unusual for newlyweds to honeymoon without a chaperone."

A rush of laughter slashed the silence. Mourning had a few more things to say, but Clint laughed, then whispered in a tone audible to her alone, "You might as well save your breath, angel. They won't believe you."

She wasn't about to be swayed, however. "I'm not his bride, I tell you. He's lying. I wouldn't marry him if he were the last man on earth."

"Now, darling, don't be angry with me," he said with a humoring shake of his head and a laugh plainly directed at the multitude. "I promise no more cards. From now on, all my time will be lovingly devoted to you alone. Will that make you happy, sweetums?"

"*Sweetums?*" she succeeded in choking out before foaming rage overtook her. "Are you out of your unoccupied mind? Why I'd rather . . ."

Clint clamped a hand over her busy mouth. "Now, darling, I *know* what you'd rather do, but these good folk here probably aren't interested. Those kinds of things should remain private, just between the two of us, don't you think?"

"*Mmmff, mmmff!*" It was no use.

Steering her away from the crowd, he guided her to a large assemblage of crates that were stacked out of the way of passengers. "Oh, no you don't," he said when she tried to bolt. His other arm went around her. "We're going to discuss this until we get it resolved. Now, tell me just what . . . Ouch! You little vampire." He glanced down at the mop of abundant curls bent over his arm. She was hanging on for dear life; her tiny sharp teeth clamped tighter than a sucker fish on his forearm. "Is this your way of conveying to me that you're hungry, or could it be in some small way you're becoming attached to me?"

She released him immediately, almost spitting his arm out of her mouth, then drawing back.

"There's no reason for you to cower at my shadow," he said. "I won't murder you. We have a rule in Texas. We never sacrifice young virgins above the age of seventeen."

"Good. We have a rule in Tennessee. We ignore *rude* people."

"You're still angry about the chaperone?" he asked.

"I'm still angry about the chaperone," she said, "*and* I intend to stay that way."

"It wasn't my fault."

"Wasn't it?"

"No, it damn well wasn't. It was her decision."

"Eventually, yes."

"What do you mean eventually?"

"I mean *eventually* she decided she didn't want the job, but only after you did everything within your power to see that she reached that conclusion."

Nothing short of a direct revelation from God could have persuaded Mourning to believe Clint had been innocent of intentionally provoking Miss Colby, whom he insisted on calling *Miss*

Coldbitch, to decline. No! not decline. She *adamantly refused* to accompany them. "You went out of your way to be rude to her."

"I did not go out of my way to be rude to her. The old crow was asking for it, and she's damn well lucky I didn't haul off and belt her one."

"*You* probably would," she said, looking him in the eye, daring him to deny it.

"I probably would what?" he asked innocently, his eyes probing hers in that way that made her deliciously uncomfortable.

"Strike a woman," she said, elevating her chin as if daring him to strike her.

"Don't tempt me, angel. You stand a damn good chance of being the first."

She gave him an undignified snort. "Well, that's just wonderful. Now we're regressing to woman beating."

"Don't forget your biting."

She ignored that. "What am I supposed to do for a chaperone? Pull one out of a hat?"

"We've been through all of that. You don't need a chaperone. You're enough to drive a man to drinking by yourself. Lord, what would you be like with an accomplice? You sure as hell don't need reinforcements." He studied her. "Besides, you've got me. You don't need anyone else."

"That's about as safe as leaving a baby with an alligator. You happen to be the primary person I need protection from." She turned away from him.

"I've never forced myself on an unwilling woman yet. You, angel eyes, of all women are safe with me."

"I won't go one step further without a chaperone."

"Why?"

She spun around. "Because it isn't proper. It just isn't done. A lady doesn't travel with a man she isn't married to."

"Well, don't expect a proposal from me. I draw the line there."

A little arch of her brow told him how ridiculous she thought he was being. "I asked for a chaperone, not a jailer," she huffed.

"Cute. Very cute." He gritted his teeth. "Look, I'm not any happier than you are about this."

"Then why did you run Miss Colby off?"

"I did not run the bitch off," he bellowed, rising on his toes, as she did, just to see if it made any difference, "I told you, she made her own decision."

"Oh, sure she did," she said, waving her arms around, "after you offered to show her your collection of scalps and told her Indians went crazy over her shade of red hair. Who wouldn't?"

This time, he didn't have an answer for that, so he followed her example and ignored the question. "I told you . . . you don't need a chaperone. That tongue of yours is defense enough. Who the hell would want to get close to a woman like you? Who the hell could?" He paused for a moment, then started up again. "You've got more armor than a damn crusader. Any man who tried anything with you could get lost forever in that maze of clothing. Hell, I've never seen such a collection of petticoats, corsets, and starched drawers. That alone is enough to discourage the most desperate of men. And then there's the matter of those damn bloodhounds of yours, slobbering everywhere they go."

"My clothing," she said primly, "is certainly none of your concern, and you leave the pups out of this." She eyed him speculatively. "Just why are you so angry?"

"I'm not angry," he said angrily, "you're the one who's angry because that frozen lump of ice changed her mind."

"I'm not angry," she screamed, "I'm fed up. I am sick and tired of your foul tongue and disgusting disregard for everything that's sacred and decent. You've done nothing but rage and curse since the day I met you, and I'm sick of it, Mr. Kincaid. Do you understand that?"

They looked like a couple of whooping cranes going through the mating ritual with all their bobbing up and down, and suddenly the whole thing seemed absurdly funny to him. It was damn strange, how he could be fightin' mad at her one minute only to find his anger had turned to sidesplitting humor—and it was happening again. He fought for control as she continued her tirade.

"You have been behaving—"

"Rather boldly," he interrupted. She flashed him a hot green stare and he grinned. She was coming round now. He liked her when she was all stirred up like this. Damn if he didn't.

"Yes," she said stiffly, rather shocked that he was agreeing with her, "and you have said things that were . . ."

"Improper." His grin was growing wider.

"Yes, improper. I know you're not accustomed to . . ."

"Being around a lady." He was shaking now.

"Yes, being around a lady." She stopped suddenly, glaring at him hotly. "Will you *please* shut up and let me tell you?"

He tried. God knows he did. But he just couldn't contain the laughter building up inside him. And finally, giving way to it, he doubled over.

And so what had started out as a discussion had ended up a full-blown argument with neither one winning and neither one retreating—two foes, perfectly matched. That was the pattern all their arguments had taken of late: a normal conversation giving way to biting words and accusations that neither one really meant. And when it got out of hand one of them would steer their words to safer ground, turning in the direction of the sarcastic teasing they had both come to enjoy. Their arguments seemed to be a form of bantering foreplay, a ground testing before the actual mating began.

If what she felt when she entered New Orleans was breathtaking excitement, then what she felt when she entered Port Lavaca was regretful disillusionment. To say there existed in Mourning a twinge of disappointment was putting it mildly. Her thoughts were lingering more in the territory of horrified revulsion.

When she mentioned her disappointment to Clint, he merely shrugged. "You'll get used to it." Then he walked off, leaving her sitting on a blistering beach.

They had arrived in Port Lavaca hours ago. Even before they docked, she could tell it was a flat, miserable place where the sun beat down with a metallic glow, searing everything it touched. As far as the eye could see there wasn't a tree to be found. Mosquitoes as big as sparrows were swarming in confusion with herculean-size flies. Mourning eyed the endless shoreline with trepidation; even the water looked dirty. What kind of place was this? She pressed her sweat-soaked handkerchief to her neck, and for the hundredth time cursed her stupidity in knocking her parasol overboard.

She surveyed her miserable surroundings once again. What was she doing here in this extension of the underworld, sitting in the scorching sun like a lizard upon a rock, waiting for him? She had no earthly idea when he'd be back; she didn't even know where he'd gone. It was bad enough that she had to suffer, but the poor pups, they were dying inside that hot basket. She had carried them to the beach repeatedly and dipped them in the water to cool them, wishing she could dip herself.

"I know you're hot, you poor babies," Mourning crooned, opening the lid on the basket that contained Romeo and Juliet. Two wiggling, wrinkled lumps rolled over the top of the basket, turning it on its side as the pups fell over their feet and scrambled to her side. Finding no shade, they tumbled over each other, frantic to return to their basket. She watched them whimper and wiggle their fat little bodies until they were out of the sun. It was too hot in this hellhole for a dog.

Her temper was soaring faster than the temperature. *Why* did he find it necessary to park her on an uncomfortable crate in the broiling sun? *Who* did he think he was, leaving her sitting here for hours? And *what* did he mean when he'd said, *If you value your life, Miss Howard, you won't budge until I return*? That had been at least two hours ago, perhaps more. Just how long did it take to make arrangements to ship two trunks?

At that moment, the object of her wrath stood at the window of the freight office watching her. *Miss Howard, you are some obstinate woman,* Clint thought. She was decked out like a Christmas tree from top to bottom. Hell, this was Texas and here she was cinched up tighter 'n a tick in her whalebone corsets, with a dress that would've made a Puritan look licentious. Not an inch of skin showed anywhere. She was covered from head to foot with long, tight sleeves with little white cuffs, a high collar so stiff it could've stood alone, a hundred or so petticoats, and white gloves. Nobody in their right mind would show up in Port Lavaca in white gloves. And that hat. It did absolutely nothing to shade her face, which was, what any fool knew, the primary purpose for wearing one. But not Miss Howard; hers was purely decorative, or it had been earlier in the day when she'd first put it on—now it was pure, unadulterated, unadorned distraction. Why, even the artificial flowers had wilted. Shaking his head sadly, he resumed his conversation with Hank, his old friend who ran the freight office.

Mourning stopped fanning herself and held the fan against the sun as she squinted toward the sky, trying to determine just how long she had been sitting here. Lord, how on earth could her mother live in an inferno like this? It was worse, much worse, than she had ever imagined. She slapped her neck, feeling the bite of another mosquito, and tugged at her high collar, trying to raise it higher. She wanted to cry, but she was too dehydrated.

What little breeze there had been remained anchored in the harbor with the packet; the air on land was sultry and deathly still. Sea gulls circled overhead, their incessant screams as irritating as the multitudes of flies that swarmed. Mourning raised her arm to shield the sun from her eyes as she looked back toward town, watching for a glimpse of Clint.

It wasn't really even a town. Port Lavaca was just a collection of adobe huts, a freight office, a small moth-eaten hotel, a livery, one general store, and a cantina. Filthy barefoot children played in the dirt while mangy half-starved dogs slept nearby.

"Heeaaah! get your rusty ass a-movin'." The foul oath was followed by a loud crack. Mourning jumped, one of the wilted daisies falling off her crushed straw hat. Turning in the direction of the repeated curses, she watched a fat gorilla of a man snap a long whip over the heads of a team of oxen that were straining at their tracings. The cumbersome beasts lumbered along, pulling a wagon so loaded, it looked as if it could topple over any moment. The wagon pulled away from the freight office, revealing Clint. He was standing on the wooden walk in front of the freight office, talking to a fairly civilized-looking man. Seeing her, Clint waved her in his direction, and she was more than happy to head his way.

Leaving Hank at the shipping office, Clint headed toward Mourning, knowing she was mad by the way she walked. She was stomping toward him like a new recruit in tight boots, swinging that infernal basket of hers for all she was worth.

She drew up short, hands on hips, angrily taking in just how cool and refreshed he looked, not a bead of sweat on him anywhere. "Do you have any idea," she choked out, "just how long I've been sitting on that stupid crate?" Her voice wrestled with a sob to see which would come out first.

Clint leaned his head back, squinting up at the sun. "Oh . . . 'bout two hours, I suspect."

"You are absolutely right," she said. "Two hours. Two long, hot, grueling hours. And just what have you been doing while I was frying in this miserable heat?"

"Well, let's see . . . first," he said with infuriating calm, "I went to the shipping office to make arrangements for your trunks, and then Hank and I went to the cantina for a drink, and . . ."

"A *drink,*" she squawked. "Did I hear you correctly? Did you say a drink?"

"I did indeed."

"You mean to stand there," she shrilled, "and tell me that you went for a *drink,* while I sat outside on that hot crate in the middle of this . . . this . . . den of iniquity!"

A crowd of less-than-desirable critters had begun to collect around them, and any southern-bred lady knew it was highly unheard of to make a spectacle of oneself in front of others, but it was something that always happened to Mourning when she got angry —really, really angry: she forgot all about being a lady. She was hot, sunburned, and tired, and this clodhopper standing before her, grinning like a baboon, was cooler than a cucumber, and she'd never wanted to slap anyone so much in her entire life.

Clint laughed. "Sweetheart, you couldn't have gone in the cantina, even if I'd wanted you to."

"Don't you get familiar with me, you slick-tongued reprobate. Why, may I ask, couldn't I go in the cantina? They let you in, didn't they? Then, they can't be too choosy."

He laughed. "They don't allow ladies." He shook his head in amusement. There she was again, standing on her cute little toes.

"Well . . . just what do you call that?" She pointed to two *señoritas* who chose that particular moment to walk out of the cantina.

"Sweetheart, those aren't ladies." A roar of laughter went up from the crowd. She was blood-drawing mad now.

"So, you just went ahead and had your fill of drinks while you let me die of thirst," she shouted.

"If you were so thirsty, why didn't you go get a drink?" he said.

"Because, you pig-headed baboon, you told me not to leave that stupid crate," she said. Her fury was on the verge of getting the best of her and she was finding his humor infuriating. "Why didn't you bring me something . . . anything . . . a lemonade, a drink of water . . . *tequila*?"

"*Tequila.*" He choked, and then he made the gross error of laughing. In her anger she hauled back and kicked him on the shin as hard as she could, wishing she had her parasol to really do some damage.

"Ouch! Damn you, you little hellion." Before he could grab

her she kicked him in the other shin, and while he hopped around on one foot and then the other she stomped off. He caught her, slinging her over his shoulder like a sack of potatoes, and walked toward the livery. A roar of approval went up from the crowd. "I let you kick me once and get away with it, buttercup. I won't make the same mistake again."

"Put me down, you sadistic worm." She began to pound his back and kick her legs, that is, until he applied the palm of his hand firmly to her bottom with a loud smack. Before she could scream a vile accusation at him she felt herself falling, and then she landed, with a splash, in the horse trough. Her words drowned in the slimy green water, and a booming chorus of laughter greeted her when she surfaced.

He stood before her, slim-hipped and lanky, his feet planted wide apart, arms crossed over his chest. "You said you wanted a drink," he drawled. "I'm only too happy to oblige you."

Any decent woman would have run to cover herself, but being a decent woman was the last thing on Mourning Howard's mind. Ignoring the crowd of people gaping at her, and their ribald comments, she stood up, wiping a long, green strand of slime from her cheek, and smiled sweetly at him. He tilted his head, studying her. She couldn't hoodwink him that easily. She was up to something, as sure as shootin'. It went against her grain to take something like this sitting down. That little face that smiled sweetly at him was not fooling him; she was madder than a hornet and ready to draw blood . . . his.

She smiled again and held up one hand, and with a crook of her index finger, motioned him to come closer. When he stepped in front of her, she looked again and motioned him closer still. When his head was just inches from hers, she spat a shower of water directly in his smart face and boxed him in the ear. A roar of laughter couldn't drown Clint's string of oaths.

Before he could grab her, she twisted, then fell over the side of the trough, jumped up quickly, and slapped against a bald man wheezing with laughter. The next thing Clint knew, he was looking down the seven-and-a-half-inch barrel of a Colt Dragoon. "Don't you come one step closer or I'll blow a hole in you," she said between gasps for breath.

Clint's astonishment was strongly etched across his features. *Where the hell did she get that pistol?* His eyes shifted to the empty holster of the wheezing man. *Fool woman.* He'd lay odds she didn't know the first thing about firing a pistol. Hell! She couldn't even hold it right. Her frail arms were already trembling from over four pounds of loaded Colt. The tip quivered, then drooped toward the ground like a divining rod, and he made a move toward her. The flagging tip was hastily righted.

"I may not know much about shooting this thing, but a fool could tell from this distance my aim doesn't have to be too good."

Looking puzzled but amused, he stopped. "Where I come from a man learns to listen to a lady packing a Colt." A round of laughter went up, and Mourning had to force herself not to look. *He's quick, Mourning Kathleen. Keep your mind on what you're doing.*

The sun passed behind a cloud, the kind that comes up with the heat, but Mourning was too tense to feel any relief. Cool and collected, Clint didn't appear to be suffering from the heat any. Perhaps it was the clothes he wore. He had patently shed his gentleman image with his fine clothes. He stood before her, looking dangerous in the rough, contemptuously worn clothing of a man who spent a great deal of time in the saddle. The clothes made his body look hard and rangy, and emphasized his raw appeal.

"You've got two choices, buttercup. Put the gun down or shoot. We aren't going to stand here all day." He took a step closer and Mourning took a counterstep backward. "Watch out for the step," he warned.

Don't listen to him, Mourning. He's lying—just trying to distract you. She took another step back and discovered he hadn't been lying.

10

Hurled like a launched projectile in retrogression, her balance the first to go, the rest of Mourning soon followed. She shrieked, and the pistol flew like a javelin from her hand. Then she went sprawling like a stuffed toy, landing in an inelegant heap. A thunderous, deafening report ripped through the heavily suspended silence.

Approaching like doom, Clint jerked to a stop, his hat blown off his head. A team of horses broke their lead and ran, out of control, down the street. The cause of all this commotion scrambled to her feet and stared at him, pale and frightened. Pandemonium swarmed around her. With wildly pounding heart she was battered with shouts and curses, the terrified scream of alarmed horses, and the splitting crash of an overturned wagon. Disoriented, she lifted her eyes with laborious effort, to the horrified blank expression of Clint Kincaid, his finger poking through a strategically placed hole in his hat.

"I . . . I don't imagine you'd accept my apology," she stammered nervously.

Slowly and silently he replaced his hat. His frigid smile extended all the way to his eyes, which pricked her like slivers of ice. She had never seen that smile before. It went beyond anger, to something stark and barren, like a soul without a spirit.

"Don't look at me like that," she said nervously. "I wouldn't really shoot you, you know . . . I was just frightened. Why won't you say something? What can I say? What words will appease you?"

His stance was loose and easy, as was his voice. "Words?" It was difficult to believe that his sugar-over-poison words came from the same lips that had once wandered over her skin so hotly. "My dear, words are a poor choice—a rather ineffectual tool in the face of adversity. Haven't you heard? Many women, many words . . . many geese, many turds."

Terrified, she gathered up her skirts and fled, threading and weaving a zigzag pattern through overturned wagons and scattered debris and across dried wagon ruts—dodging screaming children and barking dogs as she headed for the beach.

Amid the melee of confusion of jeering hoots and shouts from amused bystanders, Clint was after her, his fateful hand coming from nowhere to snatch her by the hair, just as she hit the first waves. "What the hell do you think you're doing? Swimming to San Antonio? It's impossible, you know."

Twisting his hand around her thick flaxen coils, he wrenched her arm and hauled her back to the beach, clawing and screaming, as he did his best to wrestle her to the hull of an overturned boat. For a small woman she possessed an inordinate amount of strength.

The explosion came like the wind of winter howling down a chimney, and Mourning was sure her bones cracked like pipkins when he shook her. "I've seen more brains on a piss ant!" Clint shouted through gritted teeth. Ruffling gusts of wind sent his hair rippling in silken waves over his brow. "I hate to be the one to do this, God knows you hate me enough already, but someone has to teach you sensible control. . . . That was a damn crazy-fool thing you did. There were women and children out there, someone besides me could've been killed. When are you going to learn; your brain is there for some purpose other than filling up the space between your ears. Don't you ever use it?" She tried to give him a placating smile, but it failed miserably. "No need to cower before me like a pathetic waif. Neither that nor tears will save you now." He studied her critically. "What are you going to do next? Apologize and beg for your hide?"

Her eyes widened with expectant hope. "If I did, would that mean you won't hurt me?"

"No."

All hope died. Mourning squirmed unsuccessfully against his steely grip. "What's it to be, then?" she said, not really thinking he would do damage to her person. "Drawn and quartered? A flogging? Cat-o'-nine-tails?" Her voice was pitiably childlike and frightened.

"No," he said pensively. "I'm going to do something someone should have done a long time ago. I'm going to blister that cute little butt of yours, Miss Howard, until it's as rosy as cinnamon tea. And, in case you're considering it, an apology might lessen your punishment."

"The only thing I'll apologize for is not blowing your arrogant head off."

"No, don't try to get away again," he grunted, straining against the unbelievable energy she possessed. "You do, and it'll only be harder on you."

"You can't spank me. I'm not a child."

"Aren't you?" he said dryly.

"You aren't going to spank me!"

He didn't answer, but sat down on the overturned hull, dragging her across his lap. Oblivious to the crowd, which by this time had grown in number, Clint threw her skirts and petticoats over her head, exposing her waterlogged drawers, which clung enticingly to her pink, rounded bottom.

"Let me go, you monster . . . you pig . . . Owwww, stop it . . . owwww, Clint, stop. . . . I'm going to tell my mother . . . owwww."

Stiff with anger, Clint shouted at her, "You won't get the chance to tell Caroline, because I'll tell her first, you little wildcat. When you're sorry I'll stop."

"Stop it!"

"Apologize and I will." Again and again he brought his hand down, slapping hard against her thinly covered bottom. Staunch in her rebellion, Mourning stubbornly refused to say the words that promised salvation. When he asked her again, she spat at him. Anger, hot and furious, slushed through him, swelling to thick surges of violent intensities that closed all reason behind a crimson curtain of rage. He saw red.

Unaware of approaching danger, and too stubborn to desist, Mourning clamped her teeth together, gritting back the burning pain. He could beat her to death, but she'd never give him the satisfaction of hearing an apology from her lips. Never . . . never . . . never.

Clint maintained his blistering castigation and Mourning persisted, with the same dogged perseverance, in her refusal to utter the paltry few words of apology.

Through the red mist of blinding rage Clint saw that the curious onlookers had ceased to laugh, every faint suggestion of amusement having vanished from their faces. A few people shook their heads and turned away.

He paused, and he heard Mourning's wrenching cries. She was sobbing uncontrollably. "No more, please, no more."

Throwing her skirts down, Clint pulled her up, turning her across his lap. With a dismissing glare he dispersed the crowd.

When he found her face amidst a riotous confusion of golden hair, she gave him a hurtfully bruised look that he'd never forget. Her eyes shimmered with tears, her lip quivered, and breathing erratically, she stared at him in a mortally wounded way.

"Forgive me," he said, regretfully. He placed his hands on her face and buried his face in the musky dampness on the side of her neck. An act of heartfelt contrition.

Her slender arms went around his neck and she buried her face, in the space between his collar and neck. Absorbed and comforted with the soothing scent of his warm body, she was stirred with a sense of pleasure and guilty remorse. Overcome with a sense of shameful wrongdoing, she sobbed repeatedly. "I'm sorry . . . I'm sorry . . . I'm sorry."

"You poor absurdly remarkable girl," he whispered. "Shhh. Don't try to talk, angel-eyes." He drew her intimately close, pressing his face against the thick tangles of her hair. She clung tightly, her body shaking with spontaneous cries as her tears became lost in their soaked clothing. "Love, I didn't mean for it to go this far," he whispered.

As she began to gain control, he felt her trembling body stiffen against him. "Are you going to be okay?" He drew back and cupped her chin in his palm, lifting her cherubic face.

She scowled and angrily slapped his hand away. "Don't."

She gazed at him with the mien of a woman scorned as she said in a low voice, "I can't remember ever despising anyone as much as I do you."

Her childish switch from acute remorse to hardened obduracy was so obnoxiously captivating, it washed over him like a soothing balm. Unknown to her, this extravaganza of infantile deportment did more to arouse the benumbed spirits of two fated souls at the crossroads of their relationship than anything she could have done. Clint saw it for what it was: a linking bond, a resurgence, a kiss of fresh life into a savage attraction between them.

He smiled into her hair. "I'm sure you don't." He shook his head. "It's your own fault, you know. Can't you tolerate luke-warm? Must everything be hot or cold? Temper tantrums and childish pranks are one thing, but what you just pulled . . . No self-respecting man would sanction that sort of behavior, not even from a woman. I know you're furious with me, but you're more angry with yourself."

She gave him a wide-eyed stare, momentarily stunned by the truth of his words. It wasn't a pleasant feeling, to be caught with your drawers down. He had skewered her and now he was holding her over the coals. Knowing he was right made her all the more angry. "You didn't have to go to that extreme."

"Extreme?" He laughed. "Lady, extreme is all you understand. You have spent your entire life going to extremes. But that's the key, isn't it? Miss Mourning Howard has free rein to play with the emotions of others, but no one has ever dared to give you back what you dish out. That's what galls you about me, isn't it? You have finally met someone who won't cower before you like those mindless, doting saps you toyed with in Memphis."

"That's not true . . ." She doubled up her tiny fists and pounded his chest with each word: "It's not true!"

"Yes it is, angel, and that's why it hurts. Mourning, you are such a child and obstinate to a fault. When are you going to grow up and realize life isn't a game? You and I are constantly at cross purposes because for once in your overprotected, overindulged life you've met someone you can't dominate, and it chafes you to the core. I'll tell you something else. You enjoy these little sparring matches with me because those childish emotions that rule you, for once, are pushed to the back, allowing your feelings as a woman to come forth. It excites you . . . makes you feel provocative and just a little wanton . . . and *that,* my lady, scares the hell out of you."

"That's a lie!"

"Is it? The woman in you responds to the man in me with such intensity, it scorches the starch on those pristine drawers of yours. Shall I show you?" His head lowered menacingly toward hers, and for the first time in her entire life Mourning did not have a plan for a counterattack.

"Get away from me," she shrieked, pushing at his chest.

His mouth closed over hers. She lay motionless, her teeth clamped together, her lips locked tight. He took her lower lip between his teeth and bit, lightly, but enough to get her attention. "Who taught you to kiss?" he said with an amused chuckle. "That was reminiscent of licking the frost off a cold window when I was a child. We're going to try it again; this time I want you to pretend you're sucking the juice from an orange."

"*Sucking the juice from an . . .* You're disgusting!" she snorted, squirming and pushing to no avail.

"But you like it," he teased, a grin splitting his face.

"I don't."

"Shut your adorable mouth and kiss me." He kissed her again, and when his tongue pressed against her lips she clamped them firmly until she felt the gentle pressure of his teeth biting her lip and she relaxed.

"That's better, but still nothing to write home about." She raised a hand to box his ears but he blocked it. "This time put your tongue in my mouth."

"You're not only disgusting, you're revolting! I'd sooner stick my tongue up a pig's snout!"

"Good God, stubbornness to that degree borders on the ridiculous. Now, if you want those two pups to come any farther with you, *give me some tongue.*"

"Dear Lord, you're a maniac," she moaned.

"Only when I'm around you. Now, give me a good, tongue-thrusting kiss, or we'll be here all night."

She closed her eyes, vowing to *lie back and think of England,* but when his lips touched hers and the warmth of his tongue invaded her mouth, England became a very small country that was very far away. His hands went around her. "Relax and put your arms around my neck." He pressed her against him, and when she didn't respond, he said, "Remember the pups."

He wanted to laugh at the way her slender arms slipped around his neck, inching forward just enough to submit, yet remaining reluctant enough to maintain her stubborn pride. His mouth slanted across hers, and she could tell by the tugging pressure that he wanted her tongue in his mouth. That thought set her

heart springing and thumping like the wild zigzag course of a
black-tailed jackrabbit. Remembering the pups, her tongue inched
slowly forward. It was an exercise in contradiction: opposites were
attracting, black was white, everything false was suddenly true,
and Mourning was left feeling like a round square.

She collapsed against him. The sudden heavy softness of her
relaxed body against him suspended his thought process, immediately transferring all available energy to technique. And what technique! The manner in which he used basic physical movements to
effectively express himself left her teetering between compliance
and revolt.

He caught her more firmly against him, intensely aware of her
physically: the weighted yielding of her breasts against his chest,
the soft musculature of her back and shoulders, the solid firmness
of her rounded buttocks. He lifted his hands to her shoulders.
Following the line of her arms, he slipped to the underside, coming
to the warm cove between her underarm and torso. His fingers
caressed the contours of her waist, lying small and firm above
softly rounded hips—slim as a reed yet undeniably feminine.
Touching her with his sensitive fingers, he let them travel over her
slowly and, with gentle pressure, urged her rigid arms away from
her body.

Mourning trembled like a new fawn when his palm slid up her
ribs to gently cradle the supple incline of her breast. Her primary
reaction was staggering shock, then came the frantic eddying of
eccentric embarrassment, a deviation from the established pattern
embarrassment usually took for her. What washed over her now
was an odd, almost whimsical feeling of secretive shyness. This was
not the awkward bashfulness of childhood, nor the coy *no* of a
woman who has decided in advance to yield. Neither was it indeci-
sive shame that skittered across her, but a timid tendency to shun
participation, making her hesitant to commit herself. Her natural
instinct told her this beautiful, exciting moment would disappear if
she looked at it too closely.

Secretive little cries pulsed from her throat, responsive to the
confusing change within her body. Instinctively she reacted to
what was practiced knowledge to him; the way his sensitive fingers
moved upon her breast. Bathed in a sense of warmth and faint
excitement, a deep sensation of desire began to swell and expand
until, compounded with deep pressure, it grew to a conspicuous

degree. For a twinkling moment she had the delirious feeling that he would know what to do to stop this maddening feeling.

She pushed her doubled fists against his chest, trying to break the contact of mouth against probing mouth, breast beneath questing fingers. "You've punished me enough," she whispered. "Let me up."

"Angel, I can't, not now," he said with unbelievable softness against her tumbled curls. The sensitizing touch of his searching, inquisitive fingers was so routing, a numb feeling persisted even when his fingers had ceased to deliver the exquisite torture.

Already her lips suffered separation from his with a searing need to have him touch her soul once more with the heat of his kiss. Mourning gave a mewling little cry of frustration that he read correctly. A study in perfectionism, his kiss was flawless and seductive, proficient and unequivocally accurate; so accurate that when he gave the warmth of his mouth and plunged with quick intensity, there was an immediate physical reply like a gunnery burst upon her center of impact.

She gasped. "When you kiss me like that, I fold up like a sensitive fern."

His responding laughter was punctuated with nibbling bites around her ear. "Delicate beauty," he murmured. "Together we can make your body sing."

Before he was through, Clint not only had her body singing, but singing *appassionato con fuoco* (with fire and passion). Her extreme sensibility to his physical stimulation was made manifest by the stirring of her softer, pleasanter, more feminine emotions.

Her feelings were so fragile, they responded to every pleasurable motion of his gifted touch with a voluptuous charge of passion. The indolent movement of his palm traced heated concentric circles, soaking like a cool, healing unguent against fire-ravaged skin. Sensitive to the fluctuating pressure and motion of his knowledgeable fingers, she had the capacity to react to him but lacked the power to reason.

The sun was setting, a flaming ball falling behind the horizon bathing them in rose and gold. The play of prismatic color from her hair blinded him as much as the fire from her fresh, untutored response. Control had always been his strength, his power; an effective and reliable technique of self-restraint enabling him always to remain disciplined and even a little detached. That was why he

first attributed the rasping sound of irregular breathing to her. The
subsequent discovery that the labored sound did indeed belong to
him was jarring. That sort of disquieted acceleration of heart and
lung action was normally activated during intense arousal and sexual peak. To be so fired by one so young and inexperienced was
rare for him.

When a silvered shaft of setting sun bathed her face, Mourning became aware of the uneven roughness of the overturned row-
boat's planking against her back. Somehow, sometime, during this
fervent mating of mind and passion, Clint had eased her out of his
lap to lay her on the boat, his body hard above her. Nipping at the
heels of that realization came another one of mammoth consequence. Her first indication was her sudden awareness of the movement of air against unprotected, uncovered bare skin. Her breath
shuddered and groaned to a stop. Her wide-eyed stare lowered to
the general vicinity of the air movement, to stare, in horror, as his
hand closed over her no longer virgin breast. For a moment, the
contrast of his nut-brown hand against the snowy whiteness of her
breast left her stunned. Then came slow-dawning reality. *Mourning
Kathleen, why didn't you watch those hands?*

Clint was so lost in the fire-dragon-green eyes and the warm,
supple flesh beneath him that he continued on his collision course,
guided only by his desire to un-virgin more than one trembling
breast.

Mourning was smart enough to know when she was outfoxed,
outgeneraled, outmaneuvered, and outfought. Diversionary tactics
were useless, as were prayers, threats, struggles, and tears.
Drugged by his assault on her physical and emotional being and
stretched in a paroxysm of sensuous bombardment, she collapsed
like a sand castle at high tide.

The effect of passivity was instantaneous. He lifted his head,
the caress of sea breezes touching her lips with a cool reminder of
the warmth they had shared. Afraid of what chastening anger or
indifference she might find in his powerful, expressive features, she
turned her face away.

Overhead, a solitary gull floated on a wind current while the
flat waves of ebbing tide slapped the beach with punctilious effi-
ciency. A lazy little breeze, moisture-laden and carrying droplets of
seafoam, sprayed their golden skin, twisting the silken strands of
their hair together in a damp tangle of love knots.

She watched the hurried progress of a fiddler crab scurrying sideways across the rippled smoothness of the beach. She felt Clint stiffen, then roll away. She knew he was standing before her, looking at her sprawled there like an insignificant piece of driftwood. She felt stupid and absurdly out of place.

After putting her clothes in order, she found her way to her feet with all the grace of a newborn moose. Her voice was a jerky whisper. "I better find the pups." Slowly she began to walk up the beach. The abrupt closure of his hand upon her arm forced her to stop what little movement her stiff legs were capable of.

"Don't wallow in visionary thoughts of unchaperoned seduction—it won't happen again," he said in a mature, sensible tone. "What happened—it was my fault . . . a foolish mistake. Don't let it concern you."

Tears stung her eyes. She pulled away from him, only to have him grab her more firmly. "Don't look so downtrodden, angel, your virtue is still intact."

Tired and defeated, Mourning found her thoughts swirling in jumbles. Miraculously, a whole and complete sentence formed in her mind. *"Virtue, though in rags, will keep me warm,"* she said vehemently.

He watched her swing away from him and run up the beach. "So," he said with a slow grin, "the little rabbit reads Dryden." It was another scrap of information about a woman-child of baffling complexities, and he filed it away with all the others before turning his steps in the direction she had taken only moments before. Women, he mused, are almost impossible to understand. *This* woman he would be puzzled to understand even if he possessed the wisdom of Solomon.

11

It took three days to load the freight wagons, and three days in Port Lavaca seemed like three years to Mourning. Of course she had nothing to do, and idleness, besides being the devil's workshop, was boring.

Clint, of course, stayed busy. And for three whole days he had been in a good mood. He had not taken offense at one thing she said, and considering they were mostly tacky things she mouthed about Texas—Port Lavaca in particular—that was quite a concession. At least Mourning thought it was.

Mourning knew she had been irritable and cross, snapping at him for no reason, but Clint took it all in good humor. He was careful to explain where he would be and what he would be doing before he left, giving her an idea of the time he planned to return. He took all his meals with her, and told her after each one how sorry he was at her having to wait so long in a hellhole like Port Lavaca.

"Cheer up. We won't be staying here forever," he told her one evening as they walked back to the hotel after dinner. "We'll be leaving before you know it."

Just as he'd said it would, the morning of their departure, after taking its own sweet time, finally arrived. With all the problems that had beset her thus far, Mourning greeted the day with the same eagerness she would a case of the grippe. If something bad hadn't already happened, it would.

A few horses stood swishing their tails in front of the shipping

office, the occasional stamp of a hoof ringing hollow against rut-
hardened streets that were crowded with loaded freight wagons
and sweaty, swearing men. Men that would soon be traveling with
Mourning and Clint, and their own wagons' freight—three in all—
to San Antonio. Listening to the commotion, Clint stood, casual
and relaxed, just outside the freight-office door, his gaze holding
the figure of the golden-haired girl making her way up the street.

He stood alone on the outer edge of the men, who stopped
working to watch her approach. The early-morning sun did little to
illuminate his face, which was dark and shadowed beneath the low-
riding brim of his hat. He was what he looked to be, fearless and
hard, with an undercurrent of low-simmering violence that could
be set to boiling in a twinkling. He appeared to be just another
lonely drifter leaning against the porch, whittling inconspicuously
on a piece of wood. Seemingly engrossed in his task, no one took
much notice of his eyes, which quietly sized up every man.

A few of the men working alongside the wagons stirred, while
others mumbled or scratched their faces; a few of them even spit;
but all of them watched the elegantly dressed lady step out of the
shadow of a low-overhanging porch into the brilliant sun. A
"click" fluttered past their ears when she opened her parasol to
protect pale, rosy skin, the like of which most of these rough, rangy
critters had never seen before, except maybe on a peach.

There wasn't a man gathered there who returned to his work
while she sashayed down the street. And she was something to
watch too, all properly decked out as if she were going to prome-
nade the park instead of starting on a long, grueling trip, bouncing
around in a freight wagon for several weeks.

Clint shifted his weight to his other leg. These homespun men
had never seen a lady of her caliber, dressed in frills and ruffles,
smelling like a rose, and blooming just as pretty as one under that
white eyelet parasol she carried. There was trouble in the air, he
could feel it. His attention was centered on three troublemakers
who had done little work and a whole lot of talking. They looked
innocent enough, but it was an old game, one he'd played too many
times before to be tricked. As if it were none of his affair, he just
kept on whittling.

"Ooowhee! Hey, Lucas . . . get a load o' *that* prissin' up the
street," Ollie said, then whistled, giving Lucas an elbow to the ribs.
Ollie Simmons was a big, soft-bellied, dirty fellow with a badly

scarred bald head (he had once been on the wrong side of a scalping) and at least two weeks' worth of itchy beard. Ollie was a loudmouth drifter prone to bullying, and nobody liked him. But they were afraid of him. Especially when he was with Milo Tompkins and Lucas Gregory.

Lucas was a short, stocky man with coarse features, black greasy hair combed long over a balding patch, and watery, pale blue eyes. He drank a lot, cussed a lot, whored a lot. Lucas spit in the dirt before answering. "Hell, Ollie, you just now seein' her? Why, I saw her so long ago, ole John Thomas here's done got ready." He rubbed his crotch with a movement that was somewhere between a scratch and self-stimulation.

Milo, the most dangerous of the trio, was a tall, lanky fellow with red curly hair and a pale, freckled face. An ex–Baptist minister, something had gone wrong, something that turned him bad. Everyone in Port Lavaca wondered what it was, but nobody had the guts to ask him. His shifty eyes were black and hard, and he had a habit of always hitching his gunbelt, as sort of a reminder that he knew how to use it. "Chicken shit, Lucas," Milo drawled, "that John Thomas of yours stays ready because you're always a-rubbing on it."

A volley of rowdy laughter went up around the wagons that set every stray dog to howling. Most of the men returned to work when the last faint sounds were carried off in the swirling eddy of a breeze. As the gentle vibration of deep voices settled once more, Clint's eyes riveted on the three braggarts, who continued to slyly watch Mourning, who was getting uncomfortably close.

Hank stepped off the porch. He was a wide-shouldered man with kind eyes and a soft, drawling voice that belied the strength of the man behind it. He stood at the side of the closest wagon, smoking a cigar, his deep-set blue eyes watching Clint, knowing the boy was no fool—he'd seen those icy eyes sizing up the situation. Normally Hank was a man who didn't interfere in another man's business, but Kincaid was like a son to him, and no matter how good a man was with a gun—when he was outnumbered three to one— well, it only seemed fair to even things up a mite. Hank crushed his smoke under his shin boots and stepped up on the porch. "Clint," he said in a low, rumbling whisper, "watch your step. Trouble's a-brewin'." When Clint nodded, Hank added, "And Milo's got a gun."

"Thanks."

Hank stepped inside the office and leaned against the jamb while following the progress of the beautiful young woman.

"Well, strike me dead and bleach my bones, ain't that the little filly what changed her mind 'bout hirin' us?" When Lucas stepped in front of Mourning, blocking her way, Hank's eyes flicked over to Clint, who stopped whittling but made no move to intervene.

"Excuse me, please." Mourning sidestepped and started around him when Lucas's hand shot out to detain her. Hank looked quickly at Clint, just in time to see him release the piece of whittling, which dropped to the ground, his thumb moving, kinda slow-like, across the sharp blade of the Bowie knife he was still holding.

"Hey, there, little lady. Whatcha got under this pretty little umbrellie you got here?" Lucas slurred. Mourning tried to move around him, annoyed at first, then panicked with alarm when she could not. Stubby fingers closed around her parasol, and Mourning found herself tossed about like a sack of potatoes. She began to back away when Lucas appeared preoccupied with twirling her parasol around his head, a sudden spurt of bravado coming from the encouraging comments of his two friends.

"Why'd a purty little thang like you wanna hide under this here umbrellie?" he said, reaching to pat her cheek. " 'Fraid we'd be mad 'cause you up 'n' fired us 'fore you hired us?" Mourning flinched and drew back a step, only to find her way blocked by Ollie, who grabbed her arms.

"Don't be in no hurry to leave, honey. We just want to talk . . . nice and friendly-like," Ollie said with a leering grin. "Thought maybe you wanted to reconsider us for the job you had."

Lucas dropped the parasol. "Damn your hide, Ollie. The gal's mine. I got first go with her. You kin have her when I'm finished."

Ollie flashed a toothless grin. "Shouldn't have to wait long . . . you bein' so quick on the trigger 'n' all."

Once again, Mourning found herself ignominiously tossed like a sheaf of dried cornstalks as Lucas reclaimed his prize.

"Let me go, you filthy pig!" Mourning said, feeling she was going to be ill when he slid a slovenly kiss across her neck.

"Hey, Lucas," Milo interrupted, "we don't have all day. You'd best be bringing her along so we can discuss business."

"Whose business we gonna discuss first?" Ollie drawled.

Mourning screamed when Lucas reached for her skirt, but his hand never touched her. Without a warning his shoulder slammed against the side of the wagon as Clint's Bowie knife found its mark, pinning his arm against the splintered wood. The handle, still protruding from the muscle above the elbow, shuddered to and fro before slowing to a dead vibration.

Ollie shoved Mourning away as Clint came off the porch. Clumsy quick, like a grizzly, Ollie rushed Clint, swinging a low right. Clint met him halfway with a powerful fist that caught him square in the mouth, knocking out two teeth and sending him to his knees. He was spitting blood when Clint grabbed him by the collar, hauling him to his feet, his legs flapping like a string puppet. Ollie held out his hands, signaling he'd had enough. Clint was breathing hard, and his eyes were hard and narrow as they scanned the not-so-powerful bully, watching him fold like a bad poker-hand.

Milo, sly and weaselly, inched over to Lucas, who was tugging at the handle of the knife that still held him pinned to the wagon. "Who the hell is that?" he asked Lucas.

"Some guy that'll be travelin' with the freight wagons to San Antonio . . . name's Clint . . . that's all I know."

Clint whirled, facing Milo, who held up his arms in surrender. "I don't want no trouble. We just wanted to ask the little lady to give us a chance for the job she had."

"Job's been filled," Clint said.

"By you?"

"By me. Any problem with that?"

"None worth mentioning," Milo replied.

"Take these two worthless bastards and get moving, then." Clint yanked his knife and freed Lucas's arm with one swift motion. He glanced at Milo as he wiped the knife against the leg of his leather pants before shoving it into the scabbard at his waist.

Milo turned as if he was going to leave. He had the kind of look a rattler has just before it strikes. His fingers twitched when his hand started for his gun. Clint's cleared the holster before Milo had a chance to move. Hank's voice stopped him cold. "Don't try it, Milo, Kincaid's fast."

Jolting recognition flashed across Milo's face, a low mumble went up from the men standing around. Milo's face was tight and a little white around the gills. "Kincaid . . . Clint Kincaid?"

Hank stepped off the porch. "The same," Hank said in a low voice.

Milo whirled and backhanded Lucas, knocking him to his knees. "You stupid dumb shit!"

"Aw, Milo, why'd you go and hit me for?" Lucas whined.

"Next time," Milo said through clenched teeth, "you tell me a man's name, *tell me the whole goddam name!* you stupid louse."

"I didn't remember his last name, Milo; besides, does it matter so much?"

"It matters, you brainless bastard! Clint Kincaid has killed more men than you could count on both your stupid hands. Any man that draws on him is tired of living."

Mourning turned a round-eyed stare upon the man she thought she knew. Whatever Clint Kincaid was, one thing was obvious: This crowd of men recognized the name and were backing off—way off. The crowd was buzzing now, and Mourning could hear snatches of their words. *Wild . . . brother . . . Comanches.*

As far as controlling emotions, Mourning was lagging way behind Clint, who seemed in perfect control. What she heard people say about him was astonishing. What she witnessed, even more so. His moods could change as fast as his draw. For three days he had been as tame as a house cat, turning vicious at the drop of a hat. She had spent weeks getting to know this mysterious man, only to find that now he was a bigger mystery. Her surprise, however, was soon squelched by his mocking words.

"Close your mouth, unless you're catching flies." Mourning whipped her face up to find Clint standing alone by the wagon, observing her with a flat, level stare. The empty expression on his face looked more hardened the closer he got.

"Why are they so afraid of you?" she heard herself whisper in a high, squeaky voice. "It's true, isn't it? You've killed people? Lots of them, haven't you? Are you a desperado?" He looked arrogantly uninterested in what she was saying, but seemed to find pleasure in her blossoming discomfort. Before she had been worried about being alone with a scandalous rogue, but now she realized she was traveling with a man who could kill with the same composure he used to swat a fly. Looking into the cold ashes of his eyes, she could almost hear the shrilling of alarm bells warning her away.

Alarmed by something she saw in his expression, Mourning was panic-stricken. Clint didn't notice. But Hank did.

Hank, whose full name was Henry Arnold Stonehauser, directed a disturbed stare at the frightened cherubic face surrounded by honey-butter curls. He was an old friend of John Kincaid, the two of them having served together in the war against Mexico. Fortunately for them they were with the troops at the Battle of San Jacinto, not the ill-fated group of heroes who died defending the Alamo. Having lost his own family to Indian raids while he was fighting, he strung along with Kincaid after the war. He'd been there beside him ever since, taking to John's two motherless pups like they were his own.

It was the oldest of the litter he was concerned about now. Rolling back the years and digging in the cobwebbed vaults of his memory, he brought forth images of Clint, a child too beautiful to be a boy, and his equally pretty brother, Cad. The two of them ran as wild as two Indian ponies.

Not that John hadn't loved the boys and provided well for them, but a man does a poor job of being both Mama and Papa.

An exasperated sigh from the young woman with Clint drew Hank's attention. Women had not played an active role in his life for several years, at least since his insides were all busted up breaking horses. Incredibly beautiful though she was, there was some other quality he sensed in her that held his interest. There was a newborn freshness about her, like she had just been discovered inside a fresh-shucked ear of corn, all bright golden yellow and squeaking with healthy vitality.

The young girl's troubled green eyes kept flicking at Kincaid. What was she to him? Surely this golden sun-princess was too young, too innocent, too well bred to be of interest to a man of Kincaid's ilk. Whatever their relationship, it was a stormy one, judging from the way she cast fearful eyes at him.

Keeping his thoughts to himself, Hank watched Kincaid approach and the girl shrink.

"Would you care to enlighten me as to the occasion of your obvious acquaintance with such lowlifes?" Clint asked.

Silence followed while she snatched at fragmented words floating pell-mell in her jumbled brain like a dog snapping flies. Somewhere a dog barked and a child cried. And then, miraculously, she found her words. "I didn't hire them."

"Wise and independent thinking for a change? Out of character for you, isn't it?" he said in clipped tones. "Let's take this game

a little further. What was the job you had that needed filling . . .
a job you obviously found me incapable of performing?"

She dropped her hands to her side, limply signaling defeat. "I
was inquiring about a chaperone. . . ."

His hands flew out and yanked her against his body, so hard,
the breath heaved from her lungs. Each angry muscle, every furious inch of bone, was screaming against her. He smelled like
saltwater and wind and sunshine, his breath was faintly edged with
tobacco.

"You wanted a chaperone," he repeated. "I'm tempted to call
them back and let them have you . . . in the biblical sense . . .
but that would be a waste, wouldn't it?"

Before she could answer, he whirled, jerking her along beside
him. "Where are you taking me?"

"Does it matter? You were looking for men. Won't I do?"

"Clint!" Hank yelled, heading toward them.

"I don't want to have words with you, Hank, so keep your
nose out of this!"

"Have you lost all sense of decency?"

"Not around those that deserve it," Clint answered, giving her
arm a firm yank. Mourning could hear her shoulder joints cracking
like chicken bones.

Hank studied the birdlike frailty, the huge green eyes, of the
trembling girl. "Is she with you willingly?"

Clint threw back his head in cold, ruthless laughter. Intense
anger colored Hank's features, not subsiding when Clint spoke.
"Willingly with me? No, not willingly . . . nor am I willingly
with her."

When no one said anything Clint continued. "Confusing, isn't
it? She's thrown with me, but she doesn't want to be; I'm stuck
with her, and I don't want her." Clint made a mocking bow in
Mourning's direction. "Do let me introduce you to Miss Mourning
Howard, whose illustrious connection to me stems from the fact
that her mother married my father. My illustrious connection to
her, however, is my stupidity in agreeing to bring her to the ranch.
You saw the types she prefers to me."

"This is Caroline's daughter?"

"In the flesh . . . every succulent, ripe inch of it. Amazing,
isn't it . . . a woman with the golden-tinged face of an angel,
having to hire men."

Mourning's simmering emotions began to bubble and boil. "I was looking for a chaperone, you blithering idiot! You know . . . female . . . lady . . . woman. I don't know how those three circus freaks found out about my inquiry." She threw up her arms in helpless surrender. "Everyone in this ridiculous town seems to be suffering from overscorched brains. I never spoke to those men. A girl came to my room last night asking about the job and I told her it had to be a woman. I don't know why you're so angry with me for wanting a chaperone. I was only trying to protect my name and my virtue."

The rest of their conversation settled down to mild tongue-lashings, and Hank left.

Mourning spent the next five minutes skimming the surface of the street as Clint dragged her behind him, all the way back to the hotel. "Why are you bringing me back here? I've already packed my valise. You said you'd send someone for it."

"I thought you were interested in protecting your virtue. If that's your intent, put on some decent clothes."

"Decent clothes? What on earth are you talking about?" Stopping in the middle of her thoughts, Mourning stared at him as if her eyes were lying. "You have the nerve to stand there, bellowing like some battling ram, telling me to wear decent clothes? What's wrong with my clothes? There isn't an inch of skin showing anywhere," she said with a bewildered look.

"No," he said, ruffling his fingers through the rich tones of his hair, "no, there sure isn't any skin showing. These men could handle that. They see plenty of skin all the time. What they don't see is a refined lady, all scrubbed and glowing pink and smelling like a flower bed. Then here you come, ruffled and frilled up to your pert little nose, parading around and making them realize they've never even seen a real woman, let alone touched one."

Her eyes were bright as shamrocks, and the heated glow of her cheeks stood out against otherwise shocked, pale skin.

He clenched his jaw and hardened his resolve. "Get in there and put on something less flamboyant, and for Christ's sake leave off the friggin' gloves, flower-bedecked bonnets, and frilly parasols. Cover your body without drawing every man's attention. I've ruined one man's arm today because of you . . . I don't intend to try for two. Now, move!"

"You know what you are? Crazy! that's what," she screeched

as she stormed to the adjoining room and jerked the door open. "I am forced to travel with a man as mad as a March hare," she said simply, and then slammed the door so hard a cross-hatched picture fell off the wall and crashed to the floor, its frame splintering into pieces.

Stomping to the valise she had just packed, she jerked out her drabbest dress, calling him the vilest names she could think of while changing. "Overbearing brute . . . thick-skulled toad . . . arrogant oaf . . . insensitive goat . . . foul-mouthed baboon."

Clint leaned against the door, listening to her sputter. He grinned at her expletives, understanding the need for such release. It was strange, the kinds of things he found captivating. Ironically, it was when she functioned at her most unrestrained level that he seemed to find her most enchanting.

She was a thorn in the side, a pain in the ass, an albatross around his neck. Her tongue was sharp, her words witty, her logic shrewd, her mind clever, and her humor unbounded. She was a paradox of sterling quality; she was an incongruent accumulation of comical contrasts and preposterous contradictions that came together like an absurd enigma. Trying to reason with her was like trying to back-talk a couple of sage hens. How could one tiny woman be such an argument to herself?

Mourning swallowed her pride, her misgivings, and anything else in the vicinity, and stepped into the room quietly. "Am I to be buried in hot sand or stretched out, tacked down, and left to cure in the sun like prime tobacco?"

Clint's magnificent gray eyes were softly dappled. A twist of a smile stretched itself over his shapely mouth. "Been reading up on your Indian torture games?"

"Yes, do you play?"

A grin touched his face. "Miss Howard," he said gently, "I would love to do more than play . . . with you." He enjoyed this witty and teasing conversation between them, making her steam and get all riled up. Because the only way he could shut that adorable mouth of hers was to kiss her into oblivion.

Mourning was so frustrated, she didn't know whether to clap her hands over her burning ears or his overworked mouth. In the end, she did neither, but decided to stop his line of reasoning with a few startling facts. "Talking like that, I'll have you know, is not the way to a woman's heart."

He was beside her quickly, taking her rose-petal cheeks completely between his palms, forcing her to meet his eyes. It was harder than he thought—taking her in his arms. "My sweet, winsome angel. I was never concerned with winning your heart." His eyes sparkled as he chuckled in amusement. "Actually, I wasn't aiming that high."

This sudden turnaround was so unexpected, Mourning was unsure of his exact meaning. He stroked her cheek with the curve of his finger, his steady gaze was light—almost effervescent. Fortunately, or unfortunately, Clint was feeling charitably inclined toward explanation.

He moved his hand to cup the back of her head, tugging her face to his. The penetrating warmth of his breath fluttered through the curling filaments of her hair, swirling them like crisp golden leaves before a whirlwind. Then his lips began to test the texture of the delicately sensitive skin at the side of her face. They moved in a teasing circular pattern over her silken lids, following the perfectly arched line of her brow, and down the line of her small determined nose. His words reached her through a luxurious purple mist. "Yes, my adorable little mudbrain, I meant what I said . . . literally. My target was lower . . . much lower." He brought his hard mouth down to cover hers, letting her feel the extent of his desire. Her hands, pushing against his chest, were converted to tight-fisted pounding when his next words were drawn forth in a scorch of passion. "Yes," he whispered, "my intentions were definitely lower."

Fresh color, the shade of candied apples, rose to her cheeks. Choking with fury, she was speechless, which was all right, since most of Mourning's thoughts were unprintable, unspeakable, and for a lady: unthinkable. When her words did come, they spilled out like apples from an upset cart, tumbling and rolling without forethought or direction. "Good! Why don't you aim really low . . . say, under my foot!"

Mourning whirled dramatically and marched to the door, yanking it open, only to see she'd opened the door to the adjoining room.

Between fits of laughter, Clint managed to choke out: "The door for grand exits, Miss Howard, is over there." He moved to the door. "Leaving so soon?" he taunted, giving her a mocking bow.

"I've seen all of you I care to, *Mis-ter* Kincaid." Holding the door open wide, he watched her charge from the room like mounted cavalry.

The corners of Kincaid's silver eyes crinkled in amusement. "You ain't seen nothing yet, spitfire," he whispered before closing the door.

12

Six times he fanned the hammer with his hand. Six red ribbons floated to the ground. The blurred action of his hands stilled long before the ear-ringing roar of gunfire ceased to rebound inside her head. She watched in wonder as he tied six more ribbons to the tree. *What kind of man can shoot like that?* She was no marksman, but any fool could see that hitting six tiny fluttering ribbons from that distance with a pistol took talent . . and an incredible amount of it.

He turned and walked toward her, long-limbed and lithe, moving with the soft-padding grace of a jungle cat. His walk fascinated Mourning: the long-gaited stride, the rolling action of his hips—so subtle in a blatant sort of way. His hips. She remembered a conversation she'd had two days ago with one of the drivers—a young kid named Joe.

Two weeks on the trail and the freight train of sixteen wagons had inched their way from Port Lavaca to Goliad. Plagued by difficulties—an overturned wagon, another buried to the wheel-hubs in a sandy stretch of road, and five days of persistent rain—all time-consuming and making progress slow. And two days ago, an hour before making camp, another misfortune. This time a broken axle. Hank sent two hands into Goliad to have the axle repaired and send a telegram. Two hours later, Mourning, busy washing her hair, stood with soap running into her eyes as she watched Clint and several drivers ride out of camp. They had not returned by the time she was called to dinner. While eating with Joe, she had stupidly asked where Clint had gone.

"Well," Joe drawled, "you might say he went to pleasure the ladies."

"Pleasure the . . ." she choked out. *"Humph!* that sounds just like a man talking. I bet that's not what the ladies call it."

"Aw, I don't know about that. I've heard some ladies say Clint makes love like a prairie fire: comes out of nowhere, leaving a trail of smoldering ashes behind him." Joe tossed his coffee into the fire; his dark eyes, gilded with humor, studied her carefully. "How's it you don't see what all them other gals see in Clint? I've never seen a woman what wasn't calf-sick over him."

"Oh, I get sick all right," she said, throwing her coffee into the fire as Joe had done. "Nauseated!"

"Shore don't understand that none. I hear tell his hips got more action than a repeatin' rifle. When Clint rides to town you can hear the triumphant twang of bedsprings for miles."

Walking up quietly and unobserved, Hank said, "As one can the twang of your big mouth, Hawser. I know one loose-tongued bastard what'll be eating dust come morning."

Grinning widely, and not exactly a paragon of remorse, Joe listened as Hank lectured him. Mourning stared round-eyed as Hank smacked Joe on the side of the head with his hat, then whispered something in his ear. They both laughed. Then Hank slapped Joe on the back and walked off. Joe explained how *eating dust* meant Joe's wagon would have the distinction of being the last, and getting the dust of all the wagons before it. "Until someone else gets on ole Hank's shit . . . er, black list," he said with much humor.

Now Mourning was thinking she didn't know much about repeating rifles, but Joe had been right. Clint's hips did have a lot of action. Even now, her eyes were drawn to the smooth action of his hips, moving rhythmically like the slow-swinging pendulum of a grandfather clock.

When Mourning allowed her eyes to travel up the elegant length of his body to his face, Clint was watching her, his mouth in that tugging stage just before the smile comes. He knew what she'd been watching. Heat flamed across her face. "Why don't you wear two pistols like some men who do?"

"Oh, is that what you were doing? Imagining what I'd look

like with two pistols strapped to me?" he asked, stopping in front of her, *that* part of him at eye level.

She swallowed and looked away. *Why is it,* she asked herself, *every time I talk to him, it's like spitting into the wind? Everything I do or say comes back to hit me in the face.* "No, of course not. I just wondered, that's all."

He grinned. "I have a matched pair of these, but I only carry the other one when I'm expecting trouble or if I'm traveling alone in unsettled country."

Mourning was sitting on a rotted tree-stump in a cluster of bluebonnets, watching the pups tumbling over, around, and between clumps of Indian grass and bluestem. Her discarded bonnet lay to one side, stuffed with clusters of spring flowers, some yanked so energetically, they had clumps of earth still clinging to their hairy roots. Overflowing with color, the kinds of flowers she had picked were as varied as their colors: lavender gayfeather, pale yellow black-eyed Susans, Maximilian sunflower in deep shades of yellow, the pale blue of wild aster, brilliant red splashes of Indian paintbrush—she had even added the dark golden tones of goldenrod, which made her sneeze.

Mourning tucked her legs under her calico skirt and propped her chin in her hands, watching Clint talk and handle his Colt. *I must be terribly infatuated with him,* something inside her said. *Why else would I receive so much pleasure from watching him?* Relaxed and playful, she appeared younger than she was; curled like an enraptured child at her grandfather's knee, listening to stories of the war.

There seemed to be no end to his knowledge about the things they discussed: people, animals, travel, Indians, ranching. As she watched the fluid movement of his hands, she thought about the changes this man had brought into her life.

As they traveled, Mourning spent more and more time with Clint, who seemed to have infinite patience for teaching her about survival in this raw and unruly land.

An extended journey like the one Mourning was on, which would last two months, was the ideal opportunity for a sheltered, gently reared young lady to shed her cloak of refinement and meet life on even terms. The men on the freight train were helpful and tolerant of her natural curiosity. No question was too silly or childish to be answered, often with more vigorous background material than necessary. Oh, they loved to tease her. Once when she'd inquired about an opossum, she also was told that the male opossum copulates with the female's nose. A fact she heartily doubted, but Joe Hawser swore on the grave of six ancestors, it was the gospel.

That in itself was probably the biggest change. Two months ago, little Mourning Kathleen would have been struck deaf and dumb to hear that kind of talk.

If Mourning found the men of the freight train interesting, she was as much of a novelty to them as they were to her. A refined lady was a rarity in these parts, and everything about her intrigued them, from the slow sensuousness of her southern drawl to her aristocratic carriage and puzzling need for cleanliness. Sitting around the campfire at night with tin plates balanced on their knees, the men often forgot to eat, so absorbed were they in observing her strange manners. She began to form a fond attachment to these exotic men and their flamboyant garb. They were rough and a little uncivilized yet quiet and very private at times. Shy and often self-conscious, they became poised and self-confident in the saddle.

Drenched in the perfume of spring flowers, she floated in a magic time-frame until the playful yelp of a pup made her aware her mind had been drifting. She gave Clint a treasured smile.

"Welcome back," was all he said. He handed her the pistol, observing the warm, sleepy look she had, like a furry cat chased from his warm spot on a sunny windowsill.

She took the Colt from him and almost dropped it. Her head was bent in serious study, her hands trembling with the reality that what she held in her hand was used to kill people.

"Four pounds and one ounce," he said, laughing at the startled look on her face. "Navy Colts are heavier than other pistols."

She glanced down at the shiny Colt. *A .36-caliber nickel-plated Navy Colt,* he'd said, *with carved horn handles.* Even his initials, G. C. K., were engraved on the backstrap.

"What do I do first? Is it loaded?"

"Yes, it's loaded, so don't point it at me, for God's sake!"

She giggled and drew her shoulders up in simulated innocence and he tweaked her little nose. "Now, the first thing you do is take a bead on your target."

"Take a bead?" she questioned.

"Aim."

"Oh."

"Keep your hand steady," he said when her hand trembled under the weight.

She made a move to bring her other hand up for support.

"No, don't use your other hand, it'll slow your reaction time. Waiting for the support of your other hand could cost you your life. You'll get used to the weight before long."

"There's way too much to remember," she said in a faintly dejected tone. "I'll probably be dead anyway before I can remember all that. I can't see a desperado killing time while I run through my checklist: take a bead, keep your hand steady, don't use both hands, don't point it at anyone"—she paused and looked at him— "unless you intend to kill him," she said in a seriously gruff voice that failed miserably to sound remotely like Clint. But it was effective.

Clint's eyes traveled from her fragile hand gripping cold metal and followed the incline of her swanlike arm to the strikingly beautiful face. There was so much color to her face, like a field of flowers: the vivid green of her eyes, the apricot-hued skin, coral lips and rose-petal cheeks, and a cloud of hair that covered every color from gold to silver.

A clump of clumsily braided flowers she had carelessly tucked behind her ear were showing signs of wear and tear, and they began to slip their anchor. With an insignificant movement of his hands he reached across her and untangled the star-shaped blooms and tucked them securely into place. That was all it took for the blood to pound against her ears and her respiration to reach the pace of one suffering from altitude sickness.

He moved behind her, his arms closing around her shoulders, his hands, firm and steady, over hers. As it always did when he was near, her temperature began to rise, her heart began beating a thump ahead of itself, and her breath was trapped somewhere where it had no business being. *How can I concentrate when he's standing so close to me?*

"Don't shut one eye. Learn to aim with both eyes open."

She twisted her head to observe his impassive countenance, her nose wrinkling as she frowned against the brilliant sun. "How'd you know I shut my eye?"

"Lucky guess."

She fired, shooting a limb off a tree at least eight feet from where she aimed.

"You're no William Tell."

"Rome wasn't built in a day."

"Again."

She fired again, not even hitting a limb this time. "You're making me nervous."

"Again," he said, ignoring her comment.

She continued to fire, missing each time. After the sixth miss, he took the pistol from her and began reloading. "This may have been a mistake," he said as he pulled six more bullets from his cartridge belt and shoved them into the cylinder. "I should've known better than to try and teach a stupid woman how to shoot."

"I'm not stupid," she tossed back at him, "I'm just inexperienced."

He snapped the cylinder into place, brushing his palm against it, making the cylinder spin with a clicking sound, and then handed it to her. "So now you've had some experience. Hit the target."

She was so angry, she could have spit and hit the target. She held the revolver and raised her arm, pretending the red ribbon was his mocking mouth. She fired, almost afraid to look.

"Better. Now hit it again."

"Again?" she chirped. "Did I hit it?"

"Weren't you watching?"

"You mean I really hit it?" she asked, astounded. He nodded with a faint suggestion of a smile, holding her with a long, lazy gaze, then told her to do it again to make sure it wasn't an accident the first time.

She hit three out of the next six, then four out of six. He made her practice until she hit six out of six. Her arm was so tired and stiff she didn't think she could hold the pistol any longer.

"How'd you manage to improve so fast?"

"I pretended you were the target," she said brightly.

His eyes glinted with repressed humor but he said nothing as he removed six more cartridges from his belt, handing them to her. "Now you load it and then I'll show you how to clean it."

Mourning cocked a suspicious brow at him but took the pistol once more and opened the cylinder as he had shown her. Clint lounged against a tree, watching her: the studious frown that furrowed her brow, the way she blew a stray curl away from her face, the cute way she held her mouth when she was concentrating, her soft exclamations of *Oh blast it!* or *Botheration!* or *Hang it all!* whenever she did something wrong, but his absolute favorite was the heart-melting smile she sent him when she got it right.

Enjoying watching her when she wasn't aware, he observed her every move: slipping the cartridges into the chambers, snapping it back into place, twirling the cylinder just as he'd done. The sun was warm and golden on her hair, and he took a bead on her, thinking what nice full breasts she had. He was comfortable here with her, and just for a moment he knew a feeling of belonging—a sense of home. She was smiling at him now, holding up the gun proudly.

"Now unload it and start over again, just to be sure you can do it."

She frowned slightly and then shrugged, going back through the motions. Something tickled her nose and she wiggled it. It came again, this time she twitched, then blew softly, her hands too full of Colt and cartridges to do any effective swatting. Glancing up, she saw childish delight swimming in his eyes, and her eyes drifted down his arm to rest upon the blade of grass between his fingers. A blush spread quickly and she gave her attention to the pistol in her hands. Safely diverted, she tried conversation. "How did those men in Port Lavaca know you?"

"Word travels, though not always accurately."

"They said you've killed men . . . a lot of them. Is that true?"

"Anyone living where we do can claim a few notches on his belt. Often it's shoot or be shot."

"Why did you find it necessary to kill? I mean, what were the circumstances? I know you wouldn't just murder someone." When she glanced at him his eyes were regarding her intensely.

With a quirk to his brow, he asked, "And how do you know that?"

Casually, she answered, "I just feel it.

"No, I wouldn't just murder someone. Most of my killing has been renegade Indians and men who've run afoul of the law . . . or self-defense."

She finished and placed her hand behind her back and bent

back to ease the stiffness. The move put her breasts in sharp outline, and he felt a gentle stirring of desire.

"You all through?" he said, ready to get her back to camp.

"Yes," she said proudly, and handed the Colt back to him,
butt first, just as he'd taught her.

He wanted to kiss that precious mouth of hers.

"Let me shoot just a few more times."

Another hour passed with Clint instructing and coaxing, until
she was consistently hitting the target. Clint's words of praise left
her befuddled and tipsy as a titmouse. It was the same feeling she'd
had when she consumed too much of Aunt Harriet's fox-grape
wine. Little did it matter that an entire band of Comanches could
carry off all sixteen freight wagons before Mourning could load six
cartridges.

Spending a sunny spring day in pleasurable companionship
with Clint was like a quick ascent in an air balloon. Still dizzy from
all the whirling, Mourning flashed him a smile that was so beautifully received, it left her giddy as a whirling stick. Their eyes met
and held, then she looked away.

"Are there really those kinds of ants?" she asked in a hushed
voice.

"Ants?" he repeated. "What kind of ants do you mean,
midget?"

Twisted mottes of wind-shaped trees stirred in generously rising breezes that fluttered about her skirts and ruffled the sleeve of
his shirt. Pale fading shadows of lingering day had crept across
slumbering hills to weave muted colors into glowing tapestries of
color. Standing against a backdrop of primeval beauty, she possessed an untouched wildness that Clint found irresistible.

A long shiver passed over her and he stared at her strangely.
Her green eyes were earnestly concentrating, her dainty lips were
twisted in pained confusion.

"What is it, Mourning glory? Can you tell me?"

Her hot little eyes bored into him with an air of vexation and
her face bore the expression of a frustrated child trying to explain
the Greek alphabet with a five-word vocabulary. "The ants," she
whispered, as if it hurt her to say the word.

"I know it's the ants, angel, but you must help me. I don't
understand. What ants? When? Where?" Fighting to understand,

to help, he came up with all blanks. "Mourning, can you tell me what ants?"

Twin dots of rosy color crept forward and he sensed her discomfort. He wanted so much to help her, his desire was approaching insanity. He tried to think back, when he'd been a child and had difficulty explaining things, but was unable to find a parallel experience.

Her color deepened. Her vivid eyes snapped shut, and with a martyr's dedication she whispered. "The *ants,* Clint. The ones with the brains."

He closed his eyes, and for a moment he bathed in the luxurious wonderment of what a treasured joy had clubbed her way into his life with an ax handle. Moments passed before he heard her little sigh of annoyance and opened his eyes. He found her, a sparkling dewdrop, shimmering like a rainbow crystal on the outer edge of his soul. Her head, tilted to one side in irritation, her expression was humbling. *"The ants, Clint. The ones with the brains."* Her words came in a flood of emotion, understanding saturating him with the need to laugh. He knew now, exactly which ants had caused her so much discomfort. *"I've seen more brains on a piss ant,"* he had said. Not wanting to cause her further discomfort, he decided direct was the only approach. "You mean my reference to piss ants?"

Her hand, sweaty and smelling of puppies and gunpowder, was instantly clapped over his mouth.

Consumed by laughter, he struggled with the gripping sensation, not daring to look at her, knowing her expression would send him toppling into irrepressible spasms. Still violently shaking, he lifted his hand to stroke her cheek with the back of his fingers. "To answer your question, it would be my guess that those particular ants . . . the ones of which we are speaking, are not more endowed with brains than any other types. As for the name . . . I don't think the term I used is . . . In other words, it's not the scientific term."

The concentrated color of her cheeks embellished a perfect smile that both surprised and enchanted him. Her eyes were bright and deceptively clear, yet deliciously twinkling with humor. She leaned forward, poking his chest with one slim finger. "You will notice," she said with a sparkle, "I am *not* laughing at your mistakes. Nor am I railing," she added. "Let that be a lesson." Her nose replaced her finger as she buried it against his chest. His arms went around her, effortlessly.

Her head dropped back and he caught it in his wide hand. Lips warm and demanding closed over hers with a kiss so passionately tender, she felt her soul being searched.

His fingers began a slow, rhythmic search in a lock of honey-gold hair that played around the satin skin of her throat. The trembling reaction of her skin communicated the effective significance of that one move. He fitted her closer to the hard contours of his body. Blindly, she moved closer. His hands began to play across her, slipping from the softly rounded shoulders, down the slender length of arm, going under to grip her waist, then further to cup her buttocks. She melted against him, a perfect match to the angles, lines, and contours of his body; she left no void unfilled. Her hands went around his head, her fingers sliding through the silky hair that brushed his collar.

"Oh, buttercup," he whispered, "what are you doing to me? No, love, don't pull away. What you're doing isn't painful, not in the sense you think." His lips moved hungrily over the fragrant curve of neck, her name coming like a chanted plea from his lips.

"Look at me, angel-eyes." He pressed a light, lazy kiss on her trembling mouth, then drew back. "I want you," he said, his gaze steady and penetrating, and she knew he did.

She wanted him too. She wanted every glorious, wonderful, unknown thing those three words engulfed. They were in such agreement there, but one difference lay between them. Large and cavernous, gaping like hungry jaws, lay the chasm that placed them so far apart, they might have been on different planets. She wanted him, wholly, completely, almost desperately; but she also wanted him properly. And that put them on opposite poles.

The feel of his mouth, warm against her trembling skin, was painfully sweet. Her body began to sing with tension. "Let me make love to you, Mourning. Sweet angel, let me do to you what spring does to cherry trees."

There was an aching pause.

Clint looked down into her eyes, heated with distress, not missing the blush of color forming perfect circles on alabaster skin. Had he shocked her? "Don't leave me now, angel. Come back."

The green eyes snapped shut, distraught whimpers floated up from her throat. Her frustrated words, when they came, seemed painfully extracted. "Just in case you don't think I know what I know, I just want you to know that I know it."

Dear God, don't let me laugh. She's so painfully serious. Suffering the agony of untold torture, he savagely beat back the laughter that tried to consume him. Intoxicated on the bubbling charm she filled him with, his mind floated about him, making it difficult to act rationally. "Tell me, Mourning glory. What is it you know?"

A rebellious little curl slipped across her cheek, catching in her lashes. He brought his hand up to her face, brushing the curl away, tucking it with the wilted flowers behind her ear.

"I know," she said seriously, "just what the spring does to cherry trees, and if you think I'm going to do *that* with you, you're badly mistaken."

"Why don't you tell me what it is about cherry trees and spring that you find so offensive?"

"Bearing fruit," she snapped quickly.

Previously submissive laughter refused to stay submissive any longer. When the spasm passed, he said, "I can fully understand, angel-eyes, just why that might be offensive to you. Let me assure you, that, while the idea has merit, I was speaking in more poetic terms. I believe the idea I had in mind was one of blooming."

"Oh." It wasn't long before her brow furrowed. "How was I supposed to know? You always have those *procreative* things on your mind."

"Which is," he managed to say before his shoulders shook and he was consumed with laughter, "a most unfortunate place to have it.

"No, don't run away. Come here, you little tiger cub." He tucked her body against his warmth, his mouth covering any protest. (There weren't many.)

"Man cannot live by bread alone. Are you two infants going to starve to death, or shall I wave a white flag and see who surrenders first? Is that some kind of record you two are setting? Seeing how long you can go without air?" It was Hank's voice, and Mourning thought she would like to strangle him, but Clint had already pulled away.

≈ 13

Two weeks later, the wagon train arrived in Falls City. The freight on several of the wagons had shifted, and rather than run the risk of losing it, they spent an extra day there to reload the wagons. The second night there was one of those dark, moonless nights when you can't see your hand in front of your face. Prismatic ribbons of color leaped high, as if trying to escape the bed of coals lying white-hot and silent against the dark of night. The silhouette of a man, outlined sharply against an orange halo, stirred the slumbering coals to life. The fire, snapping with renewed vigor, hurled showers of crimson sparks that spiraled upward, borne on the wings of rising heat and woodsmoke. The glow of the rekindled fire cast a burnished gloss on the leathery faces of the men hunched around its warmth.

Beyond the firelight was a cluster of wagons; drab, dusty, and piled with freight. Mourning sat in the back of one wagon, its freight shifted to provide space for her. Her eyes traveled around the deeply shadowed faces. She knew them all well now, scrappy young boys and wizened old men whose lives were shaped by the caprice of weather, the harshness of an unforgiving land, the smell of horse sweat. They were all her friends—Joe, an innocent vagabond cut from a hard piece of hide; Matt, the strapping and courageous man who never had a chance to be a boy; Will, a sad-eyed loner with little speech and a big heart; Buck, the reckless kid with galloping dreams floundering in stagnant water; Curly, the weather-beaten and bowlegged old man in search of solitude. An incongruous group of men with an unbelievable close-knit harmony of spirit, they possessed a sentimental homesickness coupled with a yearning drive to see what lay just beyond the horizon. They were as nostalgic as the ballads they sang—songs described in maudlin metaphors about living, unfulfilled dreams, and dying alone.

The backwoodsy twang of a mouth harp lingered like a sweet memory, then faded away. The boisterous singing was over now, the last dying notes lingering with sadness and a poignancy that could be felt. She dropped the canvas and lay back, finding the hushed undertone of men talking as comforting as the happy gurgle of a stream. There was a wild shout of laughter. Someone cursed. She smiled, stretching like an overfed cat, when she recognized the husky lilt of Clint's voice. It must be a good story, the men were talking later than usual tonight. She usually heard Clint settling down to sleep before now.

It was Clint's habit to bed down under her wagon so he'd be close if she needed him. Mourning lay among the stacked barrels and crates, feeling the stab of loneliness that comes to a woman sleeping alone. Mixed feelings of attraction and dislike fought like two tomcats in her mind. Mourning tried to analyze her feelings for Clint, but found the task of sorting multiple conflicting emotions too difficult. Forcing her thoughts away, she began to listen to the tales the men were telling—stories of grisly events and violent skirmishes with Indians. Before the recounting of ghost-dance atrocities ended, Mourning fell asleep.

She slept fitfully, her body asleep, her mind plagued by visions of captive Anglo women tortured without mercy by bands of savage Indians. Like the snapping of a sprung trap, a terrible wailing like a banshee pierced her consciousness. Mourning's eyes flew open in horror as she listened to the bloodcurdling scream rend the air, again and again.

The first logical explanation that jumped into her head was that there were Indians out there somewhere close who had captured a white woman and were now well into the advanced stages of torture. She lay there, for what seemed to be hours, afraid to breathe. It was a grueling task; to lie there quietly and listen to the agonizing screams of the poor woman.

Realization, when it came directly to her, roared like a cyclone through her mind; if she could hear the woman, so could the

men. Did they hear her? Were they going to help? That thought
scared Mourning witless—she wanted to help the woman, but she
didn't, by any stretch of the imagination, want to be left alone and
unprotected.

When she could stand the suspense no longer, she rolled over,
pulling her pallet aside to expose the cracks below. Squeezing one
eye shut and staring with determined effort, Mourning was unable
to see anything. She called to him softly.

"Clint?" When he didn't answer she repeated the call, louder
this time. "CLINT?" Still no answer. Stealthily, she backed out of
the wagon, butt first, stumbling over her long nightgown as her feet
dangled over the tailgate. Around her everything was a flat, dull
black. Trembling bare feet touched moist earth. A shudder passed
over her; in that vast darkness lurked tarantulas, spiders, snakes,
scorpions, and God knows what other crawly things. When both
feet were steady on the soft earth and no painful bites were felt, she
lowered herself to the ground and crawled under the wagon on all
fours.

Clint's bedroll was there but he wasn't. When it came again,
the scream was much louder—obviously closer. Mourning scrambled into his bedroll, pulling it over her head. The warm smell of
Clint's body still clung to the bedroll and she burrowed deeper.
Newfound security and peace vanished with the next scream.

Feeling vulnerable outside, she dug her way out of the bedroll,
trying to hurry back to her pallet inside the wagon, but her knees
kept crawling up the inside of her gown, which grew tight around
her throat. To prevent strangulation, Mourning backed up. Necessity being the mother of invention, she hitched her gown up and
tucked it into her drawers. One more scream added the necessary
momentum, and she shot from under the wagon, colliding with one
of the redskin devils as she came up.

Assuming that the unidentified arms lurking in the dark belonged to a woman-torturing, half-naked savage, she fought valiantly against being the next volunteer. Clawing and kicking with
amateur gaucheness, she was overpowered.

"What the hell?" Clint's ragged voice cut the air.

Relief of tidal-wave proportions flooded her. With trembling
arms she clung to him like a terrified clingfish.

"I don't think this is what Ovid meant when he said, *Women
can always be caught.*"

"I'm so glad it's you," she whispered.

"Who in the hell did you expect out here this time of night? Ivan the Terrible? Mourning," he continued, "I'm getting . . . *mmmmmmm.*" This time her hand, when it clamped over his mouth, did not taste of puppies and sweat.

"Shhhh!" she whispered.

His face looked a bit gruesome in the play of shadow and red-glowing light from the dying embers of the fire. His body stiffened, low vibrations of anger infused his voice. "Just what are you doing out here?" His fingers closed with insistent pressure around her arms, giving her a firm shake. "Dammit, Mourning. Didn't I tell you to stay in that wagon, no matter what?"

"Yes, but you don't understand . . ."

"No, I don't. Amazing, isn't it? My failure to understand your idiocy seems to be the rule rather than the exception. I'm beginning to think you don't understand either, just how important it is for you to do as I say. I do know you're going to keep this up until one of us gets hurt, or killed . . . and if I'm *lucky,* it'll be me." He shook her again, harder this time. "When I tell you to do something, by God, you better do it. Both our lives could depend on it. Don't second-guess me and don't think of a better plan . . . *just do it!*"

"Okay! But don't shout so loud!" she whispered, looking around.

"Loud? You don't know how lucky you are even to be hearing me at all. Don't you realize that I had my Bowie knife out ready to slit your lily-white throat, when just by accident my hand touched that frizzled mop you call hair?"

"Keep your voice down," she whispered.

"Why, for God's sake?" he whispered back.

"Because they'll hear us," she whispered more softly.

"Who will?" he whispered even more softly.

"The Indians," she whispered in a barely audible tone.

"Mourning!" he snapped loudly. "I'm getting pretty sick and tired of your games."

"*Shhhhhhh.* Believe me . . . this is no game. I don't know how you missed hearing those horrible screams." As she related her story, she could see that the sympathy she'd expected would be a long time coming.

He finally remarked cynically: "Indians?"

"Yes, Indians. I could hear them torturing some poor white woman and her screams were . . ." She could feel his body tremble, and when she looked into his face he began to rock with spasms of laughter. She looked at him as if she'd just seen bats fly out of his belfry. Drawing herself up piously, she snapped, "I fail to see the humor in the suffering of a fellow human being."

With that comment and the hysterical way she was acting, Clint erupted into a full-blown, gut-wrenching laugh, falling against the side of the wagon for support. Mourning drew back her foot and kicked him as hard as she could on the shin and turned away, her toes cracked in at least nine places. Clint grabbed her, hopping beside her on one leg, still laughing.

"Wait." When she continued to pull away from him, he pulled her to a stop. "Wait a damn minute." She stopped and watched him gain control of himself. "What on earth made you think it was Indians you heard?" He fought to suppress the laughter that gripped him as he continued, "And where did you get the idea that they had a white woman?" His warm gaze strayed to her slightly puckered mouth, to the glint of irritation in her eyes, and then to the cotton gown that was comically tucked into her drawers. Humor danced in his eyes.

Swelling with righteous indignation, she poked a finger against his chest. "From her screams, you bloody fool. Obviously Indians wouldn't be torturing an Indian woman." Even in the face of being scalped, the way his smile affected her was staggering.

"Good point," he said, raising his brows with mocking thoughtfulness. A smile trembled behind his tightly compressed lips. He drew her against him and buried his face in the tumbled fragrance of her hair. "You are priceless. I don't believe this." He laughed until he felt her tenseness and knew he'd gone too far. Not wanting to irritate her further, he quickly checked his mirth.

The mournful scream came again. "There it is. You heard it this time, didn't you?" she said, squeezing him for all she was worth.

Indecision hung like a weight in the back of his mind. He thought a moment longer, then shrugged. "We better get out of the firelight," he whispered, then felt her tiny hand steal into his as she whispered back:

"Come on in the wagon and then you can look out under the canvas."

The interior of the wagon was dark, but it wasn't difficult to see her sitting on her heels, the snowy gleam from the whiteness of her gown covering her statuelike form. One small foot peeked beneath the ruffled hem; he allowed his eyes the pleasure of roaming over the delicate curves of her body. Her large, lustrous eyes were turned upon him; her voice, though quiet, was startling—so absorbed was he with the almost perishable beauty of her—alone and pure, like a young hyacinth.

"I don't hear it anymore," she whispered. He didn't speak, and she wondered if he was feeling as self-conscious as she was. The pale firelight came through the split in the canvas to stroke his hair like the silken touch of a woman's hand, and throw the sculptured face into high relief.

"Do you want me to go?" he asked.

As if on cue, a long, continual moan broke the silence, and he almost laughed when she hastily shot back, "No! Please . . . please stay!"

"Would you like me to light a lamp?"

Again her answer was frightful and quick. "No. They can see us better with a lamp."

"They?"

"The Indians."

"Yes, the Indians."

"I know you should go help that poor woman, but I don't want to stay alone."

"If it is a woman . . . no one could help her now," he offered, hoping it was what she wanted to hear. It was; somehow making her feel a bit better about selfishly wanting to keep him with her. "You scared?"

"What a stupid question," she whispered back, "of course I'm scared. I'm scared to death."

"Come here, then." He was sitting on one end of her pallet now, and she on the other.

"Wh-why?" She turned the startled eyes of a trapped gazelle upon him, then looked down to inspect her fingers.

"If you're scared," he whispered, "come here and I'll hold you . . . nothing more." It came again, the scream. She shot into his arms and he gathered her to him, resting his chin upon the luxuriant curls that lay on top of her graceful head. He could feel her heart fluttering against his chest. Marble-cold, and just as stiff, her arms were curled viselike around his neck. "You cold?" he asked.

"A little," she replied.

He pressed a kiss upon the top of her head. "Lie down." In the dark he couldn't see her frown, but he felt it.

"I'm not *that* scared!" she said in her stiff, cold little way.

He smiled. "I'm not going to take advantage of you. I promise I'll stay right here," he said.

"You won't break your promise, will you? You won't touch me?"

"Not until you're ready for me to," he answered, with what she thought was unnecessary cheerfulness. "If you're cold, get back into bed and cover up."

She lay upon the pallet, clutching the covers tightly under her chin. Neither of them spoke. After a few minutes she saw the canvas open and he slipped outside. Mourning wanted to ask where he was going, but was afraid the answer might be embarrassing. A few thumps of her heart later she heard the mournful wail again. "Clint?"

"What?"

"Where are you?"

"Here," he answered, climbing back into the wagon.

"I . . . I think I'm ready," she said ruefully.

"Ready for what?"

"Ready for you to break your promise . . . you know . . . the one about staying where you are . . . and . . ."

"And touching you," he finished, stretching out alongside her. He didn't speak, and she couldn't, so they both lay there in nerve-racking silence, each wondering what the other was thinking. With perfect timing another shriek came, and she thumped against him, his arms going around her, his hands rubbing up and down her back. He smelled faintly of tobacco, and she knew he had stepped outside for a smoke. Silence again.

For a moment she was exasperated with her own inability to make conversation and ashamed of the direction her thoughts were taking. Here she was at last, right where she wanted to be, worrying that he might not act the gentleman, hoping that he wouldn't. To force her mind off that, she began thinking about him. What does he like for breakfast? Is springtime his favorite time of year? Did he like her? A lot? Has he ever grown a beard? What does he look like without any clothes on . . . no, no . . . not that! She wasn't curious about that. It was no use, once the thought was there, in her mind, it rose faster than baking-powder biscuits. "Clint?"

"Hmmm?"

"Do you sleep naked?"

His head shot up so fast, hers thumped against the floor. "What kind of question is that for a lady to ask a man?"

"It's all right with me if you do. I think I should like to try it myself. Anna and I discussed it once, but it was in the middle of winter and . . . oh, well." She realized she was getting off the subject. "Well, do you?"

"That is none of your business."

"You do, then." She sounded satisfied, and then she added, "I'm glad you do."

"Shit!" he moaned, and threw his arm over his eyes.

"Manure," she corrected.

"Mourning," he said firmly, "I know being around a bunch of rough-talking men doesn't set a good example for a young lady. But you must realize discussions of this nature aren't proper. . . ." He felt her hand touch his arm lightly and his words came out in a tormented rush: "And you are making it damn hard"—he almost choked on the double meaning—"for me to be-have myself."

"Clint?"

"No!"

"What do you mean no? You don't even know what I'm going to say."

"Whatever it is, the answer is no. Now, go to sleep."

"Would you like to make love to me?"

"Godamighty!" he groaned, giving his head a negative shake while other parts of him jumped in agreement.

"Well? Would you?"

"Mourning, I'm warning you."

"Well, tell me and I'll be quiet."

"Yes, goddammit! Now, shut up!"

She smiled into the darkness, thinking surely the rich, con-tented feeling saturating her with a sleepy glow could only be equaled by a kitten with a tummy full of cream. "Clint?"

"No more questions," he groaned.

"Tell me what it's like to make love."

"No," he croaked. "I can't." Something inside him kept saying, *Tell her! Tell her!* Tell her . . . Hell! He wanted to show her.

"But I want to know."

"I'm sure you do."

"Weren't you curious before . . . I mean, the first . . ."

"Yes, I was, but I didn't discuss it with a woman."

"Who'd you discuss it with?"

"It was a long time ago, I don't remember."

"Yes you do, you just don't want to tell me. I thought you were my friend."

"I am." He wanted to be more than her friend, he wanted to lose himself inside her and never come out.

"Then you should tell me, because if friends . . ."

"Oh, hell! It's wonderful to make love . . . great . . . fantastic . . . quite the jolliest thing you'll ever experience! Now, does that answer your question?" He prayed to God it did, because he was losing control fast.

"What do you do first?"

"Dammit! Mourning, that's enough!"

"Do you just kiss and kiss or . . ."

"Yes," he groaned, and rolled over her, his mouth crushing down on hers. Her arms went around his neck, and he pressed painfully against her. Oh, God, she felt good, so good, and he wanted her.

But he stopped.

He must be crazy, he told himself. He could've had her and he knew it, so why the hell didn't he?

"Why'd you stop? Don't you want to kiss me?"

"Yes. I want to do more than kiss you . . . but it's wrong, Mourning. Now, go to sleep."

"Clint?"

"NO!"

"Kiss me, just once more . . . please."

"No, and that's final!"

"Is it because I don't do it right?"

"No . . . no, it's not."

"Well, why . . ."

"*Hellfire!* Just once, do you hear me? Just once," he said, more softly, "and no more." His lips teased lightly across hers until she pulled his head firmly against hers. His hands were itching to go under her gown to where he knew she'd be wet and warm. He pressed against her, his tongue doing all the things his body couldn't. The kiss became long and deep and passionate. When he broke the kiss, because he would take her if he didn't, she didn't argue.

"Thank you," she said, and smiled up at him and snuggled into the crook of his arm and closed her eyes.

He felt her fingers slip between the buttons of his shirt, and when she touched his naked skin he nearly leaped out of it. How could she go to sleep at a time like this? No one would ever believe this if they heard it . . . hell, no would believe it if they saw it!

He kept rubbing her back until her breathing was regular and he knew she was asleep. Before he realized what had happened his hand suddenly rubbed bare, honest to God, naked skin and he nearly went through the top of the wagon. Her gown had crawled up and her soft skin was burning a hole in his hand. Two inches! Two measly inches and his hand could be right where it was dying to go. This must be hell, because he was in eternal torment.

He wanted to pull away. He even tried to pull away, but before he knew what had happened his hand had eased around and cupped her breast. It was the sweetest, most painful torture imaginable to keep his hand on just her breast when it wanted so badly to slip lower. She was asleep, for God's sake! What kind of lowdown character molested a sleeping woman? *His kind did.* That was a sobering thought, and he groaned with self-disgust. He had to protect her from himself. *She's family,* he reminded that part of him that wasn't bothered in the least with the prospect of molesting a sleeping woman. *She's Caroline's daughter,* he thought, and that was like a cold pan of water in the face.

He stayed there for a long time, holding her pressed against him, his hand still in the sweetest place. When the pale lavender streaks of morning colored the sky, he kissed her gently and slipped from the wagon. It was probably the most difficult thing he'd ever done, and the most honorable.

Mourning woke once when she heard the men stirring. She recognized Hank's voice sending Curly for firewood and Buck to feed the stock. Matt and Will announced they were *headin' for the river,* which Mourning knew didn't necessarily mean a bath; but not knowing the code these men used, she wouldn't dare ask where they were heading. She'd done that once, and when she inquired where Matt had rushed off to, Joe had chirped, "He's taking a piss."

"Illiterate bastard," said Buck, who was shaving by the wagon. He popped Joe with a towel that left a trail of shaving foam across his back, then gave him a shove with his foot. "Watch your talkin' 'round ladies. Holy smokes, you think any lady is used to talk like that? You don't tell a lady a man's gone to piss. You've got to use gentler words with 'em."

"Sorry, Mourning," Joe said, with an elegant bow. "Will's gone to return some of his person to Mother Nature."

Footsteps passed by the wagon and Mourning recognized Will's voice. "You think it's gonna rain today, Matt?"

"Yup. Tell by the way the frogs is croakin' . . . gonna be a real turd floater."

That, Mourning decided, was reason enough to wait a while longer before getting up. She rolled over and pulled the covers over her head.

She woke again, sometime later. Like a playful kitten, she bounced out of the wagon, greeting Joe and Hank as she approached the campfire.

"Coffee?" Hank asked, holding the pot toward her. The pups came bounding out of the brush, in hot pursuit of a cottontail.

"Fun-lovin' little beasties, ain't they," Joe said. The terrified rabbit saw them and turned sharply, scrambling back the way it came. The pups, however, couldn't quite negotiate the sharp turn with the same finesse as the rabbit and went tumbling end over end.

Mourning lowered herself on an upended crate next to Joe and curled her hands around the steaming cup, sipping slowly. "Did you hear the woman screaming last night?"

Hank lowered his coffee and looked at her curiously. "What woman?"

"The woman the Indians were torturing last night . . . I don't know how you could sleep through it. I was terrified before I found Clint. I was ashamed to ask him to stay with me instead of helping her, but . . ."

"Weren't no woman screaming last night," Joe interrupted. "What you heard . . ."

"Don't be plowin' in someone else's field, boy," Hank said, casting him a silencing look.

Mourning looked from Hank to Joe, then back to Hank. "It was a woman, Joe. Clint said she was too far gone to help. It was kind of him to say that; it made me feel a little better about wanting him to stay."

Joe jumped to his feet. "It ain't right, Hank, your not tellin' her. She don't know no better." He turned to Mourning. "It was *mighty* kind of him, considering that weren't no woman you heard last night."

Mourning felt like she'd just been jerked out of a frozen fishpond and dropped into a bucket of hot coals.

"You're wrong, Joe. It was a white woman being tortured by Indians. Clint would've told me if I was wrong."

"Maybe so, but that weren't no woman, I'm tellin' you. I heard it too." He looked at her contritely. "I'm sorry, pet, sorry as I can be." He shoved his hands in his pockets, walked a few steps, then turned. "What you heard last night was a screech owl. No woman being tortured, but a lonely ole screech owl."

Joe wouldn't lie to her, she knew that—but Clint would. He lied! It was the match that fell into the powder barrel; there was bound to be an explosion.

Clint heard the sound of something crashing through the brush like a wild boar. Before he could reach his gun Mourning came marching, hell-bent for breakfast, between two bushes, not bothering to push them out of her way. He watched openmouthed, his razor suspended in midair, soap lathered all over his face as she stomped to the rock where he'd put his pile of clothes. His mouth dropped another two inches when she swooped them up and hurled them into the river.

"Hellfire! What are you doing? Are you crazy? Those are my damn clothes!" he yelled, watching them float around the bend and out of sight.

While he was busy wiping the soap from his face she was busy stomping toward the limb his Colt and gunbelt were hanging on. With one quick movement she jerked it off and flung the whole thing into the water.

"Godamighty!" he roared, dropping his razor and holding the towel he'd wrapped around himself as he watched her march up to where he stood. "Woman . . . that is war when you mess with a man's gun," he shouted. "Just what in the hell is eating you?" Before he could get out another word she wound up her arm and came at him with everything she had, landing a bruiser on his cheekbone. The impact sent her back as if she'd fired a musket, while the vibrations rippled up her arm. While he was still reeling from that blow, she wound up and cracked him another one on the other cheek and then yanked the towel from around his hips and marched to the river. Clint watched his towel float out of sight.

Without another look at him, for which he was thankful, since he was standing there naked as a jaybird, she marched to the line of trees and disappeared from view, leaving him standing there in a dire predicament.

Clint waded into the river to retrieve his gunbelt, which thankfully was heavy enough to sink in the shallows, while he pondered just how in the hell he was going to get back to camp without being seen running around in his birthday suit. Fifteen minutes of searching along the creek bank turned up a small towel of postage stamp proportions. It wasn't much, but it was infinitely better than naked.

It was half an hour later when she heard him coming, approaching the wagon with the stride of a savage. "You are going to clean this or so help me I'll clean it myself and then shoot you with it."

"Go to Halifax!"

"I'm warning you. Clean my pistol!"

"When shrimps learn to whistle!" Brazenly, she added, "I have no intention of touching you or anything that belongs to you." She retreated a step.

"Lady, you spit those words out again and you'll be eating them. Now, clean my damn pistol!"

"Perhaps you didn't hear me."

"CLEAN IT NOW!" he bellowed. And she questioned the wisdom of carrying this any further. They shot daggers at each other, sparks flying, his jaw set in an angry clench, her eyes huge, her lip trembling.

His breath coming quick and angry, he spoke in short, rapid spurts punctuated with painfully long pauses. "Pick . . . up . . . the . . . gun . . . *and clean it now!*"

She picked it up and held it between her thumb and index finger as if it would bite. Clint ran his hands through his hair and walked to the back of the wagon, and placing his hands on each side of the opening, he spoke to thin air. "What in the hell possessed you to do a stupid thing like that? That's my pistol, and in this part of the country a man can get killed for even touching another man's pistol, let alone flinging it into the goddamn creek!"

"Shut your foul mouth and get out of here."

"When hell freezes over!"

"Just because you felt at liberty to paw me last night gives you no free rein to use your filthy language."

"And I told you before, I'll talk any damn way I please, and if you don't like it, put your damn fingers in your ears!" he roared. "And another thing, that's a *piss-poor* excuse to ruin my gun, because *we* both know the real reason you are sore at me."

"You are talking in riddles," she shouted, standing on her toes. "Last night you took advantage of my fear, *knowing all the while,* that it was a *screech owl*! I bet you got a good laugh out of that! Was it hard to shave while you were laughing so hard? Well, I'm sorry you didn't slip and cut that *lying* throat of yours."

"I never lied to you!"

"Ha! You didn't tell me the truth . . . that's the same as lying, in my book. You let me go on thinking there were Indians out there so you could paw me like some . . . some . . ."

"I did not paw you!" He laughed wickedly. "I may have kissed you a few times, but if you'll remember, you're the one that pressed the issue. I broke it off two or three times and you just wouldn't give up." He stopped pacing and stopped in front of her, his hands on his hips.

"You want me to tell you what really peppered your prissy little tail? It wasn't my *taking advantage* of you . . . or my kissing you . . . or anything else that happened. What has really chapped that tarnished little mind of yours is that you melted like butter when I touched you, and in your book that is sinful and wrong . . . but not if you can lay the blame on me. Well, you'd be lying through your teeth if you did, because we both know you wanted it as much as I did. You were all hot for it last night, lady, and don't you try to deny it."

"I did not want it, I'm not even sure what *it* is. You are forgetting that you're the one with all the experience around here, not me."

"Well, if it was experience you were after, you sure as hell were on the right track, 'cause you came mighty damn close to finding out, firsthand. You're just damn lucky I stopped when I did or you would've had enough experience last night to write a book on it!"

"Stop it! Stop it! Stop it!" she cried, putting her hands over her ears and turning her face into the canvas. "Don't you think I know why you stopped yourself last night?" she said softly. "Do you think I'm that stupid? I know you stopped yourself because I'm unattractive to you." She wanted to cut out the tongue that had uttered those words as soon as they'd left her lips.

His eyes bored into her back and for a moment he was speechless. He studied the narrow shoulders sagging in rejection, the golden head bent with humiliation, and the tiny fists clenched with self-anger. "You are wrong," he said finally. "You have no idea how wrong you are." He stopped himself from touching her golden head. "Mourning."

"Leave me alone." She flinched when his hands closed around her upper arms. "Get out . . . and leave me alone."

"I can't do that," he said gently. "I can't leave you thinking what you're thinking."

"Why all the concern for me all of a sudden?" What was motivating him now? she wondered. Pity? Because she'd made a fool of herself by allowing him to make one of her? "Oh, never mind. Just get out. I don't want to argue anymore." With a sigh she added, "It doesn't matter anyway."

"Yes it does, dammit! Now, look at me." He turned her in his arms to face him.

It was best to convince him, if possible, that his rejection meant nothing to her. Mourning stiffened her spine and lifted her chin, forcing herself to look at him steadily. It wasn't easy. Their eyes made contact. The anger and blinding rage was gone from his eyes.

His hands rested on her shoulders, then shifted to her neck. She did her best to remain unmoved, but his hands were doing all manner of things that made her want to lay her head against his chest. She was acutely conscious of the touch of his fingers, the soothing warmth of his voice—in spite of her concentrated effort to ignore them.

Arms, warm and strong, enveloped her, and his head lowered to kiss her hair. "Don't do this," she said, looking at him, unable to move when his head bent and his mouth stopped the words she should have said. He kissed her with a gentle tenderness that she would have thought impossible for him to feel. When his tongue, lazy and stroking, invaded her mouth she pulled away. "Please stop. You don't have to do this."

"I know." His hands moved to cup her face when she tried to look down. Tilting her head back, he kissed her again, his hands slipping around her, pulling her tightly against him. His breath was soft and warm as it brushed across her face, and he spoke soothing words that were like a balm into her mouth. "Don't fight me," he groaned. "You were wrong, you know." His hips ground against her, and she could feel that he was hard against the muscles of her stomach. "I care . . . I care too damn much."

"No, don't," she whispered, pushing against him weakly.

Once again he silenced her protests with his mouth, knowing all the while he had to stop this. *If I let her go, she'll hate me for rejecting her again,* he reasoned. *She'll be ashamed of what's happened, because she can't understand that there can never be anything between us. I don't want to hurt you, buttercup.*

But hurt her he must, so he had made up his mind to stop. Before he could act on his decision, he felt something warm pour over his bare feet and he broke away.

"Damnation! What the hell's going on now?"

At his exclamation she jumped back, shame gripping her.

"Dammit!" he shouted. "I warned you. This time it's gone too far!"

"What are you talking about?"

"Your stupid dogs, that's what I'm talking about," he roared, jerking Romeo off the floor by the ruff of his neck and angrily thrusting him in her face. "This little son of a bitch just wet on me!"

With a small cry of anger she snatched the pup from him and dumped him into the basket. Her eyes shooting sparks of green fury, she said hotly, "What's the matter? Can't you find something to be angry about that *I've* done? Am I to be blamed for acts of nature as well?"

Her sudden fierceness, and her slender loveliness, sent a shot of desire through his body, inciting deep primitive passions. He had neither the inclination nor the willpower to be gentle or tender. "They're *your* dogs, and I *warned* you about keeping them out of my way . . . before we left Memphis."

"They *are* out of your way, you bastard. This happens to be *my* wagon that you're standing in." That profanity was a shocking word for her to utter, but she was so hurt and confused that words came to her lips without prompting. His presence here in her wagon was a flaming reminder of everything that had happened between them. Guilt for her shameless behavior that had lain dormant suddenly sprang to life. "Just get out of here and leave me alone." She shoved him with an unbelievable strength that surprised them both, delivering a few angry blows to his chest before he could control her.

With both of them panting and breathing heavily, he pinned her with her back against him, both of her wrists trapped in one hand. "We are less than two weeks away from San Antonio. There are times when we will be together and must, at least, act civil toward one another. See that it is in the presence of others. Stay away from me, Mourning. I am warning you. If you are foolish enough to get in my way again, you may regret it. You have a remarkable talent for staying out of my bed, *querida*. Use it to stay out of my life."

PART THREE

Time, in the turning-over of days,
works change for better or worse.
Pindar, *Odes* (5th c. B.C.)

With wonderfully steady hands, Mrs. Harper poured the last kettle of steaming water into the tub and Mourning let out a loud *ya-ow!*

"What's the matter, child?" Mrs. Harper asked gently. "Did I get the water too hot?"

The beet-red face in the tub replied weakly, "No . . . well . . . I mean . . . it's just that it's already so hot in here, I'm beginning to think a cool bath would've been better." Her strength was fast dissolving away into the water's heat, leaving her limp as a dish mop and brightly flushed.

"Oh, no, that it wouldn't," Mrs. Harper answered good-naturedly as she slipped the dented copper kettle on the blackened hook by the fireplace and returned to dealing deathblows to a head of cabbage she was chopping for dinner.

Mourning guessed Mrs. Harper would have to be what one would call pleasingly plump. She almost laughed out loud when she remembered Clint had said Mrs. Harper had more rolls than a bakery shop and arms as big as a chimney flue.

Mrs. Harper disappeared behind the table, and Mourning guessed she was looking for a cooking pot, judging from the rattle and clatter of pans and the comments she made to herself. "All right, I know you're in here somewhere. Don't think you can hide from me. Humph! I knew it, it's not here." She stood up, moved to the end of the table, and disappeared again. From somewhere near the cupboard, her voice drifted back to Mourning. "Ah-ha! Here it is." Mrs. Harper's head popped back up. "As I was saying, it's always better to have hot things in the summer and cold things in the winter . . . not so much of a shock to the system that way. I remember my mother always told me: *Hot when it's hot, and cold when it's cold.*"

The covered pot on the stove boiled and rattled and then bubbled over with a steaming hiss, and that put the lid on Mrs. Harper's proverbs for the time being. While Mrs. Harper was busy scolding the inconsiderate pot, Mourning jabbed a few brass pins into her heavy hair to hold it up out of the water. Then she sank back into the tub, sighing luxuriously and closing her eyes.

It was a day for discoveries, Mourning discovered, as she inhaled deeply. Her nose could tell her about the warm kitchen full of smells—smells rich and varied that twined and twisted and wound themselves into one whole and pleasantly satisfying smell that spoke of home and belonging. She opened her eyes.

It was a happy room, full of gleaming, polished plates that winked from the shelves, and old copper pots, rich with the deep patina of use and age, that hung from the exposed beams overhead. Nets of onions and garlands of leathery red peppers hung on the walls, and bundles of dried herbs poked over the tops of woven baskets. The merry whistle of air from a teakettle on the stove was as comforting a sound as the purr of contented cats. She was nestled safely here in this long, rambling house that surrounded her warmly, like the deep softness of a pair of old fleecy slippers on a snowy morning. It was an unexpected feeling, one that she was surprised to feel in this hostile land.

Savory smells, a steaming bath, and a hot summer afternoon were overpowering foes, and while Mourning tried to discipline her thoughts, the sleep-inducing forces that worked against her eventually won out. She sank back in the tub, allowing her mind to drift.

The past two weeks had passed like a trip to the dentist: painfully and slowly. It was only at times like this that Mourning allowed the bitter joy of treasured moments of passion to creep forward from her memory. Often it was difficult to sort fact from fiction, reality from fantasy, as she asked herself if it had all been real—the time spent with Clint, the remembered intensity of desire, and the secret feelings he had put her in touch with.

It was still an unsolvable mystery to her, the reason Clint had left so abruptly, without saying good-bye. One moment her senses were reeling from the feel of sun-scented skin and glossy raven hair; the next thing she knew, she was shoved into her mother's embrace like a basket of dirty laundry. No matter how she tried, Mourning could not gloss over the expression on his face the last time she saw him.

After embracing her mother, she had turned, smiling and light-headed with exuberance, to look up into Clint's bridled expression and indifferent gaze. He didn't bother to look at her, but spoke to Caroline. "I believe safe delivery fulfills my obligations in this undertaking," he said in a voice as arid as the Sahara. "Tell John, if he needs me, I'll be at Tierra." That was the last time she had seen him.

Clint had taught her desire, then left her with repressed feelings and almost-impossible-to-suppress longing. At first she refused to believe he had left as he had, then she began to wonder if he had ever looked upon her with anything but indifference. Finally came the naked truth: He hadn't closed his heart to her, he had never opened it in the first place. If she had one wish in life, it was to be able to look at him with the same cool detachment and closed expression that he had turned upon her.

The whole experience had left her feeling like a hen that could only lay hard-boiled eggs. Nothing she did seemed to come out right. Pulling her tiny nose out of the bubbles, she inquired heavenward if things were always going to be this way for her. There was no immediate answer. God, it seemed to her, had the most vexing habit of looking the other way when he heard she was coming. With fortitude that surprised even her, Mourning closed her mind to what was negative in her new life and concentrated on the positive.

She sat in the huge copper tub, in a hospitable kitchen, and listened to a mockingbird twittering his jubilant little song. On the braided rug beside her tub lay her two wrinkled pups with tails no longer than a corncob madly thumping the floor. The lid on the iron pot clattered and the teakettle whistled. Outside the window the roses tangled round the trellis, and a paisley-winged moth was fluttering in and out of the dark, glossy leaves. She was here, with her mother, where she had waited so long to be. Caroline looked younger and seemed happier than Mourning could ever remember, and filled with the joy she felt at having Mourning with her again —well, there just wasn't any way Mourning could help not feeling that way too. They were together again, doing chores together,

playing piano duets, and talking until the wee hours of the morning. It was so good to be with her again, and now cousin Anna was
coming for a visit—these were the things she had to be happy
about. With the exuberance of girlhood, Mourning was suddenly
filled with the joy of living and the delight of summertime. Before
long the old sweet feeling of belonging and familiarity began to
creep back into her heart. Texas, it seems, wasn't really such a bad
place after all.

With the friendly feeling that comes with a sense of belonging,
she once again broke into conversation with the jovial housekeeper.
"Mrs. Harper, are you sure no one will come in here?" Mourning
draped her arm over the tub to scratch Romeo and Juliet, who
promptly shoved two damp muzzles against her hand.

Mrs. Harper did not look up. "Of course not. I've locked all
the doors, and none of the men come in the house except John, and
he's not here, or Cad, and he's not due back from Houston until
tomorrow . . . or Clint, and the good Lord alone knows where he
is." Mrs. Harper wiped her hands on her apron and checked the
bread dough rising in the kitchen window.

Mourning continued. "What's Cad like?"

Mrs. Harper fished inside a crockery pot, pulled out a handful
of raisins, offered some to Mourning, and when she declined,
popped the handful into her mouth. Mourning waited patiently for
her to finish. The last raisin put away, Mrs. Harper said, "Two
years younger than Clint, that makes him . . . let me see . . .
twenty-six. They favor some, same gray eyes—well, Cad's may be
lighter . . . and Cad's hair . . . it's definitely lighter, might call
it a sandy color. Takes that from John, I guess, since Isabel's hair
was black as pitch . . . like Clint's. Cad's tall, but lanky, not as
muscular as Clint. Cad's the mischief maker, always teasing, flirt-
ing, happy. You'll like Cad." She smiled wryly. "One thing though
. . . don't ever call him Cadwallader. The boy hates that name
like poison. I've seen him mop the floor with many a face that said
his full name . . . 'course I can't recollect none of them was a
girl, now that I think on it."

Inquiry, Mourning had learned, was decidedly easier with
Mrs. Harper than with Caroline. Not wanting her mother to know
of her feelings for Clint, Mourning had been delicate with any
questions directed toward Caroline. With Caroline and John in San

Antonio for the week, Mourning was relaxed and loose with her quizzing.

"How long have you worked here?"

"Lands, child, I've been here since Clint and Cad weren't much bigger than those pups of yours. I took care of them too, after their poor mama died. My dearly departed husband worked for John before we married. When my Max was killed, Mr. John put me to work right here in the house, and it was a good thing he did too, because Isabel went on to her reward soon after Cad was born, leaving those two little boys with no mama."

"Was she pretty?"

"Lord, yes, she was a beautiful little thing. Like a Dresden-china doll and not much bigger. That's what killed her, if you ask me, being so small, and all. Those were mighty sad days." She stopped butchering the cabbage and reflected a moment, shook her head, and started up again. "Caused a pack o' trouble between Mr. John and Don Orlando too."

"Who is Don Orlando?"

"That's Cad and Clint's grandfather. Gruff and stern as they come. Throws fits if he doesn't get his way. If that doesn't work, he starts throwing other things. Comes from one of those famous families that has tree families of kings, or maybe it's families of tree kings . . . no . . ."

"Family trees with kings?" Mourning offered.

"Yes, that's it. When you go in his house there are hundreds of pictures of people who've been dead hundreds of years. Doesn't make much sense to me . . . keeping pictures on the wall of people you don't even know."

"Where does he live?"

"He owns Tierra, a big place just south of here. It's what you used to call a hacienda, but nowadays folks just say ranch. But it's a big sucker. Back in the old days it was called *Tierra del Oro,* which means Land of Gold. It will all belong to Clint and Cad when the old Don dies."

"I didn't realize Clint was half Spanish."

"I guess he is . . . never thought of it that way, since the family's been over here for years . . . well, I think it was Don Orlando's grandfather that had some kind of land grant from the King of Spain, that's how they have so much land."

"What was the problem between Don Orlando and John?"

"He blamed Mr. John for Isabel's death . . . 'course it weren't Mr. John's fault. He loved her something fierce. Nearly killed him when she died. That's why it took him so long to remarry. Surprised the socks off me when he came back from Tennessee toting Caroline. He was a mighty good father to them boys too. But I sure wish he'd met your mama sooner so they could've had a woman's hand in rearing them. Mr. John allowed them to do pretty much as they pleased, and I mean that included plenty of mischief." Mrs. Harper smiled slyly at Mourning. That brought Mourning's chin up out of the water.

"For instance?" Mourning inquired with an innocent air as she folded her fingers over and examined her nails. There was nothing a mischievous young woman like herself enjoyed hearing more than the pranks of a fellow partner in crime.

In case Mourning might come up with the wrong idea, Mrs. Harper declared promptly that her boys were full of life but were never, by any stretch of the imagination, mean. "No, they were never mean," she assured, "they just did lots of little ornery things like riding their horses up on the porch and roping the laundry off the clothesline." Mourning lay back in the water, giggling.

"Laugh if you want to, Miss Priss, but what I'm telling you is the truth. The good Lord never created two wilder young ruffians than Clint and Cad. It was a mighty big relief to see those two reach manhood. . . . I was certain if they didn't kill themselves, they'd kill each other."

Mourning felt a tiny prick of discomfort; those words were getting painfully close to sounding like her own childhood, and she wasn't about to pooh-pooh someone else's behavior when she, herself, was guilty of the same miscreant doings. With all the grace of a master yachtsman she carefully steered the conversation to calmer waters. "Did Mama tell you my cousin Anna is coming to visit?" She lifted her feet to rest on the rim of the tub.

"And I've got her room all ready too, the one right next to yours," Mrs. Harper answered proudly, while unsuspectingly following Mourning's flawless lead to another topic of discussion. "I believe your mama said she would be here next month."

"Three and a half weeks to be exact."

"Oh, fuddle! Will you look at that!" Mrs. Harper exclaimed with disgust.

"What's the matter?" Mourning inquired, sitting up in the tub.

"Why, I spent all morning gathering what I needed from the garden and root cellar, and here I didn't even hoe any potatoes." She picked up her bent-willow basket. "Well, I'll just have to go back. It's my own dumb fault. You just keep soaking, child. I'll be back in three shakes of a lamb's tail."

The bath was progressing nicely, the water having cooled to an endurable temperature, when it suddenly occurred to Mourning: Mrs. Harper did not lock the kitchen door when she left. She leaped from the tub like a spawning salmon and slopped a wave of water across the floor, which sent Romeo and Juliet scampering out of the room. She had time to wrap the fluffy section of flannel toweling around her and lift one slim leg over the tub when the back door flew open.

"Ho-ly shit! It's a naked woman!" a voice exclaimed.

That remark spun her around. "Oh, no!" Mourning groaned. "Not another one."

"Not another what?" the face that belonged to the voice asked, with a smile of Texas-sized proportions.

"Not another foulmouth," Mourning answered, looking critically at the youthful male who stood heartlessly cheerful just inside the back door. As she looked up at him he let out a long *woman-admiring* whistle and used his index finger to slide his hat back on his head.

"Hon-neeee-y!" he said with a wide grin. "Are you the new kitchen help? 'Cause if you are, I can tell right now I'm asking for a transfer out of the pasture."

The loudmouth looked to be about twenty-five, dressed in typical cow-tending fashion. A blue shirt, wrinkled. A pair of dusty pants, tight. A red bandana, and a well-worn hat. His hair was sandy brown and his eyes were a soft gray, sparkling from the same exercise that put the color into his cheeks. His mouth was well formed, twinged with humor—tiny creases to each side indicating it was a mouth that smiled often. Intruder or no, she liked him right off.

When she didn't answer right away it didn't seem to bother him in the least. "What *are* you doing in here?"

"I was *trying* to take a bath," she said, irritably.

"I can see that," he drawled. "I'm just sorry as hell I didn't get here a minute sooner, before you reached that towel. Boy, that would've been some sight too, I'm guessing, from what I can see." He took a step in her direction, his long, well-formed body moving fluently.

She narrowed her eyes at him suspiciously. "What do you think you're doing?"

"Coming closer, so we can get better acquainted."

"You're close enough," she warned, when he stopped in front of her.

"Not for what I have in mind," he said, grinning, as he lifted his hand and captured one of her fallen curls in his hand. "A woman like you that's this soft on the eyes has got to be soft on the—"

"My Lord," she interrupted, wailing at the ceiling, "is this entire godforsaken country full of amorous loudmouths?" She jerked her head, reclaiming her curl, and stepped back. "I am getting rather tired of being manhandled and leered at by—"

"Listen, firebrat, no need to get so feisty." He took another step toward her and then stopped dead in his tracks, folded his arms across his chest, and studied her for a moment. "You're not from around here . . . are you?" There seemed to be a new light in his eyes as if he'd suddenly hit upon something and was dying to share it with her.

"No," she stammered, "I'm not."

"The accent," he said slowly, "it's southern . . . Memphis?"

"Yes, how'd you—"

"Well, I'll be damned," he said, and then threw back his head with a loud hoot.

"That," she said in dry tones, "is a much overused phrase around here."

"Is it, now?" he said, with grand admiration. "You must be referring to my articulate brother." One of those eyes as gray as cat's fur closed, giving her a flirtatious wink. "Am I right?"

"If you're referring to that filthy-mouthed firstborn of John Kincaid, then you are correct."

When his laughter subsided he shook his head in wonder. "It *would* be my luck," he said suspiciously. "You aren't Caroline's daughter by any chance, are you?"

"Yes. Are you . . ."

"Cad Kincaid, at your service, ma'am." He bowed most polite like and picked a peach out of the fruit bowl, offering it to her first.

"No thank you," she said, wishing he would leave so she could get out of the kitchen.

"What's the matter," he said, teasingly, "afraid you'll drop your cover if I toss this to you?" He made a mocking move to toss the peach and then laughed.

"If you don't mind," she said with irritable preciseness, "I'm not exactly dressed to receive visitors." Growing nervous under his careful scrutiny, she hastily looked down at the tips of her toes.

"Nope," he said, shutting one eye and examining her with calculated ease, "I guess you're not, but then I think women cover themselves way too much anyway."

"Will you please leave."

"Okay, firebrat, but tell me one thing first. How'd you and Clint make out on the trip . . . judging from the way you're talking, I gather you two aren't on the best of terms."

"Does a dog like fleas?" she replied with wholehearted conviction.

"Don't you know, little firebrat, that opposites attract?" He stroked the back of his hand lightly across her pale cheek. "You aren't in love with my brother by any chance, are you?" he asked, his voice softer, his manner much changed.

This question was not only highly infuriating, but unflatteringly close to the unhappy truth, so Mourning pulled the plug on the final restraints of her temper. "You are the rudest person I've ever met, with perhaps the exception of that loggerhead brother of yours. Why, I'd sooner fall in love with a flying hatchetfish than that ape!"

"Listen, firebrat, you sure overreacted to that question, so there must be some merit to the thought. Being an honorable man, I'll take my foraging elsewhere and leave the grazing of your fair pastures to my brother."

Before she had time to organize a clever reply, the soft thump and scratch of padded feet rounded the kitchen door and slid across the polished floor, landing with a thud against the toes of Cad Kincaid's dusty boots. Romeo and Juliet sank razor-sharp puppy teeth into his pant legs and sat back on their haunches, ferociously shaking their wrinkled heads and growling for all they were worth.

Of course, she should have used that opportunity to faint or remove herself discreetly from the kitchen, but the hilarity of the tiny pups tearing into Cad like a treed coon freed her spontaneous laughter, which seemed to override any thoughts of escape. And so, instead of a ladylike departure, she leaned against the table laughing as Cad unsuccessfully tried to free his well-punctured pants from the duo's snarling grip. As she stood there laughing mirthfully and shouting her encouragement to Cad, Mrs. Harper came bounding into the kitchen like a one-legged kangaroo and was greeted, not by the swooning of gentle southern charm, but by a wildly laughing half-draped form that looked as if she'd just stepped out of a Tintoretto nude.

Mrs. Harper took one scowling look and jumped on Cad like a chicken on a june bug. Cad already had his hands full with the pups and seemed to be having a devil of a time warding off Mrs. Harper's blows and keeping in an upright position. She boxed his ears and dusted his behind. "What do you think you're doing in here?" she said, dragging the pups away. "Don't you have any manners at all, you overgrown ruffian? You better thank your lucky stars that all you're getting out of this is a good cuff on the head. This is Caroline's daughter, and if you don't think I will give a full report to Mr. John when he returns, you better guess again." Mourning folded over in another fit of giggles as she pondered that statement, wondering just how long it had been since anyone threatened to tell his father on him.

Mrs. Harper yanked the hat off Cad's head and began liberally swatting his head and shoulders with it, beating him as he backed toward the door, too weak from laughter to move fast enough to avoid her wide sweeps. Yanking the door open, he paused just long enough to give Mrs. Harper a resounding smack on the bottom. "You're just mad," he said, giving her a quick peck on the cheek, "because I didn't catch *you* that way." He snatched his hat from her hand before she could whack him again and was down the steps when the door slammed.

Mourning dashed to the window and pulled back the gingham curtains just in time to see Cad mount his horse from the rear and fan her hip with his hat, causing the animal to dig in and leap forward at a run.

* * *

On a bluff two miles from the house Cad reined in and watched the meandering movement of an approaching horseman. With a war-whoop of recognition he dug his spurs into Jezebel's sides and rode like the devil to meet his brother whom he hadn't seen in seven months.

With a stop that threw a cloud of dust on their reunion, Cad dove at his brother, knocking him off his horse and sending them both crashing to the ground. To the unknowing eye, an all-out free-for-all was taking place, but to anyone who knew Cad and Clint it was simply a greeting between two brothers who were very, very close and hadn't seen each other in a long time.

"Well, you good-for-nothing son of a bitch! It's good to see you," Cad said with loving contempt while circling his brother like a stalking cougar. "I sure hate to admit it, but I've missed your ugly hide around here."

They continued to circle each other warily while they talked, each one ready to spring the moment an opening appeared. Behind Cad's back, Clint could see Conquistador chewing on the lariat tied to Cad's saddle. Tired of that, the stallion nipped Cad's mare, Jezebel, who responded by squealing and going into a bucking frenzy. Cad's eyes flicked in that direction briefly and that was all the opening Clint needed.

After the tackle, they rolled to the bottom of the ravine, Clint winding up on top and pinning his lanky brother to the ground. "Tell me again," he touted playfully, "just how much you missed my handsome face."

Cad hooted with laughter. *"Handsome?* You're about as handsome as the backside of old Juan's mule."

Clint grinned broadly. "I believe handsome wasn't all you said . . . wasn't there something about being what every woman dreams of?"

"Yeah, just like she dreams about a good case of cholera."

With a laugh, Clint released Cad and stood, extending his hand and pulling him up. After locating their mounts they rode toward Citadel at a slow clip.

"How was your trip to St. Louis?" Cad asked. "Do you think it'll be profitable to drive cattle that far north?"

"There's a definite market and the profit would be large if the cattle were still in good shape, but the biggest problem I can see right now is the threat of war. The situation is much worse than we thought."

"Would you fight," Cad asked his brother, "if it came to war?"

Clint narrowed his eyes. "I suppose if Texas joined in I would. What about you?"

"Same here. Probably won't consider it my business unless Texas joins. . . . If she does . . . well, I'd go."

They rode for a while in silence, and then Cad, always the more verbal of the two, started the conversation up again. "Where have you been?"

"Don Orlando's," Clint replied, looking at Cad before he added, "Have you met Caroline's daughter?"

"The hot-blooded firebrat with green eyes?"

"You've met," he said dryly.

"Since you're the lucky one who brought her to Texas, why don't you tell me what you think of her?"

"She is, without a doubt," Clint said, not at all admiringly, "full of more harebrained escapades than a barrel of monkeys, and not, by any stretch of the imagination, as easy to keep up with." His deprecations and caustic remarks continued until they reached Citadel, and those remarks were extensive, verbose comments that no lady would ever want repeated about herself—even if they were true.

When Clint finished, Cad let out a long whistle. "That bad, huh?"

His brother looked him squarely in the eye. "Any man who tangles with that wildcat doesn't have a snowball's chance in hell of coming out unscathed."

≈ 15

Cad and Clint were leaning against the fence, talking with a short, squat man when Mourning rounded the corner of the stables. Romeo and Juliet were loping along beside her, their long tongues dangling while their oversized paws slapped the pathway with a muffled thump. Mourning was running to stay ahead of them, her white petticoats fluttering around her knees, her laughter announcing her arrival. Seeing the three men standing by the fence, watching her, she immediately stopped, sending the pups tumbling end over end.

There was Clint Kincaid, in the flesh, looking better than any demented devil had a right to. Leaning with catlike grace, he had one perfectly muscled arm braced against the fence rail, and the heel of his boot hooked over the lower slat. The incredible impact of him standing there whole and hearty, more attractive than ever, caused a streak of sour rebellion to run down her back like the stripe on a skunk. She toyed with the idea of whirling around and beating a hasty retreat, but common sense got the better of her and she stood there, eyeing Clint as seriously as he was eyeing her. They stood there like two opposing warlords trying to decide whether to attack or retreat.

The visitor glanced at Mourning and down at the pups, who tilted their heads to one side and then growled at him ferociously. "What the hell is that?" he said, taking a step backward.

Mourning frowned, a look that was mimicked by her pups.

"Oh, sorry, little lady, I wasn't referring to you but to those two beasties beside you. They look like a mixed-up cross between a brown bear and a prune," he said, throwing his head back with a loud guffaw.

While the men were laughing, Mourning was, by this point, getting awfully tired of hearing comments about her pups. She frowned with disfavor at the dumpling of a man who was bent in such a way that he looked as if he couldn't decide whether to stand up or sit down. She wished the pups were big enough to give him a good scare.

Clint made a hasty introduction and Cad added that she hadn't met Ben before because he had just returned from his brother's funeral and that she would be seeing a lot of him because he was Citadel's right-hand man.

The pups soon grew tired of looking ferocious and Romeo began to chase his tail. Dogs, it seemed to her, always had the most delightful diversions, while all she could do was stand here trembling as if she'd eaten goose tansy weed. Unable to stay out of their game, Ben hunkered down and the traitorous pups bounded toward him with canine enthusiasm, jumping and pawing his arms and leaving gritty paw prints on his sleeve.

"I've never seen any critters that look quite like this . . . do they ever grow into all this skin?" he inquired, while his gnarled and twisted fingers scratched and patted the thick folds of skin on the squirming pups.

Clint's penetrating gaze swung quickly to Mourning and his eyes studied her face. All the things she'd been doing over the past weeks to forget him were, she learned, about as effective as a leaky umbrella in a rainstorm. She lost her train of thought for a moment, but recovered. She looked away. "They're bloodhounds and they're supposed to be wrinkled."

Ben grinned up at her. "Both males?"

"This one is, he's called Romeo; the other one is Juliet." She smiled at him.

"Brother and sister?"

"Yes, they're from the same litter—they're related, so I can't breed them." *Stupid, stupid, me! Why did I say that?* Color, hot and intense, flooded her face. She knew better than to look up, but she did anyway, and was greeted by the brothers grim, who grinned as if they knew something she didn't. Ben rescued her from the throes of scarlet embarrassment when he started up the conversation again. It was a move that endeared him to her forever.

"What do they do . . . besides eat?"

"They're hunting dogs."

Ben scratched his head with a puzzled look on his face. "Why, I'd think a big ole cat would tear these dogs to pieces."

"Probably so, bloodhounds are used primarily for tracking game, or . . . sometimes humans. They're unsurpassed by any other breed of dog in scenting ability. Besides"—she bent down and ruffled their heads— "they are so affectionate, they make wonderful pets." Romeo gave her a lick that would have washed the faces of ten dirty children and she laughed delightfully.

It was obvious that Ben was as fascinated with the pups as they were with him. "Don't suppose you'd let me take the little fellers with me for a while . . . would you?"

Any friend of the pups was a friend of hers, and Mourning gave Ben a smile that would have melted snow at twenty thousand feet. "Of course I would, but," she added cautiously, "if they get you into trouble, don't say I didn't warn you."

Ben grunted his thanks and called the pups after him. Mourning watched until the last wagging tail disappeared inside the barn.

"Hello, Cad," she said with a smile. "We missed you at dinner last night."

"Good morning, firebrat," he said with good-humored charm. "Clint and I had some . . . er . . . work to do and we didn't come in till late."

Mourning could well imagine what kind of work Cad was referring to. She glanced at Clint, he met her stare with his beautifully shaped eyes, and she looked away. She wondered how she must have appeared to him, running up the path, skirts flying, acting like a silly child. Just seeing him had sent all manner of trilling little melodies humming along her nerves and set her heart to pounding.

When she didn't give Clint a hello, he sighed resignedly and straightened. "Don't I get a greeting, buttercup?"

Tall and perfectly formed, he stood before her, his back to the east, the sun spreading around his squared shoulders and shooting his hair with silver. Slate-gray and smoky, his eyes were subtly stirring her to remember things that were best left forgotten. He was studying her as Mrs. Harper would study yesterday's pot roast, trying to decide whether she wanted to dice it into hash or throw it away. *Mourning Kathleen, why can't you look at him with the same sealed expression he turns on you? Must you wear your heart on your sleeve?* She felt suffused with warmth, and a slight queasiness lodged in the bottom of her stomach. With more courage than she felt, she said, "I wasn't aware that you were a person who placed any grave importance on greetings or *farewells,* especially when . . ." She clamped her hands over her mouth and giggled when she saw Ben come out of the barn stumbling and tripping over Juliet, who was running under his feet, and with Romeo pulling on his pant leg. It was quite a while before he made it to the toolshed.

"Well," Cad said, giving her a broad wink and turning to follow Ben, "I think I'll mosey on with Ben. I'll be ready to check the water in the south pasture whenever you are, Clint. See you two later."

Mourning turned to walk in the opposite direction when she felt the warmth of Clint's hand on her arm. She pulled away and continued down the path. "Don't leave yet . . . I want to talk to you," he said, but she was already stepping over the tongue of a nearby wagon. He hurried toward her, just a little chafed because he was glad to see her and she didn't seem to give a damn one way or the other. Why the hell wasn't she glad to see him? He'd been gone for weeks. Hadn't she given him a second thought while he was away? Clint found that just a little irritating, because he'd sure as hell given her some thought . . . plenty of it.

"Just wait a damn minute, will you," he demanded, catching up to her.

"I wondered how long it would be before you had to resort to vituperative language . . . you seem quite incapable of speaking without it." She was slamming those tiny feet of hers down so hard, he was sure the heels of her shoes were going to snap off.

"Look, all I wanted to do was talk to you for a minute . . . okay?" He gave her that infuriatingly attractive smile, and she wanted to throw her arms around his neck and kiss him into the middle of next week, but instead she gave him a sour, mocking smile.

"Okay, so talk." She rammed her hip out of joint just so she could put her hand on it in a most impatient manner, and all he could think about was shoving her backward into that wagon bed and spending the afternoon there making love to her.

"Well, I . . . I thought . . . dammit! you've got me stuttering worse than a tongue-tied fool."

She arched a brow at him and her muteness spoke for her. He paused, pondering over whether he should grab her and show her just what he was feeling or continue to stand here floundering way off course and expressing himself with ineffectual speech. Thinking she'd be more receptive to the latter, he said, "I'm glad to see you, dammit, but you act like you couldn't care less."

"Kincaid," she said slowly, "from what I have gathered it is quite common for you to disappear without a word to anyone, and then suddenly reappear without notice like someone sprinkled your backside with fairy dust. Are you saying you expect me to throw myself at you each time you return from one of your disappearing acts? Well, I won't. In other words," she articulated carefully, "my reception is no worse than your departure." Her words had miserably failed to carry the exact degree of hateful censure she had desired, hateful censure not exactly being her forte. To her eternal chagrin, her cheeks pinked and she vowed never to wear another bonnet so her skin would tan unblushingly dark.

He grinned with newly acquired insight. He knew now what had gotten her tail over her back; she was hot because he'd left without giving her a proper good-bye. Hell, he wanted to give her a damn proper hello. Wasn't that just as good? His chest expanded mightily with this newfound knowledge and he cocked his head toward her in a most compellingly attractive manner.

She almost smiled, but steeled herself against his entrancing charm. She wasn't about to fall into the carefully laid snare of this overzealous Don Juan.

"Look," he said beguilingly, "I didn't mean to leave without a word, it just worked out that way. I just thought we needed some time and distance between us, that's all."

"So, what's all the clamor about, then? You saw fit to leave and now you're back . . . it's as simple as that." She turned to go, but once again his callused hand came out to stay her in a firm clasp over her upper arm, and she paused, reluctantly, and gave him a begrudging look of disapproval.

"I think it's important," he said with an uncomfortable and uncertain note, "that we put forth our best effort to be amicable.

There's no point in making the entire family scene unpleasant because we are constantly at each other's throat."

"Oh," she said, gaining insight, "I can be *amicable* all right, you just make sure you keep your behavior on a brotherly note."

Damn! That wasn't what he had in mind either. How come she always twisted every little thing he said around to where he couldn't even recognize his own stupid words? He ran his fingers through his hair. "I just want us to make an effort to be friends, okay?"

He looked childishly sincere and she eyed him speculatively. She felt a lump rising in her throat when she looked into eyes as gray as rain sliding off a tin roof. She didn't know if she could be his friend, at times she felt as if she wanted more than that, but all *more* ever turned out to be was this constant fighting between them. "Okay," she said, turning away from him, "so now we're friends."

When she reached the gate and stretched out her hand to unlatch it, she felt the scalding heat of his hand on her arm once more. *If that clodhopper asks me where I am going,* she thought, *I'll scream.*

"Where are you going?"

"Ohhhhh!" she huffed, and stamped her foot. "I knew it!" she shrieked, "I just knew it!"

"Now what the hell did I do?" he said, really dumbfounded.

Being a female, she had a mind that worked like one, so she ignored his last question and answered the one before it. "I'm going to the dairy barn to see the twin calves that were born yesterday."

He watched her sashay into the barn, his eyes moving like the pendulum on a clock, watching the sway of her hips until she disappeared around the door. He made a move to turn around, then he paused, shrugged his shoulders, and said, "Oh, what the hell," and followed her.

She was greeted by a broad, glistening nose and a sandpaper tongue as the mother Holstein lowed softly and leaned her head across the slats to give Mourning's hand a raspy lick. One calf was swishing its tail and nursing hungrily, while the other, smaller calf lay weakly in the corner, its head lying forlornly against its legs.

Mourning tugged and pulled the weaker calf until she had it nestled on her lap and immediately the tiny little creature weakly turned the warm velvet of its nose against her apron and began to gently root and nuzzle into the pockets and folds of it, batting its head against her side impatiently.

Here was life in its purest and simplest form, fresh, new, and unafraid. It was creation, the beginning of life, and Mourning was enchanted, yet at the same time she was never more piercingly aware of her own unfruitfulness as a woman. Never before had she felt the stabbing, searing pain of an unfulfilled woman, the female forlornness of having no mate; and like the curse of barrenness, she felt as dry as dust.

Something within her tightened around her heart and she was overcome with loneliness—filled with the yearning desire to mate, to join together with one man, to bear his children, to be his companion. A strange dissatisfaction was gripping her, foreshadowed by hopelessness.

She looked down at the helpless creature curled on her lap and felt all the sadness in her soul pour forth, and she fought the overwhelming impulse to cry out her wretchedness.

She was in this flushed and overwrought state when he arrived. He watched her for a moment, finding the fluttering of her hands across the soft hair of the calf strangely sexual.

"So very precious, my soft little baby," she cooed, and turned the gently curled head to rest in her lap. He knew she had not seen him, so her words were not for him, and perhaps for this reason, because they were straight from her heart, not meant for human ears, they moved him with such force.

Still unaware of his presence, she said, "Did God ever create anything so wonderful as a tiny, innocent newborn?" And then she answered, "I think not, my tiny little wee one." She bent her head of golden curls against the calf and nuzzled it the way a mother would.

She was unfolding before him like the petals on some rare, exotic flower that bloomed only in the deepest and darkest jungle, away from probing eyes. He was washed with the exalting thrill of discovery, the unveiling of a fragile treasure; matchless and priceless, one that comes along only once in a blue moon.

It was as if this blooming had sent thousands and thousands of tiny little runners and creepers, like tangling roots and vines, out to twist and wind themselves around his consciousness and estab-

lish themselves like tightly gnarled roots that cannot be withdrawn.

He felt an immediate constriction around his heart. His first
reaction was to break this thing that had imprisoned him and to
run as if the very devil were after him, but she sensed his presence
and turned toward him.

"I can't get him to stand up," she said, glancing shyly at Clint
as if she were afraid of revealing something of herself to him.
"Could you help me?"

As he opened the gate she tugged and encouraged the tiny
nursling to stand on wobbly stiltlike legs, but they folded beneath
him and he collapsed, once again, into the hay bedding.

"Why won't he stand?" she said in a frustrated tone.

The man behind her laughed and crouched down, knees wide
apart, and placed his hands with confident ease around the belly of
the tiny calf and raised him up, his pitifully thin legs dangling like
the wooden limbs on a marionette. The heavy lids lifted and the
calf gazed, with empty brown eyes, at the man who held him, and
then lowed brokenly—the eyes falling closed. With a gentle touch
Clint lowered the calf back to the hay and steady fingers felt along
hollow bones and weightless feet before he sat back with a sigh.

"What is it?" she asked, alarmed. "What's the matter, Clint?"

"This calf hasn't been nursed," he said, turning toward her.

"No!" She grabbed him by the arm. "Please . . . can't we do
something?" she pleaded.

"There isn't anything we can do. It's too late, he wouldn't
nurse if we held him to his mother."

"But a b-bottle," she stammered, "we could give it a bottle."

He shook his head and rocked back on his haunches, studying
her profile, his eyes following the trail of a tear rolling in a crystal
droplet down her cheek.

He stood up and moved away to the other side of the pen. For
suddenly he felt the quickening of a raw flame leaping up in his
loins, a flame that he had hoped was quiescent, one that time away
from her had quenched. He pushed up barriers against it, but the
flame leapt forward as if feeding on the very barriers he had
erected, and gained momentum. It danced around him, circling
and enticing him until he turned once more to look at her.

She was still holding the calf, but the back of her hand was
pressed against her mouth and her shoulders were hunched for-

ward. He knew the calf was dead. She looked so lonely and afraid that tenderness shimmered across him, stirring to life the latent desire in his loins and rousing it to exquisite wakefulness.

Unaware that he had even moved, he crouched beside her once more, moving the lifeless calf from her lap, and placing it gently in the bed of hay. The fusing heat in his loins raced heartily now.

He glanced uncertainly at her and saw she had turned her face into the crook of her arm and cried brokenheartedly. He forgot he was older than she was, or that she was Caroline's daughter, or even that she was an irritable pest, a fly in the ointment. He cupped her chin and turned her face to him and then lifted his hand to trace the path of tears with the roughness of his thumb, but when he touched the baby softness of her cheek that big callused lump in his chest thumped painfully against his ribs, and he felt acute compassion for her. *My little yellow buttercup,* he thought, *what are you doing to me?*

He knew he should drop his hand from her and leave right then, right that very moment, but instead he put out his other hand and cupped his fingers around her shoulder.

"Don't cry," he said softly. "There was nothing you could've done. The calf wouldn't have lived, that's why the cow rejected him."

But his words didn't make any difference, and the tears continued to pour forth as if her heart were broken and life weren't really worth living. And he watched her silently, with the clumsy, groping understanding of a man who did not fully comprehend the misery that dwells in the heart of an unfulfilled woman; he did not know how to comfort her with words. And so, in the manner of a man, he gave comfort in the only way he knew.

His hand slipped down the smallness of her shoulder, and traveled lightly over the gently grooved line of her ribs, caressing and stroking, and continued down the curve of her hip. Traveling upward, his hand gently and softly caressed the firmness of her breast, moving to the softness of her belly, calming and coaxing with intuitive sensitivity.

He felt the whispering stir of her body's awakening, the loosening of the bands that restricted her. "Come with me," he said, in a gentle coaxing voice.

And moving behind her, he drew her up and led her quietly to

the tack room and soundlessly crossed the room. He left her standing motionless as he opened a chest and removed a fringed Indian
blanket and spread it across the stack of feed sacks.

"Sit down," he urged gently, and she looked at the face of a
man resigned to his fate, her own blank and without expression.

He shut the door and plunged the room into dimness. She
heard the crunching steps of cracking grain and felt the gentle
pressure of his hand upon her arm.

With yielding acquiescence, she sat on the blanket and felt the
tender, prompting pressure that guided her backward. She felt the
heat from his body as he moved alongside her, and then it came,
the hesitant touch of uncertain hands, touching and moving
blindly, searching for her face.

The same hands that had thrown a knife with such deadly
precision moved with unaccustomed gentleness, caressing and
stroking her face and throat with inexhaustible patience, and then
she felt the gentle assurance of a soft kiss upon her cheek.

The kiss, by virtue of its soft, subdued gentleness did what no
amount of force could have persuaded her to do, and she lay un-
moving, somewhere between the harsh and glaring lights of reality
and the soft, muted colors of a dream.

Desire for her raced through him, leaving his nerves humming
so violently that ignoring it was impossible. Christ! What was he
doing? She was innocent, she was Caroline's daughter, and he was
ten years her senior. She was no more than a baby . . . no more
than six years old when he humped his first woman for God's sake!
But no amount of self-chastisement would quench the impossible
desires or the gnawing ache he felt for her.

Two conflicting emotions were struggling within him, tearing
him apart. He threw his head back in anguish, shutting his eyes
tightly, his mind telling him to stop, his body telling him to proceed full steam ahead. He was torturing himself, but he could not
stop; it was impossible.

The months of being around her, of wanting her, of self-de-
nial, had finally eaten through his thin veneer of self-control.

He pulled her to him slowly, cradling her head tenderly
against the comforting strength of his shoulder. She uncurled toward him, fluttering small and birdlike, moving and settling closely
and affectionately against his length, fitting her warm curves into

all the aching chasms of his body, and when she'd settled comfortably, he pressed her close, as one would nestle a kitten in his arms.

He liked her like this, soft . . . warm . . . helpless and nestling, melting like something tiny and so precious in his arms. He felt a quickening within him, a sense of going beyond the yearning, craving desire he felt for her, but something infinitely more penetrating, more beautiful; too beautifully pure and delicate to express with mere words.

"Clint," she said softly, and the sound of her saying his name like this rippled across his skin like rosewater; cool, soothing, and fragrant. The sensual, soft tones of her voice intensified the blinding frenzy that swirled within him.

He looked at her with eyes that were as dark as obsidian granite and dilated with desire. "Do you know what it means to be a woman?" he said, his voice low.

"No," she said tentatively, and shook her head, her eyes glistening, her lips wet and warm.

He groaned and pulled her closer. "I want to make you a woman," he breathed against her mouth.

She quivered at the potency of his words, which were spoken softly, openmouthed against her, and she closed her eyes and became lost in them. He was different than he had ever been before, and her inward resistance and anger toward him blew away with the gentle stirring of his breath against her face, like chaff in the wind.

His warm tongue came calling then, and found she had melted her mouth opening tentatively, like the first offering of peace, a hesitant testing. The inviting thrill of his warm tongue was habituating her with a foretaste, giving substance to nebulous ideas; and unable to resist, she followed his lead and kissed him back with all the queer awakening of a newborn thing. How perfectly it felt to lie with him like this, how beautiful and strong, and she whimpered softly and clung to him because she knew it could not last. A sudden inkling of awareness crept through her and lingered like a firm, ripe peach just out of reach . . . waiting.

He began to whisper things into her mouth. "I want to kiss you all over. I want to spend all night removing your clothes," he said in a raspy voice. "Do you know what you do to me? I want you. God help me, but it's all I can think about."

He turned the palm of her hand to his mouth and she felt the soft, breathing wetness, and the muscles in her belly grew taunt.

"I dream about what it would be like to make love to you," he said, imagining the color of her skin, like gleaming ivory velvet beneath him. He twisted and shifted his weight until he was lying fully upon her and she knew the feel of the hard length of him through her skirts, and it felt so right, she fought the impulse to touch him, not because she was too timid, but because she was afraid of the unknown.

Her arms slid slowly up his cotton shirt, feeling the tensely coiled muscles. He claimed her in another kiss, this one longer and deeper, his hardness pushing against her, pressing into her belly and the intermittent pain-pleasure of it broached insanity. Her legs were weak and there was a tremendous pressure building within her—something gloriously and wonderfully painful. She made a tiny sound, deep in her throat, and felt her back arching against him.

"Oh, God," he groaned, "that's it, sweetheart, you feel it, don't you? I've dreamed of you like this, responding to me like this, sweet . . . sweet."

His words became incoherent as he kissed her again and again, pressing her breasts flat against his chest, her breath leaving her. The ribbon in her hair slid to the ground as his hands dug into her hair, and the sound of his breathing was ragged and out of control. His tongue twined around hers, asking . . . searching.

Oh, God, she was so ripe and ready. He couldn't seem to stop kissing her. She kissed him perfectly, but then why shouldn't she? He'd taught her how to kiss a man . . . taught her the way he liked to be kissed, and she had learned all he'd taught her and was teaching him a few things in return.

He knew it would be good between them, he could feel it oozing out of every pore in his body. She was one hell of a woman, and taking her would be something close to fireworks on the Fourth of July. It hit him painfully then, like a sharp punch to the gut. He couldn't take her here on a grimy Indian blanket in the tack room. She deserved more than that, his little yellow buttercup.

Sweat popped out on his forehead, and from the agony of it, it could have been blood. He held his breath and clenched his jaw in an effort to master the powerful desire that chewed at him.

Finally, he rolled off, and away from her, flinging his arm across his forehead in an effort to control his raging body, his ragged breathing, his desire to kick his own butt over the nearest fence for being so damn chivalrous and downright stupid.

Occupied with fighting his own war, he fought to bring himself under control before he turned to her. It was a mistake, for those few brief seconds were more than enough time for her to feel the abject humbling rejection that now engulfed her.

When he had his wits about him, he turned to her and saw immediately his gross mistake. For she was masked with indifference, although obviously deeply hurt. He couldn't leave her like this . . . neutral and blank . . . unresponsive. Where was her fire and vinegar, her adder's tongue? Where was the woman who boxed his ears and dumped his clothes into the river, or who called him every name she could think of? With a tenderness that was unfamiliar to him, he struck the final blow. "That went a little beyond what I had in mind when I suggested friendship," he said with a strained voice, and then stood up and walked to the door.

He opened the door and then glanced quickly over his shoulder, and saw the huge tears glistening in her eyes before they rolled down her cheek. He was suddenly sorry he'd hurt her, it wasn't what he'd intended. He'd wanted to make love to her—how'd it turned into this?

"Mourning, I . . ."

"Don't say anything else," she said like a scolded child. "You couldn't possibly say anything to hurt me any more than you already have."

Damn, this isn't going right, but Cad was waiting, he had to leave. Perhaps he could talk to her again tonight. He watched her make her way outside, and once she stepped into the sunlight, she turned and looked at him, her eyes suddenly cold. "You know, my grandmother always said *if you lay down with dogs, you get up with fleas.* Funny, I never understood what she meant until now."

$\approx$ 16

The house at Citadel had not rocked with such window-rattling noise since Santa Anna's cannons thundered by some twenty years before. Now the grand old house literally shook at its very foundations the first week Anna Ragsdale arrived, and if that wasn't enough to send it crashing to the ground in a smoldering heap, Melly had accompanied her sister.

Now the dignified and gracefully aging house was like a grand old dame who had discovered the fountain of youth—bathing in its golden elixir, becoming saturated with a rare and treasured perfume that only comes in the spring of life . . . joie de vivre. With the buoyant delight of effervescent youth, young voices echoed through its great shadowy hallways; voices that whispered secrets, or laughed jubilantly; voices that bubbled and sang, and plotted . . . spoiling mischief.

The great front door slammed behind them and rattled on its brass hinges as the girls, all three wearing light green dresses, blew through it like three off-course hurricanes, setting the sparkling prisms on the foyer chandelier to tinkling, then to teetering precariously before two of the crystallized rainbows plunged to the floor. Mrs. Harper charged into the parlor breathing fire like a cudgel-wielding Scotsman, her broom whistling through the air. Brandishing her broom and shouting her war cry, *You've done it, you've done it!* she came face-to-face with the trio who had, by this time, displayed themselves in a blameless and innocent manner on the horsehair sofa, sitting quieter than a silent cuckoo.

Mrs. Harper paused momentarily and then scowled, a scowl that Mourning had grown to interpret as one of doubtful suspicion, before she flew into one of her blustery rages that signified nothing. And as it often is with youth, a thousand stampeding buffalo couldn't have trampled the girls' mirth as they watched their beloved Mrs. Harper swell and huff, nearly popping the already overstressed buttons off the front of her stiffly starched dress.

"Your mama's going to be spittin' mad when she and Mister John get back. That chandelier came from . . . from . . . from one of those far-off places and . . ."

"Ireland," Mourning offered, and Mrs. Harper gave her a look that bespoke ill for her if she gave any more solicitous help.

"Just where were you three headed at such breakneck speed, if I may ask," she said, giving one final sweep of the broom to the gleaming oak floor, removing all traces of the shattered prisms.

"To the library," Melly chirped, and Mourning gave her a stare that condemned her to eternal silence.

Mrs. Harper, who only looked as if she were born yesterday, elevated her brows to a questioning height before speaking. "To the library? And what might the three of you be finding to interest you in the library on this fine summer morning?"

"We wanted to read," Mourning suggested, valiantly trying to cover her strong desire to burst into laughter at the expression on Mrs. Harper's face.

"Read? Humph! That'll be the day," said Mrs. Harper before she waved them out of the room. "Be on with you, then, but mind you, no more running in the house."

Melly had the audacity to curtsy, and from Mrs. Harper she received a healthy swat from the broom. It was something extra to add to the hilarity of an already ridiculously funny morning, and the trio exited the room, huddled together like a cluster of green grapes.

They filed past the sun-gilt window like tin soldiers on parade, talking and laughing gaily, until the lid was clapped on their bubbling spirits. Stricken with horror, they watched Cad and Clint round the corner of the house, walking with angry determination toward the front door. The winsome trio scarcely had time to right their rumpled clothing and pull the leaves and grass from their hair when the front door closed with a loud click and the booming sound of angry boots echoed down the hallway.

"Uh-oh," Melly said, turning quite pale, "here comes trouble."

"Should we make a run for it?" Anna asked, always the advocate of *common sense being the greater part of valor,* and common sense always told her to avoid trouble at all costs.

"We'd never make it, they're coming this way," Mourning whispered. "Here they come . . . prepare for a blasting."

The furious sound of boots was nearly upon them, and they stood there, petrified and stricken, lined up like felons awaiting conviction.

"And it was such a fine morning too," Anna said softly, on reflection. "I'm really not in the mood for a severe dressing-down."

"Well, you better get in the mood, because here comes *double* trouble," Mourning warned in a whisper. "Brace yourself."

The time for the dressing-down came too soon, and the blasting began promptly at eleven o'clock, when Clint crashed into the room followed by Cad, who stopped to lean with casual indifference against the marble mantel with an amused twinkle in his eye and a predisposition to clear his throat whenever one of the girls stole a glance in his direction. Clint stopped in front of them, one thumb hooked through his belt loop, the other hand hanging at his side, crushing a pair of leatherwork gloves that he repeatedly slapped against his thigh. It was the meter of that repetitious slapping of leather against his leg that caused the immediate dryness in Mourning's throat.

It wasn't what she willed herself to do, but the pull, the attraction, was there, uncontrollable, and for the smallest fraction of a second, wildly out of control. Her eyes were forcibly drawn to his. She felt defenseless and open to attack when his luxurious gaze joined hers. For a shimmering moment, she had the extraordinary suspicion that meeting her eyes had hit him with the same unbridled potency. But then with the same impartial appraisal one would use to assess the value of a chipped cup, he gave her the once-over, as if there were no doubt he would toss it out with yesterday's garbage.

There had been a sudden shift in the winds of fortune and the trio stood like three censured penitents humbly awaiting the ministering of last rites. Fixing her eyes upon a cluster of marble fruit, Mourning steeled her nerves to meet the first inevitable blow to her budding independence. The words, when they came, were like a shower of broken glass.

"I don't suppose," Clint said, glaring hotly at the cowering trio huddled before him, "that you three paper skulls would know anything about three horses in the stables that were ridden . . . and I mean *well ridden,* this morning?"

Feeling as though she'd been passed over for canonization and selected for martyrdom, Mourning ventured, "Would you believe . . . no?"

"No, I wouldn't," Clint responded, his lips twisting with cynical amusement, his words punctuated by the slapping of his gloves against his thigh. "You have been told repeatedly not to ride out alone. You three rattleheads can't seem to get it through your heads that this is dangerous territory. This entire country is crawling with bands of renegade Indians and Mexicans. And now Cheno Cortinas and his band have been spotted near here, and that man's first name is *trouble.*" Clint's eyes narrowed, projecting an arresting look. "You might not find it so exciting if you happen to cross paths with one of these bands."

Melly had always possessed the uncanny knack of picking the most inopportune times to giggle, and today being no exception, she giggled.

Clint gave her a quelling frown and her mouth snapped shut faster than a spring trap. "What do you find so entertaining, Miss Mouse?"

A flutter of wind sent the limbs of the old apple tree scraping against the window, and Melly said, "We saw a band of men this morning and we were excited. We were so excited, we ran all the way back to the barn. That," she said proudly, "is why the horses were so tired."

With the quicksilver speed of Mercury, Clint's expression turned frightening. His eyes pinned on Mourning, he asked, "What happened?"

"We saw a group of men on the ridge," Mourning began, "and when they saw us, they started after us."

"Probably some of our hands," said Cad, pushing away from the mantel.

"No! No, they weren't," Mourning said. "They weren't vaqueros, but they weren't Indians either. These men had a leader that rode in front. He spoke in Spanish and pointed at us. That's when they started after us."

Mourning had fully expected Clint to accept her story as he would the imagined childish fantasy of a three-year-old. To the contrary, he slammed down his gloves on a nearby table with such force, the oil in the lamp sloshed from side to side. His eyes looked angry. "When were you going to tell me this?" Not waiting for an answer, he asked, "The leader of this group—did he have a red beard?"

"He had a beard, it could have been red . . . or brown. He wore a hat, so his beard was shaded. Besides, we didn't look that long. We left."

Clint said tersely, "That's the first intelligent thing I've heard come out of your mouth."

Cad interrupted. "Cortinas?"

"That would be my guess," Clint replied, with a black look that made Mourning feel like a naughty puppy who'd just puddled on the carpet.

"You three are not to leave the house again without an escort . . . on horseback or on foot. If it happens again, *just once,* for whatever reason you three featherheads can construe, you will polish all the silver trim on every saddle and pair of chaps at Citadel. Do you understand?"

A thick gasp came from the threesome simultaneously. This was surely a punishment of unparalleled cruelty, since there were in the neighborhood of seventy-five saddles in the tack room, and each saddle had a chap-wearing rider, and with the Mexicans' love for silver concha, every piece of equipment at Citadel was loaded to the gills with ornate silver trim; more than enough to keep them busy for months, perhaps years.

"Do you understand?" he repeated more firmly, and three curly-haired heads bobbed affirmatively.

"Well, now . . ." he said, and the cousins breathed a sigh of relief, as if given a last-minute reprieve from execution. But then he added, "I'd like to know where you went," and they felt like men condemned to hang twice.

"We went riding," Mourning answered, hoping and praying that would suffice, knowing all the while it wouldn't.

Cad cleared his throat again, and it was obvious that Clint

was more firmly convinced than ever that he was dealing with a moron.

"Out riding," he repeated, stepping agonizingly close to Mourning, so close she could feel the frost of his breath crystallizing his words. He lifted a golden curl from her shoulder and stroked its shimmering length thoughtfully and then laid it against her breast. Mourning felt a lashing whip of pleasure in her chest, followed by anger at his persuasive control over her emotions.

Mourning, like her cousins, was dressed in green, but the vivid hue of her gown couldn't compare with the fiery shimmer of viridescent eyes that watched Clint closely.

They were a rare handful, this trio of trouble standing at full attention before him like three uniformed members of a regiment, the varying greens of their riding gowns intensifying the esprit de corps between them.

His eyes flicked back to Mourning, who was so seriously endeavoring to be the last word in nubile maturity, only to end up such an adorably enchanting chucklehead, he wanted to laugh outright. He loved her this way, trying to get the better of him, the cogs in her little mind churning and whirring with ideas . . . he could almost hear them. He had missed the lively banter they had so skillfully developed between them while they traveled; perhaps that was why he had been constantly nipping at her since John and Caroline left. He watched her face grow hot from his close scrutiny, the color creeping out from under her collar and inching upward. He should do the gentlemanly thing and let her off the hook, but she had to learn not to ride out alone. And besides, when had anyone ever accused Clint Kincaid of being a gentleman?

"Now that we have established that point, where did you ride?" This time his chilling look was directed at Melly, who was much easier to frighten into admissions; in fact, the way Clint was devouring her with his murderous glare, she would have admitted to anything and then signed her name to it in blood. Giving her his most murderous stare worked, and Melly spilled the beans.

"We rode to a cabin down by the creek," she said, nervously clenching and unclenching her small fists.

"And why did the old log cabin by the creek hold such fascination for you three muddleheads?" Clint asked, not releasing poor Melly from his paralyzing stare.

"W-we were looking for a p-place to b-bury a trove t-treasure," she said hurriedly.

"That's treasure trove, nitwit," Mourning corrected.

Cad had a coughing attack and Clint adroitly replaced the twinge of humor that flirted around the corners of his mouth with a freezing, unfriendly smile. His piercing eyes on Anna, Clint asked, "A treasure trove? What, may I ask, is a treasure trove?"

"Well, it's what we call a box of things you want to keep, but they're secret things . . . you know . . . things you'd die if anyone saw them . . . they're sort of . . . uh . . ."

"Personal?" Cad offered, and Anna sent him a look that fluctuated between pure adoration and eternal gratitude.

"Yes. Just a collection of things that have special meaning to no one but us."

"I see," Clint said with a slight trace of mockery. "And this treasure trove, was it yours?"

Anna glanced at Mourning, who was incapable of lifting her eyes any higher than the second row of braided trim on Anna's skirt. "No, it's Mourning's. We all had treasures back in Memphis, but Melly and I left ours, so we put some of our things in Mourning's and then looked for a good place to hide it. Naturally we didn't want anyone to come with us, because they'd know where it was."

"Naturally," Clint said dryly, and then raised his hawkish brows and looked at Mourning.

The breathlessly handsome nearness of him, as well as his line of questioning, made Mourning's stomach churn. Perhaps he was genuinely concerned about their safety—one glance at his eyes affirmed that. But then again, why would he be concerned about their personal safety when he looked on the verge of murdering them himself?

Mourning stood there with her heart in her mouth, waiting for the ax to fall, but as she steadfastly considered the bounty of his face, she was alert to the softening of his harsh features, the warmth in his smoky eyes. Suddenly she wanted the *other* Clint back. This one was making her as comfortable as a speared fish.

"Were you successful in finding a hiding place?"

Her fingers were cool on her face as she brought her hands up in an unsuccessful attempt to cover her blushing discomfort. Possible ideas for looking elegantly bored were planted in her mind, but none took root, leaving her thoughts barren, her face blank.

He stood there in confident control and she resented her own inadequacy. By now her mind was so rattled and flustered, she had forgotten the question he had asked. As if reading her thoughts, he said, "I asked you if you had found a suitable hiding spot for your cherished hoard."

With a prevailing spirit of camaraderie, Melly and Anna leaped to her defense. "Yes," they answered in unison.

"I see," he said, rocking back on his heels and looking at Cad, who raised his shoulders in a shrug.

"Is that all, sir?" Melly quaked, nervously biting her lip and looking up at him as if he were capable of turning her to stone.

"Yes, that's all," he said, sternly resisting a smile, "but I meant every word I said about polishing saddles." He took one more look at their blanched faces and sighed. "All right, you can go now."

Properly rebuked, they bolted with a run of Olympic qualifications, attacking the door at the same time. Passing through the door simultaneously being a physical impossibility, they backed off and went at it again, this time lined up like three little green peas in a pod, and scampered to the parlor as if they were being pursued by a thousand scalp-hungry Apaches.

Feeling the knee-quaking relief of one just rescued from the den of a starving lion, they collapsed weakly against the closed door to whisper among themselves. Minutes later Melly left the room and detoured through the kitchen to fetch the egg basket, and then scampered down the pathway toward the henhouse, encountering Cad and Clint on her way.

"Well, mighty mite, where are you skipping off to in such a hurry?" Cad inquired.

"To the henhouse to gather eggs," she said, sounding like something fresh out of a nursery rhyme.

Cad smiled, tweaked her nose, and raised his brows in question at Clint. "But the eggs were gathered early this morning."

"Oh, I know that."

"Then why are you going to gather eggs when you know there won't be any?"

"Because Anna and Mourning wanted me to. Anna promised

me her blue satin ribbon and Mourning is going to give me her
cupid bookmark."

"Oh, that does make a difference," he said warmly. "In that
case you best be on your way."

"This bears looking into," Clint said with a sigh, and both
brothers retraced their steps to the house, going in this time by the
back door and moving quietly.

Mourning and Anna waited until the house grew still and
then slipped down the hallway and into a small, compact study.
Mourning sat in the red chair by the globe and Anna parked herself on the oaken settle by the fireplace and propped her feet upon
the fender, much as she would have done if it were a blustery day
outside and she were sitting before a crackling fire.

Anna listened with passionate intentness as Mourning detailed
her discoveries to her.

"You have something in a book to show *me*?" Anna said,
curiously looking around at all the shelves jammed with leather-
bound books. "Whose room is this anyway? I've never been in here
before."

"It's Cad and Clint's study, that's why there are two desks in
here. The big oak one in front of the window is Clint's and the
inlaid one behind you is Cad's. As for the books, I assume they
belong to both of them, since this is where they handle their corre-
spondence and accounts and such." She tucked her feet under her
skirts.

"Anyway, the night before you came, I was so excited, I
couldn't sleep, so I came in here and sat on that small tufted stool
over there and began to leaf through several books, trying to find
one interesting enough to read, yet dull enough to put me to sleep.
Well, that's how I discovered them."

"Them?"

"Yes, there are two of them. I removed a few books when I
noticed two books had slipped behind the stack and were hidden
from view. I picked them up and didn't leaf very far when I realized the books most assuredly had *not* slipped behind the stack, but
were hidden there intentionally, and when you read them you will
see why."

"You mean they are *wicked* books?" Anna said, scooting to
the edge of the settle, her eyes wide, her mouth rounded into an
astonished O.

"The wickedest."

"You mean, as wicked as the French postcard you have in your treasure trove . . . the one of the lady in her underthings?"

"Worse than that."

"Oh, my goodness," Anna cried, "I didn't know they made worse."

"Well, now you know. Do you know what happens when ladies scamper about in their underthings and are accosted by gentlemen and robbed of their virtue?"

"No, what?" asked Anna, wide-eyed.

"*That's* how you get a baby."

"A baby!" Anna exclaimed, scooting farther out and nearly falling off the settle. "You mean you must scamper about in your underthings in order to have a baby? I can't imagine my mother doing a thing like that! Why, *I've* never even seen her in her underthings."

Moving to the tufted footstool, Mourning carefully removed several volumes and stacked them neatly on the floor.

"I see them, I see them," Anna cried, jumping up out of her seat as if she'd just seen the parting of the Red Sea and the children of Israel walking through. "Those are the ones you're talking about, right?"

"Shhhhh! I think I hear someone coming. Quick, take this book and hide it under your skirts and I'll hide this one."

They waited for several seconds, and hearing no sounds, Mourning let out a sigh of relief. "Much ado about nothing," she said, looking up at Anna.

"Milton," Anna guessed.

"Shakespeare."

"Oh, fiddle. I never could get those English authors together with all the things they wrote, but I do remember that Queen Victoria was only eighteen when she became Queen. Can't you just imagine being crowned Queen of England at our age?"

"If we get caught with these books, we may be crowned in an entirely different way," Mourning pointed out.

Mourning placed her book, *Memoirs of a Woman of Pleasure,* in her lap and let it fall open where it would, explaining to Anna that this added a certain element of mystery. The book fell open on page eighty-two. "Now, listen to this," Mourning said with matchless artfulness and calm.

"*I twist my legs round his naked loins, the flesh of which, so firm, so springy to the touch, quiver'd again under the pressure; and now I had him every way encircled and begirt . . .*"

The cut-crystal humidor on the table next to Anna crashed to the floor when Anna fell back with an astonished gasp. "Let me see that." Anna's lips moved silently as her eyes skimmed the page. When she finished, she said in a weak voice, "Do you think Cad and Clint have read this?"

"Of course, you ninny! Who do you think these books belong to?"

"I'll never be able to look either one of them in the eye again," Anna wailed, and fell back against the settle.

Mourning eyed the shattered humidor and the shreds of tobacco, then began picking up the scattered fragments and handing them to Anna. "You better run from every man you see, then, because they all read these books."

"Do you really think they do?"

"As faithfully as we are devoted to *Godey's,*" Mourning responded.

Anna stood up with a confused look, then sat back down, turning over the volume she held and studying it thoughtfully. "Do you know what will happen to us if we get caught?" She opened the book and flipped over a few pages.

"It depends on who does the catching. If it were Mama, she'd read it with us. If it were Cad, we'd get a good scolding. If it were Clint . . ."

"He's the one I'm worried about."

"Me too," Mourning confessed. "We'll just have to take care not to get caught, and if we do . . . what's the worst thing that could happen to us?"

Anna clapped the book shut with a snap. "There are any number of horrible things . . . a thorough flensing for one, and the bad thing about it is, he would have every right! Young ladies *do not* read literature of this type, and those that do should be bound and gagged and thrown from the nearest bridge."

They lapsed into mutual silence, each with her own visions. With a sigh, Mourning stood and moved to the window. "You're right . . . we shouldn't be reading these; besides, I find I rather like *not* knowing." Deep in ponderous thought she watched a squirrel scamper across the yard and zip up a tree; she gave the globe a spin. As if a new idea had dawned on her, she turned toward Anna with a wide smile. "But on the other hand, you know what Shakespeare said."

"You know I don't," Anna confessed.

"*'Tis needful that the most immodest word/Be looked upon and learned.*"

"Meaning we should go ahead and read?"

"Meaning we should go ahead and read," Mourning repeated. They returned to the settle and reread the passage they had read earlier, finding it was still as clear as mud. When Mourning reached the phrase, *I had him every way,* Anna interrupted with "Just how many ways are there?"

Mourning looked around the room as if she'd find the answer written on the wall. "As many as you want, I guess."

"You mean you don't know?"

Mourning sprang to her feet. "Anna Claire Ragsdale! I'm still trying to figure out kissing!"

"You could ask Clint."

Anna broke into ripples of laughter at the expression on Mourning's face, which only gave added dramatization to Mourning as she collapsed against the desk with a fit of giggles.

Suddenly Anna stopped laughing and was staring at Mourning as if she were naked. Mourning followed the direction of Anna's terrified gaze and turned to look her mentor in the face—only there were two of them, and the brothers stepped into the room.

"Sit on it" was all Mourning had time to say, but alas, the eye was quicker than the hand in this case and they were unfortunately caught red-handed.

"I hope we're not interrupting anything," Clint said, holding out his hand for the object Mourning was so desperately trying to hide. "No, please don't insult my intelligence by slipping those volumes under your skirts. Don't look so persecuted, angel. Cad will relieve Anna of her literary burden as well."

This time, Mourning *seriously* considered throwing herself out the window.

Cad whooped with laughter. "*Perfumed Garden of Shaykh Nefzawi!* My God!" Turning to Clint, he asked, "Isn't that the one about the sheik who was the undisputed authority on the acrobatic ability of the Hindus?"

Clint frowned. "Who?" The line of his brow suddenly went up

at least two inches. "Oh, yes, I remember. The woman who could hold an oil lamp aloft on the soles of her feet and keep it burning during the entire procedure."

"That's the one. What have you got?"

"Memoirs of a Woman of Pleasure," Clint replied, looking at Mourning and Anna standing rigidly before him. "You two termites have been busy, haven't you? Are you reading for information or pleasure?"

"Both," Anna stammered, and Mourning gave her a quick frown. "What I meant to say," she amended, " was that *both* of those books just happened to fall out while we were looking for a book of . . . of . . ."

"Gardening," Mourning interjected.

"Etiquette," said Anna.

The brothers Kincaid raised their brows simultaneously. "Gardening and etiquette," Clint repeated, "my, my, quite an endeavor. Tell me, do you plan to use good manners while you sit there like two *blooming* idiots, expecting me to fall for this?"

Mourning glanced at Cad, who smiled endearingly at her but offered no help. She must have looked near the point of desperation, because he suddenly took pity and spoke. "I wonder if you two even understand any of this mischief you have been reading?"

"Actually, we didn't have time to read much, but still, we didn't understand a word we read."

Cad grinned and flipped through the pages of the book. "I remember reading this the summer John went to Mexico City," he said, having the same habit as his brother in calling his father by his given name.

"Are you going to tell Aunt Caroline and John?" asked Anna, looking at Clint with a beseechingly hopeful expression.

"I fail to see the advantage of that."

It was at that precise moment that Mrs. Harper bounced into the room. "Here you are," she puffed. "I've turned the house upside down looking for you. Clint, Miss Whitworth is here . . . said you were expecting her. Will she be staying for dinner?"

"Yes," was Clint's clipped reply, and then he turned to Cad. "I'll see to Eleanor if you'll get these two lined out and occupied with something a little less educational." He gave Mourning a brittle smile and left the room.

When the girls were alone in Mourning's room, Anna fell

backward across the bed and exclaimed with a calf-sick sigh, "I think Cad is devilishly handsome, don't you?"

"Yes, but I don't want to discuss that right now."

Rolling over, Anna watched Mourning pace back and forth in front of the cherry armoire, setting the draperies at the window to fluttering each time she passed. "What *do* you want to discuss?"

"Eleanor Whitworth!"

"What do you want to discuss about her? I don't even know her."

"Neither do I, but didn't you notice how cleaned-up Clint was? And then Miss Whitworth shows up and suddenly he couldn't be bothered with us anymore."

The door opened and Melly peeked in and then followed her nose into the room. "Can I come in now?" she asked. "Golly, why are y'all so sad-looking?"

"We're trying to figure out who Eleanor Whitworth is," replied Anna in a worried voice.

"Oh, I know about her," Melly said grandly.

"You do? Tell me what you know," Mourning said, grabbing Melly by the arm and dragging her to the bed so fast, her feet didn't touch the floor. Anna rolled over and made room for them to sit down beside her.

While Mourning's nature was to rush into things without stopping to consider the consequences, and Anna went to any length to avoid unpleasantness, Melly was the eavesdropper, who felt the best way to deal with a situation was neither advance nor retreat, but simply find out all you can and then use it. Being the youngest and told repeatedly, *Young ladies should be seen and not heard,* she did a great deal of listening, and such was the case this day.

"I'll tell you if you'll give me your plumy fan."

"Melly Ragsdale!" Anna snapped, "I'm ashamed of you."

Melly hung her head and said, "Oh, all right, I'll take the jar of carmine lipsalve, then."

"You'll get the cupid bookmark, and that's all; and if you don't hurry up and tell me, you might not get that," was Mourning's hasty reply.

"I heard Mrs. Harper talking to Ben in the buttery. She said *that* woman had more cunning than a dog had fleas and she'd set her cap for Clint, and he'd better watch his *p*'s and *q*'s or he'd find himself walking down the primrose path with that scarlet woman."

"Scarlet woman!" gasped Mourning, who found out, when she questioned Melly further, that Melly didn't have any idea what a scarlet woman was. And that was a tremendous relief to Mourning, who didn't exactly know either, having drawn a rather hazily distorted picture herself. After much debate, the cousins decided scarlet women were wicked women who obviously wore scarlet gowns. Mourning made a mental note to sneak back into the study and see if their informative books offered any more enlightenment on the subject.

There was no time to speculate further. The girls had promised—and one never broke a promise—Mrs. Harper that they would pick dewberries, and time was wasting. So, while Clint entertained, in whatever manner he saw fitting, Miss Eleanor Whitworth in the parlor, the girls swung across the fields behind the house toward the woods, baskets swinging and curls bobbing.

It didn't take the irritable heat of the torrid afternoon long to replace the chipper moods of the three with sullen irritation, and by the time they returned to the house they were not in their most sociable moods. Baskets brimming with delicious dewberries, a fact attested to by the dark berry-stains on their bodices and the darker-than-normal rosy hue of their lips, they marched single file through the front door and into the foyer, where they were met by Mrs. Harper.

"Why, for goodness sakes, did you come through the front door looking like *that?*" she queried.

"Because it was closest and we were broiling hot," Mourning answered truthfully, the red blush of heat on her face proving the validity of her words.

Unfortunately a bee that had somehow become buried in the berries dug his way to the surface and crawled up Mourning's arm and stung her as if he held her personally responsible for his ill-fortune. Mourning squealed and dropped her basket, which Mrs. Harper made a valiant dive for, but missed, crashing into Mourning, toppling them both flat on their bustles, and sending berries rolling all over the floor, some rolling as far as the parlor.

"What the hell is going on out here?" Clint roared as he stormed into the foyer, smashing berries underfoot, and was greeted by three stained berry-pickers, one of whom was sprawled with Mrs. Harper on the berry-sprinkled floor. Anna and Melly looked up at him sheepishly and smiled through stained lips.

Mourning glanced up at Clint, and then at the beautiful dark-haired woman dangling from his arm, and she knew hate at first sight.

Poor Mrs. Harper made three attempts to right herself and was finally pulled to her feet by Cad, who had just walked up behind them. While Mourning gaped, like a startled rabbit, at Miss Whitworth, Clint glared at Mourning. Eleanor looked smug and Mrs. Harper was much put out. Cad, as was usual for him, took a backseat and observed, while Anna and Melly had a good look at the *scarlet woman* standing beside Clint.

With a sigh of solemn irritation, Clint ran his fingers through his hair and said, "I suppose now is as good a time as any to introduce you to Miss Eleanor Whitworth."

"Where's your scarlet gown?" Melly asked.

Eleanor tried to smile. "I don't have a scarlet gown."

"But I thought you were a scarlet woman!" Melly said, with a degree of mixed disappointment and puzzled fascination.

Mrs. Harper was so red, Mourning feared an attack of apoplexy as she yanked Melly by the arm, through the berries and down the hall to the kitchen, and Cad cleared his throat while Clint's mouth teeter-tottered somewhere between a smile and a snarl. Unfortunately for Mourning, he teetered when he should have tottered and gave her a look that said he held her fully responsible.

Struggling to her feet, Mourning opened her mouth to deliver a crushing speech, thought better of it, and opted for a dramatic and stately exit, which would have been the wiser choice, except that Clint, following Mrs. Harper's example with Melly, disentangled himself from his clinging vine and dug his fingers painfully into Mourning's arm and dragged her, red-faced and mortified, into the library, kicking the door shut behind him.

"You," he snapped, "are cursed with long hair and short brains. Why in the name of heaven did you drag that menagerie of miscreants through the front door? Don't you have anything better to do than spend your time in wasteful endeavors like reading smutty books and teaching young children vulgar terms?"

"But I didn't teach it to Melly, she taught me."

He looked at her then as if he were positive he was dealing

with an idiot. "You have more cheek than a one-legged ballerina, expecting me to believe that!" He grabbed her by the wrist and gave her a good shake.

Mourning thought that someone must have dropped a bag of black cats in her path. Nothing was going right, and in spite of it all, she was frighteningly dizzy, whether from the sun, too many dewberries, or Clint's physical attractiveness—it didn't really matter.

The man with the face of a Michelangelo statue and the sting of a scorpion then said, "You don't have to writhe at my feet like a freshly dug worm. Speak up, I know the words are rolling around in there with all that sawdust somewhere. God knows how you love to twitter like a sparrow."

"You're cracking my arm," she squeaked. He threw her arm back at her. She glowered at him and rubbed her wrist.

"I'm sorry about what happened," she said, valiantly attempting to regain some of her shattered dignity. "We went to gather berries so we'd be out of your way. We thought you'd be gone from the house by the time we returned, and we were so hot and tired, we didn't think about it being at all improper to come in the front way, and then the bee stung me and I dropped my basket and . . . Oh, I don't know," she said, rubbing her wrist and fighting back the urge to cry.

He stared at her as she whimpered like a lost puppy, and reached for her. She came willingly, pressing her nose against his chest. He had the feeling her nose was cold and wet. As it always was when she ground it into his freshly starched shirt.

It was too much: the heat, the berries, the confusion, the shocking discovery that Clint had a woman, the general Greek godliness of him . . . It was just too much, and Mourning began to cry. "I hate it here. I hate Texas. It's nothing but black funnelclouds, barren enormity, and hailstorms. I don't know why the Mexicans wanted it. I'm tired of savages and wild beasts, and crude men, and wolves and scorpions . . . and . . . and you. I want to go home." She sobbed against his chest. "I want to take rides in the park and go to tea parties and wear pretty bonnets and dance. I want to be normal again."

She was doing it again, tugging at his insides, making him want to kiss that adorable face and to hell with the consequences.

Somehow she had managed to burrow under his skin worse than a chigger, and it would take more than scratching to remove her.

"It only seems that way because you are so young," he said softly. The hands that knew how to do so many wonderful things lifted then and cupped her face. The room began to whirl around her, and she was drowning in sweet, warm sensations.

"You are a handful," he said, one finger outlining the shell of her ear, his other hand doing crazy things along her throat, making goose bumps pop out on top of goose bumps. "And you're as wavering as the wind, so I never know fully how to deal with you. I know what I should do with you, and then I know what I'd like to do with you. Do you understand what I'm saying?"

"I . . . I think so." *Good Lord! Am I not capable of complete thought or speech? Must I stand here bleating like a startled sheep? Where is my tongue when I need it? Why is this happening to me?* "Wednesday," she whispered in answer to her own question.

"What? . . . Wednesday? . . . But today is Friday," he said.

She sighed. "I know. I think I'm having all these problems because I was born on Wednesday."

"What," he said, looking at her strangely, "does being born on Wednesday have to do with your problems?" A smile tugged at the corners of his beautiful mouth.

"Because Wednesday's child is full of woe."

"Oh," he said, smiling fully now, "well, that certainly explains it, then." His arms went around her and pulled her against the wild thumping in his chest. "So, Wednesday's child, whatever am I going to do with you?"

She stood weakly against him. "I don't know, I'm too confused."

"That makes two of us then . . . a well-matched pair, wouldn't you say?" His eyes, of their own accord, lowered to her breasts. "Forget what I said earlier, I . . ."

"No, you were right."

He looked at her curiously. "Buttercup?"

It sounded strange, the way he'd spoken it, as an endearment. She glanced up and searched his face briefly, her eyes seeing the battle he was fighting within him.

"Little buttercup," he said, barely a whisper this time, and the sound of it was so beautiful, she wanted to catch it and press it between the pages of her *Book of Verse,* and then bury it in her treasure trove and save it for a time when he didn't stand before her. But he was here now, with his clear gray eyes clouded with troubled thoughts, looking for answers to questions that had no answer, trying to speak words that were better left unsaid.

"I think Miss Whitworth will be wondering what's happened to you, and it's not polite to keep a lady waiting . . . not even a scarlet one."

∽ 17

Like foolish French children who cry because they want to play
with the moon, Mourning watched Clint and Eleanor ride through
the front gate, knowing she craved what was wholly beyond her
reach. The foolish French children are told: *Il veut prendre la lune
avec les dents*—he wants to take the moon between his teeth—but
Mourning, pressed as she was, couldn't find anything as clever to
salve her bruised feelings. Sadly, the only words that came to mind
were: *Plus il en a, plus il en veut*—the more one has, the more one
desires.

Eleanor, who rode sidesaddle, was clad in a deep burgundy
riding habit and wore an elegant hat with a flowing scarf perched
on her dark, glossy curls. Clint rode beside her, dressed in his usual
rakish manner: chaps, spurs, worn hat, blue shirt—handsome as
sin, infinitely desirable, and as out of reach as ever.

Jealousy. There was no denying she felt it, this most ignoble of
all passions, which feeds upon suspicion and leaves one feeling
alone and abandoned against a smiling enemy. Green-eyed with
this affliction, Mourning followed with those eyes the pair who
rode slowly and talked much. Jealousy.

> O! beware my lord, of jealousy:
> It is the green-ey'd monster which doth mock
> The meat it feeds on.

Mourning had recognized this jealousy for what it was and made the decision to give it no room to breed, when Eleanor's horse bolted and ran a few yards before Clint overtook her, easing his horse in front of hers, grabbing the reins, and bringing her horse to a stop. This put their horses face-to-face. As Mourning continued to watch, Eleanor encouraged her horse closer, pressing her leg against Clint's, and then she leaned over to put her hand over Clint's hand, which rested on the saddle horn. They remained in this position for several minutes, apparently lost in conversation, then Eleanor lifted her hand to Clint's face. A few more words were exchanged before the pair continued down the road and out of sight. *Trifles light as air/Are to the jealous confirmations strong/ As proofs of holy writ.*

Today Mourning's head was crammed with fanciful assumptions, and it mattered not one wit that they lacked factual reality. He was out there with that scarlet woman, doing whatever it was men did with scarlet women; and just thinking about it sent her stomach plunging to her feet, where it lay, bulky and heavy, like a lump of unrisen dough. Sadly, she turned and made her way to the dining room, where Anna and Melly were waiting.

After the cousins had eaten, Mrs. Harper reluctantly agreed to allow the trio to make dewberry jam, not completely convinced they knew all they claimed about making jams and jellies, but willing to *let them have a go,* as she had said. Mourning was decidedly ready to involve herself in digging dusty old jars out of the root cellar and washing dewberries until her hands were stained purple.

Never had such unorthodox and unknown methods for jam making been employed in Citadel's kitchen. Mrs. Harper was busy cutting up rashers from a side of bacon, which was nothing more than an excuse to stay in the kitchen so she could listen to the girls chatter, which had, of late, become a favorite pastime of hers.

"Melly, come over here and stir these . . . and don't you dare stop, or the berries will sink to the bottom and scorch," Mourning said, leaning across the table to hand the wooden spoon to Melly.

"Melly, why are you so lethargic this morning?" Mrs. Harper asked.

"I'm not lethargic," Melly said lethargically as she took the spoon Mourning extended.

"Oh, yes, you are," Anna replied, "and I know why."

Mourning paused with the sugar scoop suspended in midair. "Why is that, Anna?"

"Because she was spying on Clint and Eleanor last night when she was supposed to be sleeping."

"So what if I was," Melly answered, taking the spoon from the kettle and turning to face Mourning and Anna. "I bet you'd like to know what I saw," she said with an impish grin that said she'd seen plenty.

"Of course we wouldn't," snapped Anna, "that's gossiping, and besides . . ." Anna put down the jar she was drying and tucked a stray lock of hair in place as she looked quite sternly at her sister. "You're not stirring and the berries will scorch, Melly. As I said, that would be gossip . . ."

"Oh, do be quiet, Anna," Mourning said a trifle crossly, "this is a matter of family interest and of the gravest and utmost importance and therefore could not be considered gossip." She turned to Melly. "Tell us what you saw?"

Mrs. Harper's knife, which had been moving briskly, was suddenly poised in midair.

"Well . . . after we went to bed they walked outside and strolled around the yard and just happened to sit on the bench under the oak tree. They talked for a while, but I couldn't hear what they said, and then they started kissing, and after a while they got tired of that and Eleanor stood up and dragged Clint to the stables . . . I guess she wanted to go for a ride."

The knife Mrs. Harper had been holding in a state of weightless suspension dropped to the counter with an exploding clatter, rolled noisily around, and then fell to the floor with a loud thump.

Anna glanced at Mourning, and Mourning glanced at Mrs. Harper, and Mrs. Harper began to pulverize that slab of bacon, poking and jabbing at it as if it were her worst enemy.

Mourning yanked the egg basket off the hook by the door and shoved it into Melly's hands. "Melly, go gather eggs."

"What about the berries? Won't they sink?"

"I'll stir while you're gone," Mourning said, taking the spoon and stirring briskly. Turning, Mourning saw Melly had not moved.

"But I gathered them this morning," Melly protested as Mourning pushed her toward the door.

"Do you want my plumy fan or not?" Mourning replied hastily, and Melly bolted out the back door.

"I just hope your wardrobe is large enough to last until Melly and I go home. However will I explain to Mother her coming home with half your belongings?" Anna said speculatively.

As soon as Melly disappeared through the door, Mourning turned to Mrs. Harper. "Who exactly is Eleanor Whitworth?"

"A good-for-nothing whose vanity overrides her virtue is what she is," snapped Mrs. Harper. "You'd best not cross swords with the likes of her . . . that woman has a she-devil in her bosom and venom in her blood. She'd fairly chew you up and spit you out and look around for more."

"Has she known Clint long?" Mourning asked quietly.

"All her life, although she's only been after him since he came back from going to school in Scotland. I believe that was when he was twenty. Her pa owns a ranch about twenty miles from here, and she always has him drop her off here when he goes to San Antonio. Says she's afraid to stay at the ranch with him gone, but she just wants to be around Clint. She's been after him for years; thinks she'll chase him till she gets caught . . . 'course that boy's got more sense than to tangle with the likes of her."

"Judging from what Melly saw, I'd say they've already tangled," Mourning offered lamely.

"Oh, she's a cunning seductress, of that there's no doubt, and I'm sure half the men within fifty miles of here would take her on in a minute, but she's always had her cap set for Clint. She told me that herself."

"She did? Does Clint know?" Mourning asked, leaning forward and putting her elbows on the table, her chin resting in her palms, her backside swinging back and forth in an established rhythm.

"I'm sure he does, he's no fool. Of course, I never told him she said she was going to marry him . . . figured it was none of my affair. The only thing that concerns me is that she wants that boy bad enough to get him any way she can, and I don't think she is above trapping him into marriage."

Mourning's mind was suddenly crowded with fertile ideas as to what *trapping him* meant, and her mouth popped open.

"Don't you be askin' me how she can trap him into marriage, Miss Full of Questions. That's one can of worms we are not going to open today," Mrs. Harper said, giving Mourning a look that put the quietus on what she was going to ask.

Mourning's mouth snapped shut, but her mental machinery was set in motion.

"Cad and Clint are both having too much fun chasing anything wearing skirts to settle down with any one woman right now. They've sowed plenty of wild oats, but they ain't showin' no signs of lettin' up anytime soon. Any little gal that tries to snatch up one of them is fairly wastin' her time." She delivered another fatal blow to the bacon. "Oh, they might act interested for a while, but I've seen them operate for too long. They enjoy the chase, but . . . well, it's sort of chase 'em, catch 'em, and leave 'em."

Even the sweetest milk can turn sour, and what had been an interesting discussion had suddenly become as bitter as wormwood, causing Mourning and Anna to lose interest in discussing Clint and Cad any further.

Mourning was staring unhappily into the bubbling pot when Melly bounced back into the kitchen with an empty basket.

"Got no eggs, just like I thought," she chirped. Noticing the chilling silence, she asked, "Did I stay gone long enough?"

Mourning couldn't resist a smile and gave her a hug, taking the basket from her. "Yes, you did, you little termite. Now help us finish the jam and then you can go to my room and get my plumy fan."

On the stove a huge iron preserving-kettle brought forth bubblings and gurglings with a vague suggestive steaminess that permeated the kitchen with a clinging sweet aroma. Anna was lining up the glass jars she had sterilized while Mourning readied the lids. Melly had resumed her job of stirring the boiling kettle.

"I remember helping my mother put up whortleberry jam when I was just about your age," Mrs. Harper said.

The girls giggled, not because it was funny but because of the way Mrs. Harper said *whortleberry*. Somehow it came out more resembling the guttural noise of a male turkey, and when Mrs. Harper carried the bacon out to the buttery to keep cool, the girls began to strut around the kitchen bobbing their heads up and down like turkey gobblers while they said *"whortleberry . . . whortleberry . . . whortleberry."*

At half past eleven, Mourning stood on the kitchen table, her apricot and white muslin dress up to her waist, showing a well-shaped leg outlined beneath a pair of ruffled white drawers from her thigh downward. Bright-eyed drunk on youthful gaiety, Mourning had escaped completely from the unpleasant happenings of the adult world to a world of make-believe. Gobbling and flapping, she jabbed the feather duster in the twisted knot of hair on top of her head, to make herself a more believable turkey.

At that moment, Anna and Melly declared her quite the largest and the grandest turkey-tom ever, and a prime candidate for the dinner table. Chased between gobbles, by Anna and Melly, Mourning scampered around the kitchen, and running out of places to go, climbed upon the kitchen table. Weak from laughter, Mourning was easy to subdue as her spirited cousins scampered behind her, captured her, and declared joyfully that they were going to lop off her head and serve her for dinner.

Just at that moment, Cad walked in the room, coming in through the back door. His surprised eyebrows elevated and he grinned. "Bless me, there's a bunch of wild Indians on the kitchen table."

"We're not Indians, we're turkeys," Melly chirped.

When Clint came, Mourning was standing in the middle of the kitchen table, her skirts still tucked inside her ruffled drawers, Anna and Melly, on each side, holding her a laughing and gobbling captive while they sang a rhyme from childhood: *Birds of a feather flock together/And so will pigs and swine. Rats and mice will have their choice/And so will I have mine.*

"All right, Mourning, before we serve you with cranberry sauce and dressing, who do you choose?" Melly sang.

"Choose Cad," Anna said, and jumped to the floor, dragging Cad by the sleeve to the table to stand in front of Mourning. Climbing back on the table, Anna said, "Do you think she looks like a turkey?"

"Absolutely," was Cad's answer. "Of course she's a little shy in the drumstick."

Mourning laughed as she was dragged struggling to the end of the table to be prepared for the beheading. Mourning had just assumed the stance of a most terrified turkey while the man who possessed the remarkable knack for encountering her at her most idiotic moments stood leaning against the door jamb, watching her.

Everything began to happen at once; Mourning stood with her turkey feather duster still in place, the morning light catching the contours of her face, just as she glanced around and saw Clint, aloof and in complete control, staring at her.

Anna, following Mourning's strange stare, and seeing Clint, said, "I think we'd better get down."

Clint stepped farther into the room. The only words he spoke were, "Mourning, get down, you look like a blithering idiot," and he strode heavily from the room.

Anna and Melly scampered from the table and Cad lifted Mourning, depositing her on the floor before him. "You can open your eyes and close your mouth, sweetheart, you're on the floor."

Mourning curled her mouth into a little bow. "Oh," was all she said, and no one on this green earth could possibly understand the effort that one word took.

"Mourning," said Cad. "Pay no attention to my brother. He's always like that when he has to entertain that harridan he's been with all morning."

His eyes traveling from one brightly flushed face to the other, he laughed. "I never knew before just how much work went into making jam," he said with a widely curling mouth and eyes dancing with humor. "No wonder it leaves you so exhausted." He pinched the top of one of Mrs. Harper's crusty buns and, finding it to his satisfaction, started to pick it up and received a slap to the wrist by Mrs. Harper, who came clucking into the room. "Those are for lunch, so keep your sticky fingers to yourself," she scolded.

Cad's reply was lost in a bloodcurdling shriek that sounded like something that had escaped from the smoldering pits of hell. No human throat could possibly have emitted that torturous sound. Expecting the absolute worst, they dashed to the front porch and found Eleanor flattened against the wall of the house, screaming hysterically, while Clint came running from the stables.

Cad was first to reach her. "My god! What's happened? Are you hurt?"

"No!" she shrieked. "He's trying to attack me with that dead thing hanging out his mouth. . . . Get him away! Please!" She shrieked again and threw her arms around Cad's neck as everyone looked to see Romeo, a possum dangling from his mouth. It was a cute little possum too: curled body, lax tail, open glazed eyes, and grisly grin.

Anna crashed into the porch swing with a spasm of laughter while Mourning maintained her composure only long enough to call Romeo to her side. He trotted magnificently to her, and dropped the paralyzed possum at her feet as if it were some treasured memorial of a victorious conquest on the field of battle, and then sat back on his haunches, looking exceedingly pleased with himself.

"What in the hell is going on up here now?" Clint thundered as he took the steps in two strides.

Stabbing a finger at Mourning, Eleanor said, "Her stupid dog was attacking me."

Fighting the urge to bite Eleanor's finger of accusation, Mourning glanced at Clint and immediately wished she hadn't.

Clint looked at Mourning with what she thought was no more affection than one would have for a dirty dish mop. "I've told you time and time again to keep these dogs locked up and out of mischief."

"But he only . . ."

"I don't want to hear any lengthy explanations . . . spare me, please," he snapped. "Just put the dogs away, and now!"

Mourning, who had been standing humbly before him blinking her eyes each time he shouted, fought the urge to salute and click her heels. Instead, she yanked Romeo off the porch, almost choking the poor thing in the process. Juliet, who had been hiding under the myrtle bush, flattened herself to pancake proportions and slithered behind them.

When Mrs. Harper had taken the supposedly terrified Eleanor inside and everyone else had vacated the porch, Clint continued to stand there, longing to beat his head against the side of the house until he was out of his misery. But instead of banging his troubles away, he stood there contemplating how a man who had led, heretofore, a simple life, uncluttered with women, had suddenly found himself surrounded by them.

Mourning hid in the kitchen with Anna and Melly, vowing, upon serious consideration, to stay away from Clint, Eleanor, and trouble. She had thought she could bury herself in the kitchen for the rest of the day. It didn't occur to her that Eleanor would seek her out, purposefully trying to flame the antagonism that was flaring between them. Because of that, you could have bowled her over with a feather when Eleanor, dressed magnificently but not for cooking, entered the kitchen with all the pomp and festive display of Cleopatra's grand entrance to Rome.

Now, Mourning was practically raised in the kitchen, and coming from a distinguished southern family, she was taught at an early age the necessity of being well educated in the area of culinary arts. One large part of her education had been to use as much of a slaughtered animal as possible, throwing away only what was absolutely useless. This meant making such delectable dishes as Calves' Head Pudding, Pickled Pigs' Feet, Lamb's Head Fricassee, Sheep's Tongue, Brain Croquettes, and her all-time favorite—the one that could churn even the most cast-iron stomach—Stuffed Shoat's Head.

Stuffed Shoat's Head is just what the name implies; a dish made from the head of a shoat (which is, for the ignorant, the head of a pig under one year old). This revolting creation is prepared, along with the shoat's feet, by the following process, taken straight from Aunt Harriet's cookbook. The head is split through the nose and the bones removed. Then the meat from the feet and liver is chopped and seasoned, and the boneless head is laid open and stuffed with the meat mixture along with the yolks of boiled eggs and bread crumbs. The head is then sewn up and stewed slowly.

If you are lucky enough to survive the procedure, it is then ready to eat with a gravy made of butter, flour, and walnut catsup. It was to this epicurean wonder that Mourning was devoting her afternoon, attempting this disgusting feat solely because Mrs. Harper had stated it was a childhood favorite of hers; but her mother had never taught her how to make it, and so the secret, and the thoroughly nauseous procedure, had been lost to her.

When preparing this gastronomic nightmare it is de rigueur to dress accordingly, and that is why Mourning was wearing a stained and faded gingham dress with an equally worn-out apron. Her hair, which had been neatly braided and coiled on her head earlier in the day, was now losing its anchoring and drifting down to curl and coil tightly to her face and neck. She had repeatedly tucked the bothersome strands back in place until bits of flour stuck to her hair like glue.

The kitchen was unduly steamy and warm, having taken on an odor that was faintly reminiscent of boiled underwear. It was into this palatial dwelling where Mourning toiled, with the most wretchedly persecuted and scowling look upon her face, that the gardenia-scented, regally coiffed, and expensively gowned Eleanor strolled.

Waving her scented handkerchief under her nose, she asked, "Whatever is this disgusting odor? It smells like someone is washing their feet." With a smile that was meant to be charming, she added, while looking at Mourning, "You are wearing shoes, aren't you, sweets?"

Clint stepped into the room, his eyes traveling from Cad to Mourning before he moved to the stove and poured a cup of coffee. Moving to the far end of the table, he dropped gracefully into a chair.

An audience was the last thing Mourning needed, and what Eleanor desired most. Fanning her antagonism with insult, Eleanor spoke with false-hearted charm as she feigned interest in what Mourning was doing.

"Why, don't you look charming . . . just toiling away here in your cozy little kitchen, and all this time I had the false impression that you southern women spent your days swooning."

If Mourning had been predisposed to swooning, she would have gladly succumbed, but being from hardier stock than that, she would have to find another way to right the wrong done when the rug was yanked out from under her dignity. It had heretofore been Mourning's policy to never, never have a battle of wits with an unarmed person, but just this once she relented.

"Oh, yes," she answered sweetly, "here I am just toiling away. Would you like to join me? I have another apron right here." Mourning made a move toward the greasy apron and Eleanor scooted back.

"I've brought my own," she said, producing a clean apron that was daintily embroidered and trimmed with lace; the kind made to impress a man, not to work in.

Eleanor tied the apron around her miniature waist with a bow just beckoning to be untied, and waved her kerchief under her nose once more. "Whatever are you making that smells so dreadful? Surely it's not fit for human consumption."

"Oh, but it is," Mourning replied cheerily. "I am making Stuffed Shoat's Head . . . see!" With brazen boldness, Mourning lifted the head from the steaming kettle, its grotesquely hideous face leering and dripping as if it had just slipped from the murky depths of some slimy bottomless lake.

Cad looked up and laughed. Clint remained silent and brooding, and Mourning made it a point not to look at him.

Eleanor turned a sickly green and shook her head disgustedly.

"Would you like to try some?" Mourning said as innocently as she could manage.

"God, no!" Eleanor said, backing away and holding out her hands as if trying to stop further advancement. "I just came to make Caramel Pecan Buns for Clint. It's not my nature to brag," she bragged, "but he simply adores them, and he just swears that my buns are the best he's ever sunk his teeth into."

"We are speaking about bread, aren't we?" Cad asked, then cast a sympathetic glance toward Mourning.

Instead of feeling comforted by Cad's remark, Mourning felt more alone and confused than ever. Clint, on the other hand, was composed and collected, even giving the appearance of being entertained.

Mourning directed her attention to her cooking, and Eleanor did the same.

"Do you have any more butter?" Eleanor inquired.

"Not here in the kitchen, you'll have to get some from the buttery."

As Eleanor left to get the butter Mourning noticed that Cad and Clint were gone. Not wanting to spend any more time with Eleanor, Mourning removed her apron, hanging it on a hook by the door. As she turned, her eye fell upon the bowl of shells left from the pecans Eleanor had cracked. Mourning gave in to temptation and dumped the bowl of pecan shells into Eleanor's batter. She gave the mixture several swift strokes to conceal the shells and, experiencing a sense of satisfaction, hurried from the room.

Sunset came, the last slanting rays of light lingering pink and golden upon the back porch, where Mourning was drying her hair. She stopped fluffing it with the towel as she watched Cad make his way from the stables toward her. She smiled when he vaulted over the fence instead of going through the gate.

She watched him climb the steps, then swing down, sitting one step above her. He ruffled her hair. "I've seen you looking more cheerful," he observed.

"Believe me, I've felt more cheerful," she said rather glumly.

"So, you and Eleanor had your first little run-in," he said. "It was bound to happen, you know."

"Why do you think that?"

Unbelievable shades of amber and coral hid like sparkling

gemstones in the tangled depths of her hair. He picked up the brush and began to brush it. She closed her eyes.

"Eleanor picked you up as a threat immediately. Ordinarily she's not very nice to women in general, but to one she sees as competition . . ."

"Competition?" Mourning cut in. "How could she possibly see me as competition when all I can do is act like a ridiculous child playing at adult games? You'd think Eleanor, of all people, would see that."

"All Eleanor can see is the way Clint looks at you. I've watched her study him whenever you come within his visual range."

"Cad, do you think I should've bedded him?"

Any other time, talking to any other woman, Cad would have said yes. But this was different—a whole set of deviating considerations—not only were Clint's attitude and behavior toward Mourning different, but Mourning herself was a complete departure from the usual woman Clint kept dangling. Cad put the brush on the steps and took Mourning's chin in his hand. Looking straight into her holly-green eyes, he said, "What I think is not important, but I don't think you've been wrong in not bedding him."

"Do you think I should . . . you know, the next time . . . if there is a next time?"

Cad's eyes were alight with humor. "Oh, there'll be another time, plenty of them. I don't think you can handle being Clint's woman, Mourning. You belong to a different way of life—where there's love and marriage and children. Whatever it is Clint feels for you, it won't be hindered one way or the other by whether you take him to bed or not—unless it's used against him, to force him. Force never works with Clint." He ran a long, tapering finger down the line of her jaw. "By the time this is all over you're going to feel like someone has taken your brain out and played with it."

The sun outlined her with gilt like Italian gold leaf. Looking simply into his eyes, she said, "I already do."

Cad studied her bent head, her trembling hands folded in her lap. "You aren't in love with him, are you?"

"And if I am?"

It was a deceptively gentle question that was loaded to the hilt. He looked at her sitting there watching him, her proud carriage, the look of vain hope in her eyes. He felt a protective anger that wanted to shield her, and at the same time a sense of mounting ire at Clint for nourishing this budding feeling within her. She was young and inexperienced, but Clint knew what he was about. Poor little creature, she deserved more. He glanced back at her, wincing at the trusting, hopeful look on her face. "For your sake, I can only hope you're not. There's not much future in that. You would soon tire of being his temporary amusement."

Wearing a strained smile and trying unsuccessfully to mask her true feelings, she said, "I don't suppose there's much chance of any other type of involvement."

Christ! What was she thinking? Surely not marriage? To Clint? Lord, she was even more innocent than he had thought. Perhaps that was why Clint hadn't bedded her. Maybe this was his way of saving her. Whatever the reason, it obviously hadn't worked. Poor little firebrat, she was in love with Clint and there was no way out of that entanglement except painfully. He wished he could spare her that. "Miracles happen every day, but Clint's falling for and deciding to stay with one woman would be a diamond of the first water."

She had been right. Clint wanted no permanent entanglements, or else she wasn't an entanglement he wanted to be permanent with. She was so confused, she felt caught in a crossfire. She tried to smile, but it was difficult. It seemed as if she had lost her sense of humor along with her heart. The best she could do was give him a thin little smile. "Well, I guess it's a good thing I'm not in love with him, then."

"Yes," Cad answered. "It's a damn good thing you're not."

18

Mourning stood before the carved cherry mirror in her room and cast a long, critical appraisal over her pale lavender dress with softly gathered pleats at the throat and wrists, then retied the grosgrain bows that held the looped braids above each ear. Her frown was one of careful deliberation as she looked at her reflection in the mirror. She regarded herself critically, the fine network of shadows forming under her eyes a product of sleepless nights and too much worry. Next, she considered the more prominent purpling of her left eye—a by-product of Cad's opening the door that belonged to the keyhole that Mourning had been using to spy on Eleanor and Clint.

Life, Mourning began to think, was something she didn't understand at all, and she could only pray that God understood it a little. What fool had said, *You dance your way through life,* when it was all she could do to wrestle her way from one plateau to another? Sadly, Mourning began to imagine her life as a fast-spinning merry-go-round she couldn't slow down enough to get off.

To her, life was like the Chinese proverb *What does not poison, fattens,* and she was acquiring vast amounts of the animated promise of those words—so much, in fact, she had decided what you don't experience, you don't know. Couldn't she just remain ignorant for a while? As Tennyson said: *Others' follies teach us not/Nor much their wisdom teaches;/And most, of sterling worth, is what/Our own experience preaches.* Reflecting on this, Mourning made a discovery that, although not new, was most assuredly new to her:

One arrives at the various stages of life quite a novice. *It's like being forced to play,* she thought, *before you know the rules of the game.* Life is an expensive onion that one peels crying.

Mourning thought back to the conversation she'd heard between Joe and Buck one evening as they sat around the fire, just as she was going to sleep.

"By the time you understand life you're too damn old to do anything with what you just understood. It's like being given a comb when you're bald," Buck had commented.

"Na, life ain't so bad, it's kinda like takin' a piss in the wind—it's all right as long as you go in the same direction," was Joe's reply.

Life was indeed strange. And if life was strange—well, the people that lived it were stranger still. Life's experiences were certainly revealing some pretty weird behavior patterns in a few people she knew—one man in particular. In Clint she saw a man full of potential who approached relationships like static electricity; highly charged and capable of singeing a woman's hair ribbons off with a single kiss, yet not really progressing any further than the sexual-games or the social-ritual stage. Mourning was ready for more. She was tired of her seduction-and-retreat or quarrel-and-reconciliation relationship with Clint. She was primed for a full-blown, all-out romance, and she wasn't getting it. What she was getting was frustrated.

Clint, she knew, had all the answers to all the questions she had about man-woman relationships. He had given her a few brief glimpses, but always slammed the door before she got a good look. Probably the biggest question looming in the vaulted chambers of her mind was, *When am I going to get what Clint's body has been promising?*

The more she considered it, the more resolute she was in her resolve to rekindle the affection that had once existed between herself and Clint. Ever since that morning he caught her making a fool of herself in the kitchen, he had ignored her completely, or looked at her with the same annoyed irritation he would have for termites. She wanted them to be friends again. No, she wanted more than that—much, much more.

Frequently she wished she didn't have to behave with such well-bred courtesy at a time she would rather pelt a boy with mud patties. If Mourning had learned one thing, it was that she got a boy's attention much faster by pelting him with mud patties than she ever had a man's by appropriate and flirtatious behavior.

Mourning cast one last speculative glance at her empurpled eye, dabbed at it twice with the down puff, which she then tossed back into the cut-glass jar, not bothering to close the ornate silver lid. She had more important things to do.

By the time Mourning reached the kitchen, Anna was already there. "Mourning!" she said gaily. "Come and see. Our picnic is going to be scrumptious. Mrs. Harper has fried us a chicken, and there are six raspberry tarts left from last evening."

Before Mourning could reply, Melly walked into the kitchen with a distressfully woebegone expression on her face and sat, with a dejected slump to her shoulders, upon a stool. "You're going to kill me," she announced flatly.

Mourning sighed, pulled the dipper out of the water bucket, and took a drink before asking, "Whatever did you do now?"

"It's not what I did, exactly," said Melly, trying to look contrite, "but rather what I didn't do."

Anna stopped counting watermelon pickles. "And that was?"

"I didn't bring Aunt Caroline's fringed paisley shawl back."

"Back from where? What were you doing with Mother's paisley shawl?" asked Mourning.

"Don't you remember? We used it the other day . . . you know . . . when we buried our treasure trove. We covered the treasure box with Aunt Caroline's paisley shawl so no one would see it. I left it on the table in the cabin." Melly began rummaging through the basket. "What are you packing? Are you going on a picnic? Can I go with you?" When no one answered she glanced at her sister, who was not exactly regarding her with affection, and then at her cousin, who gave a believable imitation of the Grand Inquisitor.

After a series of questions from Mourning, Melly was piqued. "Well, don't look at me like that, we'll just have to go back to the cabin and get it," she said, suddenly in a hurry to leave the war zone.

"And Clint will boil us in oil if he catches us," Mourning replied.

"And Aunt Caroline will do worse if we lose her paisley shawl," Anna added.

Then Mourning said, "Whatever we do, we aren't going to tell

Clint. We'll just have to find a way to leave without arousing his suspicions. If he finds out . . . well, he can be a most vicious and nasty beast at times."

Anna gave Mourning a bracing pat on the arm and said in a quaking voice that she and Melly were not afraid of Clint Kincaid and would stand by her no matter what.

Melly flew off her stool. "I'm afraid of him," she said in a convincing voice. "I'd rather tell Aunt Caroline I lost her paisley shawl than have *him* give me a dressing-down."

"Melly Ragsdale!" Anna snapped. "You mean to stand there with your teeth in your mouth and say you aren't going to help get back the shawl that you lost?"

Melly nodded.

"Ouch!" said Melly, briskly rubbing the spot Anna had just pinched. "I'm glad I lost the shawl and I hope you get caught." She flew from the room.

The picnic was canceled. The next day and a half found Mourning and Anna making every attempt to get away from the house undetected while every avenue they found open was suddenly blocked. They were growing anxious—it was absolutely necessary to get the shawl before Caroline returned. Patience, it seemed, was a virtue of which neither one of them possessed an abundance.

After dinner the next evening, Mourning and Anna were sequestered in the library. Seated on opposite sides of the huge George Washington desk, their golden heads bent in heavy concentration, they wrote furiously, expending finalities of eloquence. The great hall clock chimed eight o'clock. If the cousins heard it, they gave no indication as they continued to send the quill pens scratching busily across the page, reaching the end, only to be drawn back to start again. This fury of activity continued for several more minutes, until Anna, apparently at the end of her thought, stopped her scratching and looked up at Mourning. Noting the sudden silence of Anna's quill, Mourning glanced up.

A knock at the door caused both their heads to jerk around. Quickly they began to shuffle and stack papers. Mourning had just pulled out a narrow side-drawer to stuff the papers into when Clint sauntered into the room, long-limbed and gorgeous, still wearing his chaps, spurs, and gunbelt. Mourning followed the progress of the silver star-shaped rowels on his spurs that made a *ching, ching* sound as he crossed the room. He stopped at the end of the desk and hooked his thumbs in his belt loops, looking rugged and tough.

"You just come from the pasture?" Mourning asked, wondering what he wanted and why he stood there smiling as though he knew something naughty.

"Just this very minute. I'm on my way to clean up."

"You missed dinner. Why were you out so late?"

"The fences were down in the south pasture and half the herd had slipped through, we had to round them up . . . kept at it until seven." His eyes traveled over the desk and then back up at Mourning. "What are you two working on so secretively? Some witches' brew to give Eleanor?"

She had been enjoying his company until he mentioned Eleanor's name. It was such a casual little statement to cause such a strong reaction. Nothing had gone right today. She should have known a day that started out with her putting her underwear on backward would go downhill from there. Mourning bristled. "Eleanor is already a witch," she mocked, "she doesn't need any help from me."

Clint's eyebrow raised and his eyes held a happy glint. "Are we jealous of Eleanor?" The happy glint became an amused twinkle and he chuckled. "Don't get your dander up, imp." He tapped her on the nose before turning to pour himself a drink.

It wasn't humor that surged through her. Furious that he was laughing at her, Mourning jumped to her feet, intending to march from the room. Clint slammed the drink down before it reached his lips. In three short strides he closed the distance between them, his hand reaching down to pick up hers.

"Why don't you and Eleanor try to get along. You might find you have something in common," he said, stroking her fingers lightly.

"And what might that be? You?"

"Among other things."

"Ha!" she managed to get out through the chaos that was erupting between her vocal cords and her speech center. She was too distressed to study his purpose in mentioning Eleanor's name. It was unbelievable—the amount of heat entering her body from his hand—absolutely unbelievable. No, crazy is what it was. She was going crazy. He was already crazy and that was enough. If she joined him, that would make two crazy people in this house. One crazy person in a family was enough. Two crazy people in a family was one too many. Even one crazy person in this family was one too many. She could go crazy thinking about it.

She was getting angrier at him by the minute, so angry that the cluttered passages between her brain and vocal cords cleared. "Eleanor and I couldn't possibly have anything in common . . . we don't even make the same kind of cookies."

For a moment the pure colors of her face dazzled him, an exquisite mixture of gold, rose, and cream that opened like an oyster shell to reveal two priceless emeralds. He studied the smallness of her hand, turning it over, seeing the ink stains. Gazing down at the lovely bit of resistance standing before him, he asked quietly, "Writing?"

"Snooping?" she replied.

He glanced at Anna, who jumped as if she'd been shot. "What mischief are you two up to? Don't tell me you're writing love letters. Anyone I know?"

While Anna blushed bright red and moved to the sofa to fluff pillows, he pressed a moist kiss in the palm of Mourning's hand and then folded her fingers over it, as if she could hold the feeling of his mouth against her hand. Her eyes traversed his face with its skin tanned to saddle-brown by his hours in the sun. His hair was longer now than she had ever seen it—heathenish, and somehow enhancing his virile male rawness. Each second passed like an hour.

His eyes remained locked with hers, and he was unable to draw them away. He felt something inside him being pulled toward her but he resisted the attraction. His eyes glanced toward Anna, who was beating the poor pillows unmercifully. The spell was broken.

"Anna," he said, and she glanced at him.

Clint's look must have struck a responsive chord in Anna, because she jumped, then blurted, "We're writing our Last Will and Testament."

"You two catch something terminal?" he asked, grinning broadly. "I hope it isn't catching."

"For your information," Mourning said blithely, "I'm declining with a lingering affliction."

All trace of humor vanished from Clint's face. His eyes held a warm, intense look. He stepped closer and spoke softly. "And what might that be, buttercup? An affair of the heart?" His clear gray eyes searched hers in that maddeningly inscrutable manner he always seemed to use on her. And then his face took on another expression, one completely new to her, and he looked at her strangely and then said, "Me too, Mourning mine . . . me too." And then he turned and left the room, much in the same manner as he had entered it.

She watched the unbroken rhythmic flow of lean and corded muscle as he took his leave. He was as good-looking from the back as from the front; like a Donatello bronze, he was flawless from any angle, and a thing of matchless beauty to watch. There was a classical calmness to his movement, a calmness laced with an underlying feeling of emotive power. He was like any other man; merely a mass of bone, muscle, and connective tissue, and on any other man this mass was lumped together, scarcely more than a tenement of clay; but on Clinton Kincaid something magical had happened somewhere along the way, producing instead a masterpiece of precise planning. Why was there such a sheer carnality contained in the curving sensuousness of living muscle moving with a tight tenseness, or the action of muscle on bone, the flex of taut buttocks? Why was this one man stamped with such a hallmark of individuality, making all others seem poor imitations?

The door shut behind him with a click, jarring the cousins' minds back from their intensified study of human anatomy, their eyes blinking as if coming out of a trance.

"My goodness!" Anna exclaimed, flushing hotly. "Is that legal?"

"It should be outlawed," Mourning replied sourly, returning to the desk and falling limply into the chair.

Where there's a will there's a way, and the next afternoon the cousins found a way to slip off, undetected.

The cabin lay nestled in the oaks and looked just the way it had when the girls had been there the week before. A blue jay screeched and flew from the treetops, a squirrel darted across their path, as the two figures on horseback made their way down a seldom trod pathway toward the small log cabin. The creek was slow and sluggish at this time of year, green with algae, the top smooth as glass and littered with dandelion pods and stilt-legged water bugs, so light they could walk on its glossy surface.

"You may not care one whit about Clint Kincaid," said one of the pair, "but I know you'll be glad to see the last of Eleanor."

"Did you hear that?" Mourning asked, her breath quickening.

"I didn't hear anything. I think you're just jumpy."

"No. I'm sure I heard a horse. We're in all kinds of hot water, you know, if we get caught this time."

"Well," Anna said optimistically, "we'll just have to take care not to get caught."

They reached the tall stand of stately oaks—ancient, judging from the diameter of their massive trunks—and the twining length of twisted branches—some so low to the ground you could sit on them.

The cabin itself rested at the creek's edge in a small sunlit clearing. The chinks in the logs were sparse; weeds and a sagging front door added to its abandoned, dilapidated look, as well as shutters hanging by a thread. Silvery, silken webs of lacy spider-netting stretched across broken window panes and swayed gently between the rough-hewn posts on the warped and buckled front porch that looked questionable to walk upon.

"I wish we had this closer to the house. Wouldn't it be fun to fix it up? Sort of a second home, a place to stash our wills and such . . . away from snooping eyes," Mourning said, wiping a cobweb away and stepping upon the porch.

"I don't particularly like this place, to tell you the truth . . . it gives me the willies," Anna whispered, following Mourning closely.

They pushed open the door, which creaked eerily, and they were greeted by a dismal silence. Stepping inside, Anna right behind her, Mourning looked cautiously around the solitary room. "Someone has been here."

"What do you mean?" Anna asked while trying to peer over Mourning's shoulder. They crossed the room, stopping at the fireplace, the light filtering through the dirty, broken windows coloring the stones different shades of gray.

"Look," Mourning whispered. "Someone has used the fireplace since we were here last and there are cups on the table."

"I think we should go."

"Stop standing so close to me . . . it's too hot in here for that," Mourning said as she looked around the room. "I don't see the shawl . . . Melly was sure she left it on the table."

"Perhaps whoever laid the fire took the shawl. I think we should go."

"You said that already."

A long, thin shadow stretched over their heads and climbed up the rock wall of the fireplace. "You're right," Mourning whispered without turning around, "we should go."

Apparently Anna neither heard her nor noticed the shadow. "What if they're still here?"

"Yes, what if they're still here?" the shadow repeated, and stepped through the narrow doorway.

The cousins whirled around, each turning in a different direction and then coming together with such force, their breath was knocked out of them with a loud *whooosh!*

"W-wh-who," Mourning croaked, sounding like a tongue-tied owl, and then she tried again. "Who are you?"

"I might be asking the same of you," the shadow answered, stepping closer.

After a hasty introduction of Anna and herself, Mourning felt a harassing necessity to explain why they were there. It was a fault of hers, this fundamental desire to talk the horns off a billy goat when she was nervous . . . and she was nervous.

She glanced again at the man standing before her. He wasn't much taller than she was, but he gave the impression of reaching greater heights. His face was tanned and weathered as if he spent a great deal of time out-of-doors, and his eyes were brilliant blue and piercing, but rather friendly. His nondescript brown hair had none of the reddish highlights present in his full beard.

"Who are you?" she repeated.

"Juan Nepomunceno Cortinas, at your service, but you will want to call me Cheno . . . everyone does."

The cousins could not have been more startled if they had just been introduced to the Emperor Constantine himself. Undaunted by his identity, and not wanting to pass up the opportunity to grill the first *real* celebrity she had ever encountered, Mourning invited him in, which really didn't amount to much, since he was already in, but he did not seem to notice.

Mourning gave him close scrutiny, which seemed to amuse him, and encouraged by the half smile, she set about her questions. "I know who you are," she stated flatly. "You are a bandit like Quantrill and Bloody Bill Anderson."

"I beg to disagree," Cheno said with a warm smile. "Those men are wanton killers, while I am a mere border bandit."

Mourning's mind was whetted; standing before her was a foe worthy to have a battle of wits with, and she searched her mind for all the tidbits about Cheno Cortinas she had stored there. "It was in the paper about you, you killed a man in Brownsville."

Cheno grimaced. "You are a veritable storehouse of misinformation. I shot a man . . . I did not kill him."

"Why?"

"Because it has been entrusted to me to break the chains of slavery."

"You're an abolitionist?"

"Not in the sense of which you are speaking. I am not involved in the question of slavery between black and white, but between Mexican and American."

Mourning made a face. "I didn't know there was a problem of that nature. What kind of trouble are the Mexicans having with the Americans?"

"There seems to exist one set of laws for the Americans and another completely different set for the Mexicans; naturally the laws for the Americans are far less rigorous. The Mexicans are being persecuted, the old Spanish Land Grant families are finding their titles in jeopardy and are losing their lands to courts or crooked lawyers."

"What are you doing here?"

"You are full of questions, aren't you?"

"It's the only way I learn, since no one will ever volunteer anything to me."

"I am here because of the shooting incident in Brownsville that you so charmingly referred to a moment ago." He began to move around the small cabin, building a fire, putting a pot of water on to boil for coffee. He motioned the girls to the table and they sat down, arranging their skirts modestly about them. He was friendly, but he was still a bandit—and a man.

"Who was the man you shot?" Mourning asked.

"Robert Shears, the sheriff of Brownsville, and I might add, a very wicked man."

Mourning whistled. "Boy, when you get into trouble, you do it up proud. Shooting a sheriff is no laughing matter. I bet you feel like you just grabbed a bobcat by the tail."

"Very aptly put," he said, laughing.

"Why did you shoot the sheriff?"

"I live on my mother's ranch, the Santa Rita, just outside Brownsville. I ride into town daily for my morning coffee. Two weeks ago the sheriff arrested a Mexican for drunkenness, but then brutalized him viciously. The man had been a former servant at our ranch and I intervened, mildly at first, I might add."

"What happened then?" Anna asked, finally overcoming her desire to run or faint.

Cheno looked at her as if he were surprised she could talk. "The sheriff began to scream insults at me and I shot him in the shoulder and put the Mexican behind me and galloped out of town."

"So what are you doing here . . . hiding?" Mourning asked, giving him an inquisitive but charming smile.

Cheno poured the coffee, which looked more like blackstrap molasses than coffee, and placed a cup before the cousins. Thinking he might find it an insult if they didn't drink it, and knowing what he did to people who insulted him, they drank the bitter, foul-tasting brew. He took a long, thoughtful sip of coffee before answering her question. "Partly hiding, partly gathering men, supplies, money."

"Why do you need money? The paper said you were rich," said Mourning.

"Any money I have access to is in Brownsville, and I can't go back there until I have men and supplies to back me up, and men and supplies take money."

"How are you going to gather money from Americans when you are fighting against them?" Mourning inquired.

Cheno grinned a knowing grin. "That, my inquisitive little *gatito,* is one question I will not answer. Suffice it to say, a plan has just been dumped in my lap." He placed Caroline's paisley shawl in her hands, and then advised them to leave, saying nothing of his presence once they reached the big house. Sworn to secrecy, no two government spies could have made a more cryptic departure.

19

An ounce of prevention is better than a pound of cure, or so Mourning had always been taught by Grandmother Howard, who put a great deal of faith in sententious sayings—being a veritable walking collection of admonitions herself. Grandmother Howard also had another proverb that applied to her grandaughter's aptitude for doing everything the hard way: *Nothing worth learning can be taught.* Applied to Mourning, this translated: *Experience is the best teacher.* In that sense, Mourning was a well-educated woman, having gained the majority of her experience from that old and well-established institute of learning, the School of Hard Knocks. It was fortunate for Mourning, indeed, that at times she possessed unparalleled finesse in adroitly finding her way out of an entanglement as easily as she managed to become ensnared in the first place.

And so, having cleverly slipped from the house without attracting Clint's attention, and having successfully located her mother's paisley shawl, not to mention skillfully maneuvering their persons away from a notorious border bandit, she was led to her eventual discovery of the truthfulness of yet another proverb: *Every solution breeds new problems*, which is nothing more than a corollary to the fact: *If anything can go wrong, it will.* Unfortunately, this had a tendency to be the rule, rather than the exception in whatever endeavor Mourning undertook. With the addition of Cousin Anna, things had the inclination to go from bad to worse.

It was not by pure, unadulterated malice that the cousins found themselves out after dark, but rather due to a series of unsolicited misadventures, which all their misadventures were, in their opinion. Grandmother Howard would have said this was confirmation that whenever you set out to do something, something else must be done first.

Reaching the clearing where they had left the horses, the cousins were astounded to find the horses gone. How, Mourning wondered as she stood with a quizzical look on her face, could anyone misplace anything as large as two horses?

Admitting to herself they had been negligent in leaving the geldings untied, Mourning had no idea that one hasty oversight would extract such payment. Over two hours had elapsed before they located the two geldings in a narrow, dry creek bed. There is a proverb for this also: *Everything takes longer than you think.*

Owing to this unscheduled turn of events, evening was upon them by the time they located the grazing horses. Unable to find their way in the failing light, Mourning remembered Clint had once told her, *A horse, fortunately, has more sense than its rider. Given his head, your mount can locate water and find his way home.* They gave the horses their heads. The full moon was out, dipping and dodging in and out of clouds, casting eerie purple shadows with groping forms across their way.

"Mourning?"

"What?"

"You scared?"

"A little."

"Good." Anna, like misery, loved company.

It was a damp night, where a heavy mist curled like long, bony fingers between the tree trunks, keeping low to the ground as it threaded its way across the unfamiliar terrain like slow-flowing lava. There was something strange about this night, something Mourning couldn't quite put her finger on, but some sense of dread filled her with an anxious restlessness. The horses sensed it too, and began to sidestep, nervously tossing their heads, snorting frequently. It came to her abruptly, the reason for her unrest. Silence. Hanging like an oppressive curtain all about them was complete silence. There were no sounds, no noisy night-creatures, no rustling, no scampering—nothing but dead, disquieting silence. *Think, Mourning Kathleen, think,* Mourning reminded herself. *Did Clint teach you anything about this? A sign,* he had said, *animal sounds can be a sign. When danger approaches, animals have*

enough sense to lie low and remain quiet. If you don't hear them,
Mourning, rest assured something is wrong. Dead wrong. Did he
have to use the word *dead*?

Further rumination was cut short when the foreboding quiet
was shattered by a snarling scream that rent the darkness, rising up
from the denseness ahead, getting louder and louder, rolling from a
snarling crescendo to a pitch of fiendish savagery, then riding away
on the wind, drifting across the valley with the heavy mist. Instantly, the horses were in a frenzy, rearing and pawing the air,
fighting against the tightly checked reins that restrained them. The
scream died away and the horses, although uneasy, continued to
pick their way through the tension-riddled darkness. The paroxysm of gripping fear returned when the shriek came again, closer
this time, followed by a low, guttural snarl that vibrated through
the night, ending with a husky rattle.

"Mourning," Anna whispered with nervous dryness, "what's
that?"

That, Mourning knew, was no screech owl. Relying on the
information Clint had given her, she said, "I don't know, it could
be a bobcat . . . a very *big* bobcat," she added, vowing if she got
out of this alive, she'd stick so close to home, they would hang
shingles on her.

Bitterly repenting her rebellious folly, Mourning promised if
God would deliver her from yet one more mess, she would try to
think twice before jumping into her next scrape. It was an interrupted prayer—a low, coughing growl froze the current of her
blood. Slowly she slid the .44 Henry from the saddle holster, laying
it across her legs, and sent a quick message of gratitude for Clint
Kincaid and his foresight in teaching her how to use it. For once in
her life she was actually glad Kincaid hadn't always treated her
like a lady, for no lady she knew could even identify a .44 Henry,
much less load and fire one.

The horses stopped abruptly, dancing nervously, refusing to
go farther. And then she saw it, illuminated in the moonlight, the
silvered feral shape of something huge, crouched on a thick, jutting
branch not fifteen feet away. This was no bobcat. It was much too
large; from the way Clint had described them, this could only be a
mountain lion. Anna saw it too, and whimpered, "Oh, God,
Mourning."

The bulk moved, soundlessly, going farther out on the branch, and paused, tense and alert; crouched and waiting for the urging of primal instinct. The horses went wild, rearing and pawing, fighting frantically against any restraint. In the confusion Anna's mount gained enough slack to get the bit between his teeth and bolt. Mourning's gelding tried to follow, rearing with such terrified vigor, he fell over backward, hurling Mourning against the trunk of a tree. She felt her back slam against the twisted and wrinkled trunk, the bark's abrasive roughness scraping and clawing as she slid down its length. The ill-fated gelding rolled and twisted on the ground, struggling to his feet as a rasping scream split the oppressive silence. The crouching bulk sprang from the tree, claws spread wide, long, yellowed fangs glistening with prophetic significance. The tawny cat hit the terrified gelding, who screamed shrilly and jackknifed, throwing them both to the ground. By some strange twist of luck, the gelding broke loose and started to run. But the cougar was quick. Too quick. The huge cat followed, crouched low to the ground, moving with great speed. It leaped again . . . the horse went down.

Once again the silence was shattered by a terrified scream from her gelding. Mourning had been around horses all her life, but she had never heard one scream like that. It was a scream that mirrored the horrors of perdition, coming shrill and violent from an anguished throat and cutting through the night, rolling on the mist, across ravines and pastures, through wooded areas, and finally dying away in the hills beyond.

The gelding was up now, the bulk clinging to his back. The moon drifted from behind the clouds, full and bright, and she could see it clearly now—a cougar, huge, with slitted yellow eyes, his knotted shoulder muscles and razor-sharp claws tearing chunks of flesh, his fangs sinking into the blood-soaked withers of the gelding. The gelding was in a frenzy now, bucking and pitching, slinging droplets of blood like fine buckshot, peppering everything around. Mourning felt the warm, life-sustaining fluid splatter across her face and arms, and she watched in a trance as the gelding, screaming and pawing the air wildly, was unable to unseat the beast that rode him to his death. He went down, and it came quickly, the moment of death, when razor-sharp fangs sank into that vital point, perforating the jugular, severing it with one fatal bite, the gelding's final scream bubbling to the surface on a torrent of blood; and then he was still. The struggle was over.

It grew quiet then, and the huge cat continued his death-lock hold on the throat of the gelding; and then, with a growling snarl the mighty cat released his prey. Aroused by the taste of blood, he paced back and forth, hissing and snarling and circling the butchered horse. Mourning knew she didn't have much time before the cat turned on her, and she searched the grass-covered ground for the Henry. She must have done something right in her life, for her hand had no more than closed over the stock of the rifle when she heard the low, vibrating growl of the yellow demon.

The bloody carcass of the gelding lay between them, blood still pouring from a dozen wounds as the cat sat back on his haunches and pawed the air, swatting at her as he spit and hissed his warning. His yellowish eyes were slitted with hate, the smell of blood in his nose, the taste of death on his tongue. He rose up, out of his sitting position, his front paws alternately pressing the torn grass as he crouched, his tail lashing and whipping behind him.

As the cougar sprang, clumps of grass and dirt showered the brush behind him from the powerful thrust of his hindquarters.

She raised the rifle, remembering everything Clint had taught her, hearing it so clearly, as if he were standing beside her. With a calmness that would later surprise her, she fired.

The cat screamed but did not stop, and for a moment she thought she had missed; but then it turned a somersault in midair and hit the ground a few feet from her and rolled into a tight coil, flipped over, and jumped at least five feet in the air, twisting like a fish trying to throw a hook. Hissing and snarling, the cat landed on his feet again, staring at her with renewed hatred, his eyes narrow and yellow-green, his tail lashing at the darkness.

Clint and Hank had spent many nights around the campfire telling her unbelievable stories about the stamina and endurance of the cougar, stories of the remarkable vitality of this mountain lion, and how it could be fatally wounded, bleeding from several bullet holes, and still find the extraordinary strength to attack again. She had never believed the stories of course; they were simply tall tales, tales men told around campfires for entertainment. But now . . . Oh, God, now she believed . . . she believed.

For a moment she panicked. *Oh, God, Clint, I need you now. Where are you?* The thoughts were not cold when she felt his presence, heard his soothing words instructing her. *Don't panic. Stay calm. Breathe deep. Aim and fire as if it's the only shot you'll have.*

*Don't think about anything else. Take careful aim, buttercup, and
remember I'm right behind you. Draw a good bead, squeeze the
trigger slowly.* The blast from the Henry startled her. Had she
fired?

The cat jolted, but did not go down, only continued to look at
her through narrow, hate-filled eyes. She could see the blood gushing from the mortal wounds, its sickly sweet smell cloying at her
nostrils, and she felt a wave of nausea pass over her. The smell of
death hung heavy in the air as the cat continued to stare at her, his
scream turning to a bloody gurgle in his throat, his tail still lashing
and whipping behind him. His scarlet body glistened in the moonlight as a shudder ran through him. Still he would not fall, but
started toward her, taking three steps before another shudder rippled through him and he fell. This time he did not get up.

There was a loud buzzing in her ears; she suddenly felt
weightless.

When she came to, a blurry form huddled over her and she
heard the anguish in her cousin's voice as she sobbed, "Mourning,
don't be dead . . . please don't be dead."

"I'm all right," she whispered, accepting Anna's help to rise
to her feet.

"Come on, let's get out of here, my horse is tied just down the
draw."

Mourning stared at the grisly scene as they passed by, the
huge cat still frightening, even in death.

They rode in silence, staring ahead numbly, seeing nothing
and trusting the gelding to take them home. The mist was heavier
now, rising higher to envelop the tall trees, casting an iridescent
glow around the moon, bathing everything in a heavy dew that
clung in fat droplets and glistened against their clothing and hair
like sparkling brilliants. They topped the crest of the hill overlooking Citadel and did not pause, but rode straight to the house.

They slipped into the kitchen and out into the hallway, pausing to listen for sounds. Hearing none, they removed their boots
and quietly tiptoed down the hall to the stairwell. "You go up first,
and I'll be right behind you," Anna whispered, "just in case you
get dizzy."

Mourning nodded, too tired and drained to argue. The stairs
creaked twice during their ascent, and when they reached the top,

they paused momentarily to listen. Hearing no sounds, they slipped silently by Clint's room.

When they had ridden down the hill overlooking Citadel, the house appeared dark; yet now, as they slipped past Clint's door, a faint light spilled out from under his door into the hallway. They hurried on by, stopping at Mourning's door.

Mourning turned to Anna. "I can't believe after all that's happened, no one saw us."

"There is no need to fasten a bell to a fool." The voice came from the darkness. Two startled gasps broke the silence, followed by two pairs of boots hitting the floor with a thud.

"I can explain," Mourning croaked miserably.

"A talent you've polished to perfection, no doubt." Clint's words were chilled and devoid of emotion. Cad stood beside him looking concerned.

"We were in the barn with the dogs," Mourning offered, praying he would spare them the discomfort of challenging their flimsy excuse.

"A good and believable story, except I was in the barn not twenty minutes ago . . . looking for you, I might add." She felt the soft caress of his hand brushing her cheek and then lifting a curl from her shoulder. "And the lingering dampness that permeates your hair . . . what of that?"

"I'm getting awfully tired of this constant and harassing necessity for explanations every time I move. But, if it will satisfy you, we took the dogs hunting," she offered, a little awkwardly and with deep guilt. "We went farther than we realized and it was quite dark before we started back." Her words seemed to roll off him like water on a duck's back. The darkness prevented her from seeing more than just the faint outline of his face. The silence was extended to ridiculous proportions, and she began to feel the stinging pain of the scrapes to her back. She was tired, her nerves were frayed, and she wanted to go to bed.

"Sometimes I think you're blinded by the brilliance of your own imagination, Mourning. A lie comes so easily to those lovely lips of yours . . . do you find yourself actually believing your own prevarications?"

She stood there, in the temper-charged atmosphere, cudgeling her brains for some retort, something clever to say, and when no inspiration came, she seriously contemplated becoming a nun. "I'm

tired and would like to go to bed. I see no reason to stand out here
and beleaguer the issue with you further. I told you we took the
dogs hunting; if that doesn't suffice, then I . . ."

"It would, sweetheart . . . except the dogs have been with me
all evening." Cursing the impotence of her mind, she stood
before him, pathetically, like a butterfly caught in a glass jar—alive
but hopelessly trapped.

"You were left in charge of the ranch, not me. I don't owe you
any explanations of my whereabouts. I am home and safe, that
should be the end of your concern. I'm not a child."

"Unfortunately, there's no proof of that," he said glibly. "I
am responsible for you, whether you like it or not, and until you
show some sign of being something besides a fool who constantly
places her life in peril, I shall continue to monitor your coming and
going." She heard his sigh of exasperation, and could see, in her
mind's eye, his beautiful hands running through his silky hair as he
always did when he was frustrated.

"What do you want me to do?" she said, choking back the sob
that had been dwelling in the back of her throat and seemed to be
growing larger and larger with each breath she drew. She was
trembling now, her ordeal with the cat still holding her in its grip
as surely as if the big cat himself had suddenly sprung, swift and
noiselessly, back to life. She had completely forgotten about Anna
quaking in the shadows behind her, nor was she aware that Cad
was there until he spoke.

"Clint, why don't you let them go to bed and hash this out in
the morning?"

There was a long, penetrating silence and then Clint sighed
deeply. "All right. Cad, you take that other miscreant who appears
to be speechless as well as mindless and see that she goes straight
to her room and stays there . . . even if you have to crawl in the
damn bed with her."

There was a startled gasp, and the whispering rustle of skirts,
and on the shadow of that came the hurried tread of departing feet
scampering down the hallway as Anna fled to her room. Her hasty
steps were interspersed with the smooth, rhythmic thump of
heavier boots as Cad followed her. A door opened, and voices
spoke softly. Glancing toward the sound, Mourning could see the
silhouetted outline of Cad and Anna as they talked briefly, then
disappeared into her room and closed the door behind them.

Ordinarily Mourning would have dashed to her cousin's defense, determined to save her virtue at all costs, but tonight she had problems of her own, and they were looming threateningly before her in human form.

The pain in her back was becoming more intense now, and the world began to shift and move, or was it she? Her hand slipped from the folds of her skirt and pressed against Clint's chest for support as the churning in her stomach began to rise.

"Don't think your provincial attempts at seduction will get you out of this predicament. Although I am surprised that after spending half the night with your lover, you would still seek another's company . . . but then, that is the beauty of the female body; to be aroused to its zenith again and again."

Even if Mourning had been feeling up to snuff, she would not have had the faintest idea what Clint was talking about, and on this particular night she didn't even care. Unfortunately, Clint mistook her silence for guilt.

A hand closed around her arm and she lowered her forehead against the firm, consoling warmth of Clint's chest. "You're chilled," he said. How could she be chilled when she was burning up, she wondered, as her teeth began to chatter.

"There is nothing to be gained by standing out here all night. I swear, Mourning, if you had a brain, you'd take it out and play with it," he said unkindly. "What kind of man would allow you to traipse around the damn countryside in this dampness for half the night? And what crackbrained woman would want to?"

"There were no men . . . we were alone."

She barely had the strength to stand up, and as another shiver racked her body, she leaned against him once more. "Please," she croaked pitifully.

"Ah! Are you so eager for it, then?" He placed one hand behind her elbow and pushed her bedroom door open with the other. "Come, then, sweetheart. God knows how long I've been wanting to do this . . . and didn't."

She must have moved, for suddenly she was in her room, and heard the door snap behind her as the bolt was rammed home. The room was no lighter than the hallway, and she could barely make out his silhouette as he turned toward her, his hands sliding with familiar ease across her body and moving to the row of buttons down her bodice.

"Please, Clint."

"I hope to please you, sweet . . . at least I promise to do my damnedest."

"Clint, please help me," she sobbed, and slumped against him. "Please," she whispered brokenly, "don't be angry with me . . . I can't take any more tonight . . . I can't . . . I can't." Her body shook with a violent trembling, passing directly to a hysterical fit of dry sobbing.

Suddenly she was absorbed into the comforting warmth against his chest as his hands gripped her upper arms and pulled her against him. She felt her insides twist with love, and tears sprang forth. "Oh, Clint," she sobbed, and slipped her arms around his waist, holding on for dear life.

"My God! Something terrible must've happened to you tonight . . . what was it? Tell me who the son of a bitch was . . . by God, I'll kill him!"

Her reply was a sobbing, confused murmur of strange and wild, almost foreign-sounding words he couldn't understand, but her agonized cry was something he could fully comprehend. He had never seen a woman so distressed with unmanageable fear . . . distressed to the point of emotional excess. He buried his face in the crook between her neck and shoulder and kissed her gently, murmuring soft and gentle words as he slipped his hands around her.

She jerked and whimpered with pain.

He froze.

"Your back is soaking wet."

He moved away from her and she heard the strike of a match, a red glow illuminating the sharp angles of his face as he lit the kerosene lamp beside her bed. And then he turned toward her.

"Jesus H. Christ!" he said, his eyes searching her blood-splattered clothing and face. Suddenly Clint was at her side; the hands that moments ago had caressed her body seductively now searched it frantically, seeking the source of all the blood.

"Mourning, what happened?" His tone was gentle and concerned, and all she wanted to do was cry.

"Turn around, and let me see your back." She half turned, half stumbled, and then heard Clint draw in his breath sharply. His explosive outburst bounced off the walls.

"Son of a bitch! You look like you've been dragged through

half the countryside on your backside." She felt him lead her across the room to her bed.

"Lie down on your stomach and let me see to your back."

"Don't you think Mrs. Harper . . ."

"Mrs. Harper, my ass! That woman would spend the first hour asking questions."

Mourning was in no condition to argue and she obeyed without another word. He split the back of her camisole with a loud rip, then uttered another one of his famous imprecations before commanding, "Lie still," and then he was gone.

She didn't hear him return, but felt his fingers touching her back. "Keep wiggling," he said stiffly, "and I'll give you a bruise on that chin that'll keep you asleep for a while." He touched her back again. "Why are you squirming so? I haven't touched your cuts yet."

"No, but you've ripped my clothes off!"

"Good godamercy! I'm looking at your back, for chrissake! Besides, you don't have a damn thing I haven't seen. At least a million times."

"Well," she said with an angered huff, "you may have seen a million naked bodies, but I haven't had mine looked at once! Kincaid, what are you doing?"

"Lie still, dammit! I'm trying to clean the dirt out of these wounds so they don't get infected. What in the name of hell did you run into . . . or what ran into you?"

"A tree."

"A . . . no, never mind, I'm not going to get into that right now. Just lie quietly."

Clint finished tying the cloth strips in place, and then dropped the clean gown over her head. When he had tucked her in, he sat beside her and took her hand in his. "Are you sure you can lie on your side like that? Wouldn't your stomach be better?"

"This is fine."

"Do you want some more brandy?"

"No. I'm pie-eyed now."

He cocked a brow, but said nothing. "Now, I want to hear . . . from the beginning, exactly what happened."

She told him everything—well, almost everything, leaving out only the small part about Cheno Cortinas. After all, they had promised not to tell a soul. When she reached the part about the cat springing from the tree, Clint stopped her.

"What did you say?" he said doubtfully, looking at her as if she'd just won first prize in a liars' contest.

"You don't have to look at me like I'd just eaten a bowl of worms!" she snapped. "I said a huge . . . gigantic . . . enormous cat sprang from a tree and killed my gelding and I shot him." He still looked at her as if she had straw for brains. "Kincaid," she said with obvious irritation, "you do understand the word *cat,* don't you? Like fangs? Long claws? Growling and spitting?" When that didn't seem to register, she sat up in the bed, looking at him. "Why can't you understand what I'm trying to tell you? I'm talking about punctured jugular veins, and blood, and dead . . . D . . . E . . . A . . . D, like departed, gone, deceased, finished!"

She would have gone on, because she was wound up tighter than an eight-day clock, but she glanced up at him and saw the amusement tugging at the corners of his mouth. Inevitably, he threw back his head and gave a shout of laughter.

When the laughter died away, he began to look at her strangely. His eyes burned like glowing coals, scorching her skin wherever they touched. Was it his voice that was heavy, making her feel stupid and groggy, or was it the brandy? He was hypnotizing her with his narcotic voice, and shivers ran across her belly, her heartbeat approaching impossible speed.

"I'm going to kiss you, Mourning Howard," he said softly. "You know that, don't you?" Clint watched her mouth tremble, her tongue nervously wet her lips, as she nodded her head slowly.

He lifted his hand to her face, gently pushing her hair back, then lightly, gently, he trailed one finger down the bridge of her nose, down to her lips, where he paused, feeling the soft flutter of her breath, watching the slight flaring of her nostrils, the dilated eyes.

The tip of his finger followed the line of her mouth, stroking, teasing, driving her pulse to a frenzied rate beneath her white cotton gown. She studied intently the face above her, the dark eyebrows, the ring of black that separated the gray iris from the wintry part of his eye.

Then she felt his hands slide from her face, down over the bodice of her nightgown, until she arched her throat and threw his heart into confusion. His thumbs began to stroke the line of her jaw, his first kiss following the flutter in her throat down to the moist V between her breasts.

He slowly kissed his way back across the line of her shoulder, his breath rapid and hot in her ear when he took the tip of her lobe between his teeth. His touch exploded within her, leaving her so fragmented, she would never find all the pieces. Just when she was chasing her scattered thoughts he lowered his demanding mouth across hers and his tongue entered hungrily.

It was a slow, lazy kiss, the kind that penetrated and probed and explored, and she had never dreamed anyone could do such wonderful, magical things with his mouth. It was a peaceful, relaxing kiss—one that caught her completely off guard by its subtlety, rendering her powerless and stunned. It was a delicate, elusive kiss in which his tongue teased and flirted with hers, cunning and skillful, penetrating deeply and so thoroughly that when he finished, she had little doubt that she had just been exhaustively and painstakingly kissed. In all respects it was the kiss of a man who should be awarded an academic degree for proficient skill and mastery.

With a sigh she relaxed completely and went limp, thinking what a kisser he was.

It began like the low moving rumble of thunder rolling over the hills in the distance, gaining momentum until it spilled forth with the sharp loudness of a clap of thunder, jerking her from her euphoric state. She frowned, thinking he picked the strangest times to laugh, just when he had kissed her into oblivion.

"So, I'm a good kisser, am I?" He looked down into her shadowed face with its closed, tightly squeezed eyes, her determined little chin, the look of absolute mortification on her face.

Her heart turned a flip. "I don't know what you're talking about." Embarrassment burned in her heart that she could possibly have uttered those words aloud, and she felt the need to look away. He stopped her, splaying his fingers on each side of her face, his thumbs wiping away the tears of shame that collected in pools below her eyes. She squeezed her eyes like a child, hoping to shut him out.

"Come on, admit it. You liked my kisses." He laughed heartily, enjoying her immensely, as he so often found himself doing. He watched her determined little face. She didn't like to be caught at anything; it rubbed her fur the wrong way to be bested, to be placed in a vulnerable position. He knew what her next move would be. She would huff and spit at him, drawing his attention away from what she had said, like a mama quail distracting a predator from her babies. And if he persisted in reminding her of her words, she would swell up like a toad, refusing to talk at all. He was learning. He had all her little defenses mapped out, knowing her vulnerable places and her weakness. She was like an ostrich, craning her neck to peek at life, but thrusting her head in the sand the minute it got uncomfortably close.

"I don't like anything about you, especially your kisses."

His brows shot up and a lazy, insolent smile crept across his face, going all the way up to his eyes, and then he started to laugh.

"Oh, you . . . you . . . you make me so mad!" she stammered. "You are so smug, thinking you are the last word just because you know how to kiss! Well, let me tell you something. It's nothing to brag about. Anyone can learn with enough practice . . . even a baboon!"

"Come on," he teased, "show me. Show me how you'd teach a baboon how to kiss." He was grinning widely now, ready to come back at her when she wound up and smacked him, a misaimed blow he feinted expertly, and then nailed her in a viselike grip.

"Gotcha now!" His smile was wicked, his hands getting dangerously close to places they had no right being, his breath fanning the wisps of hair against her throat. She battled him, pushing and twisting until he saw her grimace of pain.

"Why are you doing this to me?" she choked.

Watching the mercurial expressive face before him change, the answer hit him like the slap of a cold mackerel across the face. He knew instantly why he'd done it. He'd been furious over her blatant refusal to obey him, choosing instead to ride off unprotected, nearly getting herself killed. But still, that wasn't it. He was jealous of the smooth, trusting friendship she had formed with his brother. He had never made her bubble and laugh the way Cad did, nor could he hug or kiss her affectionately without her freezing up, but Cad could. A strange sensation fluttered through his loins, and he knew the overpowering urge to mate—not just to lie with her in the carnal sense, but to mate, to give her a child.

She felt the soft change in him. When he rose and turned down the lantern, she watched him.

"I'll leave the lantern low and both our doors open. If you need anything, just call out." He stood there, just above her, looking down at her with dark eyes, his hair ruffled, the look on his face open and vulnerable. He appeared strangely warm and softly beautiful to her, standing there in the golden bath of lamplight. It made her want to take him against her and hold him.

He leaned forward and softly stroked her face.

"Angel-eyes, I think you just learned a valuable lesson tonight."

Flustered, she could only mutter, "Which was?"

"Mother Nature is a real bitch!"

20

It was no great surprise to Mourning that the morning following the most trying day of her life was the day her mother and John picked to return to Citadel, riding into the yard just as Clint and Cad were leaving to locate the dead horse and cougar. John decided to go with them, and Caroline, upon discovering neither girl was seriously hurt, gave them a caustic scolding strong enough to remove varnish, and then assigned a sufficient number of chores to keep them occupied until they were at least thirty-five. Melly, who was innocent of any wrongdoing, except for the grossly overlooked fact that she was the one who left the paisley shawl in the first place, was allowed to go outside and play, while the confidante of bandits and slayer of cougars had been banished, along with her cohort and second in command, to the library, to give it a thorough cleaning. Armed to the teeth with every cleaning device known to man, from Indexical Silver Soap to hartshorn, the cousins laid siege to the room, determined to leave no stone unturned as they vigorously attacked with mops, brooms, and feather dusters.

All was progressing rather nicely; book bindings were relieved of their dust, the pewter lamps gleamed, and the desk had been waxed to a mirror shine. The fireplace was swept and its fender polished, with at least one full hour being devoted to the coils and frills of the peacock screen. Next, they led a full armored charge against the leaded windows, removing every trace of grime, magically transferring most of it to their white aprons. Not content to stop there, they trotted outdoors to clean the other side, stopping by the kitchen on the return trip.

As they filed through, Mrs. Harper was making gingersnaps, and the aromatic pungency of the ginger combining with the sweet smell of molasses was more than two ordinary girls could ignore, and these particular girls, not being in the least ordinary, had to stop. On cue, they went into action. "Mrs. Harper," Mourning chirped, "my hair seems to be caught on my button, could you loosen it, please?"

She turned around so Mrs. Harper could get at it while Anna stuffed gingersnaps into her apron pockets. Now, this action was not completely necessary, for Mrs. Harper was a generous soul, and finding immeasurable delight in every scrape the girls got themselves into, she would have given them the entire pan of cookies if they had but asked. But of course that would have taken all the fun out of it, and any fool knows, cookies given freely, in no shape, form, or fashion, remotely compare with the delicious tantalizing flavor of snitched ones. "I don't see anything," Mrs. Harper replied, checking each button. "Perhaps it's come loose of its own accord."

Mourning moved her head from side to side, checking. "I guess so, I don't feel it anymore. Thank you," she said, dimpling sweetly and giving her a peck on the cheek. Mrs. Harper clucked in disapproval as she looked down at the cookie sheet, eyeing the empty spaces as Mourning and Anna gave her a quick curtsy and some fancy footwork before they shot through the door.

Giggling, the cousins burst into the library like two popped corks as the china shepherdess clock on the mantel chimed. With a sigh of counterfeit fatigue they fell back against the velveteen horsehair sofa, with its slightly sagging springs, for a short rest, Anna producing six slightly misshapen gingersnaps.

Nibbling between snatches of conversation, they did not pay much attention to the approaching footsteps until it was too late and Clint stepped into the room. Mourning had a mouthful of cookie and had just picked up another when Clint walked in, so for lack of a better solution she shoved the entire cookie, which was rather large, into her already stuffed mouth, looking like a squirrel with his entire winter hoard crammed between his jaws.

Clint walked to the immaculate desk, which had been swept clean of all papers, ledgers, pens, and the like, and stopped. Glancing over the spotlessly clean surface and not seeing what he sought, he turned. "I'm looking for a bill of sale for . . ." He paused in mid-sentence to stare at Mourning.

The object of his astonished gaze was frantically trying to rearrange the wadded lump of gingersnap so she could speak. Regrettably, the gummy glob was cemented between her teeth and her jaws, causing them to protrude conspicuously.

"My God," he said suddenly, "don't tell me you've taken up chewing tobacco."

Clint sat on the corner of the desk, his interested gaze falling upon the indignant face of the owner of the grotesquely swelled jaws as he crossed his arms and patiently waited.

Mourning worked frantically—chewing, pressing, poking, shoving . . . trying every clever trick to dislodge the gooey mass. She tried to flatten it against the roof of her mouth, but it began to slip down the back of her throat, almost gagging her. Afraid she was on the verge of strangulation, or worse, she applied suction. That worked like a charm, only when the sticky agglomeration decided to pull loose, it did so with a loud *slurp,* sounding like an old pair of galoshes being laboriously extracted from mud.

At last, near the point of tears and embarrassed to the point of self-destruction, Mourning squeezed her eyes tightly and swallowed. The glutinous clump, with the texture and consistency of a monstrous lump of unrisen dough, sank like a ten-pound lead weight and lay heavily in her stomach.

"Anna, why don't you get a glass of water for Mourning?"

Mourning sprang to her feet, humiliated beyond belief, desiring nothing more than to put as much distance between herself and Clint as possible.

Extending a hand to detain her, Clint drew her against his chest and she turned her head away, too ashamed to look at him. Tucking her head under his chin, Mourning slid her hands inside his jacket, her fingers gliding over the starchy smoothness of his shirt. Her tactile sense told her his muscles leapt reflexively, and somewhere behind the veil of withdrawal she had draped around herself, her woman's instinct told her that she struck a responsive chord within him. Any other time, that would have brought a flickering flame of pleasure leaping inside her, but too overpowering was the abject wretchedness within her crushed spirit to respond.

His shirt was cool against her heated face, the pressure of his warm hands stroking and comforting her soothed her blistered emotions like a balm. She felt a sob collecting at the back of her throat and brought the back of her hand against her mouth to prevent its leaving.

"Mourning, Mourning," he said, pressing a kiss against the fragrantly coiled braids on top of her head. "Whatever am I going to do with you?"

"I know," she sniffed, "it's utterly hopeless . . . I'll never be normal, and I want so much to be normal, and I try . . . . I really do, but . . ." She couldn't go on, and she looked despairingly at him.

She presented such a rueful face that he smiled with tender understanding and pressed a healing kiss against her smooth plaits. "Shh, buttercup. Don't cry, sweetheart. You are normal"—he grinned widely— "a little strange perhaps, but normal nevertheless . . . refreshingly so."

"I know I'm *normal,*" she said, her voice tinged with anxious confusion, "but I'm not *normal* normal."

He pushed her away from him and lifted her chin, gazing down into her upturned face, and placed a kiss against her red nose. "Whatever you are, my treasure, I like it, be it normal or normal normal," he answered, a smile curving across his painfully handsome face.

"Well," she said heavily, "it's nice to know that, because I might as well tell you right now that your behavior toward me, most of the time, smacks of strong dislike." She tilted her head to one side and looked doubtfully at him, trying to judge how he was taking all of this.

"Does it?" he said in a surprised tone.

"Yes, it does," said Mourning, watching the light dancing in his eyes, the devilishly charming curl of his smile. "You are just having fun with me right now," she said, eyeing him suspiciously, "but you get positively furious with me when I do something wrong."

"Only when you endanger your life," he said truthfully.

"Oh, really?"

"Truly."

"If that were the case, which we both know it isn't," she said knowingly. She stood defiantly straight and slender as his eyes considered her. "What about your constant irritation toward me whenever you're around Eleanor? Surely that isn't a danger to my life." She watched him speculatively, reading his thoughts. "Don't think you can humor me into thinking differently, because I know my presence is a source of great vexation to the two of you."

"You don't know what you're talking about."

Mourning looked at him for a second or two before she turned to leave the room. Better to depart now, before she lost her temper. Let him defend his relationship with Eleanor. It was what she'd expected. Why should she be surprised? He permitted her one small, insignificant step before he grasped her arm with unbelievable strength.

"You aren't going anywhere."

"Why not? I would think you'd be glad to get rid of one of your problems this easily."

"I never said anything about wanting to get rid of you. I believe I said I wished you'd grow up. You're a very beautiful . . ."

"Thank you," she said haughtily, "that's the second time I've been told that today." There was little doubt in his mind who the other bastard was.

She smiled, watching his jaw clench and his face darken with anger. While he was caught in baffled confusion, she drove the point home. Glancing down at his hands, which were still gripping her arms tightly, she said, "Was there anything else you wanted to say?" She watched this arrogant, cocksure, handsome man who was accustomed to having his own way, knowing her only defense against him was her clever mind and sharp tongue that could wheedle him to blind fury.

Putting his hand beneath her chin, he tipped it up and slowly bent his head to her. "Not with words," he said softly. His lips came down to court hers in a long, tender yet demanding kiss. His hands tugged at the braids wound around her head until the lemon-scented mass tumbled to her shoulders like a bubbling cascade of water flowing over rocks. His words came soft and gentle to her ear. "Lord, you are sweet."

He kissed her throat, which arched gracefully, his lips traveling across the untouched softness of hidden places. The contact of their bodies moving together was as shocking as it was natural; his hard and well-developed, hers soft and pliant, touching each other with mind-fracturing intensity. Her response to him was as innocent and unaware as a timid snowmouse. He drew back; her eyes were closed, her lips parted slightly.

He studied her pure face, pleasuring himself with the sight of her. She'd opened to newly awakened desire like the unfurling of a fern frond beneath the penetrating fingers of the sun.

She came up on her toes, pressing her lips against the taut sun-kissed skin of his throat before pulling away, disturbed at the warm flood that washed across her, like waves coming one behind the other, leaving her body soft and open. Far down inside her she felt a stirring, like a timid creeping nakedness emerging. Her eyes fluttered open, and met his startled yet vibrantly anticipating gaze.

"Do that again," he whispered. "Touch me with your lips." And then, so softly, he urged, "Kiss me just once more, angel—angel-love."

The soft, swirling heat of her gaze drifted over him like a shower of fragrant rose petals as she lifted her hand tentatively. He smiled with his eyes, his head bending to press a kiss against the fingers that were trembling with uncertainty. She moved her hand to touch his lips, using one finger to brush softly back and forth against the fleshy pad of his lower lip. He wanted to crush her against him, but this was her first attempt at initiating anything between them; awkward and inexperienced, her touch, in its simplicity, thrilled across him with complex rewards. Her eyes on his, intently she lifted her face to his, her eyes fluttering closed, her lips parting slightly before they touched his and his eyes following her lead. Passion-drugged by her shy seduction, he was mindless with desire when he felt her tongue trace the seam of his lips and timidly slip inside. It was a subtle, gossamer kiss, tempting and beguiling, spiced with the sweet fragrance of pure innocence. Desire spun through every membrane, and for a brief moment he lost complete control of his skyrocketing senses. Crazed from desire, he fought the concentrated flammability of passion spreading faster than fire through dry grass.

He stiffened and she broke away, obviously shaken, her face flushed. Self-consciously she said, "I'm sorry . . . I didn't do that right, did I?"

Clint attempted to smile while he brought his screaming body under control. He pulled her against him, kissing the rosy spots of color that marked her flawless skin. "Angel mine, there was enough rousing heat in that kiss to fuse my belt buckle to my backbone." She began to laugh. "Come here, you golden-haired temptress." Suddenly she found herself back in his embrace, his tongue drawing hers into his mouth, caressing and stroking her to weightlessness.

Sprinkling a trail of hot, open kisses across her cheek, following the curl of her ear, the sensitive flesh of her throat, his hands began a second assault against her flagging ability to withstand the force of her violent compulsion to yield.

Wild, unpredictable sensations were running out of control within her, leaving Mourning trembling against him with violent intensity. The room spun and tilted as he pushed her back against the desk, following her down and covering her trembling body with his own.

"Clint, stop, you can't . . ."

His mouth was hard and silencing. His tongue teased and tormented with soft promise, then retreated, until Mourning was lost in a fever of naked desire.

The touch of strong, roughened fingers on the naked softness of her flesh roused her drowsy senses. She began to mumble, "No, Clint . . . no," and push frantically against him.

"Don't," he ordered with a groan, as he intensified the wild, devouring kiss while the flame-kissed heat of his hand slid across her breasts, teasing and touching them to agonizing tenseness.

Touched and kissed mindless, Mourning was still drifting in a bath of sensual sensations when he stopped. Her opiated consciousness gradually returned and she gazed at him to see his eyes concentrating on the stark whiteness of her breasts.

He lifted his gaze to hers, holding her as he brought his palms up to brush lightly against her passion-teased breasts. "You can't possibly know," he said with a low, vibrating husky tone, "what it's like to touch you here . . . where the flesh is pure and white and untouched, like snowcaps on inaccessible mountains." He leaned forward, pressing a warm, moist kiss on each feverish breast before hesitantly tying the ribbons of her chemise. "Sometimes," he said softly, "I forget there is so much standing between us, the age difference, who you are, what I am . . ."

She lifted a finger to smooth the troubled frown from his brow. "The only thing between us now is an infinitesimal bit of displaced muslin dress, a ravaged camisole, and the quill pen that's gouging a hole in my back. Let me up, you ridiculous man."

He helped her put her clothes in order, but her hair was hopeless. They were convulsed with laughter over her blighted attempts to do something with her wild hair, when he drew her against him and kissed the top of her head. "I know I should be sorry, but I'm not. If I'd done what I really wanted to, I would've taken more than a few hairpins. I find myself thinking of little else."

Poking her finger with brazen impertinence against his chest, she said with sassy impudence, "Is that so? Well, my bonnie braw lad, I ha'e been doin' some thinkin' o' me own, and 'tis a sorry lass I am wi' your cowardly ways. Hav'na ye heard: great desire obtains little."

His thunderous laughter drowned out the sound of the door opening when poor Anna Claire Ragsdale entered, carrying a glass of water. The stricken look on her face sent Mourning into peals of laughter.

"Here's your water, Mourning," she said, looking from Clint to Mourning and then handing her the glass.

"Now," Clint said, giving Mourning a twinkling look. "I am still looking for a bill of sale for ten head of cattle that I left on the desk. Do you know where it is?"

"I do," Anna answered, sweeping around the desk. As Anna dug through the drawer, Clint's gaze drifted to Mourning, who smiled impudently and stuck out her tongue, suddenly struck with an impulsive dash of wildness. Clint's booming laugh brought Anna's head up, and she directed a bewildered look at the grinning pair. With a huff, she removed the bill of sale from the drawer and handed it to Clint. With a brief thanks, he swiftly left the room.

With elevated brows, Anna turned her questioning stare upon Mourning. "My lips are sealed," Mourning said with a giggle before she twirled and collapsed on the sofa. "Until tonight."

With the promise of being informed of the reason behind her cousin's strange behavior, not to mention what set Clinton Kincaid to grinning like a hyena, Anna let the matter drop.

Jumping to her feet, Mourning began to clean the floor with a mixture of boiled linseed oil and burnt sienna while Anna finished polishing the brass plant-stand.

"We only have the music room left and then we're finished. Mama said we would have a family gathering in there tonight after dinner, since it's Eleanor's last night here." Mourning stopped the sweeping movement of her arms across the floor. "Did you know Mama said we have to perform for that overuddered cow?"

Anna paled. "I don't think I can play in front of Cad . . . not that he ever notices me," she added woefully.

"Perhaps you should do something to get his attention," Mourning suggested.

"Mourning, we've done nothing all week but get his attention," Anna groaned, then added, "his attention and everyone else's. I think we need to lie low for a while until some of this blows over. No need to press our luck."

"That's not the kind of attention I was referring to," Mourning answered, having polished her way to the library door and then pausing to proudly admire the gleaming floor.

She began to give everything a final going-over, fluffing a pillow here, flicking a bit of dust there. "You need to be more seductive . . . that's what Cad told me to do around Clint."

"Well, I haven't seen any proof that it's worked . . . all you've gotten from your efforts so far is a black eye from peeping through keyholes!"

"Nevertheless, I think you should do something glamorous to let him see you as a woman, not just a girl who's always getting into trouble." She gave the lamp a final whisk with the feather duster and then started on the collection of lead soldiers in the fruitwood display-case. The thought flashed through Mourning's mind as to why she didn't take her own advice, but she quickly replaced that thought with another, more pleasant one, like what she might wear tonight.

"Just what could I do that would be glamorous?"

"Like playing the piano tonight . . . and wearing something really seductive and irresistibly low-cut."

"You mean something like Eleanor would wear?"

"Sort of."

"Mourning," she snapped, throwing down her polish cloth and placing her hands on her hips, "you know I don't have anywhere near the necessities to hold up a gown like Eleanor does. If I put on a dress that low-cut, it would hang to my knees!"

Mourning began to look rather heartsick herself. "Now that you remind me, I don't hold a candle to her in that department either. Perhaps if we . . ."

"No and no, and double, triple, quadruple NO!" cried Anna.

"What do you mean, no?" puzzled Mourning. "You don't know what I was going to say. I was only going to suggest we stuff our bosoms with socks, like Drucilla Smathers—"

Anna interrupted her again, speaking adamantly. "Mourning Howard, I will go along with almost any harebrained scheme you cook up; in fact I have, lots of times: I helped you put the itching powder in Horace Plover's long johns hanging on the clothesline. I'm the one who held Mrs. Hambeltonian's corset until you could climb the tree and hang it from a limb, and I let that horrid Elmer Blathersby hold my hand and kiss my cheek just so you'd have enough time to put sneezeweed in his snuffbox, but this is where I draw the line. I absolutely and positively refuse to stuff my bosom with anything!" She snatched up her polish cloth and began to vigorously rub the brass stand. "The very idea," she said, sounding just like Aunt Harriet, "just what would a man think if he suddenly found that the well-endowed woman he had courted suddenly went flat as a pancake on their wedding night? Just what would you do then?"

"You could always toss him the socks," Mourning choked out between fits of laughter, and fell back against the overstuffed chair.

21

At precisely ten o'clock the next morning an elated little mocking-bird was sitting on the clothesline, bursting at the seams with joyous song; a color-splashed monarch butterfly was fluttering in and out the kitchen window; Mrs. Harper was up to her elbows in sourbread dough, singing three off-key verses of "Onward Christian Soldiers"; and the three cousins sat on a pink and blue wedding-ring quilt in the shade of a sweeping oak, placidly shelling black-eyed peas. Or rather Mourning and Anna were shelling black-eyed peas. Melly was absorbed in some fascinating research of her own—experimenting to learn the exact amount of pressure to exert and send a pea, squeezed between the forefinger and the thumb, flying, more often than not, into the cheek of the other two inhabitants of the quilt.

Mourning was drifting, her mind profoundly occupied in daydreaming, when Melly let fly with another pea, this one *zinging* across the quilt with the speed of an exploding bullet. It scored a direct hit on the smiling countenance of one daydreamer, who was marvelously separated from reality, ripping the gauzy veil that surrounded her thoughts and cruelly jerking her screaming back into the present. "Melly Ragsdale!" Mourning shouted. "Will you make yourself scarce!"

"But Aunt Caroline wanted me to help . . ."

"I *know* that, featherbrain! But you aren't shelling peas anyway, and I'm sick and tired of being the bull's-eye for your target practice. Why don't you take Romeo and Juliet for a walk?"

That suggestion in itself was a stroke of genius, solving two problems simultaneously: Melly and her pestiferous ways, and the hounds, who were having a field day yanking the wet and shredded end of the quilt, shaking it every which way but loose.

Upon hearing the sound of their names, Romeo and Juliet dropped the ragged edge of the quilt and bounded toward Mourning, Juliet lightly jumping over the bowl of shelled peas and Romeo stepping directly in it, toppling the bowl and sending the peas rolling.

"Melly, go chase yourself—now!" said Mourning, enraged and dismayed that in her wonderful daydream Clint had been just two words away from scandalously ripping her clothes from her body and professing his undying love when Melly shattered the dream forever.

When Melly didn't budge, Anna chimed in. "Melanie Elise Ragsdale, I'm going to slap you into the middle of next week if you don't make yourself scarce."

Melly, her impish face bright with confidence in her immunity, joined the romp with the pups. Giving one of Melly's plaits a vicious yank, Anna glared frostily at her sister, who stated that she was ready to leave anyway and sashayed across the yard, her blue satin sash trailing limply in the grass behind her. She paused just long enough to call the dogs, who bounced behind her, long ears flopping up and down in time with their jogging lope, Romeo chasing and barking at her sash.

"Sometimes I find it hard to believe we are sisters," Anna said wearily, watching Melly remove her sash and drag it across the lawn for the dogs to chase.

Mourning stopped picking up peas to look at Anna and then follow the line of her vision to Melly. "She reminds me of myself . . . I think that's why she irritates me so." She grinned at Anna. "Vexatious little brat!"

"Good morning," said Caroline cheerily. "What did you two say to Melly to send her ripping away from here in such a hurry?"

Mourning and Anna glanced at each other, and Caroline, remembering her own irritation with Harriet when she was younger, understood. Not waiting for an answer, she continued. "Eleanor's father is here and she's leaving. I want you two to come say goodbye."

"Of course, Mama," Mourning said, while thinking she'd sooner tell Eleanor to take a long walk on a short pier.

"I must say, Mourning, your attitude does indeed surprise me," Caroline said, studying her daughter's profile with a smile.

"Why is that?"

Caroline gave a light laugh as she winked at Anna. "Oh, I don't know . . . perhaps I just thought you'd either be overjoyed finally to be rid of Eleanor and tell her good-bye, or balk at acknowledging her presence at all by refusing to bid her farewell."

Mourning kept her head straight ahead, but cut her eyes in Caroline's direction. "I can't help it if I don't like the woman . . . in fact, I can't stand her." Especially after last night, Mourning added, under her breath.

Last night! What a fiasco! What a disaster! Truly the worst night of her whole life! She was mad all over again just thinking about Eleanor in her figure-hugging red satin gown, so tight, it seemed she'd had to have been melted and poured into it—not to mention the plunging neckline that displayed enough bosom to supply ten flat-chested women.

"If you promise to keep a secret, I'll tell you something," Caroline said with a tone of high intrigue that demanded and received the cousins' full, undivided attention.

"If it's a derogatory or inflammatory remark about Eleanor," Mourning exclaimed, "I'm all ears."

"I wouldn't go quite that far," Caroline said with a laugh, "but I don't really care for her either, and John shares my sentiments. . . . No, that's not true . . . John detests her. I'm sure you've noticed how reserved he is around her—said it tests him sorely just to be civil to her. Last year he threatened to disown Clint if he even suggested marriage to her."

"Was Clint contemplating marriage?" asked Anna in a surprised tone, for she rather liked and admired Clint, thinking he had more sense than to marry someone like Eleanor.

"Who knows?" replied Caroline with a shrug. "John was on a 'give me grandchildren' binge last year . . . drove Cad and Clint wild with his pestering them about it. Finally, one day in exasperation Clint said, 'How do you know I haven't already given you several grandchildren?' and that really set John off!"

Mourning felt as if she had just swallowed an enormous lump of lead that dropped to her stomach with a thud. She had purposefully forced herself *not* to think about all the women Clint had known, and there were legions of them—that is, if she were inclined to believe all the stories she had heard, and she was. Of course he probably had children—a whole long line of little woodcolts, strung all the way from California to the East Coast.

"Does he?" Anna asked curiously.

"There's always that possibility with all the wild oats Cad and Clint have sown, but I've never heard rumors to that effect and I think Cad and Clint are both aware of where babies come from and have taken precautions."

Both girls came to an immediate standstill as if they had suddenly glimpsed Sodom and Gomorrah and turned into a pillar of salt. Mourning's mouth flew open—bursting with the need to ask the question taking rapid root in her fertile little mind. Anna's own mind was plowing furiously only a few furrows behind Mourning's.

With a laugh, Caroline looked at the gloriously innocent faces of the young women on the threshold of discovery. "Before you ask, I'm not going to explain anything else. Not today, at any rate."

"But . . ." Mourning protested, finally finding her words.

"Not today, and that's final." To make sure they understood she meant what she said, Caroline lengthened her strides and left the cousins walking slowly behind her, gears grinding and wheels whirring as they pieced the bits of information they had just gleaned into the large *Puzzle of Knowledge*, finding they still had too many missing pieces to see anything clearly.

"Why don't we walk really, really slow and arrive too late to tell her good-bye?" Anna suggested.

"No, she might use that for an excuse to stay another day, just to bid us farewell."

"After the way she behaved last night, I'm surprised she didn't just sneak off before sunrise . . . I would have," Anna said reflectively. "I still cannot believe she had the audacity to perform a dance like that in the *music room*, of all places."

"Where would she perform a dance like that? We don't have a perversion chamber in this house," Mourning said gloomily.

Shaking her pert little head with horrified disgust, Anna said, "I still can't believe it."

"I can believe it," Mourning said, remembering the way Eleanor's body flowed like water over rocks. "She had more writhing moves than a dying snake." Mourning reflected back upon the twisting, coiling moves; the way her serpentine body wound around Clint's like an overpassioned python. Mourning also remembered how she wanted to do something equally disruptive to draw Clint's attention to her, but all she could think of was falling out of a tree. Unrolling her sleeves and rebuttoning the white cuffs, she said, "I'm actually happy to tell her good-bye. It means I won't have to see her spiteful face around here anymore."

Rain began to fall upon her very soul when Mourning saw Clint holding a tearful Eleanor, sobbing and clutching, while she despaired of having to leave. The vivid green dress Eleanor was wearing, Mourning thought, was just like the woman it clothed—clinging and tasteless. Seeing the cousins, Eleanor pulled Clint's head down and kissed him full upon the mouth before she turned toward them with a breathless exclamation, "I was just telling Clint good-bye."

Before she could answer, Mourning saw Cad step forth and take Eleanor's arm and hand her into the carriage. "Really? Is that what you were doing, Eleanor? I am relieved, for a moment there I thought you looked just like a cat sucking the breath from a sleeping babe."

When the carriage pulled out of sight, Mourning turned to see Anna being led reluctantly away by Cad, while questioning gray eyes studied her intently. Moved by the spirit of prophecy, knowing Clint was sharpening his mental fangs to pounce hungrily upon her, Mourning turned and began to inch her way toward the house.

"Mourning, I want a word with you," the voice thundered. She gave a sigh and her shoulders rose protectively around her, as if trying to shield her tender ears from the verbal abuse that would surely follow. "Don't pull your head in like a snapping turtle. Come here."

And then it happened, as miraculously as the sun peeping through dark and thunderous clouds during a thunderstorm: A smile began to dance and flirt around the corners of his sternly held mouth, bursting with the brilliance of sunlight into a full, wide grin. The shock of seeing him laughing when she had fully expected to be the recipient of a blistering lecture stopped her words faster than a chop to the throat.

"I guess you're really sad she's gone."

"Terribly sad," he agreed, straight-faced.

Her eyes flew to his, seeing his gray eyes lit with amusement. Incorrectly assuming he was flaunting his feelings for Eleanor, Mourning's face flushed while she searched for control.

"Don't you know I'm fighting the urge to take you in my arms and kiss you?" he said in a deep, velvety voice.

The look in his eyes confused her. "Have you become so accustomed to making indecent advances to Eleanor that you . . ."

"I made no advances to Eleanor, indecent or otherwise." She noticed that even while defending himself, his voice was quite seductive.

"Well, she sure accepted them."

"Mourning dove, you have been bitten by the green-eyed jealousy bug again," he softly chided.

Dumbfounded, Mourning looked away, then gave him a glassy stare. Usually she placed the man she knew as Clint Kincaid somewhere between a ruthless despoiler of women and a mind reader, but at this particular moment she felt a hint of possessiveness toward him. Admitting she was just a tiny bit jealous of Eleanor wasn't as hard as she'd imagined. She looked up at him and saw his beautifully shaped eyes were smiling.

Pulling her against him, Clint chuckled as he whispered into her ear, "It's not very pleasant to realize you've been found out, is it, buttercup?"

Cocking an impish brow at him, she whispered, "Oh, I don't know . . . it could be pleasant . . . quite pleasant in fact, depending, of course, on what you did about it."

Kincaid let loose with a roll of laughter, then looking at her with obvious pleasure, he said, "Remind me to lecture you sometime on why men take mistresses."

"Kincaid, are you plowed?" Before her stood the most confusing and unpredictable of men, capable of more moods than a centipede had legs. He was capable of whittling away her emotions until she was like finely diced mincemeat, completely unaware that he had taken a plug of anger here, a slice of resentment there, a sliver of despair, a wedge of frustration—leaving her full of more holes than a round of Swiss cheese, and leaking like a sieve.

Her face tilted upward to search his for some clue to what he was thinking, but nothing was apparent but his infectious humor.

"I asked you if you were plowed." The sun sparkled with refracted beams, plunging to the depths of her eyes, which looked at him in puzzled wonder. He drew the back of his knuckles across the curve of her cheekbone.

"I haven't had a drink in two days."

"You've been in the sun too long, then," she said as his hand encased hers, tugging for her to follow. She followed mutely beside him until they reached the edge of the small pond just down the slope of the hill from the house. He led her behind a stand of thick trees and brush.

When they reached the water's edge she thought at first he was going to toss her in, but instead he leaned against a twisted branch and crossed his legs in front of him. "Why did you bring me here?"

He smiled a smile that went clean through her, passing by osmotic action through skin, traveling through muscle like an electric current, and settling like the gentle caress of fluttering snowflakes in her bones, freezing them in place; leaving her suspended and dazed, unable to move.

Openmouthed with confusion, she felt, as usual, the necessary compulsion to speak. "Clint . . ."

One of his hands reached out, placing the tips of three fingers across her lips to silence her. "Mourning, my willful little chatterbox. Don't say or do anything for a few minutes, just try to fight the irresistible impulse to perform one of your irrational acts."

Even in disgrace she stood proudly before him, belying the dejected feeling sweeping across her as she morosely contemplated the unladylike display he had just witnessed. No wonder he preferred Eleanor's seasoned experience to her green-as-gourds behavior. At least Eleanor was aware she was a woman, while she seemed to be trapped forever in a bubble of immaturity, floating and drifting in rainbow hues, looking beautiful and iridescent on the outside but hopelessly confined to a transparent world lacking firmness, solidity, or reality. Was she confined to this existence forever, never to cross the threshold into maturity?

Beside her came a discreet but nevertheless false cough. Mourning turned to confront Clint's cool gray stare. She gazed at him as if anesthetized, feeling uncomfortably aware of her crack-brained childishness, which had to be ridiculously distasteful to someone of Clint's consummate sophistication. She blushed, and knowing she was on the feather edge of disaster, she decided to try the direct approach.

Looking him straight in the eye, she immediately lost the meager supply of courage she had scraped together, for there stood Clint Kincaid, looking hale and hearty, as if he could wrestle a couple of grizzly bears with one arm tied behind him. She bought herself about half a minute, stammering and stuttering, before finally choking out the hastily composed words. "I know you'd like to kill me for the way I behaved," she said with a heavy sigh, looking at him with all the sorrowful melancholy of one about to be secured to the rack and stretched beyond recognition.

"You're absolutely right . . . I'm only hesitating until I can think of a fate cruel enough to subject you to. But it's quite difficult, you see, for all I can think of is kissing you into a stupor," he said.

Curiously, she studied the gray eyes that studied her in return, and said, "I don't understand."

He looked down into the honestly open face before him, the soft, shining green eyes, the peach velvet of her skin, the rose-petal softness of her slightly parted lips. "Mourning, my delight in disorder, don't you know it's at your idiotic worst, when you're in the very thick of one of your spellbinding feats, that I desire you the most?" His hand slipped inside his jacket and pulled out a small package. "Here, perhaps this will explain it better."

She held out her hand and looked up at him with a puzzled frown. "For me? You bought this for me?"

"For no one else."

She dropped the satin ribbon to the grass, then the thin covering of tissue, and found a silver-framed poem by Robert Herrick.

DELIGHT IN DISORDER

A sweet disorder in the dress
Kindles in clothes a wantonness:
A lawn about the shoulders thrown
Into a fine distraction,
An erring lace, which here and there
Enthralls the crimson stomacher,
A cuff neglectful, and thereby
Ribbands to flow confusedly,

A winning wave (deserving note)
In the tempestuous petticoat,
A careless shoe-string, in whose tie
I see a wild civility,
Do more bewitch me than when art
Is too precise in every part.

"Now I really don't understand," she said with a puzzled tone. "You're supposed to be angry with me . . . don't you understand, Kincaid? I'm talking about anger, you know, madness . . . fury . . . wrath . . ."

"Dudgeon," he offered.

"High dudgeon," she corrected. Her tone was so adorably clownish, it made him laugh.

"Mourning . . . captivating child . . . my cherished prize, you are the one who doesn't understand." His hands cupped her face, his spellbinding fingers threading through her hair, finding the sensitive spot on the nape of her neck, sending shivering tremors rippling across her shoulders. He felt it and lowered his head to the cove between her throat and shoulder, which she discovered was another sensitive spot, to blend the husky warmth of his whispered reassurance with the seduction of her bare skin. She moaned, her head falling back, exposing the full lustrous length of warm throat. His lips moved lower, and she felt the instant betrayal of her body rushing to meet him. She was intoxicated with his lips, lazy and thorough as they covered every inch of exposed skin and went seeking for more.

"Enchanting," he said, his voice a husky, seductive whisper. "We're under a spell now, did you know that, little Mourning? No, buttercup. Don't pull away. That's right, sweetheart. You feel it now, don't you? Come with me. Easy. Yes. Sweet. Sweet. Oh, God."

Floating away from herself, she was out of touch with reason; nothing was important but the taste of his mouth, the rough texture of his face, the fragrance of his skin. She whimpered softly and tried to pull away, but he held her to him. "It's all right, sweetheart. Am I frightening you? Okay. Tell me what you want. Too shy? Don't be . . . not with me . . . never with me. Tell me, sweet. Tell me what you like." He released her with a gentle nuzzle, his tongue following the outline of her ear, and laughed softly when she leaned toward him like a little iron filing drawn by a magnet.

As they had a way of doing when she was around him, her words deserted her and she could only blink like a frightened rabbit. His thumb was stroking the sensitized skin of her lips with a narcotic effect, and she felt her feet taking root to that very spot where she stood. "You're not playing fair," she said hesitantly.

"You know what they say . . . all is fair in love and war."

"Which one are we involved in now? You keep switching sides, so I'm always confused." She said this so mournfully that he threw back his head and laughed.

"Sweetheart," he said, smiling, his voice husky, "right now there isn't an angry bone in my body."

"There will be. Just give it time."

"You are a treasure. Did you know that?"

"Yes. One you'd like to . . ."

"Bury myself in."

Suddenly she was within the circle of his arms, with his kiss drawing away any resistance she had left. "I want you. Lord help me, I think of little else," he whispered. "Let me love you, Mourning."

A loud voice pounded in her ears with each pumping surge of the blood singing through her veins. *Let him . . . let him . . . let him . . .*

Drowning her with heated kisses, his lips traversed the course of her face, breathed soft words into her ear, and swept across the pulsing silk of her throat. She leaned full against him, feeling a great deal like a rag that had just been well wrung. She encircled him with her arms, spreading her fingers flat against his back, her other hand slipping behind his neck, tangling in his hair, pulling him closer.

He kissed her, tenderly and long, with a shattering intensity that left her crumbling, unable to stand. If he hadn't been holding her, she would have slipped to the ground. Sensing this, he drew her downward, pressing her back into the fragrantly curling clover, covering her with his weight, the flat hips grinding against her with an agonizing heat that scorched the clothing between them. His hands knew precisely where to touch to make her moan with painful intensity while the rhythm of his hips filled her with a madden-

ing throb, a throb that beat against her with the acute awareness of
something beautiful happening between them.

She was like a naked newborn, creeping forward, half afraid,
yet something was driving her ahead, something within her trying
to emerge; tiny ripples of pleasure washing forth, another, and
another, running together and overlapping, coming faster and
faster until she was consumed with a frantic need.

He felt the blistering heat of her response and knew he should
stop. But before he could collect the strength to initiate the action,
she tugged his shirt loose, slipping her hands under it, sliding them
across his naked skin. A startled exclamation sprang from his lips
and the thought of stopping, if there ever was one, was lost.

She felt the warmth of his hands cover her breasts, forming
them like clay to the contours of his hands, causing a feeling of
levitation to bubble through her, leaving her buoyant and weightless.

Suddenly, bounding from the low-lying brush nearby, came
the pant and thump of two hounds, who playfully pounced on the
pair, who were engaged in some kind of fun of their own. Mourning shrieked with surprise, then buried her head inside Clint's
jacket to evade the dogs' velvety, wet tongues as she bubbled with
laughter.

"Damn! If I didn't know better, I'd swear you'd trained these
dogs to protect your virtue, for they always seem to appear at
precisely the right moment." He rolled over and sat up, leaning
against the tree, calling the hounds to his side, freeing her from
their frolicsome attention.

Mourning rolled over on her stomach and plucked a blade of
grass, poking it between her lips as she studied the flushed features
of his face, the control he was exercising to bring his surging body
back to normal.

With an impish grin, she said, "Yes, but aren't they nice to
wait as long as they possibly can before pouncing?"

He raised his eyebrows in surprise. "Why, Miss Howard, you
aren't saying you are overcoming your prudish ways and are actually enjoying my advances, are you?"

She watched Romeo tugging and chewing on the side of
Clint's boot. "And what if I am, Mr. Kincaid . . . what if I am?"

"Come here," he said huskily.

She jerked her eyes away from the dogs and looked at his face.

"Come here, my frightened little butterfly. I just want to hold you, nothing else."

He opened his arms and she hesitated for just a moment, until she saw the teasing light flicker deep in his eyes, and with a smile she moved to him and he drew her within the comforting enclosure between his arm and the solid warmth of muscular chest.

She sighed with contentment and felt his smile in her hair, where he was busy pressing thoughtful kisses. She wondered what he was thinking. Probably what he would have done next if the dogs hadn't interrupted them, or perhaps he was thinking about her.

"Do you like to fish?" he asked.

"Fish?" she squeaked. *Fish?* she thought. *How can the big dope be thinking about fish at a time like this?* Shaking her head with wonder, she answered, "Yes, I like to fish. Why?"

"Thought I might take you with me sometime, would you like that?"

"Yes," she said, turning her head back so she could see his face. "You look funny upside down."

"So do you," he said, dropping a kiss against her forehead.

She felt his chuckle and pushed away from him to see his face. "What are you laughing at?"

He was still laughing when he began to answer her. "I was just remembering the look on Eleanor's face at dinner the other night when she served those buns of hers. Lord, but those things were awful." Clint's brow rose and his eyes held a twinkling glint of humor. "I've been wondering, Mourning. You wouldn't know anything . . . no, never mind. I'd rather not know." He looked at the radiant face watching him and felt a sudden flush of tenderness. "You handled yourself pretty well around Eleanor. She's not an easy woman to be around. I knew there'd be trouble the minute you two crossed each other's path. It was obvious she was after you."

"No, you're wrong, Clint." He looked at her sharply and Mourning continued. "Eleanor is after you, Clint, not me."

He grinned. "Yes, I know."

"She's not for you."

"Oh, ho! So you know me well enough now to be picking my women for me, do you?"

"No, but she's not the kind of woman to love one man for very long. You deserve more than that."

He looked down at her, with her head resting against his shoulders, her face turned up toward his. The sun washed her face with gold and he could see the velvety soft cheeks glinting with drops of moisture. He fought the desire to lean over and touch them with his tongue, tasting her once more. This warm intimate sharing with a woman was something new for Clinton Kincaid, and he wasn't sure how to handle it. "Well, I'll tell you what I'll do. Whenever I feel myself falling, head over heels, I'll bring the lucky lady by for you to check out, before I tie the knot. Okay?"

The moment flooded with warmth and goodness between them was gone as soon as the words left his mouth. He saw the pain leach into her eyes and felt her muscles tense, and then she was standing, calling the hounds. He followed her up. "Mourning . . ." But she was already running ahead of him, a splash of yellow, vivid against the backdrop of green, as she disappeared from sight.

"Heavens," said Melly, when Mourning entered Anna's room, "you look like you've just eaten pickled eels!"

"Melly, you always have such a way with words. Why don't you . . ."

"I know, I know, go gather eggs. It may interest you to know I was going that way anyway," she said, snatching her bonnet from the wall sconce and twirling through the door.

As soon as she had left, Anna whirled around and grabbed Mourning by her upper arms, a desperate look on her face. "Mourning, am I ever glad you are here."

"What's happened?"

"You remember I had set my easel and paints up near the flower garden this morning? Well, when I went back out there after Eleanor left, I found this tucked beneath a tube of burnt umber." She began fishing around inside her bodice. Giving Mourning a sheepish look, she said, "I know it's here."

"Are you sure it didn't fall out? There's not much there to prevent that from happening."

"At least I'm not contemplating the use of stockings like some people I know."

"I wasn't contemplating . . . merely suggesting that . . ."

"Oh, here it is," Anna exclaimed, and she unfolded a small scrap of paper and handed it to Mourning.

> If you want to know more about how I plan to gather money for my cause and would like to help, meet me at the cabin tomorrow.
>
> Cheno

"Mama will kill us," Mourning said, thoughtfully studying the note.

"Clint is the one I'm worried about. Do you think we should decline?"

"The devil take him!" Mourning snapped, deciding to go, just to spite him if for no other reason. "No, I don't think we should decline. How would we? By having Ben deliver our regrets and invite him to tea?"

"Yes, I suppose you're right." Anna dropped onto the bed, her skirts billowing around her. "If we are going, we'd better start some serious planning right now."

Mourning had at that moment a singular experience in the form of an intellectual revelation flashing through her brain. Anna glanced at her, seeing the eyes wide with wonder, the face illuminated with a wild radiance.

Anna sprang to her feet. "What is it?"

"I've just had a startling vision, a foolproof plan for us to slip away unnoticed."

"I don't know, Mourning. When you get possessed by these passionate fits of inspiration, we always get into trouble . . . *big trouble!*"

"Oh, Anna, *Damnant quod non intelligunt!*" she said, falling across the bed backward and landing spread-eagle.

"Which means?"

"They condemn what they do not understand!"

22

The first thing Mourning saw upon awakening the next morning was a black figure huddling over her bed, and she let out what would have been a piercing, bloodcurdling scream—had not the devilish apparition before her clamped a strawberry-flavored hand over her mouth. Strawberry? Something was amiss!

Before she could surmise just what kind of bandit went around with strawberry jam stuck to his fingers, she heard a familiar voice. "Mourning, it's me," Anna whispered. "What do you think of my disguise?"

Puzzled, Mourning sat up and looked sleepily at Anna, who was swathed in at least forty yards of heavy black cloak. "It's not too bad if you're applying for the position of resident vampire," Mourning said, laughing at the comical figure standing before her, "otherwise I'd be careful lest someone drive a stake through your heart."

"You think it's too much?"

"Not for the theater curtain at the Royal Globe in Memphis."

"It's just as well," Anna said with a sigh as she unwound herself. "This thing is beastly hot, and I feel like a mummy." She dropped the cloak on a nearby chaise and sat on the edge of the bed, propping her chin in her hands. "Just what did you have in mind when you said we'd disguise ourselves?"

"I was thinking more along the lines of a vaquero."

Anna's head sprang up, as did her eyebrows. "You mean wear trousers?" Anna tried her best to sound somewhat mortified, but fell short of her objective. There was no way she could disguise the excitement in her voice.

The clothes were fairly easy to obtain; two pair of britches stolen off Maria Rodriquez's clothesline, two cotton shirts stolen from the big house—one from Clint and one from Cad, because Anna refused to wear anyone's shirt but Cad's—and two hats pilfered from the tack room. Jose Valdez lost his vest when he hung it on a hook by the pump while he washed his face. Mourning used a long piece of cane to gently lift it off the hook. And Rudy Sanchez had one lifted out of his saddlebags while he was eating lunch.

Stealing two pairs of boots from the vaqueros' cabin was easy. Getting outside with them was not.

Things were progressing rather smoothly until Anna's eyes fell upon the undulating form of a robustly lush Jezebel, done in the Catholic Baroque style of Rubens. The cousins paused to study the painting. The woman was reclining upon a bed in a position that only an experienced, professional contortionist could achieve, and she possessed more pagan sensuousness than Pan himself.

"Mourning, this positively knocks your French postcard back three centuries."

Before Mourning could reply, the sound of approaching feet and robust laughter sent them flying to the window. "Oh, my stars and underdrawers!" Mourning whispered. "They're too close . . . we'll be seen if we leave now. Quick! Under the bed."

Communicating in whispers, the two conspirators, hiding under the bed, anticipated the fate before them like two criminals awaiting trial.

Two men entered, and the two collaborators heard all manner of tramping, shuffling, scraping of chairs, and then silence. Mourning lifted the blanket edge to peek beneath it. Seeing the men, she gasped and dropped the blanket. "Saint Sebastian! . . . No, Anna, don't look!" It was too late. Anna lifted the blanket and peeked under the edge, seeing the naked backside of one of the vaqueros, leaning over the table, squirming and writhing as the other vaquero extracted cactus spines from his buttocks.

It cannot be truthfully said that the cousins watched with passionately interested eyes, but there were suddenly a great many reasons why they had to check the lay of the land.

Whispering to Mourning, Anna said, "I can't bear to look."

To which Mourning replied, "I might find that more believable if you'd drop the blanket." After what seemed hours, the two vaqueros left and the two, somewhat blushing, somewhat wiser cohorts crawled out. When the coast was clear, they fled like a pair of flushed quail.

It was a hot, steamy day, not a cloud in the watery blue sky, not so much as a flutter of a breeze stirring the flowers that stood with thirsty, drooping heads. Reaching the meadow, Anna and Mourning slowed the horses, giving them a cooling before reaching the cabin.

When they arrived at the cabin, having made sure they had tied the horses, they stepped upon the porch. The door was ajar, so they peered inside. It was deserted. "Yuck!" said Mourning, grimacing as she began to pull at the sticky, silken spider's web she had walked into.

"I wonder," said Anna, hands on hips, surveying the surrounding area, "if this was just a trick."

Looking crosser by the minute, Mourning was still fighting what appeared to be insurmountable odds against the spider's web. "I think Cheno is much too busy being an important bandit to waste time writing silly notes to trick two maidens."

"You're probably right, but if he is going to put in an appearance, I wish he would hurry up, because I'm tired of waiting." Anna lowered her voice. "And I don't mind pointing out these britches are horribly uncomfortable. My legs are chafed mightily."

"So are mine, Anna. Cheno didn't strike me as the sort of gentleman who would keep two ladies waiting indefinitely. In fact, I bet he's watching us right now."

That prompted Anna to jerk her hands away from her chafed thighs, which she had been gingerly rubbing. Looking around to make sure she had not been seen, she said, "Why don't we act like we're leaving?"

The cousins returned to the horses, and Mourning had just placed her hand upon the saddle horn to mount when a hand closed about her wrist. *"Yiiiah!"* she screeched. "We've had it!"

Whirling around, she drew back her clenched fist and found herself face-to-face with Cheno himself. "You are lucky," she said, placing her hand against her chest to quell her spastic heart, "that I didn't deck you."

Cheno watched her with black shining eyes that were dancing with humor. He released her wrist. "Little *gatito,* I am quaking with fear." A slow, lazy grin spread over the mouth that had so valiantly tried not to laugh. "Come inside," he said, turning toward the cabin. "Paulo, make sure the quiet one comes also."

Mourning glanced around to see Anna being escorted toward the cabin by a very dark, swarthy man with an enormous sombrero. "We've changed our minds," she said frankly, "we waited for you so long, we can't stay any longer."

"I'm afraid you must," Cheno answered, kicking the partially open door back against the wall. Nodding to the chairs by the table, he watched silently as Mourning and Anna seated themselves. Once they were settled, Cheno propped one leg up on another chair, folded his arms across the braced leg, and leaned toward them. "Now, I will tell you why I asked you to come here."

Wide-eyed, the cousins leaned forward.

"Ransom."

"Ransom?" Mourning choked. "You mean like kidnapping?"

"That is precisely what I meant."

"But why are you telling us? What is to keep us from going . . . home and . . . telling . . . unless . . ."

"Unless I plan on kidnapping the two of you?" Cheno finished.

Mourning jumped up. "We need to go home and get our clothing, then," she said, moving toward the door. Cheno nodded and the man named Paulo moved swiftly, kicking the door shut.

"I am sorry, my little friend, but I have a feeling that you would not return. You will not need any clothes where we are going. I am delighted you chose to dress as you did today. It will make transporting you much easier."

"Where are you taking us?" the silent one asked.

"I will reveal that later. For now, we must be going."

Seven hours later, Caroline and the other inhabitants of the Kincaid ranch discovered that Mourning and Anna were missing. A thorough search of the premises did not turn up anything. When Clint rode in and was brought up to date on the situation, he promptly put Romeo and Juliet on the scent, which turned up nothing, except Anna and Mourning's abandoned clothing in the stables. As he searched, Clint wondered why they didn't take Melly. *Melly!* Clint entered the house, thundering and bellowing for Melly until she scurried from the music room. "Come into my study, you little wellspring of furtive activity. I want a word with you." She followed Clint into the study, where she revealed all she knew, which proved to be more than enough. She even produced the note from Cheno that Mourning had locked in her jewel box.

Twenty minutes later Cad and Clint were on their way to the cabin with John and several vaqueros following close behind. When they arrived, they found the two horses Mourning and Anna had ridden, with a note demanding ransom money pinned to one saddle.

"Thirty thousand dollars." John whistled. "He has expensive taste, doesn't he?"

"We aren't going to pay it," Clint snapped. "I'm going after them . . . now."

"We'll return to the ranch for supplies first," John said, looking at his watch, then at the sky. "It's getting late, and it'll be dark soon. Best thing to do is head out early in the morning."

"There is no reason to waste more time and hit a cold trail. I can make better time than a group of men. I'll gather what I need in the way of supplies on the way."

"You may make better time, but what about when you locate the women? It's my guess Cheno will head for Mexico, and once he reaches the Sierras it will be nigh on impossible to get them out. You'll need a small army," John answered.

"Removing them from a Mexican camp will be easier for me working alone and a lot safer for them," Clint argued, his tone a bit sharp.

It grew silent. The vaqueros, still mounted, watched and waited in silence to see what John would say. Cad took his hat off solemnly, and began to improve on the crease.

Concern was etched on John's face, deeper than any wrinkles. He nodded at Clint, drawing him aside for a moment. The two of them walked a few yards away, out of earshot of the others. John hesitated, then looked his son square in the eye. "What about Mourning, Clint?"

Clint frowned slightly, looking at John's weathered face. "How do you mean?"

"I mean she is a beautiful young woman. The idea of the two of you alone for what may be weeks or even months doesn't sit too well with me. I mean . . . well, goddammit, boy, what are your intentions?"

"I won't be alone with her. Anna is with her, or had you forgotten?"

"No, I hadn't forgotten, but knowing you, that is a very minor obstacle to overcome."

"You trusted me to bring her all the way to Texas. Why the sudden change of heart?"

"I didn't realize she looked the way she does, for one thing, and secondly, you were supposed to have a chaperone. I think it would be better to let Cad go."

Clint gave John a puzzled frown. "You *trust* Cad?"

"With Mourning, I do. I've seen the way you watch her, and I've heard the caustic words that you both let fly at each other. Cad is no more than a brother to her, but you . . . that's a different story."

"I'm going after them, and unless you plan to put a bullet between my eyes, you can't stop me."

"All right, but I want Cad to go with you . . . just for insurance."

Clint let loose with a string of oaths that would cure leather. "*Insurance?*" He ran his fingers through his hair and walked a few paces. "Son of a bitch! I'm talking about lives, and you're worried about insurance? Jesus! They could've been raped repeatedly by now." He kicked a rock. "*Insurance? . . . Shit!*"

Clint continued to pace, back and forth, running his fingers through his hair several more times before he paused. Turning, he walked back to John, stopping directly in front of him. There was no change in the expression on his face, but it was obvious he was furious. When he spoke, it was with bullet-hard determination. "I'm going after them . . . right now . . . and alone. I'll not risk her life with anyone else. I have to do this. You see that, don't you?" His voice was iced with possessiveness and a hard, brutal look glazed his eyes. He walked toward Conquistador, affirming once more, whether to himself or John, it wasn't clear, "She is my responsibility. I'll be the one to go after her." He collected the reins in his hand and was raising his foot to the stirrup when John's words halted him.

"Have you bedded her?"

Clint whirled, blood rage in his eyes. "That," he said, "is none of your goddamn business!"

"I asked you if you had bedded her, and since she is legally under my protection . . . it is my business."

Hitching a thumb over his gunbelt, Clint gave John an empty look, his gray eyes like slabs of cold Arctic ice. "No. I haven't bedded her . . . at least, not yet. As for what might happen on the journey home"—he shrugged—*"quien sabe?"*

"You lay a hand on her and I'll force you to marry her, Clint. By all that's holy . . . you touch her and she's yours! She'll be your wife . . . you understand that?"

The muscles bunched along his jaw. "Sure," he said mockingly. "Can't you see me shaking in my boots?"

Grinding his jaw, the veins on his neck bulging, he swung in the saddle and eased his horse around to face John. "It's been a long time since you were able to make me do anything," he said, giving the brim of his hat a yank, pulling it down securely on his head. Without a backward glance, he dug his spurs into Conquistador and followed the trail of the sun as it moved across the sky toward Mexico.

Walking back to his horse, John saw Cad mount up. "Where are you going?"

"I don't figure Clint can handle both them women by himself," Cad said with a wide grin. "Thought I'd go even things up a little."

Before John could reply, both his sons were riding west.

PART
FOUR

Loss is nothing else but change, and
change is Nature's delight.
Marcus Aurelius, *Meditations*

 23

There are kidnappings, and then there are kidnappings, and this does not bear any of the traditionally accepted earmarks of a kidnapping! Or so thought Mourning as she was borne along in a most scandalized fashion, wedged between two of Cheno's banditos.

She looked with disgust at the filthy vaquero clothing she still wore, glancing up to catch the back of Anna's head, which was bobbing up and down like a tiny cork in the throes of a hurricane. She was silently wondering why Anna's clothes were not deteriorating as fast as hers, nor looking as wretched. Of course Anna had not crawled on her belly through the cold ashes of the fire, trying to escape, nor had she jumped from her horse, rolling down a steep ravine in another attempt.

Mourning knew the men riding next to her couldn't understand English, but she began talking to them anyway. "I would like to speak to my cousin. I need to attend to some personal matters if you please," she said, exaggerating her enunciation of each word. The man next to her merely grinned widely, his gold tooth flashing brightly in the sun. Irritation was banking within her. Before long Mourning began delivering a few finalities of eloquence, but only after a few dazzling but nevertheless disastrous attempts to break formation. Growing desperate, she wondered, How does one transmit over the language barrier the fact that she needs to relieve herself?

Once she had gone beyond what even *she* would dare, and had actually pointed to her lower abdominal area and grimaced, hoping they would understand her discomfort. This the bandito misunderstood for hunger and handed her a flour tortilla.

They had been riding like this for weeks, and time had ceased to have any relativity after the second day—one day being much like another. Where was the excitement? Kidnappings were supposed to be dangerous, spine-tingling feats of daring, where the heroine was trussed up like a Christmas goose and carried away on a prancing black stallion by a dashing outlaw who strangely enough bore a striking resemblance to Clint Kincaid.

This kidnapping, she decided adamantly, was positively degrading, humiliating, and embarrassing. In no shape, form, or fashion did it remotely resemble anything romantic, dauntless, or dashing. She hadn't even been dragged screaming and swooning from her bed. She had gone placidly along, tricked and duped into her abductors' hands by her own stupidity. Oh, how would she ever live this down? It just wasn't fair. How could she be expected to act alluringly distressed while trudging along at a snail's pace on the back of a donkey—one so small that her toes were skimming the top of the ground? It was rather reminiscent of being bandied about by the scruff of the neck like a naughty tiger cub, and just as embarrassing.

Mourning had never ever read anything in *Martine's Handbook of Etiquette* that said what the proper posture was that one should assume while perched astride an ass!

When she had complained to Cheno and requested the horse she had ridden earlier, he laughed and said a burro was more surefooted in the mountains.

"But we're not even in the mountains," she screeched.

"We will be," he said, dismissing her by turning away to talk to one of his men. Moments later Anna was brought forward and Mourning was hoping they had decided to allow them to speak to each other, having been separated since their capture. "Anna," Cheno said, "you will accompany Paco and some of the men to our other camp."

"You . . . you aren't going to split us up, are you?" Mourning asked, knowing the answer.

"I am sorry, my little friends, but I'm afraid it is necessary. I know Clint and Cad Kincaid well enough to know they are probably not far behind us. Splitting up will increase our chances of keeping at least one of you until we can collect the ransom. We will make it obvious that we split our group here; that will force them to split as well. If I must fight, better to fight one Kincaid instead of two."

Mourning decided to argue the point, but there was a certain look in Cheno's eyes that warned her to remain silent. Arguing with Cheno, in the past, had not netted any favorable results, and more than likely would not this time. She was itching to find out how he knew Cad and Clint, but friend or not, Cheno had let it be known that he did not wish to be bothered with the prodding of her active mind or her insatiable curiosity. He was a man with a mission, and keeping them kidnapped until he was ready to release them was the key to the success of his mission. He would tolerate their childish whims just so long.

"Mr. Cortinas?" Mourning said, amazed at her own bravery.

"If you persist, *señorita*, I may be forced to do more than bind your hands. Your mouth would be my next choice."

"I just wanted to know if it might be possible to . . . well, is there some way . . . could we leave some kind of message so Cad and Clint would have some way of knowing *which* one of us went which way?"

Cheno's hard features softened. "Ah, so that's the way it is. It makes a difference to you, then?"

"Of course not," she snapped. "I just know that Anna . . ."

"Mourning Howard! Don't you dare blame me. You know as well as I do that you want . . ."

Cheno's laughter interrupted Anna, who snapped her mouth shut and glowered at her cousin. "Tell me, Miss Howard, which brother do you prefer to come after you, not that it matters . . . one man against so many?" He studied her face, a wide, knowing grin spreading across his own. He glanced at Anna, as if seeking confirmation of his growing suspicions. Looking back at Mourning, he said, "So, what would you have me do? Leave a sign here saying Anna to the right, Mourning to the left? Or should it say Cad to the right and Clint to the left?"

Both heads snapped up. "How did you guess?" asked Anna.

"Just a hunch," answered Cheno, drawing out his knife and reaching for Mourning. She gasped and squeezed her eyes shut, knowing suddenly she had pushed Cheno too far; he was going to kill her now, for sure. Miraculously she found herself opening them moments later when she felt her hair jerk and heard Cheno's throaty chuckle. Opening her eyes, she saw he had lopped off a nice fat curl and was securing it with a length of rawhide. Moving to Anna, he did the same, and handing Anna's lock of hair to Paco, he spoke in rapid Spanish. Paco grinned and nodded, tucking Anna's hair into his vest pocket.

"What did you tell him?" Mourning asked suspiciously.

"I told him to tie her hair in that tree over there and I will do the same with yours. Once it is apparent we have split up, the hair should clue the Kincaids as to which way you went."

"But we're both blond," Anna explained.

"True, but any man that knows you very well will undoubtedly know that your hair is very silky, while Mourning's looks more like . . ."

"I know, sheep's wool," Mourning interrupted in a woeful voice.

And so that is how the cousins came to be separated after a tearful farewell. Anna cried as she rode off and Mourning glared hotly at Cheno, who tried to humor her. "Now you can ride a horse if you like."

But Mourning merely snorted and walked to her ridiculous-looking donkey and mounted, refusing to talk to him or the stupid donkey. She gave him the silent treatment for two days before she forgot her anger and once again began chatting like a magpie, making Cheno pray for her silent anger once more.

As they rode she watched the heatwaves dancing ahead like a silvery mirror; a huge lake, cool and refreshing, but in reality only a mirage. Yet even a mirage was more pleasing to look at than miles and miles of creosote bushes, cactus, sotols, yuccas, agaves, and the ever-present prickly pear. There was no sign that a human had ever come anywhere remotely near this desolate place. Everywhere she looked there were the deformed shapes of a strange plant with long, slender, crooked, thorny limbs that grew upward from the ground for up to twenty feet. It was a dull green color, covered with thorns and small, pretty flowers. Cheno called it *ocotillo*.

"It's a strange-looking plant," she said as she pointed to a more familiar shape. "I know that one, yucca—rather useless, but yucca, nevertheless," she said, rather proudly.

"Yucca it is, and we usually call it Spanish Dagger," he replied, "but it's not completely useless. The Lipans, Comanches, and Kiowas have long used the yucca tips for needles—with some species it's even possible to break off a thorn so that a long strand of fiber peels away with it, and you have both needle *and* thread . . . and I've seen many a life saved from rattlesnake bites by using the sharp tip to puncture the bite and draw out the venom."

"Who are the Lipans?"

"The Lipan Apaches. They roam this part of the country, along with the Kiowas, the Kiowa Apaches, and the Comanches. Farther north, near El Paso, you'll find the Mescalero Apache. They're all related, although the Mescaleros are considered part of the western Apaches and the Lipans and Kiowa Apaches are eastern, because of their language. . . . They're all Apaches and all deadly, no matter what they're called."

"Have you seen any signs of them . . . lately?" She gulped.

"Not for several weeks," he replied, laughing at her sigh of relief.

Mourning's next words were lost in her throat as Cheno suddenly stopped his horse. "Don't say anything, but look, just across that *arroyo.*"

Mourning looked in the direction of his pointing finger and was startled to see a strange-looking animal—something like a cross between a horse and a cow, but with an enormous lump on its back and a rather haughty look on its face. "Merciful heavens and saints above, what on earth is that?"

"A camel," he said.

"A camel?" she echoed.

"A camel," he repeated.

"A camel in Texas? I can't believe that. There aren't any camels in the whole United States."

"Then, what would you call that?"

"I don't know," she answered, not wanting to argue the point further; besides, she had no earthly idea what that obnoxious-looking animal could be—and camels did have humps, she remembered that much. "I guess it's a camel," she conceded, "but I can't believe it is here . . . in Texas."

"There weren't any here until a few years ago. The army brought several out here to experiment with. They were named . . . believe it or not, the Camel Corps, and their headquarters is in Kerrville. This one probably escaped from there or from the army camp at Fort Stockton."

Mourning couldn't take her eyes off the strange-looking beast, which seemed to find her as fascinating as she found him. He stood there, silently chewing, as they rode by. Soon the camel was no more than a tiny dot in the background as they approached the Rio Grande near Presidio on the Chihuahua Trail. Cheno told her they would cross there because the river could easily be forded, but they'd cross at night so they'd not be seen by the many freight wagons that traveled the Chihuahua Trail from Indianola on the Texas coast to the mining capital of Chihuahua.

True to his word, Cheno halted the group just north of Presidio. Mourning could see the tiny town far below them and the river behind it, not more than a thin trickle from where she stood. They rested their animals until dark and then crossed the river, slipping into Mexico and the Chihuahua desert.

It was a sun-baked and brutal land, a place where death sat patiently and waited . . . waited for one slip, one miscalculation, one mistake—that's all it took. To make one wrong decision meant certain death; merciless, slow, and agonizing, in a place where only coyotes and buzzards would notice. And all the while, the sun smiled down upon them, cruel and unrelenting.

She learned there were any number of ways to go: choking on the alkali dust or the chalky powder that came in unbelievable sandstorms, suffering the deadly and tormenting bite of scorpions or rattlers, writhing in agony from the hideous swelling of the tongue and the horrible bloating of the body, doubled in pain from drinking from an alkali waterhole, and finally the long-drawn-out death without water—all of them real, none of them pleasant.

For over a week they rode, hearing no sound save their own idle chatter, the creak of saddles, the rattle of equipment, and the snort of horses. Mourning was filthy, hot, and cross, yet they never stopped, save to rest the horses. Her fair skin had burned and was now flaky and peeling, and her clothes were nothing more than tattered, filthy rags, and she was weary to the bone. She wasn't going to cry, she had promised herself that, but whenever she thought of Clint, she felt the tears collecting. With a sigh born of desperation, she glanced around her as she thought, *Oh, Clint, why did I disobey you? Why did you let me? Are you out there somewhere looking for me?* Her mind was flooded with the memory of his face, and the comforting flood of warmth that had come whenever he touched her. And all the times he had saved her, scolding her unmercifully until she quaked and then holding her tenderly, calming her fears. If she had only listened to him, she wouldn't be here now, facing at best a questionable future.

Having Cheno to talk to was the only thing that helped her maintain her sanity, as no one else in the group of fifteen men spoke English, and certainly none of them looked very friendly. He had laughed when she informed him of this, telling her, *But* seño- rita, *I did not pick them on the basis of friendliness. It is a good quality to have, but of little value to a border bandit.*

Cheno sat beside Mourning, balancing his tin plate on his knees, talking to her about his life. He was a strange man . . . one who gave up much, answering the call of those less fortunate. He was a striking man, educated, and from what he'd said, wealthy. He was charming, self-possessed, and very mannerly. Listening to him talk, she saw him to be a sort of Mexican Robin Hood, a champion of the people.

Cheno Cortinas had all the qualities to be a champion. He had a flair for leadership, the disposition of a gambler, intuitive insight, and genuine love for the Mexican people. To them he was a hero, to the Americans he was a pest. He stole horses from the American army and then brazenly sold their own horses back to them. He stole from the wealthy Americans and gave to the poor Mexicans. If the Americans he stole from were poor, the Mexicans he gave to were destitute. He constantly intervened in matters of persecution and went out of his way to irritate: killing sheep, running off cattle, stealing horses, and now . . . kidnapping.

"But, Cheno, why kidnapping?"

His eyes twinkled as he said, "Why not?" He would give no other reason, and she did not pry.

Cheno had been careful to avoid towns in Texas, but once they were in Mexico he seemed to relax. They stopped at several small villages, picking up a few supplies, then pushing on. After several days Mourning began to notice a change in the desolate desert terrain. It began to get rockier and drier, mountains appearing in the distance—smoky and blue, looming against the faded pink of evening sky. The only vegetation was sparse grass and a huge broadleaf plant, almost cactuslike. It had heavy bluish green leaves that tapered upward into a sharp, thorny point.

"It's the Maguey plant, used to make pulque," Cheno had answered when she inquired.

"Pulque?" Mourning said. "I've heard that name before."

Before she could remember where she had heard the name, he looked at her, his dark eyes dancing with humor. "Before you ask," he teased, "I'll tell you. Pulque is an alcoholic drink, similar to wine." Reaching behind him, he offered her a leather pouch. "Would you like to try some?"

He laughed when Mourning declined, kicking her donkey ahead at a slow, spine-jarring trot, removing her from the glint of laughter in his teasing eyes. He watched her bob up and down before slowing the stubborn animal to a walk.

They were in the Sierra Madres now—they'd been steadily climbing for several days. She sat huddled around the warmth of the fire, the evening chill having been drilled into her bones by the harsh wind. Her hands circled a dented tin cup with some god-awful-tasting stuff in it. It was wet and hot—that was all that mattered; besides, she was afraid to ask what it was . . . the last time she'd done that she'd discovered she'd been eating lizard . . . *LIZARD!* of all things—she could still be sick, just thinking about it.

Cheno hunkered down beside her. "You once said you were from the South—what were you doing on the Kincaid ranch?"

"My mother married John Kincaid several years ago. When I finished school I came to live with her. Clint—" Her voice broke, and it irritated her that she'd revealed that much to Cheno. She gave him a sideways glance and was sure he'd not missed the change in her voice. She continued as if nothing had happened. "Clint had been in Missouri and on the way back he stopped in Memphis to bring me to Texas with him."

"You going to marry him?"

"Clint?"

"That's who we're talking about, isn't it?"

"No . . . no, I'm not."

"Why? You're in love with him."

"For one thing, he hasn't asked me," she said angrily, "and for another—you're wrong, I'm not in love with him."

"You are lying, *señorita*. This is your friend Cheno, don't try to fool me."

She smiled shyly and sighed in defeat. "I didn't realize that I was in love with him until just before we left. Now I'll probably never get the chance to tell him, not that it would matter any."

"He does not feel the same, then?"

"Hardly," she snorted. "As far as Clint Kincaid is concerned I am a *willful, prankish kid, and he wouldn't marry me if I were the last woman on earth.*"

The dancing shadows from the fire played about his face, washing light and dark over his hair, accenting the reddish tint to his beard, highlighting the sparkle of his eyes. She studied his face intently, trying to guess his thoughts.

"It takes determination, beauty, and brainpower to catch a man like Clint. You shouldn't have any trouble."

"You sound awfully confident. Myself . . . I'm not so sure. There was a time I thought I had a chance with him, but now I know differently." She must have looked as dejected and unloved as she felt, for Cheno's warm hand sought hers, giving it a reassuring squeeze.

"Have you bedded him?"

Mourning couldn't help the gentle smile that possessed her lips when she remembered a time Clint had asked that question and how she had been so innocent that she had stupidly answered that she had helped Aunt Harriet bed one. Well, she wasn't the same naïve little girl she had been. "No, he hasn't bedded me, not that he hasn't come close to it, but one of us always manages to stop it . . . usually him."

"And now you're wondering if that was so wise?"

"Yes," she answered softly, "because then I'd know without a doubt that he cared for me."

"To the contrary, I think his refusal to bed you attests to the fact that he cares for you . . . very much so."

"You don't even make sense," she said, desiring to put an end to this ridiculous conversation.

"I know Clint Kincaid, and I know he has never had any scruples when it comes to bedding a woman. If he was reluctant to do so with you, he must care . . . more than you or he realizes."

"You are just making rash judgments."

"It wasn't a rash judgment. However, if I'm proven later to have been wrong . . . well, I'll apologize now, since I may not see you when that time comes. *Cadit quaestio.*" He stood, throwing the rest of his drink into the fire, and walked away.

His use of Latin surprised her. *Cadit quaestio*—the question drops: the argument collapses. Why did he say that? She grinned and called after him. "Cheno?"

He paused and turned around.

"Que sera sera," she called to him.

"What will be, will be," he translated, then with a quick salute and a smile, he dissolved into the darkness.

By morning the wind had increased to an awful roar, sand-blasting the mountain, biting at their faces, and blowing into their mouths when they tried to speak. Twice it got so bad, they had to seek cover under rocky outcrops until the howling wind subsided somewhat.

On their third stop Mourning hovered against the cool, jagged stone of the mountain, trying to shield her eyes and face. She felt the comforting warmth of an arm slip around her and words spoken low in her ear. "The wind has died a little, we are not too far now, let's ride."

It was customary for her now to follow Cheno without question. She ate when he said eat, slept when he said sleep, and mounted when he said ride. Today was no different. She mounted, wrapping a long scarf about her head and face, giving the burrow his head while she buried hers. They were high in the mountains now, the trail only wide enough for one horse or a mule, and she wondered if she would ever hear anything besides the steady prodding of hooves striking the rocky ground, the jingle of spurs, the creak of saddle leather, and the mournful howl of wind.

One minute the wind was blowing fiercely and the next moment they were riding through a small cavelike opening in the side of the mountain, and when they rode out the world was strangely quiet. There was no wind, only a green valley in a small canyon and warming rays of sunlight. Eden.

It wasn't much of a camp; three adobe buildings, a corral, two supply carts, and a few scattered tents, but it was more welcome than a scratch to an itch.

Mourning was taken to the largest of the three adobe huts, which was nothing more than one small room, but it was the first real building she'd been in for weeks. She was pushed inside and the door shut and locked. After weeks on the trail in the wide open, she found the small room oppressive.

She realized suddenly that she was alone.

She unwound the scarf from her head, trailing it across the

floor as she looked around the room with dismay. There was only one grimy window, not even covered with glass, but something greasy-looking, almost like oiled parchment. The furnishings were meager: a cot, no pillow, one blanket, a small stool in front of a tiny table with a broken leg that had been propped up with adobe bricks, a chipped pottery bowl for washing, and a tin cup for drinking—all dirty. Too exhausted to care, she fell across the cot and slept.

"Señorita . . . señorita, comida." The words slowly sank into her consciousness and she stirred, the smell of food drawing her senses acutely awake. She opened her eyes to a young Mexican girl wearing a red skirt and white blouse. She was smiling as she pointed at the table, where a bowl had been placed. Mourning walked to the table and sat down. "Thank you."

"De nada, señorita." The girl smiled hesitantly and then left Mourning to stare at the greasy contents of the bowl. The more she looked at it, the worse it appeared. What in the name of St. Sebastian was it? She stared until she decided it was either leftover dishwater or soup made with bootblack. Hoping it was the latter, she decided to eat it anyway. By the time she arrived at that decision, the grease had congealed into small clumps—not very tasty, but filling. She picked up the cup and saw it was filled with water, which she drank, noticing how tinny it tasted. She shook her head as she thought about the depths she had sunk to—Memphis was no more real to her now than Aladdin's Magic Lamp.

Her life fell into a routine. All meals were brought to her. She received a daily ration of soap and water and clean clothes once a week. She soon began to feel like a Mexican peasant in her colorful skirt, white blouse, and woven leather shoes. By her estimation she'd been there for three or four weeks. She hadn't seen Cheno in all that time and she was slowly going mad.

Mourning had been allowed outside only a few times, and trying to talk to the girl was useless, since all the girl would do was smile. It was finally due to complete and utter desperation that Mourning threw what Aunt Harriet called a *walleyed fit,* thinking the girl would probably go for help—she did.

Cheno entered her hut for the first time. "See what happens—I leave you to yourself and I hear the most unflattering reports," he said, smiling at her with understanding. "Are you having problems?"

Mourning stared at him. "Problems? Of course I'm having problems," she sputtered. "I need to get out of this blasted cabin before I go stark raving mad. Do you understand? I am talking about fresh air, sunshine, trees, water. I need exercise. I haven't had anyone to talk to in weeks! I want a bath."

"When?" he asked.

"When what?"

"When would you like it?"

"Like what?"

"The bath," he said with a chuckle.

"You mean I can have a bath?"

"If that's what you wish . . . you've only to ask."

"You mean I could've had a bath before now . . . if I'd asked?"

"Of course. I've been away, but I left orders that you could bathe and go outside if you wished. I assumed you didn't because you did not want to."

Mourning was speechless. All this time . . . she could have had a bath, a real bath.

Cheno watched her fume silently. "There is a stream about a half mile from camp, you can bathe there, but you'll have to have a guard."

"I can't bathe in front of a guard," Mourning snapped. "Let the girl go with me, she can watch."

"Perhaps the cool water of the stream will cool your temper," he said with a laugh, shutting the door just as the tin cup slammed against it.

More weeks passed and her life was so predictable, she could go through the motions of living with her eyes closed. Citadel and her mother seemed so far away, and the very thought of a certain gray-eyed rogue still brought tears to her eyes. She began to grow fearful that she'd never see any of them again. She pounded the hard cot and rolled over, facing the wall, as bitter tears rolled down her face. They were tears of regret . . . and strangely enough the one thing she regretted most was the one thing she'd fought the hardest against. Like a miser she'd hoarded her treasure, unwilling to share it, and now like an overripe fruit she'd fallen to the ground, useless and withered. She'd fought him, tooth and toenail, protecting her virginity, yet it was a hollow victory, a taste as bitter as gall. She could have shared something warm and vibrant and alive with him and she'd foolishly refused . . . and now she'd never be given a second chance.

For the first time in her life, Mourning cried herself to sleep.

∼ 24

"What do you think, Clint? Is it a trick to throw us off?" Cad's eyes were following the bob and sway of a golden lock of hair dangling from a low-hanging branch. He stretched upward, and with a smooth slash of his knife the curl tumbled into his outstretched palm.

"Hell, no. I think it's another one of Mourning's harebrained schemes. This," Clint said, calmly holding up another, more frizzled curl he had just cut down, "is what happens when two cabbageheads become overinvolved in subterfuge. They left these token indicators"—he gave the glossy curl a jingle—"cleverly implying it *might* make a difference to you and me as to which of the two airheads we go after."

"And does it matter?" Cad inquired with a grin, his gray eyes filling with laughter in spite of his weariness. Provoking and wheedling Clint had always been one of his favorite pastimes. Just because they were both dog-tired and grown men to boot was no reason, in Cad's opinion, to stop.

"Should it?" was Clint's sarcastic reply.

"In that case," Cad drawled, while reaching over to pluck the lock of Mourning's hair from Clint's hands, replacing it with the lock of Anna's he had just cut down, "I'll go after Mourning."

Clint made a disgruntled sound. "I know you aren't as stupid as you sound, little brother. You'd be wise to back off . . . way off."

"Oh-ho! So that's the way it is," Cad said.

"Just what in hell is that supposed to mean?" Clint asked, his gaze locked on the golden curl in Cad's hand, thoroughly irritated by the way his brother's fingers were caressing the lock of Mourning's hair.

"Meaning," Cad repeated with celestial innocence, "oh-ho! So that's the way it is."

Clint's smooth gaze narrowed considerably. "So now we're down to fornicating with words, are we? While you're busy wasting time, Cheno is getting farther and farther away. Just what do you hope to accomplish by all this clowning around?"

Cad shrugged, his face becoming more serious, but retaining the glinting humor in his eyes. "So who's clowning? There are two trails to follow, two girls to rescue, and two of us to do the rescuing. That means we split up here. You claim indifference as to which girl you go after, I've declared a preference. Maybe we need to discuss this. I'm ready to go while you're still trying to make up your damn mind. Now, you tell me, brother . . . which one of us is the clown? Are you sure it's me?"

Cad gave Mourning's curl another obvious caress before he tucked it safely into his pocket, throwing a grin that was guaranteed to infuriate at his brother.

Clint moved like a speeding train, catching Cad's shirtfront in a button-popping grip. An awful, ominous silence was interrupted by the crackle of tension as Clint glared at the confident face of his brother. With an edge to his voice that belied the control he tried to show, Clint said, "Okay. So now you've accomplished what you set out to do. You have wheedled me into making a choice. Don't try it again, brother . . . I don't like being a cat's-paw for anyone, not even you. We're both tired and on edge. Don't push me into doing something we'll both regret later. I'll discuss whatever you wanted to discuss, but the girl you're going after is not Mourning."

Remembering that Mourning cared for this lumpheaded brother of his, Cad tried to keep the lid on his own temper. "Who said so? You? I think you forget, brother, I don't intimidate as easily as Mourning. Is it possible for you to admit that you might just happen to care for her, or is your guilt driving you? Just how long are you willing to wait before you admit she's more than a fucksome woman to you?" The murderous rage in Clint's eyes did not alter Cad's verbal direction. "Don't wait too long, brother, or someone else will come along . . . someone who recognizes she's more than a warm piece of calico."

"You wouldn't happen to be that someone, would you?" Clint said, well aware of the fast displacement of his reason and self-control. Surely Cad knew he was skating on mighty thin ice. A few more sharpened barbs from him and they'd be settling this with their fists, the way they had done a thousand times before when they were growing up.

"Those are your words, not mine. And before I forget it, take your frigging hands off my goddamn shirt!" Cad brought up both forearms under Clint's grip, breaking the hold on his shirt. He saw the dangerous light in Clint's eye. Cad felt his own anger surging. If it was a fight Clint wanted, he would be glad to oblige him. "If you aren't interested in her, leave her alone. Don't keep dangling a carrot in front of her nose and yanking it back every time she tries to take a bite. You either want her, or you don't."

Clint laughed, a bitter, sarcastic laugh that made Cad clench his fists, fighting the urge to punch the fool in the mouth. "Oh, I want her, there's no denying that. Tell me, Cad, what's got your goat? Are you angry because I want her, or because you do?"

"You stupid son of a . . ." Cad stopped and forced himself to wait, gaining control. "She's Caroline's daughter, for God's sake! You know you can't toss her skirts the way you would some half-breed *señorita*. That option isn't even open to you, because of who she is. What I'm angry about is your stringing her along. Drink the whiskey or pass the bottle. Don't keep her existing on a chimerical diet in an illusory tower. Goddammit, Clint! She's a human being . . . an extraordinary, sensitive, wonderfully idiotic girl, not some mooncalf to be taken advantage of. She doesn't deserve to be treated that way." Cad saw that Clint was looking at him in an odd sort of way. Hopefully he had touched a nerve somewhere in that stupid callused lump.

"You don't know what you're talking about," Clint said, using a vexing tone of casual indifference.

Feeling intense exhaustion and surging wrath, Cad said, "Don't I? Are you so bullheaded that you can't see she's in love with you? Don't break her heart, Clint."

"You've never had any more scruples than I have when it comes to women. Why the sudden change over Mourning?"

"I . . ."

Clint threw up his hand as if waving Cad away. "No, don't look upon yourself as the cloistered crusader coming to her rescue. Your interest in her may not be as brotherly as you'd like to believe, my saintly little brother. Underneath that suit of armor of yours beats a heart as randy as they come. I think you're just pissed because you're afraid I may get to her before you do."

Cad's fist caught him square in the chin, sending Clint reeling into the twisted trunk of a mesquite tree. He looked at Cad with a stunned look of disbelief behind the split lip that bled like a stuck hog. A second later, Cad found himself in the same position, against the same tree, bleeding out of the same side of his mouth. Gingerly wiping his busted lip with the back of his hand, he grinned up at his brother. "Some discussion, huh?"

"It was your decision. I said we'd discuss it . . . you're the one who wanted to fuck it to death," Clint said succinctly.

Cad threw back his head with a boisterous laugh that was almost as good at releasing tension as a good old free-for-all fight. Touching his busted lip with his sleeve, he said, "I guess I had that coming, but so did you."

"Yeah. You're probably right. I guess we can both claim exhaustion." He picked Cad's hat up and slapped it against his thigh, then dropped it on his head. Grinning widely, Clint said, "No one could call you a pretty boy now. You're a mess."

"Oh, yeah?"

"Yeah."

"Well, for your information, brother, that puss of yours would stop a clock." Cad began to laugh, reducing the intensity when the split on his lip began to throb. "Damn, that's some right you delivered," he said, bringing his hand up to cup his jaw, then testing to be sure he could still move it.

Clint began to laugh along with him and threw his arm around his brother's shoulder. They walked toward the horses, which stood silently watching them as if they were total strangers. Before mounting, Cad fished the lock of Mourning's hair out of his pocket and tossed it to Clint. "Okay. You take the high road and I'll take the low road. See you at Citadel." Swinging upon Jezebel's back, Cad caught the lock of Anna's hair Clint tossed as he swung upon Conquistador's back.

After Cad departed Clint rode like a madman through Apache country, following Cheno's trail with relative ease until he reached the Rio Grande. Once he crossed the river into Mexico, the trail went cold . . . nothing. He rode for weeks with nothing to keep him company—nothing except the chestnut stallion that moved powerfully beneath him, a lock of golden hair tucked in his pocket, and his own loneliness.

He leaned forward in the saddle as he crested a butte, riding with a natural smoothness that only comes from hours astride a horse. He drew rein in the broiling sun, not bothering to look for shade. His eyes flicked over the endless stretch of desert that lay before him, lifting with a frown to the serrated edge of mountains lying blue in the distance.

Cheno had headed into the Sierra Madres, of that much he was certain. But it was a vast range of mountains encompassing thousands of inhospitable and unforgiving miles, and Mourning could be anywhere, no more than a tiny pinprick in that buckled and warped landmass. He removed his hat, wiping the sweat from his forehead with his arm, and then replaced the hat, again pulling the rolled brim low over his eyes. In the distance a heat devil shimmered in the air above the heated surface of the inferno that lay before him. A muscle moved in his jaw, and his thumb rubbed the raw edge of the reins hanging limply in his left hand. He needed a break and needed it bad. He would not accept defeat. With a nudge of his spurs he angled down the steep slope, driving himself and his horse almost beyond endurance.

Weeks passed, and still he rode on, the determination of his ancestors driving him as it had driven the Moors into Spain centuries ago. All about him lay vast and wasted land—like a woman, he thought, beautiful and beguiling but deadly if you didn't understand her.

They lay ahead . . . the Sierras, shimmering now in the dancing heat wave, no mirage, but real. His canteen was nearly empty and he was at least a day's ride from Acuna—he'd make it. His years around the Comanches had taught him to make do in the desert with little or no water, and Conquistador was getting by eating *cholla* and prickly pear, once Clint burned away the sharp spines.

It was the first week in October when he rode into Acuna; the dust lay fine and powdery, a foot deep beneath the chestnut's hooves, caking the pink satin lining of his nostrils and covering Clint with a gray film. He had been on the trail for two months now and he was hot, tired, dusty, and ready for some bit of information—any clue to point him in the right direction.

After a couple of tequila shots in the cantina, he ambled down the dusty street to purchase supplies. He had stopped outside the store, removing his hat to beat the dust from his clothes, when he noticed three pack-burrows tied to the hitching post. Running his fingers through his hair, he replaced his hat, pulling it low and stepped inside. Two *hombres* were purchasing a large quantity of provisions. A cart would have carried all the supplies much better than burrows . . . unless . . . unless they were going into the mountains, where a cart could not go.

He casually rolled a cigarette as he leaned against the counter, his hooded eyes watching the *hombres* make the last of their purchases and leave. With little effort, he pushed away from the counter and walked toward the clerk, purchasing what he needed; blankets, food, a few medical supplies.

"Looks like you just about sold out the house. Is business always this good?"

"It varies, *señor*. There are good days and bad. Today happened to be a good one." He began to wrap Clint's purchases. "Will there be anything else, *señor*?"

"No more supplies. I could use a little information."

"Where are you headed, *señor*? You wish to know a short-cut?"

"No shortcut, just information. Do you know where those two *hombres* are headed?" he inquired with a nod of his head in the direction of the departing men.

"No, *señor,* they are strangers here, and strangers do not usually state their business. We get many strangers through here . . . you are a stranger yourself, are you not?"

"Yeah," he replied, "I'm a stranger."

Loading his supplies, he rode out of town trailing the two *hombres.* It wasn't much of a lead and could very likely end up being a wild-goose chase, but it was the closest he had been to a break since crossing the Rio Grande. He trailed the *hombres* for almost two weeks before they rode into a small camp high in the Sierras.

Circling around the camp, going higher in the mountains, Clint set up a post to observe their movements. There was no way of knowing if this was a *Juarista* camp or one belonging to Cheno

Cortinas himself—just as there was no way of knowing if Mourning was even here. There were literally hundreds of small revolutionist and renegade camps, just like this one, scattered all through the Sierras. *Hell . . . this whole thing could end up being about as worthless as tits on a boar.*

He was on the mountain early the next morning before signs of activity were visible in the camp below. Everything looked normal enough—animals were fed, goats milked, tortillas made, and beans cooked. The door of one of the adobe huts opened and a man walked outside, pausing to talk before mounting and riding away with five other men. Clint recognized the red beard immediately—it was Cheno. A dizzying sense of soaring elation buzzed through him like a swarm of bees after honey. He tried to fight the sense of pleasure sweeping over him. *What if she wasn't here? What if she was . . . hurt . . . violated? No, Cheno was a cunning devil, sly as a fox—but he wasn't cruel. If Cheno still had her, she was safe—he'd stake his life on that.*

∽ 25

"Mourning . . ." He saw her the moment she stepped out of the hut. Her name came quickly to his lips, drawn with soul-ripping power from deep within him. Cankered by doubt, Clint found the sound of her name on his lips to be like the suppuration of a festering abscess draining away the purulence, allowing healing to take place. "Mourning . . ."

Finding her alive and apparently uninjured released an overflow of throbbing awareness he had suppressed during his endless search. Acutely aware of her nearness and the incredible attraction he felt for her, he battled yearning desire and craving need, hoping to conquer his body's reflexive response—a feat not only nigh impossible but also damn uncomfortable, considering the strong woman-hungry message his body was responding to. Relief, frustration, and desire; they churned within him, a boiling caldron too close to overflowing to come near.

Focusing with spirited intensity, his eyes followed her with a craving urgency as she left the camp in the company of a young Mexican girl and an armed guard. The musical jingle of her voice floated across the treetops to play upon his ears.

"Hurry up, Martina!" He heard the elfin laugh that had so haunted his memory. "I want to swim for a long time today."

The girl answered, *"No comprendo, señorita."*

"Sí, Martina, no comprende, but I'm going to keep on talking," Mourning said gaily, "even if you don't understand what I am saying." She ran ahead of the girl, pausing to snatch a flower,

then plucking the petals one by one and tossing them over her shoulder chanting, "He loves me . . . he loves me not . . ." She continued on down the path, disappearing into the thick growth ahead.

With the agility of a pronghorn Clint traversed the side of the mountain, following them. Half a mile down the trail he watched the guard pause by a twisted, weathered tree and roll a cigarette while Mourning and the girl continued around a bend to a small pool.

As Mourning approached the pool's edge Clint was standing motionless, watching each step she took as if he could not take his eyes off her. It came again, that slow, oozing warmth he felt when he was around her: unsolicited and, at times, unwanted, yet unavoidable. Spasm after spasm gripped him while he watched, dry-mouthed, as she quickly wiggled out of her clothes. She stood there, naked as a newborn, against the dappling of sunlight filtering through the twisted coils of vines and dense foliage. Against a backdrop of vivid color her slim body looked like a lonely pistil— pale against the crimson velvet of an exotic flower.

Mourning felt something powerful tugging at her with a curious tenderness that fluttered over her, like fragrant rose petals skimming lightly across her skin. "Clint," she heard herself whisper, knowing he was hundreds of miles away, but for some strange reason feeling his presence. She turned slightly, the curve of her head madonnalike as her eyes scoured the raw cliffside across from her. Seeing nothing, she turned and entered the water, where she was absorbed into the emerald depths of the quiet pool.

Slender, quiet, and quick, she glided through the water and Clint grinned widely at her uninhibited antics: dives, flips, even a couple of headstands. It wasn't enough. Not even the humor in her playful movement would sufficiently quench the desire that glimmered in his loins.

He wanted her, dammit. Tensing, he felt the return of the old idiocy; wanting to choke her for what she had put him through, yet desiring her more than he would have thought possible. He felt a new awareness; a spiraling power flowing through him; the old familiar sensation of quickening arousal manifesting itself once again, seeping like the thin curling smoke from an opium pipe . . . seductive and sweet, turning his blood to the consistency of thick honey. Slowly . . . leisurely . . . fluidly, he became aware of the soft rippling of tender emotions within him; no more than a thin trickle at first, drifting like a floating flower until it plummeted over the edge in a cascading fall, the sudden surging thrust of it stirring his quiescent passions. With it came the mounting realization of that separate part of him—his instinctive physical drive—superseded by more important emotional appeals when she disappeared, and now rushing through him with an almost nervous terror. He cared. He cared more than he realized. What had Cad said? *Just how long are you willing to wait before you admit she's more than a fucksome woman to you?* She was more, he knew that, but he just wasn't sure how much more. This new emotional upheaval gave him a whole new set of fears. He began to feel the encroaching dread. The Samson in him had its long hair, and it was Mourning. She was his most vulnerable point, having the power to cripple him mortally. He felt the constricting bands of female possession arise and seize him with a repellent force that tightened around him like a collar on a dog. It was a different picture he began to paint of himself. One that he did not particularly care for—Clinton Kincaid did not heel for any woman.

That night, as he sat by a small, secluded fire, his thoughts were about her. After weeks of gnawing raw anger, hours of searching—refusing to accept the fact that he might not ever find her, or that he would find her, but too late—he was astounded at his feelings toward her now. What he was feeling was not what he had expected. He was no longer angry, nor did he feel the overpowering urge to take her with savage violence. What he felt was a sadness of spirit, almost a repugnance to have any further contact with her. He wished he had not come after her, or even found her —he wished it to the point of hatred. He hated her childish immaturity. He hated her strong spirit and indestructible will. He was repulsed by the beauty of her face and body. And most of all he hated her feminine impudence of forcing her memory upon his mind.

Before she had come he was a free man; unattached, undisciplined, uncommitted . . . it was unnecessary that he be so. But now she had come and all that had changed and he hated her for it. He felt himself drawing away. With a ragged curse, he kicked dirt over the flames and rolled into his bedroll, her slippery, wet body still gliding through the dark shadows of his mind. *Go away, dam-*

mit! Can't you see that I loathe the sight of you? Get out of my mind, you don't belong here. But she was there, in his dreams.

The dawning of a new day brought with it the rebirth of the gnawing hunger he felt for her. He allowed that hunger to dominate his thoughts, supplanting the fears and dread he had felt the day before. He was a restless creature with a disciplined body, and a shaking foundation within his soul—one that did not always respond to the restraint that was expected, giving way to the yearning of the flesh. It was this weakness in himself that he despised. He did not like being vulnerable. To him it was a sign of weakness, and anyone knew that Clint Kincaid was not a weak man.

She was back at the swimming hole the next day, and when he'd watched all he could, he threw himself away from the sight that tormented him. He lay back in the shade, shutting his eyes, listening to the chirp of birds, the movement of the wind through the trees—anything to squeeze the vision of her perfect solitary nudity from his mind. His mind withdrew into the seclusion of the cliffs, but it was illusory. He could not withdraw from her completely. He had tried that before and he knew from experience that it was impossible. He still hated her for the confusion she had brought into his life, but it made little difference—there being such a thin, fine line between love and hate. She continued to dwell behind his closed eyes, and he felt the gradual ebbing of his resistance, the tempering of his anger. It was not her fault. She was young, unknowing, and vulnerable, not yet scarred by close sexual contact. No, the fault lay within him for allowing her to invade his privacy, for penetrating the mysterious stillness of his soul. He wished for some way to preserve the tenderness of his feelings for her, to protect the pure white fragility of her innocence from what was inevitable—the dreaded malignancy of desire.

But it was already too late. Desire quickened, and he felt the subtle awakening of his body, the stirring restlessness in his loins as the old hard passion in him came to life and he began to fight the same old battles. Giving way to the stirring propensity of his body, he lay back and thought about what he'd do if she were lying there beside him—naked, wet, and trembling like a newborn fawn.

His hands would caress the delicate, warm skin of her belly and then glide slowly down to her thighs, where the outsides would be firm and smooth and the insides . . . ah, the insides would be soft as silk and oh, so warm, with little quivers running through them when he touched her secret beauty. He would place his hands on . . . Shit! What the hell was he doing? Going crazy, that's what. Here he was—a grown man, sitting here like some pervert watching a woman undress and swim, and if that wasn't bad enough, he was daydreaming like some pock-faced fourteen-year-old. No reason to hate her, she had no control over him. There was no point in dreaming either . . . he wanted the real thing, not some vapor-and-mist substitute.

He rolled over to resume his watch, trying with no avail to look away when she left the water and dried off. Watching her use that towel was nearly the death of him. There she stood, naked as the day she was born, rubbing that towel all over her legs, arms, breasts, belly, and then . . . Oh, God . . . between her legs. Damn it all to hell . . . for a woman like that, he'd take on the whole damn Mexican Army . . . single-handed . . . blindfolded . . . one arm tied behind his back!

For the next three days he did nothing but observe, and every day it was the same . . . just what he'd been hoping for—a pattern. Convinced of her schedule, he left, riding farther into the mountains, searching for a campsite. He wanted a place to hide—a day's ride, no more, from Cortinas's camp. When he took her, he hoped they would expect him to head straight for the border and Citadel. He would head in the opposite direction, going farther into the Sierras to his prearranged hideout. After a few days, they'd move north for three or four days before turning east toward Texas.

He located a small cave, hollowed out above a small stream. Unloading his supplies, he stacked wood and brought grasses in for bedding and horse feed. He cleaned and loaded his Colts, rifle, and extra rifles. He fed and groomed the horses, checking their feet and going over the leather on both saddles, making the necessary repairs. He hunted fresh game, hanging the excess meat in strips across a willow frame to dry. He'd close up the mouth of the cave when he left, preventing any wild animals from entering his cache. When everything was ready, he ate a full meal, cooking some extra, just in case, and then he rested. He dressed and rode out before daylight the next morning, a man with a mission, leaving a trail that even an Apache couldn't follow.

It was agony, waiting for her to come for her bath. Only the calculating ruthlessness of self-discipline he had learned to force upon himself helped him to remain cold and passive, not allowing his emotions to blur his vision or cloud his thoughts. There'd be enough time for that later. When she appeared, he staked the horses at a safe distance and moved toward the pool.

Like an otter, he slipped silently into the pool, swimming underwater until he could see the pale shadow of her gliding through the crystal depths. When he grabbed her he felt her body stiffen, both of them sinking deeper when his hand slipped around her mouth. He pulled her struggling form into the shallows, allowing them to surface in the protective cover of water weeds. Her eyes were huge with fear when she looked at him, turning doe-soft and warm as velvet when recognition penetrated.

"Clint!" she breathed, with disciplined control over her shaking emotions, a result of her months under his tutelage. "You came for me," she whispered. "You really came."

There could have been no greater surprise if she had spit water in his face. Of all the things she could have said, this puzzled him the most. Why did she seem stunned that he had come for her? He looked down at the childish, water-logged face he knew so well. She was mermaid-naked and mermaid-wet against him, and he could feel the warm pliancy of her soft breasts pressing against the bare flesh of his chest with each shallow breath she drew. She seemed totally unaware of her perfectly remarkable nakedness . . . the gloriously undefiled beauty of her devastating body, and he could feel a soft rapture in the magnificent throb of rekindled passion. Her hair clung to her damp skin like twisted ropes of seaweed, and for a moment he felt a reluctance to disturb the harmony between her and the water, as if Poseidon himself would rise up from the depths and protest violently. Her arms slipped around his neck and she pressed her face against the cove of his shoulder and he could feel that her nose was cold.

"Clint," she said, over and over. As if she finally realized it was him, she began to say, "You came. After all this time, you came for me. You're really here." As if trying to convince herself of his reality, her hands traveled across his shoulders and down his arms, drifting lightly across his chest to cup his face. The look on her face was one of adoration, glazed with disbelief.

"I'm here, little buttercup. I'm really here," he said, pressing his lips against her wet head.

To have her like this, after so long, living with the fear of never finding her, the dread of the condition she would be in when he did . . . everything was suddenly of vague importance, nothing mattered but the burning contact of her flesh against his. This was not the time, and he willed himself to repress the emotion that quivered within him.

Mourning did not sense this, so she stood there, inertly looking at him, thinking, *I don't know this man, he is a stranger to me.* She was swept with a staggering flood of resentment toward him. She resented his finding her, she resented his taking so long to do it.

"Don't say anything," he whispered softly. "Finish your bath as usual and then get dressed. When you finish, call the girl." When Mourning's eyes pleaded with him, he softly kissed her wet mouth. "I won't hurt her . . . now, hurry."

He disappeared as silently as he'd come. Dazed, her mind tried to assimilate what he had said, but she was soaring on the warm current of his presence. Mechanically she finished her bath; numb and shocked, she didn't consider the probability that Clint was watching.

When she was dressed, she said, "Martina, come help me with my hair," forgetting the girl couldn't speak English. With a snort of self-chastisement she motioned for the girl to help her, jumping clear when Clint's hand slipped over the girl's mouth. A quick chop to the back of the neck silenced her.

To Mourning's concerned look, he hastily assured her, "She's okay, just out for a while. You stay here while I take care of the guard."

He returned a few minutes later and led her to the horses, pitching her a *rebozo* as he said, "Put this on, it may get cool before we can stop." For once she obeyed silently.

They almost made it. A flash of metal, reflecting the sun, glinted in her eyes, and Mourning looked quickly to see the guard, high on the ragged edge of an overhanging cliff above them. Screaming his name, she pushed Clint out of the line of fire as the resounding crack of a rifle echoed through her head, stunning her. Clint whirled, and with lightning speed jerked his rifle from the saddle. He fired, sending the Mexican falling to the rocks below— knowing the first shot had to count, he had no time for a second.

Alarmed and shaken, Mourning sank to her knees. He saw her trembling attempts to stand and pulled her to her feet, helping her to mount and following her down the narrow, winding trail. Soon the thunder of hooves and the wild, alerted cries of *banditos,* following in close pursuit, shattered the stillness.

"Stay low," he shouted, leaning flat against the neck of his stallion. When they reached a widening in the trail, Clint abruptly reined in. Without taking careful aim, he fired a succession of bullets into the side of the steep cliff that rose above the trail. The barrage of bullets zinged and whizzed as they slammed into the loose shale, causing a small landslide to cover the trail, burying it in a heap of rock and rubble, beneath a billowing cloud of dust. It would take days to clear it for passage. By the time he turned, Mourning was well down the trail ahead of him.

After several hours of hard riding they came to a narrow clearing by a small stream. "Dismount. We'll rest the horses here," he said sternly, making no move to help her dismount.

Lanky, handsome, and dangerous, he walked to the gurgling stream and knelt down, cupping his hands and bringing the water to his mouth. Before she had time to move, he said, "You'd better rest now. There won't be another chance for a while." He made no move to assist her.

He had spoken much more harshly to her on numerous occasions and it surprised him to see how his words had etched themselves across her pale, startled face. She appeared to be as shaken as he was when he watched her trembling hand close over the saddle horn and her leg slide lifelessly over the back of the horse. He realized then with a gripping sense of alarm that she needed help. She slipped to the ground before he could reach her. As he lifted her to her feet she looked at him with brightly burning eyes —unnaturally so.

"What's wrong?" he said as he put his hands on her upper arms to steady her, noticing for the first time that her skin was clammy and cold. Fine beads of perspiration dotted her lip and brow. *She's in shock,* he thought, and thinking she needed warmth, pulled her against him. "It's only a little farther and then I'll build us a nice warm fire." He brought his face against the softness of her hair. It was an instinctive act born of intense relief that pressed his lips against her soft curls.

Her voice was so soft against his ear, he almost missed her words. "I think I'm hurt."

Clint drew back and looked at her strangely. "Hurt?" he said softly, and then once it registered, he said more loudly, "You're hurt?" And louder still, "Where?"

She looked at him, squinting against the sudden brilliance of the sun angling across his shoulder. A shiver rippled across her. "It's so cold, I think it's going to snow."

"Buttercup, it isn't going to snow, it's too early. This is only Octo—" He saw it suddenly, the glazed incoherence in her eyes just before they rolled to the back of her head and her body swayed heavily against him. He shook her gently. "Don't pass out on me now, dammit . . . tell me where you hurt."

She tried to tell him, but her mouth seemed disjointed from the rest of her body and incapable of functioning.

"Mourning, tell me where you hurt."

Inside her eyes there were brilliant splashes of color so pretty, she didn't want to open them. She heard him ask again and she tried to concentrate, but a scalding pain in her middle spoiled her efforts.

"Something bit me. . . . It w-was the c-cougar."

"Dammit! You're not making sense," he said with a shaky voice.

Her head lolled back and her eyes closed as her body became deadweight. He swept her into his arms and carried her to the water's edge, nestling her as best he could in the grass. "Something bit you? Where?" He began to feel along her arms and legs, finding nothing broken, no swelling, no bites. He lifted the side of her *rebozo* and uttered a sharp exclamation:

"Son of a bitch!" Her entire side, down past her hip, was soaked in blood. She had taken a bullet meant for him and had been bleeding for hours.

Clasping her against him, he whispered into her ear. "Oh, Jesus, sweetheart, why didn't you tell me?"

It was the only time in his life that anyone was present when Clint Kincaid emerged from behind the handsome exterior he had erected to protect his privacy from trespass. His face was twisted with raw pain—the kind that comes only from caring . . . deeply. It would have meant something to her to have seen it, but she was lost behind closed lids in a world of profuse color.

He could never remember experiencing fear—pure, cold, gut-wrenching fear, the kind that knots and curls deep in the belly, growing until it consumes—but he felt it now. It was an almost comical fear, funny because it wasn't only the thought of her being taken from him that caused the shuddering apprehension, but the untimeliness of it. It was wrong. It was all wrong. There was something not finished here, something left undone; a painting sold before the final splashes of color had been added.

"You aren't going to die, Mourning. You aren't going to get away from me that easy. We've a lot of unfinished business, you and I, and it's not like you to quit. You're no coward, so don't you quit on me now . . . damn you! Don't you quit!" He couldn't go on. With a frenzy born of fear, he clutched her to him and carried her to his horse. The cave . . . they had to get to the cave.

He stumbled twice as he carried her into the cave three hours later—his body too fatigued to tell his mind it was exhausted. A tiny moan escaped her lips as he lowered his treasured little burden to the bed of grass he'd made the day before.

Gritting his teeth to the shattering point, he did what he could to prepare for extracting the bullet: building the fire, boiling water, placing medical supplies at her side, burying his knife blade in the glowing coals. Opening the medicine pouch, he surveyed the meager contents: antiseptic powder, bandages, needle, thread—not much, but it was all he had. He wished he had something to give her for pain, but wishing wouldn't make it so.

He washed his hands and removed the red-hot knife from the coals, plunging it into the boiling water and rinsing it with whiskey —taking a stiff drink himself. Locating the point of entry, he placed his finger in the hole and began to probe, feeling the tunnel the bullet had made as it barely missed her rib. She stirred slightly and groaned weakly. No time for him to get shaky hands now, he thought as he hardened himself to the task at hand. She groaned again. "I know, love, I know. I'm sorry. I have to do this."

He knew she couldn't hear him, but somehow talking to her was reassuring to him, confirmation that she still lived. "It won't be much longer now, angel."

Probing deeper, his finger stopped against the hard, flattened surface of the bullet. "I've found it, Mourning. Hang on, firebrat, just a little longer." Following the guide of his finger, he slipped the knife into her side, and after what seemed an eternity felt it scrape the metal. Blood continued to flow from her, gushing more heavily when he pulled the small twisted piece of metal from her side. He tossed the bullet into the tin basin of water. It landed with a splash and the hollow clink of metal hitting metal. He rinsed his fingers before taking up the needle that had been soaking in whiskey. She flinched when he poured whiskey into the wound, and dusted it liberally with antiseptic powder, and then moaned pitifully when he sutured the ragged edges together, using the same stitches he'd used to stitch his saddle leather when it needed mending.

When he'd finished, he drank several gulps of whiskey before collapsing next to her, falling into an exhausted sleep.

When he awoke it was dark and she was still asleep, her face hot to the touch, and her breathing shallow and rapid. She stayed this way for three days, alternating between freezing chills and burning fever, Clint following the demands of her tortured skin; building up the fire and bundling her under blankets, or stripping her bare and soaking her with cooling wet cloths.

Gradually . . . slowly, the buzzing in her ears subsided and she became painfully aware of a gnawing heat radiating from her. The cougar! His low, hissing growl punctured her sensitive ears and she screamed, "No! No! No!" and then she felt the weight of him on her and she pushed at him with all her might, fighting and twisting until she felt the wet drag of his tongue across her fevered face and she went still. It wasn't the cougar at all, but a kitten; soft and cuddly and purring. She relaxed, nestling down in the familiar feather mattress, the sound of the steamboats churning up the muddy water of the Mississippi, drifting in through her bedroom window. Memphis! She was home.

The wet tongue of the cat came again and she pushed at it. "No! Don't!"

"Mourning, sweetheart, it's me, Clint."

She opened her eyes to see Clint huddling over her, wiping her face with a wet cloth. She watched the concerned eyes, observing through blurred vision the unshaven face, the ragged hair, the tightly drawn lips. "You're getting me all wet!" she snapped crossly, slapping the cloth away a second time.

He stopped instantly, holding the dripping cloth suspended in midair, and looked at her as if he'd just seen a ghost. Before she had a chance to complain further about the still-dripping cloth, he dropped his hands flat against his thighs and sat back on his heels with his eyes squeezed tightly, his head thrown back as if in agony.

"Okay! I didn't mean to hurt your feelings . . . go ahead and wash my face if it makes you feel that much better," she said with an air of condescending irritability. When he began to look as though he were in the final throes of a fatal spasm, she said more loudly, "I said it was all right to wash my face, you big, dumb lummox."

Those were the sweetest words that had ever slipped from her mouth. She was going to be all right. He lowered his head, pressing the heels of his palms against his brow for several minutes before he finally looked at her with a helpless, washed-out expression on his face. "How do you feel?"

She was as cross as a bear and his ridiculous behavior was not helping her mood any. After a few moments of heavy concentration centered on the rough stubble on his face, she replied, "I feel rather like a pair of old galoshes left out in the rain after a good stomping. Where are we? What happened to you? You look like something the dogs dragged up and the cats wouldn't take. Do you know that? Is there anything to eat? I'm starving. Did I ask you where we were?"

"Yes, morning glory, you did," he said, grinning widely. The euphoria sweeping through him had him soaring to greater heights than any rotgut whiskey had ever accomplished.

"Well," she snapped, "why haven't you answered me?" He opened his mouth to speak, but she interrupted. "Never mind, now. I'm sleepy." And with that she closed her eyes and smiled at the fluffy kitten that was waiting for her.

Mourning had no idea how long she'd slept, but on awakening, the first thing she saw was Clint's exquisitely chiseled profile sleeping so close to her, she could reach out and touch him. Attached to that beautifully embellished face was a set of magnificently muscular shoulders. He was naked to the waist, below which the blanket left the rest to her imagination. Her eyes roamed over his blanketed form, growing inquisitively wide when he turned on his side toward her, the blanket riding low on his lean hips—suggestively low. There was a light fluttering in her throat and she found it increasingly difficult to swallow. What did he look like down *there*? From a purely inquisitive standpoint, of course—curiosity being the foundation of all learning.

Most young women have at one time or another experienced, in reality or a dream, the overpowering thirst for knowledge of that most forbidden of all subjects: *the male anatomy*. Their eventual salvation comes not from the dissipation of that shameful curiosity but more from the unavoidable lack of opportunity to satisfy their unquenchable thirst. And now, when she had least expected it, the opportunity had miraculously presented itself, and Mourning's inquisitive eyes fell upon the woven blanket that barely covered that mystery of all mysteries.

With intense anticipation and profound shortness of breath she tentatively raised her hand, and instantly a mind-boggling timidity swept over her. She jerked her hand back as if she had been bitten, thrusting it under the covers as if to protect it from the terrible and sinful unknown. She squeezed her eyes shut, but that blinking blanket was there, lit up like a Christmas tree . . . beckoning. She eyed *it* again; that area of supreme mystification, knowing that underneath that blanket lay the Tree of Knowledge, Pandora's Box, and everything she had ever wanted to know about male sexuality. All she had to do was peek beneath it.

With a woman's patient passivity she decided to outwait him. If she waited long enough, she reasoned, he would move again and the chances were good that the blanket would slip lower—and it was dead certain that it would if she helped it a little. So with trembling resolve she began to wait cautiously on what seemed to be a most harebrained and hazardous undertaking. What on earth would he think if he happened to wake up while she had the blanket up over his head? He would probably think her a little strange, but not startling. She waited, and waited. Well, patience had never been one of her virtues.

The forbidden vision remained in front of her, increasing in vividness. She was unable to fix her mind on anything else. She was overly aware of what opportunity lay before her, and staring morbidly at *it,* she saw an opportunity for the attainment of knowledge heretofore reserved for the most lewd, immoral, unchaste, or married among women. Here was the opportunity to be a real pioneer, yet the very thought of looking at *that* part of him made her throat dry. The thought of touching him made her ears ring. And the thought of fondling him launched her like a hurtling rocket streaking through the cosmos. She began to understand the tormented frustration of Eve; should she give in to temptation or not? *Give in! Give in!* something within her kept saying.

She swallowed loudly, her eyes streaking to his face to see if he had heard. He slept on, blissfully unaware of the havoc he was creating. She sighed, feeling a heaviness of spirit as she gazed

wretchedly at the blanket. Clint turned in his sleep, throwing one
leg out, thrusting *that* part of him unavoidably close. It was predes-
tined; fate had brought about this opportunity for enlightenment.
The time for confrontation with her destiny was at hand. With
quaking confidence she forced her hand to move, fumbling her way
. . . inching across the distance between them with caterpillar
speed until she touched the naked edge of the blanket. When nothing happened she expelled a long-held breath, for she surely had
expected thunder to roll and lightning to flash when she touched
the gateway to sin, which was posing as a blanket.

*Just lift it and then you will know . . . just one quick peek.
The world is full of people who don't know what you are about to
find out.* Why should she care? But she cared! She cared! It ate at
her like acid. *What can it hurt? Plenty!* She wasn't about to be led
down the primrose path of self-persuasion. She knew a little bit of
knowledge was a dangerous thing, but in this case it could be fatal!

Still . . . The little flame of curiosity licked her once more
and she experienced frustration as she had never before experienced it. Finally, fired by sheer desperation and obeying an impulse
so universally aroused in the female breast that it would be a sin
against creation to ignore it, she slowly lifted the edge of the blanket to begin her exploration of the manifold wonders of the magnificent but little known anatomy of the human male.

Look, stupid! Look! she told herself when the blanket was
high enough, but still she kept her eyes averted. At last, with the
resolve of one facing a firing squad, she turned her head and
looked! Oh, God! There is nothing as disappointing as being disappointed. Underneath the blanket he was wearing a pair of buckskins, deliciously tight and riding sinfully low on his hips, but more
than covering the subject.

Mourning at that very instant had a singular experience—a
mortifying shock like a stabbing knife to the heart. With horrible
suspicion, Mourning allowed her eyes to travel up the naked expanse of chest to the wide-open, glinting-with-humor eyes of a very
much awake Clint Kincaid. She gasped. The sound of his cracking
laughter caused her to experience some severe qualms about the
soundness of her mind and the capabilities of her good judgment
(or lack of it), and brought to a screeching halt any further
thoughts she might have had on the subject.

Caught red-handed in her peeping Tomism, and beginning to

feel deep in her repentant heart a mounting displeasure with the Creator's methods, she had no recourse but to confront him with the chilled dignity of one not long for this earth. "That," she said in her best debilitated, bedridden voice, "was most ignoble of you."

He had the presence of mind to control further outbursts of laughter. "What? Waking up, or wearing pants?"

"Your mind seems to dwell on nasty perversion," she sputtered.

He growled deep in his throat, in a lazy, sensual way. "Why, weren't you just enjoying a little *nasty perversion*, Miss Mourning?"

"No!" she squeaked, and cleared her throat, and then, speaking with more control, she said, "I was just . . ."

"Checking out the finer points of my anatomy? Shame on you, Miss Mourning . . . taking advantage of a sleeping man that way. All you had to do was ask. Here, I'll be glad to show you." He gave her a smile so warm and rich, it would make hot fudge look anemic, and then he made a move toward the buttons on his buckskins.

Mourning squeezed her eyes shut, and her face flamed from the rasping edge of his laughter. "For the last time, I am not interested in looking at any part of you. Do you want me to write it on the end of a hammer and beat it into your thick skull? Now leave me alone, I am feeling tired again."

"Do you feel bad? Is it your side bothering you again?" He laid the back of his hand against her forehead, her cheeks, her throat, and finding no fever, he left it there, caressing her flowerpetal smoothness.

Mourning looked up into the hooded fire of his eyes. "I believe when we last talked you were going to tell me where we were."

"So I was," he said.

"Well?"

"You are in a cave in the Sierras." He could not help but notice the mask of disappointment that settled over her pale face.

"We're still in Mexico, then?"

"Yes."

Her next question was never asked because she paused to listen to a low humming that became louder and louder, becoming a rapid slapping with frequent short shrieks, high-pitched and shrill.

"Clint!" she said, groping blindly for his hand.

"It's only the bats leaving the cave," he said, enjoying the nearness of her, the way she clutched his hand to her chest. "They are nocturnal animals, you know. Like you, they sleep all day and want to prowl at night. They're harmless." He kissed her forehead, savoring the cool feel of it against his lips after so many days of raging fever. "I've made some soup. Would you care for some?"

Remembering how Cheno's band had eaten whatever was available, she felt compelled to say, "If it's bat soup, I'm not hungry." It wasn't. She ate. Afterward he bathed her face and hands again and tucked the blanket around her. When he drew away, she still held tightly to his hand.

"Stay with me."

"I'm right here, not more than two feet away," he said, pointing to his bedroll.

"No, I mean stay here . . . next to me."

"Mourning," he said sternly, "I don't think that would be a very good idea."

She wrinkled her nose. "Why? Even *you* wouldn't attack a sick woman. Would you?"

He grinned. "I might not attack, but I'm sure as hell not above a little subterfuge." He stretched out beside her and smiled when she groped for the blanket and lifted the edge, inviting him inside. "That," he said seriously, "is a *very* bad idea."

"I promise I'll slap your roving hands," she said happily.

"My sweet darling girl, it's not my hand that I'm worried about." Slipping next to her, he placed one arm under her shoulder, drawing her head against his bare chest. Shadows danced across the cave walls in rhythm with the shooting flames of the fire. The bats were all out now, and the cave was quietly hushed, except for the hiss of a too green log and the occasional pop of an ember showering the darkness with pinpoints of light.

"Will they come back in the morning?"

"Hmm? Who?"

"The bats. Will they come back?"

He brushed his lips across her forehead, a tendril of her hair clinging to the stubble of his beard. "Yes, they'll be back at dawn with full little tummies, ready to sleep the day away. I'm sure when the mother bat serves soup to her baby bats, they will all screech, *If it's girl soup, we're not hungry.*"

She giggled and then gasped with pain. "I forgot," she said through clenched teeth. "It hurts too much to laugh."

"I think it would be better if you tried to go to sleep," he said against her forehead.

"I will if you promise to stay here."

He nodded and she shifted and stirred her position until she had rooted out a little nest and had nuzzled comfortably into it, surrounded by the warmth of his arms and his beloved long body —the familiar smell of him soothing and comforting like fragrant spiced-apples simmering in an open kettle.

As she grew still and her breathing grew slower and deeper, he thought about slipping away from her, thinking she would rest better, but somehow he was finding immense pleasure in giving comfort to her by just holding her near. It was a new feeling, this sharing of himself, of giving part of himself to someone else. Although he was a considerate lover to the women he bedded, he gave pleasure to them because it made it more enjoyable for him; he always received something back for time invested. The idea of enjoying a close, physical relationship with no sexual contact had never been something he would even consider, much less find pleasure in. He had always mated like an animal; it was the quality of the act itself that was important, not the person it was consummated with. And now he found himself heavily involved emotionally with a woman for the first time in his life, and he hadn't made love to her.

Mourning shifted in her sleep, sliding her smooth leg over his bristled one. Lust, raw and primitive, reared its head, and Clint felt the rousing hunger of his body's craving for her. No, dammit! Holding her wasn't enough. He wanted more, but not enough to press an injured woman. He would have to be content to hold her for now. What was the quote from Epicurus? *Do not spoil what you have by desiring what you have not; but remember that what you now have was once among the things only hoped for.*

≈ 26

The mouth of the cave lay gaping like the enormous jaws of a waking giant. Early-morning light pierced the dank interior with brilliant beams of light. It had been six days since Mourning's escape from Cheno's camp, and it was the first day she woke without her mouth feeling like the inside of a cotton boll.

Today she was feeling marvelously chipper and in the highest of spirits as she lay on her blanket watching Clint rush in and out of the cave, performing his chores. She lay perfectly still as Clint flitted to put away their freshly washed clothes, carried out feed for the horses, and carried in canteens of water. He leaned over the fire to taste his culinary concoction, which smelled a lot like venison stew, and she smiled privately as his muscular buttocks, which were pointed her way. She closed one eye, as she had seen him do on numerous occasions when he didn't think she knew, and drew a bead on him, sizing up the generous curve of his backside, the dense strength of his thighs, the hard curve of his calves—all perfectly outlined in the snug-fitting buckskins he wore. When he glanced in her direction, she closed her eyes, pretending to be asleep. Moments later she peered at him again. Holding up her thumb she drew a finer bead on him, this time much more critical in her analysis. Even in this semidomesticated state he was one fine-looking specimen of manhood. A man like Clint Kincaid would be breathlessly masculine in an apron. She stretched as luxuriously as the soreness in her side would allow and imagined him wearing an apron, then smiled a satisfied feline smile as she pictured him in an apron—nothing else . . . a glorious study in almost naked Herculean splendor.

Moments later Clint swept into the cave with all the sheer carnality of Bacchus and his riotous group after the hesitant Ariadne. Stopping just inside the cave's mouth, his arms loaded with firewood, he observed her watching him with silent mirth. Giving her a smile that would raise blisters on paint, he said, "Care to divulge the source of your bubbling cheer?"

She jumped, startled at the sound of his voice. With a puny gulp she stared into his dove-gray eyes. Her voice, like her good humor, had suddenly deserted her, leaving her mind as blank as an old maid's dance card.

"Come, now, my glib-tongued parrot," he said pleasantly, "surely you can think of something clever. Just tell me what you are smiling at?" He dropped the load of wood by the fire and walked toward her, a smooth, rolling walk that rendered her temporarily thoughtless, speechless, and witless. He dropped to his knees beside her.

"Now, love, tell me what has tickled your fancy this day. Surely it can't be that you find humor in the sight of a man earnestly at work." His hand moved forward and slid behind her neck to the baby-soft flesh that lay pure and white under her hair. Caught without warning, she was unable to repress the quick intake of breath that coincided with the brushing of her skin against his. Lacking in the urbane sophistication of an experienced flirt, her responsiveness to the sensual stimulation of his fingers was open and clownish. As his thumb stroked her ear and his fingers played in the sensitive hair at her nape, she gasped, drawing her shoulders upward, trapping his hand against her as she looked at him with eyes as big as cartwheels. *Words, where are you when I need you?*

Encouraged by his smile, she made some reference to having allowed her mind to wander and asked him if he had ever drifted away from the harsh land of reality and floated briefly in the world of fanciful daydreams. His response was that he had, as a child. Somehow it was difficult for her to picture Clinton Kincaid as a daydreaming youth.

"It's an experience I would like to recapture, however. Why don't you bring me up to date on the finer points of castle building," he said with a heart-melting smile. "If one were going to daydream, what is the first thing one would do?"

Anyone but a complete fool would not have been duped by his slow, lazy smile. Fool that she was, Mourning swallowed the bait.

"First you lie down, on your back, like me."

He stretched out next to her on his side, his elbow bent and his head resting in the palm of his hand. His questioning eyes studied her. "Then what?"

"You close your eyes, because it's like drawing the curtain between the dreamer and the real world." She closed her eyes, her lashes fluttering long and thick against her cheek.

"And then?"

"You relax completely and let your . . ." *Oh, dear, oh, dear —it is a blind goose that comes to the fox's sermon.*

His warm breath shimmered across her bare shoulders with the chilling effect of cold arctic air as he leaned forward and pressed a gentle kiss against each trembling lid. The whisper-soft tips of his fingers skimmed the sensitive skin of her throat, traveling up to trace the line of her lips, the bridge of her nose. There was something dreadfully loud pounding in her head and her once steady breathing had deserted her completely, leaving her to make do with short, erratic pants, incapable of providing enough oxygen. She was light-headed and hot . . . no, cold . . . actually, there was no feeling at all.

"Wait!" she shouted, and he winced at her volume.

"I'm right here, love, see? Feel how close I am." His fingers stroked her throat. "Mourning-love, there is no need to shout. We can discuss sensibly what it is that distresses you so." Once again he felt the gush of tender amusement when she became so obviously flustered at his nearness. Her eyes flew open and she looked at him with eyes as unconscious and innocent as a five-year-old. Emotion began to stir, and desire rushed through him with such force that he was left momentarily as startled as she was. "Perhaps I was wrong . . . yes . . . did I say we could discuss it? Sensibly? My error, sweet angel, for I am quite incapable of discussing anything sensibly at the moment."

"Stop! Let's talk a minute. I wanted to tell you . . ."

"Mourning, sweet, haven't you heard it's a foolish sheep that makes the wolf his confessor? Don't you know that you are no safer talking to me than when you are lying half naked in my arms?"

Kincaid possessed a certain teeth-gnashing giftedness for speaking proverbially—a talent that always left her stunned. As she began to gain control once more, she looked at the yawning mouth of the cave, then down at the blanket covering her . . . just barely. Distressed, she gave it a tug, only to find it pinned beneath his weight. With a small cry of alarm she began to jerk frantically at the blanket to tug it higher over the satin-smooth curve of her breasts. Her movements were pathetically infantile and oh, so obviously prompted by extreme discomfort. One hastily stolen glance at him told her that her clumsy movements had done absolutely nothing to still his increasing ardor. The grayness of his eyes grew darker as he studied her intently. His slender fingers followed the silky length of a curl that curved inward just below her breast. Reaching the end of the curl, his hand rested a moment before tracing the line of her rib. Charge after charge of electrical current jolted through her, reducing her to a mere lump of stupefaction.

"Mourning . . . Mourning. My clumsy little clown. Here you go again trying to distract my advances with your ridiculously blundering diversions. When are you going to realize that your adorably refreshing attempts are like a strong wind to glowing coal —igniting with greater passion that which you so foolishly seek to subdue?"

The soft familiarity of his voice was penetrating her consciousness, calling to her with all the innate intensity of a familiar roost to a homing pigeon.

"Leave me alone," she said, trying to sound aloof, which was pathetically more like the forlorn bleating of a fatted calf. "Don't touch me . . . please."

His hand, which had been tracing her ribs, closed warmly over one perfectly sculptured breast. "You've got to be kidding."

Nothing is more treacherous than the human body; nothing is quite so capable of betrayal, and Mourning suddenly found herself traitorously abandoned. With paralyzing horror she gazed at Clint as if she had never seen him before, every part of her body acutely aware of him with such fierceness that it was frightening. She could feel the kneading warmth of his hand through the thin blanket, while the inside of her body was like an overwound clock; springs were popping, gears were stripping, and wheels were grinding.

While his hand wreaked havoc at her breast, his lips began their own assault on her face, throat, and neck. *My lord,* she thought, *he's got more maneuvers than mounted artillery.* Mourning frantically searched for something to distract him. "I'm hot," she stammered.

"Angel-love, you must be delirious to play into my hands like that. If you're hot, by all means let's get this blanket off."

"No, no!" she shouted while gripping the blanket with clam-jawed strength. "That's not what I meant. I want *you* off." *How can I distract this odious man?* When no other idea presented itself, she merely lay there gasping for breath like a banked fish.

Meanwhile, Clint, with calculated ease, made a very thorough manual examination of her body that seemed to go on forever until in desperation she wiggled. She knew immediately that was the wrong thing to do. He whispered into her ear, "You're playing into my hands again."

Everything she said or did was a reversal of what she'd intended. When she tried to push him away, her hand slipped off his smooth chest and plunged downward, and to her chagrin Clint murmured, "Lower." Truly flustered now, she pushed earnestly against him, saying, "Get up, you big oaf. I prefer you standing erect."

"I'm doing my damnedest to do just that," he whispered, with a chuckle that shivered across her skin.

"I mean I want you up." His mouth took hers with gentle passion. When he lifted his head, his lips singed and scorched a meandering little trail across her bared throat. "Mmmm, lady bright, I can grant your wish now."

When she looked at him, he was grinning. "What wish?" His lips found the sensitive tingling place just below her ear. A pleasure-moan escaped from her throat and she felt a corresponding shiver, hard and intense, run the length of his body.

Smiling against her throat, he whispered, "It's up."

Her eyes flew open. The idiot kept grinning until she could almost feel herself on the edge of a smile. This time she was convinced that morons, like grapes, came in bunches.

"My adorable goosecap, keep looking at me like that, and it's going to stay up."

With a groan, Mourning buried her head against his shoulder, thinking she was on the verge of an emotional emergency of epic proportions.

"Come here, little virgin. No, love, I won't compromise you if that's what you're thinking." His gifted fingers played slowly with a lazy lock of hair that lay over her shoulder. Something in the intensity of his eyes spoke to her and her lips parted softly, and were parted further by his, in a long, exploring kiss. Afraid she would float away, she anchored herself against him, her slender arm curling around his shoulders.

Clint turned against her more fully, fragrant skin and tightly coiled muscle pressing against her as the smoothness of his palms cupped her buttocks, pulling her to meet him. She fitted against him like the peel on a banana, the sharp outline of him cradled against her belly, generating a dull, throbbing ache within her. She felt like a fragile leaf floating on the glassy surface of a sun-drenched pond, lazy and immobile—drifting with the current.

His breath, mingling with hers, was dulling her to inaction like a sleep-inducing opiate. The silky coolness of his dark hair was pressed against her hot skin as his lips did the most magical things against her throat and shoulders.

"Enough," she whispered weakly. "Enough . . . enough."

"Oh, no, Mourning-love, my little morning glory. We've just begun." His lips moved with precision accuracy against her trembling lips with an open kiss, light and intriguing. His lips flirted across hers, arousing her curiosity with subtle play. Sensing her interest, he deepened the pressure, his tongue playing against the seal of her lips, slipping inside with delicate penetration, carrying her with him into the swirling vacuum. His mouth still covering hers, he whispered, "See, love? What ever made you think you'd had enough? There's more. Let me show you. Let me teach you how to use your tongue."

She pushed against him. "You are disgusting. I don't want you to teach me any . . . What do you mean, how to use my tongue? No! No! I didn't mean it," she said frantically when he smiled with a degree of clever cunning. "Oh, help!" was all she managed to squeak before his lips claimed hers again.

"Help? No, love, you don't want help. I know what you want, buttercup. Let me show you. See? Yes. Oh, yes. That's it, angel. Are we sure we want to continue this? No, never mind, it's too late now. *Mmmm,* I can't seem to stop. Can you, love? No? That's good."

Her breath rate increased as well as his, and her skin trembled beneath the faint movement of his hot breath as his mouth roamed over the her throat, the glide of his hair across her cheek drawing a response of its own. "See what I mean. It's all done with subtle intrigue and movement."

"Oh, Lord! You are crazy! I can't believe you are tutoring me about kissing like it was a history lesson. A kiss is a kiss," she said flatly. "They're all the same . . . well, maybe not exactly the same, but they're all approached from the same . . . no, that's not what I meant either. What I'm trying to say is, kissing is basically . . . Oh, never mind. Have you no shame? Is there nothing you won't discuss?"

His body was shaking as his face nuzzled the hollow of her throat, his words light and tickling against her skin. "There is no one like you. Do you know that? This is the way I like you, adorably idiotic and bewitchingly innocent . . . And no, there is absolutely nothing I won't discuss," he answered, with a tone of humorous endearment. Running his fingers along the line of the blanket that skimmed the contours of her breasts, he slipped them slightly inside. *"Hmmm.* You feel good. Tell me, Mourning, love . . . morning glory . . . my little morning star . . . do you look as good as you feel?"

Taking the bait like a starving lumpfish, she answered, "I . . . I don't know."

"You don't? That will never do, angel. Shall we see?"

It was a good thing she was already lying on the ground—as it was, she felt she was slowly melting the surface beneath her and sinking lower, like a hot coal on a block of ice.

He made a move to lower the edge of the blanket and she grabbed his wrist. "No! I don't want to see . . . I've already seen . . . No, I mean you don't need to see . . . oh, please stop. You're making me feel like a mass of overkneaded dough."

"Mourning . . . adorable girl . . . my sweet angel. Am I so hard on you?" The warm current of his breath was striking her skin mercilessly as his lips continued to dwell languorously about her throat. "Now, Mourning, love . . . my wonderful, crazy girl, show me . . . show me how you've learned to kiss with your tongue." His mouth opened searchingly over hers and she felt ev-

ery part of her body swell with a deep, aching need. As his mouth
hovered over hers, barely touching the sensitive skin of her lips, she
inched her tongue forward, touching his. This kiss was as different
from their usual kiss of heated passion as the slow heaviness of a
cudgeling battle-ax is from the weightless flexibility of a sword;
light, smooth, airy—like the whisper-soft thrust of a fencing foil—
rapier-sharp and subtle.

"Mourning, sweet, you learn fast, did you know that?" he
groaned huskily, using his hands to encourage her. "Yes, sweetheart . . . yes . . . you learn very fast. Perhaps that is incorrect
. . . oh, yes . . . it is . . . I think you could teach . . . me
. . . a . . . few . . . things." He placed his fingers along the
hidden angle of her jaw and kissed her again. Hard, forcefully, and
passionate. This was no light, subtle, intriguing kiss, but an impassioned, driving thirst. Mourning whimpered from somewhere deep
inside and could not stop her hands, which slid upward to lock
around his neck, drawing him closer. With a feeling of something
like despair, she kissed him intensely and felt a corresponding stab
of longing curling deep within her.

"Mourning, sweet darling love . . . bid me enter . . . don't
keep me howling at the gates forever."

She couldn't have answered him if she had understood the
meaning of his words because she was drowning in a warm pudding—thick, creamy, and heavily sweet. Somewhere between his
howling at the gates and her slow sinking, the blanket that barely
covered her slipped lower, revealing her exquisitely splendid
breasts, lustrous in the soft luminescence of the fire's glow.

Seeing the immediate change in his expression, slow recognition dawned on her, and with a lugubrious look she glanced
quickly down. Stricken, her eyes shot back to his face, seeing what
she dreaded most—a love-glazed smile as his hand floated upward,
warmly covering her naked breast. Impassioned and panicked, she
pushed at him, but he held her in a fusing embrace, stealthily
overpowering her resistance, leaving her will blurry and indistinct.

"Clint, please . . . don't." It was a whisper lacking conviction.

"I can't, little mourning dove. Don't fly from me . . . not
now."

"What are you doing?" she squeaked.

"Thwarting your escape," he said, his lips laying waste her

good intentions as they nuzzled across her throat to the soft swell
of her breasts. "I have you in check now, love. Did you know that?
Your king is exposed to attack and must be protected or moved.
What are you going to do?"

Her arms, which had been pushing at him, were now limply
useless as his questing mouth found her breast. She arched against
him.

"Ahhh. That was the wrong move, my wild, foolish girl. I
have you now."

He could have the king. He could have the queen. He could
have the whole chessboard for that matter. Nothing mattered but
the delicious stroking of his hands, the warm, soothing phrases
that he uttered, and the lazy movement of his tongue, all working
separately, yet coming together to leave her incoherent and mesmerized.

"Checkmate. I'm sorry, love . . . it's too late. Escape is impossible now," he said, his voice a low, vibrating growl as he
moved with leonine stealth and grace to assault her lips once more,
his fingers tangling in the thick mass of hair at the back of her
neck. Using this as leverage, he pulled her mouth to his once again.
Again and again he brushed across her parted lips and felt the
timid inquisitiveness of her tongue, like the first spring crocus
peeking through the snow. "Yes, love. That's right. Now it's my
turn." But she quickly turned aside when his tongue sought hers,
blocking him with simple evasion. He chuckled.

"Do you know, Mourning bright . . . we've gone from chess
to fencing? That was a parry. Do you know what comes after a
parry? No?" He smiled, a slow, sly, almost wicked smile, and she
squeaked she didn't want to know. "It's a riposte, my love. A
retaliatory measure . . . done painlessly . . . with the tongue.
Let me show you."

"No! Please."

His face loomed over hers and everything became glazed and
foggy. She lay there in a remarkably wonderful state of raptured
bewilderment. His mouth, heavy with desire, found what it sought,
and like a fencer's quick return thrust, his tongue sought hers. It
was a long-drawn-out affair, a duel between two well-matched op-
ponents.

"Hmmmm. You fence well, love . . . as well as you play
chess. What else can you play, angel-love? I'd like to play you. Do

you know that? I'd like to spend hours preparing your body . . . fine-tuning your responses. Wouldn't you like that?"

He stopped her answer with his mouth. With a fevered response she began to kiss him, her hands kneading the smooth, well-developed muscles in his warm back, from his broad shoulders to his firm buttocks. In response to her bewitching naïveté, his blood began rushing through his body violently.

"Unbelievable, what you do to me," he said, his voice barely a husky whisper. "Whatever I was looking for . . . sweet angel, you've got it. No, don't stop. I like it . . . it's agonizingly wonderful. You know that? Yes, you do. Oh, God, yes. No, love. Slower. What ever made me think I had to teach you anything? My God . . . if this is just the beginning . . . I'll never make it to the end. You taste good, angel . . . here on your lips . . . your throat . . . *mmmm,* your breasts . . . beautiful. What about the rest of you? Can I sample the rest? Would you like that? No? It's probably a good thing. I'm not so sure I could handle that right now. This is getting out of hand . . . did I say getting out of hand? A miscalculation . . . this is already out of hand. I think we're on the brink of lunacy. You feel it? I feel it. We need to go slower, but I can't. Can you help me? No? Kiss me again . . . yes, yes . . . don't stop."

Like a piranha in a feeding frenzy, she was overcome with an intense wildness to get closer to him, not caring where she touched or where she kissed: his face, throat, cheek. Feeling the agitation of temporary madness, she began to cry out in distraction, "I don't think I feel well."

He paused. "Not a bucket of cold water, exactly, but equally effective. That should go down as an all-time classic response to lovemaking. Do you know, love, I've encountered more firsts with you than I care to recall. We have just crossed another milestone. In all of my twenty-eight years, I've never had a woman complain that my lovemaking made her sick. Kiss me again, you crazy little luna moth."

His lips brushed her bare shoulder, traveling across her throat, biting along her neck, turning her objections to vapor. Like a drop of water in a frying pan, she was sizzling.

"I've waited so long to have you like this," he whispered, "so very long . . . and now that I do . . . I can't touch you." Her mouth opened to the heavy stroking of his tongue. She took each kiss he offered, each one more potent than the last, until she couldn't tell which was faster—her breathing or the pounding of her heart. "So sweet"—he breathed against the smooth peach-velvet of her skin—"so very, very sweet."

There were no words to answer him. Her insides had turned into molasses.

He moved closer, so close, her left leg was pressed against the hard length of him and she could feel the heat of his loins burning into her skin, searing with white-hot intensity. "You know," he said with a raspy whisper, "I sat in the hills for days . . . watching you bathe in your little pool . . . naked and innocent." Her eyes widened, but he continued. "I was trying to establish your routine . . . watching you bathe was an unexpected treat."

His lips left the softness of her throat. *"Amante,"* he muttered from deep in his throat. Sweet mercy! How he wanted her . . . here . . . now. He was a magician when it came to women. He could bend their wills to his so adroitly. But where was the shared pleasure in taking her in brutal force? Strange. The one time all factors led to seduction he was stopped by his own inclinations to be chivalrous. The beauty of a butterfly was in the watching—not in the crushing of it underfoot. He wanted to possess her, but not at the cost of her destruction. Her body was ready . . . screaming. But emotionally? This was all new to her. He was moving too fast. She had been through an emotional, stressful kidnapping and a physical injury. She was like a chubby-cheeked child, a rosy person, and he couldn't do that to her. It would be like seducing a cherub . . . raping an angel.

He lowered his head, moving across her face, kissing her softly. His skin was so fragrant, like freshly baked bread, and she slipped her hands across his chest to rest on his shoulders. He was so hard, yet soft—so warm, she wanted to curl up against him and stay forever. His breath blew upon the soft, fragrant curls of her ear, setting her body adrift. When his tongue traced the line of her closed mouth, she melted into the blanket, her body a caldron overflowing with sweet desire.

As he would a fragile little creature, he held her close, nuzzling her neck, stroking her slender arm, talking in soft, dulcet tones. "One day as I watched you, I lay on my back trying to imagine what I'd do if I had you in my arms, just as you were in the pool, all slippery and wet and naked."

She shivered and he raised himself on his elbow, his eyes hot. "Do you know what I thought I would do?"

She swallowed and shook her head as he studied her incredibly beautiful eyes. "I imagined I would start at your tiny little feet . . . placing soft kisses on them, and then I would come up your smooth legs to your knees. I would kiss them and trace my tongue across the back of them while my hands touched your milky-white thighs . . . so soft and smooth, like the richest cream. My hands would slide up your thighs to your softly rounded hips, so small yet perfectly formed to receive a man and cradle a child. While my hands caressed your hips, squeezing them, my lips would touch the curls at the top of your silky thighs . . . I'd place little kisses on the soft, curling vines that hid the entrance and slide inside. . . . I'd be the first to touch you there, yet you'd be waiting for me, all soft and wet and warm.

"My hands would move to your waist, so tiny, they would reach completely around it and touch in the back. My mouth would kiss your stomach and my tongue would feel your ribs, which form a little cage around your heart, and your heart would flutter inside its little cage like a tiny, fragile bird. Then my lips would begin to climb, little biting, nibbling steps to your soft breasts, and they would taste like the sweetest honey and nectar. My mouth would be all hot when it closed over the hard little crowns."

He began biting her ear and she could tell it was wet—his breath hot and heavy—the smell of his nearness, the warm cadence of his words, making her dizzy and weak with desire.

"I would kiss you, Mourning, kiss your hard little crowns sitting there so regal at the top of the snowy peaks, like little acorns, high in the oak trees. Then I would look at your lips, love. They would be all pouted and soft and oh, so warm—just waiting for mine, as they are now. They would speak only my name, and I would look into your eyes—your beautiful green eyes—they would be the color of the Atlantic after a storm, and they would see only me."

He slid his mouth across hers and she unfolded against the caress of his hard, persuading kiss. "You're so soft, angel-love, soft as a gosling." His words vibrated across her skin. "Soft, and fragrant as an apple blossom. Oh, love, sweet angel-love." She could feel the steady drum of his heart pulsing against her bare breasts and the firm press of male flesh, warm and persistent against her inner thighs. "Forgive me," he whispered. "Darling, forgive me."

Before she could question, his hand closed over hers and taking it, pressed her palm against that part of him that was the living, pulsing core—the holder of the seed of life, the key to immortality. It wasn't at all what she expected . . . not at all frightening, but more a soft, wondrous rapture experienced only upon touching his living, secret beauty—a deep and warm contact, forming a bond.

He knew she didn't understand and he could tell by the way she held her hand against him that she was shy and unsure. "Clint? I don't know what . . ."

"Shhh. It's all right." He brushed his lips across her cheek. "Just feel how much I want you. Feel what you do to me . . . know me." He ground his hips against the softness of her hand— more overpowering because of the gentleness of it.

His upper body was naked and somehow her blanket had slipped lower down on her hips and she felt the warm smoothness of naked skin pressing against naked skin—it was so right to be this way with him. From deep within there came a new, creeping awakening—a gentle stirring like the soft swirling of snow off high-banked eaves. His head drifted to the softness of her neck, where it joined her collarbone and trailed brief kisses across it to the first gentle swells of her breasts. "I want to look at you." He whispered so softly against her skin that the words came a hairbreath from drifting endlessly into eternity, never to caress the human ear. With the slowness of something desired that never comes, his hands began to slide the blanket down her body and away from her hips, his eyes warmly covering what the blanket exposed.

And when his eyes caressed her delicately, but with an overpowering intensity that was pleasurable to him, she felt left out.

Like the parched earth, his eyes absorbed every inch of her body as if it were rain after a long drought—until they rested on the starkness of the white bandage that bound her.

His mind went numb with loss, and he threw back his head with an agonized groan, his eyes squeezed tightly—trying to shut out the pain. "You save my life and I repay you by trying to rape you."

"It wouldn't have been rape," she said softly, and he watched her with a strange gentleness.

Mourning raised her hand to the side of his face and stroked it. "Tell me what it's like between a man and a woman—what it's like to make love."

Pain shuddered across his perfect features and the answer was torn from his lips with a groan. "I can't . . . love, I can't . . . not now." He rolled away and shut his eyes as if hurting.

"Clint . . ."

"I can't talk about it anymore," he said with raw emotion, and she saw the open, exposed pain in his eyes that pleaded with her. "I know you don't understand . . . I'm trying, but it's not easy . . . it isn't something I can turn up and down like the wick of a lantern."

She slipped her arms around his neck, pulling him down to her, her lips soft and tender against his ear. "Please, Clint. I want to touch you . . . with nothing between us."

He groaned as her hand slid down the smooth expanse of ribbing, resting on his waistband, her touch fire and ice. He rolled to his back, flinging his arm over his eyes. His breath coming in short pants, his face contorted in discomfort.

"Please . . ."

"Oh, God, Mourning. Don't."

Her hand shyly eased into his and he pressed her against him, his hips anxious for the merging. "Jesus!"

The overwhelming desire to share with him overrode any reluctance she might have had. Her hand moved to the waist of his pants, slipping the buttons through the openings, releasing them one by one. He rolled to lie stiff on his side, his breathing faster and harder as her fingers finished the task and struggled with one hand to free him. His hands helped her and when she touched him, he jerked, reverting to softly spoken Spanish words—the language of his youth.

His eyes were tense and brilliant as her hand touched him, turgid and quivering—vulnerable. Sensing her indecision, his hand urgently covered hers and with an almost unspeakable motion, he showed her what to do. Caught up into the swirling pool with him, rushing along with each deepening sensation, she watched, awestruck, as his life-seed sprang forth.

She would remember forever the soft, silky hardness of him, the force of life-giving power that surged under her hand as she held him. The tempo of clamoring rhythm. The spasms, quick and powerful, like a great sperm whale rising majestically from the depths, shuddering violently, only to fall back and be consumed once more by the sea.

27

She sat in the cave listening to the rustle of leaves as the wind chased them across the dirt floor. To Mourning, it was the kind of silence that grates on the nerves, a quiet that really isn't quiet at all —not if you count the scampering noise of rodents or the slow, steady dripping of water seeping through porous rock. The damp smell of decay, rotting wood, and leaf mold combined with acrid woodsmoke from the fire to burn her eyes and throat, yet, save the occasional blinking against the offending irritant, she seemed not to notice. Outside it was misting rain, and the dampness inside the cave brought to life once more the trenchant smell of sweat that clung to the saddle blankets she used for a pillow.

Lost in thought, she watched without really seeing the shadows from the fire dancing across the cave walls, giving lifelike animation to crudely fashioned drawings that had been left there by earlier occupants—their interpretations as dead as the men who painted them. With an air of pure insouciance she stretched. Feeling fit for the first time in a week, she decided the only thing she needed was a bath as she eyed the canteens speculatively. Ideally, what she desired was a long, leisurely soaking in a rose-scented tub with millions of silky bubbles and hot, steaming water. Actually, what she got was a stingy bath with cold creek-water stored in a canteen and poured across her with a tin cup.

Clint made his way back to the cave with a rather scrawny possum thrown over his shoulder. As he approached the cave he had visions of Mourning . . . sweetly adorable, hopelessly lunatic, irresistibly wanton, chastely innocent, ridiculously naïve Mourning. She would be sleeping beneath a mass of tangled curls. A tiny fist would be tucked tightly under her chin, her uncovered pink toes would be curled inward, seeking warmth as she slept with a cherubic flush across her angelic face. He pictured her thus, as she had been early this morning when he had, with an unaccustomed feeling of protective tenderness, pulled the blanket over her exposed toes and silently left her slumbering while he hunted fresh meat.

In lieu of an angelic sleeping cherub, he encountered Mourning bathing alfresco, her eyes closed and her head thrown back as she poured a canteen of water over her glossy body. Rivulets of water ran in tiny tributaries across the alabaster skin along her throat, channeling together to run in streams between the ample firmness of her perfectly formed breasts. She turned slightly, silhouetting her curvaceous form against the dark cavern walls. It was this guileless movement of her gleaming body that gave him a full profile of her pagan sensuousness.

She looked up, because of a strange sensation of being watched, and saw him standing just inside the mouth of the cave, his face stamped with the expression of a man erotically awestruck. His flesh pierced countless times with Cupid's arrows, his dark, moorish features possessed a sort of puzzled, half-resentful look. It was as if he didn't know exactly what to do with that powerfully intense feeling of desire that coursed hotly through his veins.

Flushed and glowing with a sensual bloom, she stood before him, wide-eyed and lost. Suddenly she gave a pitiful little cry as if she had been pinched, and her hands reached blindly down and tried to cover herself while presenting her backside to him. It was a sight as breathtaking as the one she desperately tried to hide.

Her back was pure and fine, the small buttocks beautiful and gently muscled in a delicately vulnerable and feminine way. Glistening wet, she would have been a priceless choice in a collection of rare masterpieces.

"Mourning, my angel, if you didn't want me looking, bathing like that wasn't a very good idea."

"I know that now, but it seemed like a good idea at the time. You could leave."

"Yes, I could."

Seeing the naked hunger in his eyes, she gave him a rather

nervous smile, while doing her best to shield her feminine identity from the blistering intensity of his stare. "Don't come any closer."

Seeing her words were as effective as arrows fired into rock, she tried to reason with him. "Clint, think of the consequences . . . the price to be paid for a moment of foolishness."

"Mourning dove," he said, stepping closer, his eyes locking with hers in a quasi-hypnotic state of animal magnetism, "What I see would be dear at any price."

Wishing she could close her eyes and pretend she wasn't there, Mourning made another pitiful attempt to hide her nakedness. It was a good idea, but unhappily she had only two hands, and no matter what she covered, something was left on open display. In her unsettled agitated state, she was unable to decide which part of her anatomy most critically needed to be covered to cool his ardor. Struggling with her dilemma, she tried to think if Grandmother Howard had any words of comfort for troubled times such as these. While her childishly awkward movements to shield herself approached a murderously frenzied state, she could hear Grandmother Howard calmly saying, *You can never tell how deep a puddle is until you step in it.* Somehow Mourning got the feeling she hadn't stepped, but jumped, and the water was slowly closing over her head.

Reduced to the desperation of a drowning man going down for the third time, she quickly glanced up, only to discover that Clint had moved dangerously close. She wanted to flee, but abandoning all hope, she forlornly squeaked, "Oh, help!" The flower-fresh innocence of her unchecked honesty brought a sympathetic smile to his lips.

"Believe me, my love . . . help is on the way."

"No! I don't want any help . . . not from you. . . . Oh, please go away."

"Mourning," he said with a touch of humor he dredged up from God knows where, "my whimsical, provoking, laughable mooncalf. Don't you know? Can't you see . . . all this idiotic foolishness of yours is about as helpful as tilting at windmills?"

"Stop! I want to talk a minute," she said, wringing her hands, while visions of what she was afraid might happen never completely focused in her mind's eye.

"Talk?" he said. "You mean like discuss? Debate? A pow-wow?"

She nodded agreeably, but his next words sent her hopes plunging downward to reside with the discarded possum.

"Mourning bright," he said, taking another step, "a pow-wow at this point wouldn't be worth the powder it would take to blow it all to hell."

She made a quick dash for a blanket lying by the fire and had time to wrap it around her only once before he drew her against him, her back pressed against his chest. She had the crazed sensation of floating out of her body, an impulse so genuine, she was tempted to slap herself—just to see if she was real. Clint's hands were certainly roaming as if she was real. In fact, he was behaving as though he'd just purchased land and planned to stay there indefinitely.

"Mourning . . ." he whispered. "My frightened little rabbit. Why do you tremble so?"

His hands were moving with firmness of conviction as they traveled across the slight slope of her shoulder before sliding down her arms to her waist. He held her thus for long moments and Mourning found herself wondering what he was about. *If this is ravishment, he's going about it strangely.* Her panic began to subside and Mourning became slowly conscious of the potency of his hold. She felt a comforting sense of reassurance, but there was also a creeping awareness of him as a man.

Clint as a person was familiar and safe, but Clint as a man surrounded her with a smoky uncertainty. It was as if the man in him was controlled by some driving force that neither of them could fully understand or control. Once again, she was harried by the unnerving impulse to turn to him and slide her arms around his neck. It was unfair—this constant battling with herself. One part of her wanted to trust him, to open like a slumberous bud in his hands. That was the private side of her—her sensual self, naked and free of shame. Ruled by her wild and reckless heart, this part of her was tempestuous and eager and not guided by reason. Her young heart was inexperienced and slow to learn, for the heart is not always wise.

But Mourning was ruled by her mind as well; a cautious and reasoning intellect, responsive to the moral code she had been taught, which neither tried to understand, nor even co-exist with, her cheerful little heart.

Confused, she was, at the very core of her being, torn between the cold reality of her mind and the cravings of her heart. But rarely can the mind prevail over the heart, and the heart has its own brand of magic that suits the inclinations of a woman in love. Subdued by the softness in her heart, Mourning relaxed against him. "Clint . . ." The whispered entreaty of his name was a strangled plea.

His head lowered to her bare shoulder, his mouth, warm and firm, touched her with a soft kiss. The intimate flow of his heated breath made her quiver, and she trembled in his arms. Caressing fingers closed over weighted breasts and she was agonized by the pressure of it. Weakened by desire, her eyes fluttered closed, her hands gripped his forearms for support. He chuckled, "Easy, love, I'm not going anywhere."

Clint knew instantly it was the wrong thing to say. He gazed down into eyes green as grapes, flushed skin, and an upturned face that wore an expression of shameful regret spiced with anger. Snared in his own trap, Clint's mind was slow to function—intoxicated as he was from his need to bury himself within this captivating angel, with her green eyes and a rose-petal mouth spewing fire and brimstone.

"That's the last time you're going to arouse my hopeful heart and then ridicule me when, gullible fool that I am, I fall for it. Take your overactive hands off me, and don't touch me again."

"I wasn't arousing your hopeful heart."

"What were you doing, then?"

"I believe the proper term would be seduction. I was seducing you, nothing more."

His words cutting like a scythe, Mourning felt the bitter bile of dead, cold reality sting the back of her throat. Too hurt to answer, she jerked away from him before speaking. "That was a cruel thing to say. How do you manage to make everything dirty and vulgar?"

In less time than it took her to say the words, he grabbed her, once more, from behind. His voice, soft and soothing—if it was meant to salve her wounded pride—failed miserably. "My adorable buttercup. Don't ask the question if you don't like the answer."

"But it's not the question that's vulgar. It's always your answer. You're just one big, callused lump of roaming hands and wicked thoughts. Sometimes I think I'm going crazy from all of this. Do men ever think of anything moral and decent? It's everywhere I go. I can't even sleep at night without seeing Arabian sheiks, or Indian maharajas, and pirates who rape and plunder, and opium dens, and fruits."

"Fruits?" he quizzed, looking really intrigued.

"Yes, fruits," she snapped. "I'm sick and tired of being treated like something to eat. I don't like being a juicy tidbit, or a tender morsel, or honey, or ambrosia, or nectar. You've got me feeling like a cornucopia. My skin is not apricots or peaches, my bosom is neither grapefruit nor coconut, my lips are definitely not cherries, my eyes are not olive, avocado, or pea-green, and furthermore, I don't want to kiss like I'm sucking an orange."

A smile fought against his restraint, and it was more difficult than usual to quell the staggering swell of sympathetic compassion that battered his defenses. His face nuzzled the crook of her neck and then moved to her ear, where he whispered, "Would you object to a little passion fruit?"

"Not if you wouldn't object to my being a little prickly pear, or a crab apple with persimmon lips. Kincaid, what are you doing? Stop that! Oh, don't. I can't think when you do that. I just want to go home. I don't want to be educated. I don't want to know about mating. I'm not even curious. Can't we just be friends? Oh, dear, why won't you stop? I don't want to be seduced."

Lifting her heavy hair and running his lips over the sensitized skin at her nape, he said, "I think love, at this point, you don't know what you want."

Curls as yellow as jonquils tumbled in lazy coils against her cheeks that still bore the faint tinge of embarrassment. He lowered his head to kiss the creamy softness just below her collarbone. Her breath quickened to the rapid meter of his own swift pants and he whispered her name.

Raw and naked, the urgency of his whispered plea shocked her. Oh, how cruel poets and authors were, and how they lied about love being pure ideals and grand heroics, and sentimentality and romance. All this time she had looked upon love as a gift of the angels, beautiful and sacred, not to be sullied by lustful thoughts. When in reality it was a fine madness, both painful and consuming—and *filled* with lustful thoughts. Why, even Cupid himself was naked. *Mourning Kathleen, you are a lovesick fool! Why, oh, why can't you love and be wise?* She was beginning to feel like two kinds of fool: one for loving him, and another for admitting it.

He turned her to face him, his palms slipping down her back and resting on her buttocks. He pulled her upward and inward to press against him. There was little doubt in her mind just what she was pressing against, and that froze the current of her blood. It was one thing to read books about being gallantly seduced, or whisper and giggle with colorful speculations among schoolgirl friends, or even dream of being romantically ravished. It was quite another to be locked in an embrace with one's senses being battered. One was romantic. The other was frightening.

She was suddenly a tingling, quivering, trembling jumble of nerve endings. It was a brilliant maneuver, this slow, lazy sensuousness that he used to consume her. As he pressed her against him she began to feel the fusing together and dissolving into each other like alloy to metal. Intimately united under molten pressure, they were made stronger and more resilient, like fine tempered steel.

His hands slipped inside the blanket, feeling blindly for her naked skin that was smooth and warm.

"Stop," she croaked. "Stop."

"Stop?" he repeated, then softly added, "At this point, that's a physical impossibility. Mourning, sweet child, wild horses couldn't drag me away now."

She lifted her face and looked at him. "But wait . . . you can't just . . . do . . . do . . . do the act without giving me a chance."

He continued to kiss her along her hairline, stopping at her ear. She heard him chuckle. "What a paradox you are, my love. Just about the time I think I've educated you, you come up with some hopelessly lunatic and infantile comment like calling it *the act*. Lord, I haven't heard it referred to as *the act* since I wore short pants."

"How can you joke at a time like this?" she asked, pushing against him as his face continued to nuzzle her throat, making her giddy with pleasure. "Will you please stop? I can't think when you're doing this to me." She pushed once more. "Clint! Will you stop? I think I at least deserve a sporting chance."

Without the slightest intention of giving her anything that even faintly resembled a chance, sporting or not, his lips moved with incredible softness across her cheek. "My beloved angel, you talk too much," he said, and his mouth found what it sought and closed over her trembling lips and she forgot all about words. Words were such a poor choice, really.

Mourning was beginning to fill with a warmth that set all her insides humming. Deliciously drifting in a euphoric state, she became slowly aware of her unmentionables suddenly clamoring not only to be mentioned but to dominate as well. Her fingers threaded through his dark hair, she could feel his head move, his lips seeking the soft flesh of her throat.

Returning to her mouth, he kissed her, with more pressure this time, entering her warm depths with the same thrust he longed to use elsewhere. Gradually she became aware that he was murmuring something. "So, you want a chance? A showdown? Pistols at twenty paces? Or perhaps a footrace . . . winner take all?"

Here she was at the negotiating table and all she could do was moan pitifully like a scalded cat: "Yes . . . please . . . right now," which came out sounding more like an agonized *meow*.

He chuckled low in his throat.

It went against her grain, to allow him to control her so simply. It was irritating beyond belief to watch him standing there with an air of tolerant ennui, absorbing her every utterance, decoding it with simple logic; and then, understanding her basic motives, he knew her next move before she did.

"I don't know why, but I'm going to agree to your pathetic request. However, I'm going to reserve the right to choose the method of contest, and the winner takes all. There will be no right of refusal. Agreed?"

That rankled, but she was not about to let him know. Living through the next few seconds was like waiting for the millennium, but at last she said with obvious pique, "Agreed."

He just stood there, his legs spread wide apart, staring at her, all his thoughts concealed behind clear, almost colorless gray eyes. His brooding silence unnerved her, causing her composure to slip drastically. She drew the blanket more tightly against her. "What *are* you going to do with me?"

He smiled and said in a tone of compassionate amusement, "It's not what I'm going to do, my curious little lioness. We're in this together, remember? So, we're going to seal the bargain." He grabbed a handful of golden hair, tipping her head back as his mouth covered hers in a searching, moist kiss that sent tongues of flame shooting through her body.

It was a kiss that would have scorched the feathers on Aunt Harriet's ostrich boa. Mourning tried to speak, but her tongue was thick and her thoughts jumbled, so she simply stood dizzily looking at him with an expression of genuine emperor-worship.

"Cards," he said, holding her against him while his hands roamed in a most distracting manner.

"Cards?" she parroted.

"Cards," he repeated, and stepped over to his saddlebags. She watched the erotic message his body delivered as he covered the short distance to his saddlebags and began to rummage around inside, producing a deck of cards.

Spreading out a blanket, he sat down, indicating for her to do likewise. Clutching the blanket around her, she eyed him warily as he spoke. "Do you want the chance, or don't you?"

She sat down vigorously. "What game are we playing?"

"I'll deal the cards faceup. The first one with four of a kind wins," he said, shuffling the cards.

When he began to deal, she wailed, "What kind of card game are you trying to bilk me with? I've never heard of a game like that, and besides, you're cheating me already . . . you didn't even let me cut the cards."

Mourning's earlier anguishes were milk and water compared to the distress that flooded her bosom when Clint drew a pistol from under his saddle, placing it on his leg. "Haven't you heard, my love . . . the man with the gun makes the rules."

It was the final subjugation, but her volcanic desire to revolt was suppressed when she saw the well-polished and heavily loaded pistol coldly pointing at her. "Oh, never mind, just shut up and deal," she said crossly.

He watched her sitting in rosy light upon the blanket, gazing with scowling concentration as he dealt the cards, faceup. Her face glowed with impervious superiority as she let out a string of grandiloquence when he slowly flipped over the fourth ace for her. "Four aces," she shouted with a tone of joyful victory. "Four aces . . . I win . . . I win . . . I . . ." Her voice slowly trailed off to nothing when it at last penetrated her consciousness that Clint sat before her with a confident expression of roguish benevolence on his silly face. He watched her patronizingly, giving her a wry smile when she shouted with delighted confidence in her victory. Her elation evaporated as a great black cloud of suspicion cast a sense of imminent disaster upon her. Glaring at him, she said, "You can't beat four aces."

Picking up the pistol, he waved it in her direction. "Drop the blanket," he said in a slow, menacing drawl.

She squirmed. "What do you mean, drop the blanket?" she cried, in a sudden frenzy. "I had four aces, you half-wit. You can't beat four aces."

"A Smith and Wesson beats four aces," he said, waving the gun. Her eyes followed it with a look of disbelief. Calmly he replaced the cards and then turned toward her.

Mourning's reason reeled from the onslaught. For a horrible moment she looked at him approaching like some fatal volcano about to erupt. Her formerly rosy face turned white, she knotted fistfuls of blanket against her while trying to master, without shrinking, the overwhelming desire to flee. Realizing at last her inability to counteract the anticipated event, she scrambled, then bolted.

Clint caught her before she had gone three feet and drew her, struggling and twisting, against him. He pressed her head against the hollow of his shoulder and held her panting against him. In no apparent hurry, he soothed her with honeyed words and gentle caresses until he felt the gradual weakening. Clint's thumb stroked her ear before replacing it with his tongue. She mumbled inarticulately.

"Mourning, sweet angel . . . losing isn't so bad, is it?" he asked against her ear, his breath making contact with her sensitive skin with electrifying effects. Before she could reply he drew her into another kiss, full of probing eroticism.

She gripped him tightly, trying to steady the spinning sensations whirling through her. In a state of acute sensitivity, she could hear bugs walking and flowers blooming. She was in a different time zone, dining on honeyed milk and almonds, dwelling in a potpourri of fragrance. She was seeing only his face, feeling only his touch. Suddenly it was her birthday, it was Christmas, the circus had come to town. The cave had filled with people dancing around the fire—a menagerie on a merry-go-round, complete with dancing bears and clowns, ice cream and cake, tinsel and glitter.

She felt his eyes upon her, and when she looked at him, the

intensity of his gaze mated with that wildness in her. He filled her with the desire to do crazy things she'd never done before. She wanted to fly and visit the Arctic; she wanted to swim naked in the sea and eat chestnuts in England; she wanted to float down the Nile and dance with the Russian Ballet, but most of all . . . she desired him with such intensity, it was frightening.

"Mourning, my golden angel, drop the blanket." The smoldering fire banked in his loins for her had finally burst into irrepressible flames. She watched him, silent and forlorn, and he felt a tremor of compassion for her, standing there like a woolly little lamb about to be sheared.

Surprise registered momentarily across her face when she felt his arms release her. The surprise only lasted for the brief instant it took for her to bolt, the cool air touching her naked skin. She turned quickly to look back at him standing there with his foot on the blanket that had moments ago covered her nakedness. He had let her go, knowing all the while she would run; he would keep the blanket.

He watched, silently waiting for her next move, but when it came it was not at all the one he had expected. A quick gleam of surprise floated across his face momentarily before it was replaced by one of triumph. He had won, by God. He could see it in her eyes. Joy and elation surged through him, white-hot and searing, immediately followed by a feeling of aching hunger too overpowering to ignore. Her voice was soft and childlike when she spoke. "Will it hurt?"

The smile that began in his heart spread all the way to his mouth, and for one fleeting moment she thought he might have changed his mind. "My male ego," he said softly and with much compassion, "would say no, yet you're a maiden . . . untouched . . . it must be so; pride before the fall, pain before pleasure."

The fire sizzled and the foggy chill of the night air swirled around their feet, creeping across her body, evoking a shiver. Drawing her more closely against the heart that hammered insanely in his breast, he lifted her into his arms, his mouth hovering and then closing over hers. With swift, determined steps he carried her to her pallet, sliding her body down along the hard contours of his until her feet brushed the floor. "Lie down," was all he said.

She lay there on the grass bed and watched the slow unveiling of his body, naked and lean, gleaming in the flickering firelight like one of Michelangelo's own. When he finally came to her, his warm, hard body was infinitely soothing as he drew her against him, his mouth coming against hers, softly . . . gently plying her with a lazy, familiar feeling, like hot sugared caramel drizzled over warm custard.

Clint was devouring her with tiny nibbling kisses, making her feel deliciously like a half-eaten dessert. "Clint?"

"Shhh," he whispered, threading his long, talented fingers through the fine, silky filaments of the hair at her temples, baring her throat as he kissed the hollow where her pulse beat was visible.

"But, Clint . . . stop a minute . . . I need to ask you something."

He lifted his head slightly and looked at her through love-hazed eyes. "Are you stalling? Buying time? Putting me off?"

"No, really, I'm not. This is a very important matter I need to discuss."

"Can't it wait?" he asked, outlining the shell of her ear with his tongue, smiling at the catch in her breath.

"No. Well, it's something I need to know before." His distracting tongue moved to the other ear, evoking the same response from her. "You have to stop doing that while I ask you, Clint. I can't think when you're doing that."

He buried his face against her neck, his breath sweet and warm, fanning the curls against her face, sending pinpricks of delight tingling along her spinal column.

"Mourning, love, what else could you possibly need to know? Why don't you stop asking questions and let me show you? Believe me, words can, at best, only inadequately describe what we are about." When she remained quiet he raised his head and sighed. "Okay, ask me."

She looked at him in a timid, strained way, shyly trying to lose herself against his shoulder. He slipped his hands along the line of her jaw, turning her face up to meet his and kissing the tip of her nose. "Don't be embarrassed. It's all right," he said, his thumbs stroking lightly across her satin cheekbones.

"Will I know when you're going to . . . that is, when it's time for us to really . . . what I want to know is, whenever you're ready to do whatever it is you're going to do . . . you know, the actual act . . . well, will I know . . . I mean, will I know before you do it? What if I'm not ready? Will you ask me first, and if I'm not, will you wait until I am?"

Her adorable soft voice was husky, ineptly trying to sound cheerfully businesslike and unafraid, but failing miserably. He clenched his jaws tightly to maintain a straight face, not wanting to show any humor when she was so serious and self-conscious.

"Mourning, my love, by the time we've reached that point I can assure you that you will be more than ready. I wouldn't force you. No matter what I say, I would never force you. If you tell me to stop, I'll do my best, but sometimes . . . for a man . . . there can be a point where he is unable to stop. Do you understand?"

"No . . . I don't think so, but I trust you," she said tremulously, her eyes looking at him with an almost childish adoration.

"As I said, you talk to much," he said with a silent laugh. He lowered his face to kiss her again, so she would forget her fearful apprehensions.

She held her breath, the blood spurting through her veins like fire, then scalding the chambers of her heart when his finger wandered along the hollow of her throat, across the fullness of both breasts. When his mouth followed the path of his finger she expelled the breath, as all the vital liquids in her body seemed to bubble into a fine mist, evaporating like water in an overboiled pot.

When he took the fullness of her breast in his mouth, she began to feel tiny purls of sensation rippling downward where she felt a strange new stirring, like the birth of an entirely new emotion, incomprehensible and unfulfilled, but silently emerging like the unwinding of tightly coiled fern fronds awaiting their first kiss of warming sun. Her body began to blossom beneath his gentle coaxing fingers, the stroking caress of his hand, the magic of his tongue.

"Clint," she whispered, "when you kiss me there . . . I can feel it in other places."

She heard his swift intake of breath and felt the cool rush of air against her wet breast when he raised his head, his eyes liquid and hot. Nuzzling her downy soft cheek, he whispered, "What does it feel like?"

"Hard to describe," she said in short, breathless pants, "It's a new feeling, almost strange . . . something I've never felt before, like a dull ache, a red-hot coal waiting to burst into flame. I feel hot and . . ." She suddenly felt embarrassed, yet when she looked at him she felt her words were giving her a new power over him, as if somehow what she was saying pleasured him as much as his kisses and caresses pleasured her.

"And what?" he asked as he nuzzled her face and throat. "Tell me how you feel. Hot and what else?"

"Wet."

"Jesus!" he said, her words shooting through him with volcanic force. He was on a very, very short fuse, and she was pure dynamite.

"Is that wrong?" she asked tentatively.

"No, sweetheart. It's good . . . very good," he murmured. "Where do you feel it? Show me."

His hand closed over hers as it slid down the trembling flesh of her belly. She jerked spasmodically when his hand left hers to slip lower, cupping her with gentle pressure. She made a soft whimpering sound low in her throat.

"How does it feel now? The same?"

"No, it's different . . . more intense," she answered, listening to his harsh breathing in her ear.

He slipped his hand lower, his fingers entering her, staying shallow and still. He felt the corresponding shiver as she sucked in her breath and tensed. "Wait . . ."

"Shh . . ." he soothed, his lips speaking against hers. Just lie still and get used to my touching you here." He nuzzled her with his nose and began murmuring his desire, telling her what he wanted to do to her, and she found his words were having the same effect upon her as hers had upon him moments before.

When she stilled he began to move his fingers slowly. "No, Clint . . . stop . . . I don't . . ."

Her objections died in her throat as she drew a deep, shuddering breath and closed her eyes. He watched the sharp rise and fall of her breasts and listened to the quickening of her breath as his fingers moved with rhythmic magic. She began to move, slowly at first, and then her movements began to match the rhythmic pace set by the motions of his hand. She grew impatient and restless, her arms flung away from her body curling tightly around the blanket's edge, her sweat-dampened head turning from side to side.

Through a curtain of mist she heard his murmured chant of encouragement, his voice shaky. "Coo for me, little dove. Let me make you fly, little mourning dove . . . that's it, sweet love . . . move faster now . . . yes, feel it? Oh, angel, my darling angel."

She moved against his hand in unconscious passion as strange rhythms washed across her, each ripple unbearably shattering, yet the next one stronger and more intense, growing and swelling with magnetically impelling force, drawing her into a whirl of spinning excitement and filling her being with clamoring force. Her body, united in perfect concentric waves of superlative feeling, took possession of her. Suddenly, reaching a climactic point, she felt the moment of her own death and she cried out his name. From the ashes of her own flesh she felt the birth of a new being. He had opened the door to her very soul, allowing the child within to die so the woman could be born.

His eyes never left hers as he lowered his head, kissing her with agonizing tenderness, his hips grinding against her, the burning length of him searing and hard.

In her hazily confused world her thoughts were not completely coherent. She heard herself murmur, "Clint . . . aren't you through yet?"

In spite of the consuming passion that gripped him, he felt the bubbling lift of her wonderfully innocent humor. With more levity than he would have thought he could scrape together at a time like this, he said, "You may be through, love, but I've just begun."

He shifted his weight and she felt his thigh slip between her legs, pressing against her flesh, which was still acutely sensitive. She whimpered as she moved against him; the taste of his mouth, hot and wild, was intoxicating. "I don't think I'm through either," she panted. Her passionate response pushed him dangerously close.

"Are you going to do it now?" she whispered, her words faintly tense against the warm flesh of his shoulder.

But this time there was no humor in his voice; his answer, ragged and strangely thick, was spoken with great effort. "Mourning . . ."

It was a question, an invitation, a plea. The husky groan of his voice was adoring, worshipful, and she drowned in the knowledge of his response to her.

"Yes, love, now . . ." he whispered raggedly.

She felt the solid burning warmth of his loins against her, his sweat-slicked body arched in driving need. Captured in the low hum of passion, she clung with tender love to this beautiful, beautiful man.

For a shuddering moment she was frightened and tense, but his words came, soft and reassuring.

"Don't fight me now, love . . . please. Mourning . . . my darling angel, help me. Help me to love you." He entered her and she dissolved small and wonderful around him.

It was the same act, involving the same body parts, using the same moves he had used a hundred times before with a hundred different women, but it was different. So very different. Everything was the same, and yet it wasn't. There was a pure, quiet stillness within his soul, and from the dark center of his being there came a faint flickering like a tiny blue-white flame of perfect peace. Peace, strong and consuming, settled deep within the very marrow of his bones, and he felt an aching closeness to her.

Lost in a love glaze, he held her cuddled against him, his body exquisitely at rest. Clint thought Mourning, breathing evenly and lying still, was asleep, until the small body next to him stirred. She shifted her weight and he gathered her against him, small and nestling, and gazed down into her face with tenderness.

His gaze was met with anything but tenderness. It was a jolting shock to see the rather cross little frown spoiling her beautiful face when he had expected one of rapture-filled bliss.

It was another first. Never before had he taken so much care and time to give a woman pleasure, yet she looked anything but pleased. On the heels of that thought came a feeling of incredulous joy washing over him like an unexpected surf as the meaning of her irritable expression manifested itself. With the light of sudden understanding glowing in his eyes, he clapped the lid on the effervescent feeling of lighthearted humor that fizzed through him, rising to the surface like bubbles waiting to pop into peals of laughter. As he glanced down once more her waiting expression told him she was expecting him to do something. With a sense of desperate urgency he suppressed the threatening laughter as he searched for the right words, not wanting to spurn her by laughing—not when she was so open to being hurt. It was difficult. His own emotions were shadowy—not yet returned to normal, and thinking straight was next to impossible. "Sweet angel, it will be better for you next time, I promise."

"I don't know," she said pensively. "I had been told you had a lot of experience at this sort of thing, but I can see now that was wrong." She gave him a serious look. "I don't know how to say this without hurting your feelings, but . . . well, frankly, Kincaid, you need a little more practice."

To a man whose sexual prowess had been praised across eight counties and five states, that was a profoundly humbling statement. With an almost apologetic tone of polite concern he asked, "I'm sorry to hear that you were disappointed by my performance, angel-eyes. What in particular did you find disappointing . . . surely not everything?"

"No, just the second part."

"The second part?" he repeated, not fully understanding, because he had never before heard the sex act divided into parts. Realization suddenly hit him like a bolt of lightning. "Oh, the second part . . . you mean when I . . ."

"Hurt me," she finished.

This time the humor would not be repressed and he was forced to camouflage his laugh with nuzzling kisses along her cheek. "I'm sorry, little dove, that I had to hurt you, but it was only that one time . . . never again. Next time, I think you'll like the *second part* every bit as much as the first part . . . perhaps even more."

"You want to practice again?"

Inevitable laughter consumed him. "I hope, love, to prove my proficiency once and for all, but failing that, I'm not above practicing until we get it perfect."

She would have answered him cleverly, but his lips brushed across hers, sharing the swelling desire that was rising within him. When his lips wandered downward to her breast, she said in a ragged little pant, "I think being alone with you for the next month is going to be very hard." When he didn't reply, she prodded him by tangling her fingers in his hair and tugging his face up to hers. Rubbing her nose against his, she smiled impishly. "Don't you?"

"Don't I what?" he repeated between hurried little kisses across her face.

"I said, don't you think it will be hard?"

"Love, it already is."

≈ 28

The French have a saying, *Si jeunesse savait, si vieillesse pouvait!* If youth only knew, if age only could! And so, the next five days passed as a lovers' idyll. Mourning knew that time, that everlasting monster of reality, was the enemy of her happiness. She would reflect in the coming years how things would have been so very different for them if they had been given just a little more time, but fate had not decreed it.

For her their five-day idyll was a period of hopeless adoration where she ignored the gentle prodding of feminine instinct to keep separate unto herself that illusive freedom a woman has over a man. That beautiful freedom to yield sexually to a man without yielding her inner self. But she was young, she was in love, she held nothing back.

Blinded by love, she was consumed by the tender naïveté of a sensual blossoming, a coming to life of a new, whole being beneath the expert tutelage of Clint's seductive words and proficient touch. She placed herself in a position of acute vulnerability by giving way to this tenderness within her. It was a vague and confused tenderness that sparked a sense of belonging; a curious and sudden warmth, an outpouring of her soul, a gentle opening of her womb to him.

Their time together passed with dreamlike slowness, like the purring of contented cats, the twitter of sleepy canaries. It was paradise; a purple island of pink sands and violet seas beneath an aquamarine sky—golden days and balmy nights, an illusive dream, never meant to last.

She lay on a carpet of moss by a quiet little stream running cold and clear as she watched him, a glossy plumed blackbird bent over his task.

"How long will it take us to reach Citadel?" she asked, more from wanting to hear his voice than from actual curiosity.

"Four weeks, give or take," he replied, giving the pack behind his saddle an extra jerk before tying the rawhide thong securely. He removed the Smith and Wesson from his saddlebag and brought it to her, crouching low, his eyes studying hers for a long moment before he spoke. "Think you remember how to shoot this?"

"I remember."

"Good. I've put a holster on your saddle for it . . . it's not there for decoration. If you hesitate even for a second to use it, it may be too late. Remember what I've said."

"I'll remember." She lay back, lost in the burning molten feeling inside her that she always felt when she looked at him. She adored him until her knees were weak and her heart felt as if it were squeezed in a linen press. I feel like a child, she thought as she lay there, wondering if this strange new unfurling she felt deep within her womb was the creation of new life. Absorbing the idea like a sponge, she was lost in the contemplation of bearing his child, a thought that surrounded her like a down comforter when he spoke.

"Have you ever saddled a horse?"

"No, but I've watched."

"Well, watch again, and listen carefully. First rub the back of the horse to remove any burrs and then check the blanket before you put it on. Next . . ."

But she was lost in a euphoric bliss, happy as a clam at high tide, as her thoughts were in a quivering state of suspension.

Clint said something about the cinch, but the exact meaning was lost to her.

"You make it look so easy," she said, rolling to her side to look at him. "I'm sure I can do it, just like you've shown me."

He watched her with a sense of frightening awe, uneasy with the happy state of half-consciousness that had enveloped her. She had never looked so contented, nor had she ever ventured so far

beyond his reach. He felt a sense of irritation that she had slipped
beyond his understanding, experiencing something he denied himself. It was a feeling of the same emotional quality that makes a
man react like a child when a woman won't yield sexually to him.

He continued to look at her, feeling both fear and fascination
as he came under the spell of the soft intoxication of her eyes, like
the male spider enraptured of the female while mating and destroyed by her after copulation. Breaking eye contact with her, he
continued his explanation, the low, vibrating throb of his voice
caressing her like azure waves lapping against amber sands. The
voice she heard, but of the finer points of saddlery she compre-
hended not one word.

*If I could keep him inside me as a child, a part of him he could
not control.* It was a thought born of inward fear, a fear that comes
from the helpless, despairing apprehension of loving to the point of
losing oneself, becoming addicted with hopeless dependency, unable to function without it. But if she had a part of him to
keep . . .

"After you tighten the cinch, buckle the girth . . ."

She disappeared once again into the soft cocoon of thought,
basking in the warmth of his presence—drenched in glossy green
foliage and velvety, star-shaped flowers like a deciduous tree, ever-
green in the hope that winter would not soon come and strip her
bare.

His voice stopped and she suddenly realized he was watching
her with furious eyes.

"I appreciate your explaining it to me," she said gently. "You
seem to do everything with adeptness."

"So do you . . . especially listening," he said, rather sarcastically, choosing this method to extricate himself from her possessiveness. Helping her to mount up, they rode away from the small
cave nestled high in the Sierra Madres—without looking back. She,
because she was afraid she would cry if she gazed once more upon
the site of her metamorphosis, where she entered as a child and
emerged a woman. He, because he was almost morbidly sensitive
about the place where he had allowed her to trespass on his privacy, a place where he had almost succumbed to her power over
him, where her whole body, soul, and sex had almost absorbed him
to the point of madness.

Sharp, cold breaths of air came between little shafts of sunlight weaving their way through a covering of opaque gray clouds. She drew her *rebozo* tightly around her and began to absorb the beauty of her surroundings, blissfully content with herself—feeling rather like a child who lost a quarter but found a fifty-cent piece. Whatever she had left behind her in the cave, she was convinced she had exchanged it for something much more meaningful.

Clint rode away with an air of subtle arrogance, a self-assurance that he had triumphed over this woman by not becoming ensnared in her enticingly woven web of love, possession, and ownership. It was the fear that every man experienced, a universal fear of handing over his identity, the giving up of personal freedom when he heard the matrimonial yoke of bondage snapped shut around his neck, marking him forever a tractable being, an emasculated male.

He convinced himself that for him this idyllic encounter with her had merely been a period of mental attraction and sexual love, and that all the things he said and did were born of the passion of that attraction. Now he felt the beginnings of chilling remorse. Once again he remembered who he was and who she was and how he treasured his solitary life. Their joining was destined to be short-lived from the beginning, like a shallow rooted tree, flourishing in sunshine and gentle breezes; ripped heartlessly from the earth's nurturing breast to wither and lie forgotten with the passing of halcyon days. It was like the love act itself, impassioned and craving, with a brutal explosive quality; a physical experience with a climactic ending like an exclamation point at the end of a sentence.

And so they rode away like Amphisbaena, a serpent with a head at each end, pulling in opposite directions, yet hopelessly tied together.

They traveled for weeks, their minds churning and grinding with the same passionate intentness by day as their bodies did by night—each convinced in his mind that achieving his primary goal would soften the inevitable blow of their separation: she by having a part of him forever, a child to keep when he was lost to her, he by willing himself to his solitary separateness, offering him protection, a buffer against being destroyed by love.

They were two days out from the Nueces River when they came across a small army patrol from Ft. Brown. The air was dry and hot for this time of year as they sat in the rocks, watching the thin trail of dust stirred to life by the approaching patrol. Mourning felt a stirring of slight elation; it was her first view of something representative of the States, something not Mexican. She glanced at Clint; it was immediately obvious he did not share her elation. There was a serious quietness to him as his narrowed eyes followed the thin column of blue-clad soldiers. He was so removed, she felt she didn't know him. A shiver hovered around her neck and shoulders and she glanced at the approaching patrol once more, still unable to understand his reluctance, his caution. Just when she thought they should ride forward and join the protection of an army escort, Clint turned his chestnut and started back down the dry wash they'd just crossed. He was leaving . . . why?

"Clint, wait. Where are you going?"

Halfway down the slope he pulled up and looked at her. "Coming?" was all he said, and then he kicked the chestnut into a gallop. She had no choice but to follow.

When Clint finally stopped, Mourning was full of questions. "Why, for heaven's sake, didn't we ride with the patrol? It seems to me it would've been much safer."

He looked at her with all the significance he would reserve for a peahen. When she was on the verge of exploding with anger, he spoke.

"It's a feeling I have . . . something isn't right. Don't ask me to explain . . . I don't think I can, you'll just have to trust me."

"But . . . but I think . . ."

"Mourning, thinking for you can be dangerous. In the future, whenever you feel the urge to think . . . don't."

His hot words and cool look provoked her further, almost to the point of riding away from him just for spite, but for once she allowed her head to overrule her urge to react. He watched her face, a thin grin showing he was aware of the warring emotions that raged within her. "I suppose the fact that you're still here is proof that you have finally outgrown that irritating habit you have of bolting at the drop of a hat. If that's the case, get down and come with me."

"You mean dismount?" The minute the words left her mouth she felt like a mummy trapped in his own wrappings. Of course that's what he meant.

Clint walked a few feet away, then stopped and turned around, giving her one of his famous looks. As far as looks go, this one was a classic. "There are times," he said, "when your intelligence, or lack of it, completely baffles me." Before he could go further she leaped from the roan and scrambled up the embankment behind him. They reached the top and he instructed Mourning to lie flat against the ledge of a narrow overhang that protruded above a narrow canyon—the same narrow canyon that the patrol would have to pass through.

"But why should we hide right above them? I think we should hide farther away."

"That's your problem, Mourning, you try to think and the process is far beyond you. If we hide here we will know exactly where the patrol is; if we hide where we can't see them, we won't."

She snapped her mouth shut and obeyed him at once, pressing herself flat on her stomach, lying uncomfortably against the hot ground. He crawled next to her and whispered in her ear. "I'll hide with the horses a little higher up the ledge. Just lie flat and don't move." He pressed a hurried kiss against her hair and disappeared.

She remained motionless, wondering what was taking the patrol so long to pass by, but she never dared to lift her head to look. She could neither understand nor explain her nervousness; after all, they were only U.S. Calvary, but for all her fear it might as well have been Attila the Hun. Her body had reached the temperature of well-done pork when she heard the soft crunch of horses walking over gravel, the chipping of shod hooves against rock, the soft murmur of voices, as they rode down the narrow passage that passed directly below her. Her mouth was dry and her body ached from the stiff manner in which she lay sprawled on her stomach, listening to the rattle of equipment, the barking of orders, and the occasional snort of a horse.

After an eternity the noise faded and everything grew deathly quiet, yet she still remained sprawled—obedient to Clint's orders. She wondered why he found it necessary for them to stay hidden for so long after the patrol had passed, but she wasn't about to give him another chance to ridicule her. She'd stay here until she turned into jerky before she'd move.

She was being slowly broiled alive in the blazing sun and her clothes were soaked with sweat. One rivulet was particularly irritating as it trickled down her neck, giving her an itch that just had to be scratched. Carefully and slowly she began to move her hand up toward her neck. She could have milked three cows in the time it took her to inch her hand forward and wipe the offending sweat

away. Her mouth was dry and her skin itched from the rocks and
twigs she was stretched across. She eyed the sun, feeling extremely
sorry for any poor devils the Comanches might have staked out in
this intense heat.

She thought about a bath and what she'd give for one—not
just any bath, but a real honest-to-goodness bath, scented with
lavender, a bar of English Rose soap, and a sponge so big it would
take two hands just to hold it. She closed her eyes against the sweat
that made them sting and thought about herself in that luxurious
bath. She folded her arms quietly and rested her forehead against
them, but found the position not to her liking when her nose
ground into the dirt. She had just pulled her head up slightly when
she heard him, the sound of his resonant laughter reverberating off
the surrounding boulders as she scrambled to her feet. Hands on
hips she stared at him, angry enough to shove him over the ledge.

There she stood looking like something that had just dropped
out of a dust devil; hair frizzled and looking wilder than a milk-
weed pod, clothes wrinkled and streaked with sweat and dust,
grimy little hands, and a smudge on her nose.

"Just what, exactly, are you laughing at?" She was tapping
her foot with irritation.

"Was I laughing?" His teasing eyes twinkled delightedly with
suppressed humor.

"Does a leopard have spots? Of course you laughed . . . you
always laugh at me . . . and don't you dare add insult to injury
by trying to mollycoddle me by saying something stupid like you
weren't laughing at me . . . you were laughing with me."

"Just how long were you going to lie there, sprawled in that
precarious position before getting up?" With a teasing arch to his
brow, he added, "Until I came along and took advantage of it?"

She swallowed painfully, tears filling her eyes. "I stayed there
because you once warned me to always obey you—that when you
gave an order I was to follow it without question because both our
lives could depend on it. How was I to know you were g-going to
use that to make me look s-stupid and r-ridiculous just so you
could laugh at me?"

"Mourning . . ." Scruffy-looking as she was, nothing seemed
to detract from her sweet flowery face, the slender symmetry of her
figure, and the profusion of curly gold hair, under which a forehead, wide with intelligence, gleamed like fine porcelain. He was

not the kind of man who normally found this type of thing enchanting, yet on her, combined with her complete lack of sophistication, it was staggering.

"Sweetheart, don't cry," he whispered, with a strangely uneven voice. His words seemed not to matter, so he just held her tenderly, talking to her softly, touching her with tenderness, until gradually her tears subsided. When she quieted, he tried to pull away from her, but ten overweight oxen pulling with all their might couldn't have pulled her loose, as she clung to him tighter than a baby marsupial being evicted from his loving pouch. Every muscle she came in contact with drew taut and hardened against her. Lifting her face to his, she locked her arms around the back of his head, parting her lips beneath his, almost frightened at the violence of his response as he crushed her against him.

"Mmmm," he said, a smile in his voice, "this is what I like about our disagreements . . . it's so very pleasant to make up." His fingers gently threaded through the heavy coils of burnished hair, massaging the back of her neck until she relaxed against him with a contented purr.

"I feel," she said with breathless awe, "like a scarecrow that has just been taken off the rack—all sawdust and stuffed with hay."

"With this hair," he said, not hiding his soft laughter, "you could be accused of having straw for brains."

"It's all this fighting and kissing . . . I'm becoming addled from it," she said candidly.

His eyes sparkled with amusement. "Why don't we try a little diversity, then. I think we should get out of here. I've seen signs of Comanches; they're probably watching that patrol, but I'd feel a lot better if we put a few miles between us." Her head snapped up and a smile crept across his face. A smile like that, she thought, could knock an entire chorus line flat on its face.

Obeying his suggestion, she hurried to her horse, swinging herself up in the saddle just as she heard a soft hiss of air followed by a muffled thump, then the sound of Clint's voice, strangely muffled, "Ride, Mourning . . . don't stop."

She whirled to see a blur of motion as a half-naked savage flung himself from the rocks overhead. Her eyes flew to Clint, who was grimacing as he broke the shaft of an arrow that had gone completely through his upper arm. Instinctively she grabbed the Smith and Wesson, her hand trembling as she pointed it in the direction of the savage as he and Clint circled each other warily, each waiting for a break to spring. Blood was running in scarlet rivulets down Clint's left arm, which was hanging limp and useless at his side. She saw then the large knife gleaming in the Indian's hand and knew she had to shoot—but this wasn't a cougar . . . it was a human being. Murder. His words came to her, *It's not there for decoration. If you hesitate even for a second . . . it may be too late.* Taking careful aim, she fired, hitting the Indian square between the eyes, and then fainted dead away.

Two weeks later Mourning and Clint were forced to camp on the Nueces River for a few days owing to her roan's pulling up lame—a bruised cannon-bone.

While Clint was hunting, Mourning spread her dusty blanket beneath a huge cottonwood tree near the river. Stretching out on her back, she stared up into the leaves that fluttered in the gentle caress of the wind. Closing her eyes, she breathed the scents of late fall; the pungent smell of dried grass and the musty smell of leaves lying at the base of the tree, beginning their slow decomposition. There was a quiet, untouched beauty here. The soft gurgle of the river as it slipped past and the subdued rattle of seed pods speaking in quiet overtones wafted across her ears and she slept.

She was just waking when Clint entered camp, leading behind him that most haughty and arrogant of animals, a camel. Probably not the same one she saw with Cheno, but obviously from the same Camel Corps. His nose proudly aloof, the camel looked down his less than attractive nose and blinked. Giving him the once-over, she decided, then and there, he had absolutely nothing to be arrogant about. He was hideous. Of a light yellow-brown color, he had shaggy matted hair, enormous flat feet, scaly, wrinkled knees, and a monstrous long neck with a shaggy, beardlike covering.

"What in heaven's name are you going to do with that?" she gasped.

"This, dear child, is the answer to your lame mount."

She began backing up. "You can't really mean to look me in the face and say you think I'm going to ride that . . . that . . ."

"Camel."

"A grotesque reject from a freak show is more like it," she shouted desperately.

"Surely you aren't so naïve as to think I went to all the trouble to get him and bring him back just for the hell of it."

Mourning, remembering Grandmother Howard's advice, *A closed mouth catches no flies,* wished fervently Grandmother Howard were before her in person so she could tell her to suck eggs. Opening her mouth wide enough to accommodate a whole multitude of flies, Mourning let loose with a whole string of reasons why she wasn't going to ride that stupid camel and another list of undeniable proofs that strongly attested to the declining condition of his mental faculties.

She stopped for air. "Haven't you heard," Clint said, dismounting and tying the camel, "that every bird loves to hear himself sing? Are we going to stand here, hammer and tongs, grinding away at each other, or are you going to be sensible and listen to reason?"

"Humph!"

"I know he's a bit long in the tooth, but no reliance can be placed on appearance. This is a perfectly functional animal, broken to ride."

"Good," she shouted, rolling up her blanket and stomping a few feet away, "you ride him."

"Will you stop honking like a goose! Why won't you even consider it? For all you know . . ." He stopped, watching her under hooded eyes. "Oh, so that's it. Well, why didn't you say so in the first place."

"What on earth are you talking about?"

"I didn't realize you were afraid. Of course you don't want to ride something you are scared witless of."

"Scared witless," she croaked. "I am not scared witless. I just don't want to ride that haughty humpback, that's all. Why don't you ride him and I'll ride Conquistador?"

"Because Conquistador would throw you flat on your adorable little butt before you could count to three, that's why. No one has ever ridden him but me . . . or Cad. You're welcome to try."

"I'd rather take my chances with Conquistador than that queer-looking brute."

Clint leaned nonchalantly against the trunk of a tree and watched her approach Conquistador, who flattened his ears when she held out her hand to him. "Does he bite?" she asked, in a strained voice.

"Yes, but I don't think he has rabies."

"You're a big help." She took a step closer and Conquistador snorted and pawed the ground, the bit ringing against his teeth. One more step, and the stallion reared, pawing the air. Retreating, Mourning stumbled over a rock and fell backward, sprawling.

Clint sprang forth to help her up. She angrily slapped away his hand. "Don't touch me! I don't need your help."

"Touchy, aren't you? I tried to give you the easiest beast to ride, but still . . . the choice is yours."

She eyed the red-eyed fire-breathing stallion cautiously. Perhaps it was better to try a not so captivating camel than a horse determined to destroy her.

"Why don't you try the camel before you decide? I'll let you choose whichever you prefer."

She was still caught between a rock and a hard place, but it was, at least, a compromise. She wouldn't be giving in. Not wanting him to see the eternal gratitude she felt, she snapped, "Okay, I'll try the barbaric beast."

"Before you do, there's a . . ."

"I don't want any watery offerings of help from you," she said hotly. "Just be quiet and let me handle this my way." She approached the contemptuous camel with quaking knees and quivering determination as Clint touched the camel behind the knees and he folded up like a parasol. "How can I ride something that won't even stand up?" she said with a disappointed tone that she hoped overrode the elation she felt inside. Perhaps she could escape this fool's escapade after all.

"He's just making it easier for you to mount. Accommodating, isn't he?"

"I'll believe that when eggs crow," she snapped, irritated at his jovial humor.

"Here, let me help you," he said, extending his hand, "all you need to remember is . . ."

"Mounting an animal on his knees is child's play, for heaven's sake. I don't need your help."

She considered the camel for a moment, trying to decide just where to sit: on the hump, in front of it, or behind. Approaching with caution, she was totally unprepared for the snapping turn of his head, the curling back of his hairy lip that bared horribly yellow teeth and the gratingly irritating sound that was emitted. Startled, she jumped backward.

From behind her, Clint calmly offered, "Go ahead, mount up . . . it's child's play."

She would have enjoyed shoving him and his clamoring camel down the nearest hole, but she was determined to show him her mettle. She reached a trembling hand forward, touching the coarse-haired monstrosity, and calmly swung a leg over him, arranging herself just behind his long neck. This was done just in the nick of time, because the posterior end of the beast began to elevate itself, throwing her forward so she had no choice but to throw her arms around its neck. At that precise moment, the anterior end came up, and not particularly happy with where she was sitting, the camel lowered his head and shook, flinging her to the ground.

Camels, she decided, were creatures to be reckoned with cautiously. With a deadpan expression on his face while contentedly chewing, the camel looked at her through eyes as yellow as his teeth. Listening for the sound of Clint's laughter, and hearing nothing but cavernous silence, Mourning decided he had probably collapsed from a euphoric stupor.

"It always takes me a minute or two to get my bearings," she said, dusting herself off.

"You might try creeping up on him when he's asleep."

"Very funny, very funny," she said frostily. "If that's the best suggestion you have . . . I can do without it."

"Try sitting on top of the hump this time."

With the same fierce determination that pillaged Rome and conquered England, she approached the hateful hunchback, scrambling to the top of the hump, where she perched like a marble on the top of a mountain in avalanche, destined not to remain long. Rising to his feet, the camel sent her flying at a bent angle like a backfiring boomerang. Springing to her feet, she screamed, "Listen, you demented dromedary, I've had about all I'm going to take of this ridiculous game you're playing. You just think you're going to get the best of me."

"According to my calculations the camel is ahead by two points. Do you want to concede?"

"Not as long as there is a breath left in my body," she answered with breathless determination as she dusted herself off.

"Don't you have a saddle of some kind? Where did you get this mindless miscreation anyway?"

"Bought him from a miner. Yes, there's a saddle."

"Why didn't you tell me before?" she screeched.

"I tried to, but you told me to be quiet and let you handle it in your own way. I thought perhaps you preferred to ride camels bareback."

Before she could throw back a nasty retort, he threw his good arm around her, hugging her against him, bruises and all. "Before you break your wonderfully foolish neck, would you mind cooking me some dinner?"

After the bruising excitement of her adventures with the camel, the next few days passed uneventfully. Two days on the camel and she was officially declared proficient in camel riding, to the point that Clint was sure they would reestablish the Camel Corps when they discovered her advanced training. Besides her lessons in advanced camelry, they found time to settle into a comfortable by-play of bantering words interspersed with lovemaking so candidly hot, prairie fires were a constant threat, or so she was told.

With time on their hands, they escaped from the harsh realities of the world to exist in their own private Camelot. One warm, sunny day they waded in the river and Clint made a swing for her from vines, swinging her far out over the water, where the swing broke, throwing her into its chilling depths. When he offered her a helping hand she laughed and jerked him in with her, and then ran screaming when he chased her from the water. He caught her upon the grassy bank and kissed her blue, frozen lips until they were rosy and warm. He then made love to her with such unbelievable tenderness, she cried.

She gathered leaves and grasses and braided them with small seed pods, and while he slept in her lap she placed the woven garland, a crown of earthly things, upon his head. When he awoke and sat up it was all askew and she wondered why it hurt so to love like this.

He caught fish and they sat cross-legged by the fire and fed each other, their fingers greasy and their spirits intoxicated with desire. He sipped tequila and pressed her back against the blanket and kissed her until she felt the liquid heat of the tequila as it warmly flowed into her mouth, and giggled when his tongue chased a small drop that tried to escape. She doubled over with laughter at his boyish antics when he chased an armadillo, rolling in the grass convulsively when he errantly uncovered a skunk. She showed him how to call up doodlebugs and the best way to catch crawdads, and when one bit her he laughed and kissed away the pain, and she loved him so much she thought she would die from it.

After he came to her again that night she lay with his slumbering head cradled to her breast far into the night. As she gazed into the sky, the stars a scattering of fine white diamonds against a black velvet backdrop, she clutched him to her fiercely. With a love as open and vast as the land they slept upon, she took an oath, wrestling with God, like Jacob, for a blessing. The pale fingers of dawn were streaking the sky with gauzy streaks of rose and lavender when she felt at peace, knowing what she must do. And before God, she vowed her lifelong love to this man, binding herself to him more strongly than any minister's words or any band of gold could do. She took him for her lifelong mate, her husband. The vow made, the marriage consummated, the seal broken . . . she would never marry another.

PART FIVE

A mighty pain to love it is, / And
'tis a pain that pain to miss; / But of
all pains, the greatest pain / It is to
love, but love in vain.
Abraham Cowley, "Gold,"
From Anacreon

Mourning stood before the rain-spattered window listening to the slap of hard-driven rain upon the frosted panes. It was pouring down in torrents, and the mournful sound of wind wuthering around the corners of the weathered old house added to the ever present chill of the room. She stood mutely gazing, no longer a thing of fire and spirit, but a vague shadow. Her face was drawn, her eyes dull, her shoulders slumped and defeated. A trembling hand fumbled deep in the pocket of her gray linsey-woolsey dress for the little kerchief that was wadded in a damp ball. Blotting the tears that trailed across her pale cheeks, she returned it to her pocket. Her trembling hand touched the embroidered linen cover of her dressing table. It hovered briefly over the cold memories of warm moments: the pink coral beads he gave her for her nineteenth birthday, the silver chain and green enamel locket given because it was the color of her eyes, the ivory cameo pin that reminded him of the color of her skin where the sun never touched, and the rosewood music box he had given her for Christmas. Lifting the lid, she pressed her forehead against the cold pane of glass and listened to the clinking clockwork grinding out its mechanical reproduction of "The Yellow Rose of Texas."

A bittersweet depression engulfed her as she remembered the tenderness in his eyes and the whisper-soft caress of his husky murmur when he gave her the inlaid box. She'd felt like a sun-ripened berry, oozing-plump and juicy-sweet, just waiting to be picked, when he'd swept her into his arms. *Don't ever forget me,*

Mourning . . . whatever happens . . . remember every time you see this box, play this melody . . . remember.

She remembered, she remembered. How could she not? She remembered the way he tried to lighten the mood by casually calling her his little yellow rose, because he couldn't find a music box that played "The Yellow Buttercup of Texas." She remembered a man whose hard handsomeness struck her with the same refractive force as that of a light ray passing obliquely through crystal; subtle and radiant, going right through her and changing her life forever while she was completely unaware she was ever touched. She remembered a man wonderfully wild and a little crazy, with more personality parts than a puzzle and just as complicated. A man capable of dismembering her into bite-size pieces and skewering her like an Armenian shish kebab with one cutting word or reducing her to a quivering state by the fusing heat of his gaze. A man who entered her life and sent her world spinning like a top, out of orbit on a collision course, and then left her reeling from the shock of it.

She closed her eyes and brought the tips of her cold fingers to her still lips, trying to recapture the feeling of a warm, living mouth that fitted so perfectly over hers. But her body, which was so finely tuned to his, rejected the touch as an impostor. Every nerve, each tiny living cell in her body, was wired by some physical phenomena to him by an attracting force stronger than the pull of a magnet to lodestone. As a result, he was the essential nature of her, a settled habit, as intrinsic and inherent as the beat of her heart. Even now, when he was no longer here, she still felt the irresistible pull, and like a lost soul, she was so dominated by his magnetic charge that she was trapped in it, destined to float aimlessly for eternity like a celestial particle in the atmosphere.

She had tried, God knows she had tried. After he left she tried to hide everything in the house that belonged to him. She scrubbed the smell of him from rooms with disinfectant so strong, it left her hands bleeding and raw. She rearranged the furniture in his room and beat the shape of his body from his mattress until the goose feathers, driven by the force of her blows, whirled around the room like snowflakes in a Siberian blizzard. But nothing helped. He was always there, in the back of her mind, waiting with the same casual indifference, the same lean hardness, the same beloved face, that haunted her day and night and would not go away.

Tears stung her eyes and she groped blindly for her kerchief again, for she felt it coming—the sob that would not remain hidden. Up it came, followed by another and another, choking and fast, until she gave up and cried helplessly and brokenly for having lost that which she could say she had hardly ever had.

And suddenly something within her snapped. Raging anger surged through her and exploded with a violent outburst. In a frenzied rage she flew around the room, jerking every memento of him off its honored and esteemed pedestal and slamming it in the bottom of her armoire. In went the music box, the coral beads, the enamel necklace, the book of poetry, the bracelet he had woven her from camel hair, and even the Smith and Wesson.

"It may beat four aces, you lousy bastard, but it won't beat me," she screamed. "Do you hear me, Clint Kincaid? You aren't going to beat me. I want you out of my life. Do you hear me? Get out and stay out!"

But he was already out.

She fell across the bed, her tiny, pale hand ineffectively muffling the heart-wrenching sobs of acute loneliness that racked her body. Clutching the only thing of his she hadn't been able to hide, her slim arms hugged protectively the child growing within her womb, and she buried her face in her pillow while she cried. Gradually the sobs became less violent and more relaxed, the choking lump at the back of her throat began to dissolve to a hiccup. Mourning lifted her swollen eyes to the window and stared at the steel-gray sky, a color so remindful of his eyes, dark with passion. With a sense of hopeless desperation she looked sadly at the sky that seemed to cling to the lingering light of the departed day as if afraid there would never be a tomorrow. Perhaps she should just give up now, it would be the easy way. How could she live without him? What reason did she have to go on? But then her trembling hand slipped over the row of smoked pearl buttons once again, touching their cool, smooth surface one by one, down across the fullness of her breasts and lower to the distended and swollen belly below.

The sting of bitter bile rose up in her throat, and for a dizzy moment she allowed herself to think of the personal humiliation, the shame, the degrading disgrace she had suffered because of his illaudable actions. She wished she were dead . . . no, she wished he were dead. The bastard had gone—left her with a broken heart, an empty life, and a full belly, while he rode gloriously away to fight in this godforsaken war.

She could remember so vividly the way things had been after their return from Mexico. The elation of finding Anna and Cad safe and waiting for them at Citadel, the sudden threat of war, and Caroline's decision to take Anna and Melly back to Memphis. Her time with Clint had been so brief—days that lingered but a moment, then slipped silently away. How had so much joy faded to dull indifference?

Now he was gone, leaving her all alone in this big and lonely house with only Mrs. Harper for company. God only knew when Caroline would return from Memphis. Clint had left to join the Confederacy shortly after Texas seceded. Cad had left a month later, followed by John—all of them gone to fight in the same senseless bloody war.

Why couldn't she cut the memory of that horrible day out of her mind and allow her life to return to normal? She couldn't forget. She would always remember that day as if it were yesterday. A day, very much like today, dark and raining, the sky overcast with gray clouds . . .

She had been sweeping the front porch, waiting for Clint to return, watching the rain dripping through the still leaves of the trees and listening to the sound of the water running off the roof, falling into the flower bed, forming puddles.

The pastures were alive with hazy color, red, yellow, pink, and blue, as the spring flowers bloomed wildly, forming a foreground of color for the small distant figure of a horseman riding across the pasture, his silhouette dark against the faded sky.

Clint rode into the yard, his chestnut stallion looking black and slick, wearing a coat of rain. His yellow slicker was spread across Conquistador's rump like the skirts of a woman's dress, and the rain was pouring from the brim of his hat.

Mourning paused, leaning on the broom as she watched him, a smile tugging at the corners of his mouth.

"What are you going to do with that broom, buttercup? Ride it?" Dismounting in the mud with a laugh, he ran to the porch and she flung herself into his arms, not waiting for him to remove his wet slicker.

He laughed and clutched her to him, swinging her around until her feet left the porch, then set her back on her feet and pushed her from him. Pulling his glove off with his teeth, he reached inside his slicker and pulled out a half-wilted bunch of flowers. Cocking his head with a grin, he said, "For you."

"Oh, Clint . . . thank you. The colors are beautiful. What kind are they?"

He grinned teasingly, "These," he said, pointing to the tiny orange flowers, "are called Devil's Bouquet."

Her eyes were shining brightly with something funny she was dying to share, and true to her nature she couldn't contain it for long. "How appropriate!" she said, thrusting her nose into the wilted bouquet.

With a twinkling gleam to his own eyes he pointed to the delicate white flowers twined and woven throughout the larger orange flowers. "These," he said softly, "are Angel's Trumpet. They don't look too bad together, do they? Devil and angel . . . sort of like us."

Her hand trembled and he reached for her, his mouth slightly parted. There was a strange, urgent look on his face, the same look he'd had in Mexico when she was shot. He said nothing, save her name. "Mourning . . ."

His hand closed around hers and he drew her inside the house and up the stairs to his room. They had made love many times since that night in the Sierra Madres, but never in the middle of the day here at Citadel. "Clint . . . what are you doing? We can't . . . not now."

"Yes, we can. John and Cad are still in San Antonio and Mrs. Harper is over at the Palmers' place, helping with a birthing."

She lifted her eyes to his and smiled, a hasty, heartwarming smile, but he knew her well enough to see the difference: the bewildered look in her eyes, the trembling corners of her mouth, the unnatural paleness of her skin that even the diffused light filtering through a rose-colored shade could color.

"What has stolen your sparkle, my bright morning-star?"

She lifted heavy eyes to him, and immediately felt that same old magic; the dryness of her mouth, the shortness of breath. He was still leaning against the closed door, his arms casually crossed over the solid chest, the long, tapering fingers of one hand tucked beneath the bulge of a muscled arm, while the other hand lay loosely against the bight of his arm. The roseate warmth from the lamp drizzled down the long, muscled length of him like heated oil.

"I . . ." But she couldn't seem to find the words to tell him of the pensive melancholia that was eating away at her like an acid bath. He would be leaving, it was inevitable, she knew that now. Ft. Sumter had been fired upon, Texas had seceded, and war had been declared—it was only a matter of time before he left. With a tired shrug of her shoulders she whispered, "Nothing." Desire tiptoed across him, swiftly and effortlessly.

He came to her with slow, determined steps. He smiled that wicked little teasing smile of his as he reached for her. "What you need is a little honey-making. Let me fill you with honey, love."

His hands flowed over her like a warm bath, relaxing her and making her drowsy. His eyes held hers as he reached for the buttons at her throat and freed them one by one. "Close your eyes and let me take you to heaven." Her breath came in a quick gasp as his face came so close, she could see each individual hair of his incredible black lashes.

Clint's mouth came to hers hungrily, twisting over it as his powerful arms pushed the dress from her shoulders and swept her up and away to the bed, following her down and covering her with his warm, solid body.

"What if they come home early?" she said breathlessly.

"They won't," he answered.

"But if they should, Clint . . . Oh, Lord, I'd die."

"*If* they should," he grunted, slipping his clothes off, "I'll handle it." Her eyes closed and any further questions vaporized as she felt his fully aroused body brush across her belly.

He's so good at this, she thought, he should open an academy: *Kincaid's Academy for the Sensuous Seduction of Simpering Succulents.* There would be a waiting list.

He looked down at the smile, soft upon her face, and he smiled slowly as he pressed his legs between hers and kissed that beautiful smiling mouth as his hands left the heavy curling hair and slid down the length of her body to where she lay open and waiting.

She moaned when he penetrated her.

Her breathing had not returned to normal when he raised up on one elbow and looked down at her. "Why did you cry?"

"I didn't cry."

"Yes, you did," he said, leaning over to kiss the high flush of cheekbone. Um-hum, I thought so."

"What?"

"Salty."

She smiled hesitantly at his fledgling attempts at humor, and he saw through the mask she was wearing to the troubled little face below. Something had stolen her fire and brilliance, and her crazy, idiotic little manner of being so hopelessly lunatic that infuriated him to no end and aroused him to passionate heights he had never before experienced.

Was it real? Was it real, this feeling he began to feel growing deep within him? Was he losing his solitude, his privacy, his last personal freedom to her? Still, something within him cried out, lonely and afraid, always afraid, afraid of belonging, afraid of caring too much and losing himself. Yet his very soul was straining at the bonds he had placed around it, wanting to belong to her, wanting it to the point of madness—straining, straining . . .

He had her here, in his arms, alive, warm, loving—yet it wasn't enough. There was more. There had to be more. He wanted to own her, body, soul, and spirit, but he was afraid to give that much back to her. And he knew she was the kind of woman who would demand as much as she gave. No. Not now. The timing was all wrong. You can't rush into belonging. It had to grow. He had only just begun to think about belonging to her. It was a freshly planted seed, and here he was ready to harvest a crop. Patience . . . always patience. Patience and time. Be patient and wait for the right time. You can't rush it.

He felt the expanding and stretching deep within him, an elastic pulling, high-strung and tense, stretching beyond ordinary limits of endurance until he felt his soul cry out, no more. There was an instant and sudden spiraling snap he felt throughout his body. He had broken the bond. He was free. It was what he wanted. Wasn't it?

He looked down at the fresh little face that watched him, her eyes full of such blind devotion, and he felt a sense of helpless compassion. No, he cautioned himself. You have broken it. Let it stay broken. It's better this way. You have no right to hold her to you. Not with the war, the uncertainty. No, he thought, it's better this way. It's the man who should do it, because he's the stronger of the two. But deep down inside himself he felt it was because the man was really closer, in reality, to being a real son of a bitch.

It hurt him to look at her, so fair and soft and undeniably warm, so beautiful, so in love. He leaned forward and kissed her between the wide green eyes that watched him so intently. Her hand brushed his cheek and he felt a stab of desire grip him once more. Pulling her against him, soft and gently curling, he kissed her hair with tenderness. "What are you thinking?"

Mourning did not answer straightaway, but her hand slid down the smooth length of his flanks, across his firm thighs, and back up, stopping at the erect symbol of his maleness. Her eyes followed her hand and she snuggled against him, laying her head on his belly as she trailed her fingers over the hot, rigid length of him.

"I think he is standing there so proud, like a peacock, his body arched proudly, trying to get my attention."

Clint laughed and raised his head slightly and looked across the wide expanse of chest and belly, watching her. "He is part of you, but you don't really own him, do you? He has taken command of you now, hasn't he?" Her hand, like her voice, was quick and unsure, but oh, what it did to him.

She did not wait for his answer. "You no longer control him, do you? In fact, I control him now, more than you do."

He laughed. "Yes, I suppose you do. What would you have him do for you, Mistress Mourning? I'm afraid his talents are rather limited though."

This time she laughed, a deep, throaty laugh. "It was for me that he rose so strong and proud. You see?" She touched him again and he groaned and pressed her head against his belly. "See how he responds to my touch? He is my loyal subject, rising and bowing before me." She pressed a kiss in the indentation of his belly and closed her gentle fingers around him.

His hand covered hers, stilling her movement, his breath came hot and urgent in her ear. "Don't touch me now! The greedy little beggar would spill himself at your touch, but I am in control now and I have a better plan." He rolled her over quickly and slid into her with a sense of urgency as he groaned, "Oh, little Mourning, what have I done to us?" And his body once again took command of him and he gave himself up to the strange, mysterious ways of passion.

Much later, they still lay there, neither of them willing to be the one to say it was time to go, both knowing they should have been up long ago. He was still holding her; this time she was cuddled against him, spoon fashion, his arms around her, cupping her breasts. She shifted her position slightly. She sighed, and moved again. Still not satisfied, she wiggled once more. "What's the matter?" he asked, smiling at her childish squirming.

"I don't know. Something is poking my back," she answered.

He chuckled, "My aim is better than that."

She laughed softly. "It's been pretty good so far." She elbowed him in the ribs softly as she sat up, her hand groping along her back.

He erupted with laughter, and leaning toward her, he picked something off her back. Placing his hand in front of her, he opened his palm, displaying a peanut. They both rocked the bed with their laughter. "Clint, whatever are you doing with a peanut in your bed?"

"I was eating peanuts last night when I spilled them; guess I didn't find all of them." He nuzzled her shoulder. "Why don't you lie back down and we'll see if we can stir up another one."

She snuggled against him once more, her hand rubbing his chest and belly, going lower. Suddenly she grew quiet. "Oh, look, he's grown tiny and soft, curled up like a slumbering babe." She touched him and held him in her hand, fascinated with the wonder of him in his flaccid state.

Clint chuckled and kissed her shoulder. "He won't stay tiny and soft long if you continue to hold him. This is one baby that does not sleep when he is rocked."

She laughed. "He is so beautiful lying there. I don't know why I was ever afraid of him."

"Were you afraid of him then?" He rose up to look at her.

She smiled, "Terribly."

Clint laughed loudly.

She continued, "I can't decide which way I like him better. Lying there soft and sleeping or fully aroused and rearing his head." As she spoke, she could feel the soft pulsing that began to bring him to life—a gentle fluttering like the wing of a bird. Rolling across Clint's chest, she looked deep into his eyes. "I love him both ways, Clint. I love him because he is part of you and he has given me so much."

"My wonderfully complex, simple girl," he growled, punctuating each word with a kiss, "you keep touching me like that and saying things like that and we'll never get out of here. We'd better get dressed. No point in tempting fate."

But fate was already tempted, and when Clint opened the door, John and Cad were just coming up the stairs. Seeing Clint, they both started to speak when their eyes were drawn to the pale face behind him, the rumpled bed beyond.

"Oh, shit!" Clint said.

"My sentiments exactly," John said. "Well, Clint, you have your tail in a meat grinder this time. Just how long did you think you could keep forcing yourself on Mourning without someone finding out?"

Clint's eyes narrowed. "Is that what you think? That I forced her?"

"Well, didn't you? My God, what's gotten into you, Clint? In this civilized world, if you want to live with a woman like Mourning, you marry her. What do you have against marriage? You obviously care for her, or you wouldn't go to such lengths for her. I've never seen you go to this much trouble for any other woman."

"She isn't like any other woman, but I'll not have you butting in on my business. Mourning was agreeable to our arrangement. It is none of your concern."

"I told you once before the only way you could keep her. If you agree to marriage, she's yours. If not, I'll see her married to another. I'll not see her suffer the humiliation of being used by you or anyone else. If you don't want her properly, I'll fix it so you can't have her at all."

"You think a little thing like a husband would stop me?"

"It just might . . . if she were married to your brother."

"Cad?" Clint said, looking first at John and then Cad with choked disbelief. At first Mourning thought he was going to strike his own father, but then she saw him gain control of himself. "Perhaps you should have consulted Cad first. It would appear that he is every bit as surprised by your declaration as I. Cad wouldn't marry her," Clint said with grinding anger. "Especially not now, now that I've had her," he added confidently.

"That," Cad said softly, pushing away from the banister, "is where you are wrong. I would take her any way I could get her. It looks like you are being forced, brother, to marry the injured party, or lose her forever."

"Injured party? You are needlessly concerned about her recuperative powers. She has more recoil than a repeating rifle."

"Careful, brother, I can see you are starting to sweat. The pressure is getting to you. You're being backed into a corner and you're dangerously close to being forced to admitting you care. But then it goes against your grain to admit to caring for anyone, doesn't it? Perhaps you can use this as a method of escape, then. You know, a honorable way out. A reason to leave without the unpleasant task of having to admit you're in love with her."

"Oh, this is rich . . ." Clint's forced laugh was dry and scraping. "Is that what this is all about? Force? The gladiator in the ring . . . the lady or the tiger? Tell me, *brother,* am I in love with her because I've bedded her? I must hold some record, then, for the number of times I've fallen in love, because we both know how many beds I've been in."

Mourning stepped around Clint and into the hall, pale, shaken, and stunned. Clint looked at her with clear gray eyes and a tightness around his lips, but said nothing, his silence loaded and pointing at her like a pistol with a hair trigger, one little jolt and . . .

"Please . . . can't we wait until Mama gets back," Mourning pleaded.

"No!" John snapped, then more softly he said, "I'm sorry, Mourning. I know Caroline picked one hell of a time to take Anna and Melly back to Memphis, but with this damn threat of war, there was no other choice. I don't know when she'll be back, she could be cut off up there for the duration of the war for all I know. I'll see this matter taken care of now." John turned and walked down the hallway before adding under his breath, *before we have a little bastard to contend with.* "We will finish this discussion in the library."

"There is nothing more to discuss. We will work this out for ourselves. We aren't ready for marriage."

"Mourning," John said wearily. "Are you agreeable to being used by Clint like some cantina chili pepper, or would you prefer marriage?"

She felt the brutal attack of Clint's brittle eyes on her before she ever looked at him. *The hair trigger,* she thought. *This is the jolt it needed. What shall I do? A loaded question like this . . . there is no correct answer. I lose either way.* Thinking about the child growing within her, she made her choice. "I . . . if you put it that way, I'd be a fool not to choose marriage."

Eyes that had once looked at her with such softness burned, white-hot and searing, on her skin. Hands that had, a thousand times before, held her with such gentle pressure, gripped, cruel and painful, into the tender skin of her slender arms. Lips that had once kissed her with such tenderness were twisted and cynical as they snarled, "Well! That settles it, my glib-tongued seductress. Marriage at all costs? Did you see yourself as some biblical saint? Ruth perhaps?" He pulled her against him and covered her mouth with his in a heated, moist kiss that sent goose bumps rippling across her skin in spite of the audience. He pulled back and looked down at her dewy face. "Open your eyes, my love. I want your eyes open so you will understand exactly what is happening." An electrifying jolt of thrill shot through her. He was going to marry her.

Her heavy-lidded eyes opened, looking at him adoringly until they focused more clearly on the piercing intensity of his. Slowly, deliberately, he jerked her around so her back was against his pounding chest. "You wanted her. She's yours." Before she knew what had happened, he had shoved her into Cad, who, surprised off guard, barely caught her before she went tumbling down the stairs.

And so, as turbulently as he had entered it, Clint Kincaid walked out of her life.

She started after him, but Cad held her back. "Let him go. Give him a chance to cool off. You can talk to him tomorrow."

But by tomorrow he was gone. No one thought he would do it. They all speculated as to why he did and then turned to assure her she would hear from him soon. Once again they were wrong.

Her head splitting like a fissure before an earthquake, she looked forlornly around the room. Soon it became a rainbow-hued blur as the hot, scalding tears bubbled forth, right on time, with the precise clockworks of a faithful geyser.

The door opened softly and Mrs. Harper's gray head popped around the door. "You crying again, child? That's not good for your baby, you crying and carrying on like this. I know you're hurtin' and I can't say that I understand what came over that boy to leave like that. Raised him from a little feller . . . thought I knew him through and through. Must have loved you something fierce to do that."

"Obviously he didn't love me at all," Mourning said bitterly.

"I'll not believe that for a moment, and I've told you that before. Never seen that boy like he was, all tied in knots, never knowing which end was up. He suffered, I know that much. He just made a mistake, and God help you both for suffering so because of it. You need to concentrate on forgiving him. This bitterness and hate is eating you up. It ain't healthy, child. You know that."

"I've tried to forgive him, but it hurts too much," she sobbed.

"I know, child . . . I know. But don't let this destroy you. You've got that baby to think of now. Why don't you come on down into the parlor and let me fix you a nice hot cup of tea."

"I'll be down in a minute," she choked, mopping her face with the kerchief. Mrs. Harper closed the door gently, and the sound of her departing steps faded down the hall.

Mourning closed her eyes in agony, the choking, overwhelming grief gripping her once more. She couldn't eat, she couldn't sleep, she couldn't speak more than five sentences without crying. Like some demented and depraved monster he had wrapped his destructive tentacles around her and sucked the very life from her —taking her soul, her spirit, her very being, and leaving her an empty shell. How could she forgive him? She hated him with every bone in her body. "Oh, God," she cried, clutching the cheerful rose-chintz draperies, "I can't hate him . . . I want to hate him . . . I want to see him lying torn and bleeding on some lonely battlefield so he will know how I feel, but I can't . . . I can't . . . I love him . . . God help me . . . I love him still. I know there's a war, but I need help."

She slipped down the length of the draperies and curled into a small taffy-colored ball, shrunken into herself and biting the back of her hand to muffle the sound of agonizing grief that tore from her throat. Consumed by violent shivering and passing into a hysterical fit of sobbing, she cried until the tears would no longer come, and then she gradually sank into a troubled doze, broken by startled and confused mumblings of things dark and frightful.

She awoke to find a tray with fragrant tea steaming on it and a plate piled high with thick, crusty slices of dark, rich bread, generously buttered and saturated with fat, golden drops of honey.

For the first time since Clint had left she ate with a healthy appetite and afterward felt strangely light and satisfied. The honey. She smiled a thin, sad little smile as she remembered the times Clint had told her all she needed to cheer her up was a little *honey making. Let me fill you with honey, love.* She realized then that she was thinking about him without feeling the deep, piercing agony and . . . she smiled. Oh, it hurt . . . it still hurt, but the acid bitterness of it was gone, leaving a deep, smoldering coil of pain deep within her, but perhaps in time that, too, would go.

It must have been a slow day as far as wars go, because God had heard her mournful wail. In the months ahead she began to look back upon that day as a turning point—a point from which she began, slowly, to regain the sanity, the order and balance, in her life. She still found it painful to remember, but learned, in time, that if she completely blocked him from her mind, she could convince herself that she had forgotten him.

And gradually the weeks and months began to pass, each day a little easier than the previous one, and slowly she began to smile from time to time, and then more and more, until she found she could even laugh . . . as long as she blocked him from her mind. . . .

PART SIX

It is impossible to love a second time
what we have really ceased to love.
La Rochefoucauld, *Maxims*

 30

June 1865

It was a hot, lazy summer day—too hot to do anything but sit in the shade of the porch and fan. The creek had slowed to a sluggish trickle and the fish within were paralyzed to inaction by its heated laziness. Grasses drooped in the pasture and the cows clustered under splashes of shade provided by scrub oaks. Far overhead a hawk made lazy circles, riding on an updraft, spiraling higher and higher, going out of sight.

It was a sullen, quiet kind of heat, where the only sounds were the slow, steady droning of the honeybees and the occasional tapping of a distant woodpecker. The sweet smell of late summer grasses hung in the air, drifting up from the valley, where freshly cut hay lay curing in the sun.

A capricious little breeze that started from nowhere danced across the surface of the earth, catching drowsy sheep winking and blinking in the warming sun. It startled sleepy chickens, which cackled and flew upon the henhouse, and started the fat, old mama hog running in circles, squealing and grunting. It rustled the leaves of the myrtle bush, driving out four furry balls mewing and hissing at the old bloodhound that had settled into the freshly turned earth so recently vacated. Giddy and dizzy from its own circling course, the breeze spun inward and upward, a whirlwind spiraling into the summer sky on its never-ending quest across the parched terrain.

That same whirlwind moved across the pasture and along Sandy Creek. It crossed Newberry's cornfield and set old Mrs. Peterson's laundry to flapping on the clothesline before stirring up a nest of furious hornets on its way to Dome Rock. It traveled down the well-metaled road that led to Citadel, dropping a cloak of fine dust upon a weary traveler in ragged gray clothing. And then it swept over the white picket fence and rattled the screen that needed painting on the old front door, as if announcing the approach of the dusty figure on horseback.

The weary traveler dismounted and stared at the rambling old house; the gabled roof and battered shingles, the wraparound porch with its gray painted floor and sky-blue ceiling. His eyes glanced at the familiar myrtle bush by the front step, half expecting to see a pair of bloodhounds bounding from underneath its glossy leaves . . . her hounds.

The smell of dinner wafted around him and he wondered if she was in the kitchen. Weary eyes noted the bowl of shelled peas abandoned in the seat of the rocker, and a forgotten crown of braided flowers dangling from the arm. Devil's Bouquet and Angel's Trumpet—the flowers' names came quickly to his mind as he was reminded of a similar bunch of wilted flowers that haunted his past. Pausing for a moment, he dropped his meager belongings in the rocker by the front door, and ran his fingers through hair that was shaggy and way too long. Then he hesitated, wondering what he should say, how he should approach her. What if she had married? He opened the front door.

He made not a sound, save the anxious rattling of his heart, as he followed the savory smell of fried chicken down the dimly lit hallway to the kitchen.

She was putting the finishing touches on a pie, pricking a floral design on the upper crust, and then tilted her head to one side, deciding to add one more slash.

He stared at the thick, biscuit-blond braids that were crossed behind, brought up over her head, and crossed again, the ends tucked neatly out of sight. Her apple-green dress was of plain Swiss muslin with white hemstitching, and a white pinafore was tied at the back of her slender waist.

The rusty door of the oven creaked as she closed it with a bang and turned to lift the lid on the chicken that was frying. He imagined himself putting his hands around her tiny waist and kissing the fine sprinkling of curls at her nape. He pictured her turning in his arms and pressing her rosebud mouth, trembling with joy, against his lips that had thirsted for a taste of her for four and a half years.

Mourning placed the last piece of chicken on the ironstone platter and pushed it to the back of the stove to keep warm before covering it with a cloth of white butter-muslin. A dented old pot started bubbling furiously, its lid rattling and clanging, and she picked up a wooden spoon and gave it three quick swirls before clapping the lid back down and turning toward the sound of footsteps on the back porch.

A violent slam-bang of the kitchen door announced the arrival of a tangled ball of snarled buttercup curls and ruffled petticoats, with a sweet flowery face. Entering the door hind side foremost, the tiny, energetic bundle was dragging, from warm seclusion to terrifying display, a wrinkled, velvet-skinned half-grown hound pup with a tightly stretched and obviously full tummy. Unable to pull the pup's distended stomach over the threshold, the diminutive dynamo proceeded to drop down on all fours, humbly placing herself at the hound's level, and began a series of gentle, persuasive words, honeyed flattery, loving pats, promised rewards, and even a wet kiss or two—any of which would have convinced a bull he could give milk. But the pup moved not. It grew quiet. All resources and patience exhausted, the little half-pint began to sputter threats, to which the pup responded by flattening himself to the thickness of a banana peel, and when threatened more sternly, finally gave a credible rendition of a slow-dying snake.

Her own resources exhausted, her small voice pleaded for help: "Mama?"

Clint's expression, which a moment ago had been tender amusement, suddenly was a queer mixture of shrewd understanding and sickening dread.

"Katy, can't you see the pup wants to go back outside with his brothers and sisters?" Mourning answered, walking to the door and releasing the chubby fingers that were gripping the loose folds of skin. The pup came to life and bounded across the porch, and Katy gave chase.

Mourning shook her head and gave a sigh as she watched the pair romp across the yard before shutting the door. Turning back to her work, she gasped, her hands flying up to her mouth. "Oh, my God . . . Clint?" Her heart flip-flopped and then slammed against the walls of her chest. The blood in her veins, running like a bubbling mountain stream moments before, dropped to sea level so fast, she was dizzy.

It was the moment she had prepared for, for almost five years, only to find herself totally unprepared. She couldn't think of anything to say except "Clint? Is that you?"

A questioning smile revealed itself from the midst of a full beard . . . it was the same slow, sensual, mocking smile she remembered so well. He was back.

He took a step in her direction and paused when she stepped backward and he heard her faint protest. "No . . . Oh, God, no, please . . . oh, please, don't come any closer."

"Mourning, what . . ."

She whirled and ran to the door, jerking it open, and dashed across the porch. "Cad," she screamed. "Cad, come quick!"

Clint walked down the steps and paused when he saw his brother hurry out of the barn, moving with incredible speed for a man on crutches. His eyes flew to his legs, which moved unsteadily, but at least they were still there.

"Mourning, what's happened? What's wrong?" Cad shouted as Mourning flew across the yard and flung herself mightily against him. "Whoa! Firebrat. The last thing you want to do is have me flat on my back. You'd have the devil to pay trying to get me upright again." He balanced his crutch under his arm and slipped it around her shoulders. "What happened? Why are you crying?"

"I think it might have something to do with me," Clint said, walking toward them with a weary gait.

Cad's face suddenly blanched. "Clint? My God, brother, is that you behind all that brush?" Mourning turned and stepped aside, wiping her eyes on the corner of her apron, and Cad sprang forward and bear-hugged his brother. Turning toward Mourning, he held out his hand. "Mourning, didn't you know who it was?"

"I knew," she said stiffly, moving back into the one-armed embrace of Cad.

Clint swallowed as a thick, twisting feeling of dreaded fear began to coil and tighten in the pit of his stomach. He looked at the casual way Cad's arm was draped over her slim shoulders and the protective way he held her securely against him.

Tension snapped and crackled like a winter fire kindled with green logs. Clint's eyes lowered to the figure of the young girl running from behind the henhouse. "Mama, Mama, Gabe 'n' Clay said there's a strange horse tied up in front of the house and . . ." Her high, excited little voice trailed off as her eyes locked with his and she stopped next to Mourning, hugging her legs.

"She's your daughter?" Clint asked, knowing the answer, but, for some singular motive, requiring the affirmation to come from her lips alone.

"Yes."

Another obstacle. It was going to take infinite patience and iron-clad endurance to survive this footrace and surmount all the barriers between him and the final consummation of his goal. Clint theorized about what game the fates had been playing the day they sent Mourning's little celestial body careening off course and crashing into his, knocking them both off their heavenly rockers. At that moment the kitchen door slammed and two young boys came dashing out.

"Mama . . ."

Clint's eyes flew to the boy that spoke. The boy's agate-gray eyes were full of eager curiosity, eyes almost too large for a cherubic face that looked small next to a wealth of dark curly hair that needed cutting.

"Not now, Clay. You three go wash up for supper. Go on, now. You heard me."

Clay and Katy simultaneously looked at Clint. It was purely a look of childish curiosity—a benign expression on their faces. But the other boy, standing just behind his brother, studied Clint with an air of sullen suspicion. Mourning gave the young girl a swat and sent the three on their way.

The children went charging toward the house, shrieking and laughing, slamming the door behind them. Clint had sent a slow glance after their retreating merriment. Odd. The quiet boy looked back over his shoulder at him four times before he reached the back porch. Clint said nothing, but merely returned the direction of his cold stare to the pair who stood before him.

It grew quiet. So quiet, the silence was painfully uncomfortable, yet unavoidable.

The smoky depths of Clint's eyes studied her with the dissecting eye of a zoologist bent over a pinned moth. His perfect facial contours were relaxed and a slight smile sliced through the shaggy growth of beard. Mourning remembered that smile, a smile that had once trapped her. It was centered in the middle of a beautiful facade, a mask—a painted face with vacant staring eyes; no soul, no heart, no purpose. It was a face about as friendly as a school of piranha set loose in an overcrowded swimming hole.

"When was the wedding? Sorry I missed it." Clint's voice was detached and hollow, finely iced, with a light sprinkling of bitterness.

"There's been no wedding," Cad said. Clint flicked his eyes at Mourning, who quickly resumed giving her undivided attention to the tops of her boots.

"As variable as the wind, aren't you, buttercup?" Clint said. His voice was silky soft, as if it might have belonged to a henchman about to spring the trap. "I can't help but wonder how you came to justify being Cad's mistress when I exhausted every avenue of persuasion and all I got was an obligatory show of resistance."

It was a cheap shot, and he knew it, but he didn't have to worry long about her injured pride. She had a protector waiting in the wings.

And right on cue, that protector leaped on stage when Cad said, "She doesn't have to stand here and take that kind of . . ."

"No, she shouldn't have to stand here at all," Clint said, his tone hollow and resonant. "From the fertile results I've seen, she obviously functions best flat on her back."

Mourning could feel her heart pounding heavily. She gripped Cad's arm tightly as she glanced, first at Cad and then at Clint, thinking she hadn't seen so many neck muscles bulging since deermating season.

"Mourning," Cad said with a tone that indicated it was an order, "why don't you get supper on the table. Clint and I will finish this discussion and wash up at the well."

Mourning felt a welter of newly sprung emotions. Turning away, she felt the cold, ruthless scrutiny of Clint's eyes as she ran to the house.

Cad looked up at Clint, his eyes clear and innocently confronting the penetrating stare of his brother. "Well. You might as well go ahead and say it. You've been standing there looking like the last stanza of *Dies Irae* on the day of judgment. Although I don't know what good it will do. Your mind is made up, and a thousand tongues calling down solar eclipse, cataclysmic events, self-flagellation, and a good dousing with cougar water wouldn't change it."

Clint snapped forward like the backlash of a bullwhip, jerking Cad forward, sending buttons popping off his shirt and his crutches clattering. Even Cad's levelheaded control was no stabilizing force for his brother's emotional and physical exhaustion.

In a voice he found impossible to keep under tight control, Clint said, "All right. To have fathered three kids you had to have bedded her off and on throughout the whole goddamn war, you virile bastard."

Cad's transitory smile melted into a carefully controlled expression. His voice held a note of detached coolness that rolled over Clint like fingernails scraping across glass. "What has you so pissed, brother dear? The fact that I could've fathered three children by her, or that I would've had to sleep with her to do it? Tell me, Tartuffe, when did you suddenly become empowered with the spirit of chastising hypocrisy?"

"Don't put my motives on the firing line. I'm not the one who fathered her three bastards."

"Is that what placed us in this moral dilemma? The identity of the fornicating bastard that's responsible?" Cad's voice was elaborately sarcastic. "Because if it is, I can solve that problem readily enough. I didn't father her children. You did. And while we are at it, take your friggin' hands off me!"

A quick flicker of shock passed over Clint's features, and Cad saw him shut his eyes tightly as if trying to salvage some remnant of self-control. Slowly he released Cad's shirt and turned to a nearby tree, placing both hands against the roughened bark, one knee bent slightly, his head hanging low, between his arms.

Dropping his arms to his side, he shifted his position to lean slightly against the tree. A look of cool detachment settled in his eyes. "Obviously you've never heard," Clint said coldly, "the man with the short straw must be delicate in his diplomacy. You're pressing a trifle hard, Cad."

"Someone has to look out for her," Cad snapped.

"What? Are you her wet nurse? Your shining example of over-protective sentimentality is choking me. I can almost hear the golden notes of a celestial choir chiming in support of your platinum deeds."

"At least I didn't go off and leave her, apron up."

"I'm not overly fond of splitting hairs, but I'm not convinced I did either. I know barbers first learn to shave by shaving fools, but I'm no fool, brother. Unless you're speaking in a mystically divine sense, no mortal man could have fathered those three by-blows with one swift stroke, not even me."

"No," Cad agreed, "I guess he couldn't—unless of course, they were triplets."

Emotion sprang like a cat's paw into Clint's eyes and then vanished as quickly as it had come. It was as if something powerful had stung him with the agonizing potency of a scorpion. "Triplets?"

"I didn't stutter. Triplets. You know, three of a kind born at one time? Multiple birth? Three babies . . . all yours, the legacy you left her with when you rode off to war mounted on your arrogant pride. Your children, Clint . . . your sons and daughter . . . your own flesh and blood, not mine."

"So where are we now? A stalemate? We seem to have complicated and simplified matters with one fell stroke, haven't we?" Clint said, with almost painful deliberation.

"Yes, I guess we have, in a sense. Simple because you don't have to scour the countryside like some starving wolf trying to ferret out the man fool enough to infringe on your territory, yet complicated because you have wronged her, and as far as Mourning is concerned, you no longer have any territory." Cad smiled like a throned seraphim. "You know what they say about hell having no fury like a woman scorned. All I can say is, you've sure as hell got your work cut out for you, and I wouldn't want to be in your shoes right now for all the flax in Flanders."

"She's still bitter, then?" Clint asked, then added, "After all this time?"

"You might apply that phraseology, but from what I've heard, it runs more along the line of wanting your head on a platter. According to Caroline, Mourning didn't just immediately bounce back. Your leaving like you did was hard on her, so hard, they thought she might lose the baby. Doc said it was a miracle that she broke her ankle and was confined to bed the last six weeks of her pregnancy. He figured that was why she carried them as long as she did. I don't need to tell you how rare it is to have three live babies." Cad smiled an uneven grin and slapped his brother on the back. "Don't take it so hard, Pops. Just look at it as a footrace to win the fair Atalanta, and take a lesson from Hippomenes."

"I'm a little low on golden apples at the present, but perhaps there's a worthy substitute," Clint said wearily, then handing Cad his crutches, he walked with his brother to the house.

Mrs. Harper served dinner to Cad and Clint in the dining room while Mourning ate in the kitchen with Caroline and the children. By the time the meal was over, Clint learned that Cad was right about one thing, Mourning was deeply hurt and unforgiving, and right now she looked madder than an old wet hen and let Clint know in so many words that she wouldn't listen to anything he said if he chopped off both legs and threw in his arms for extra measure.

It wasn't the start he had hoped for, but it was a start. One must play one's cards where they fall.

The sun was beginning to sink; streamers of golden sunlight filtered through the twisted vines of virginia creeper that covered the south end of the front porch, falling with a metallic glitter on a coil of flaxen braids. Mourning watched the children scamper down the path with their pails. They were going up to Dome Rock to hunt *valuable* rocks. She swept the porch until the last tinkling sound of chatter drifted across the yard.

Katy perched upon a smooth, flat rock she called Gramps, because it looked like a bald head. No one knew where she hit upon that idea, having been too small to remember her Grandfather John, who was killed at Vicksburg; and of course Mourning's father, Clay Howard, had been dead for years. Childish fantasy was what everyone called it.

Katy spread her rocks out in a grand assembly faintly resembling a segmented worm, then reached into her cape pocket and pulled out a napkin, as Clay watched curiously. "What's that?"

Katy dimpled, "Nuts . . . the ones Grandma gave me." She spread the napkin on the rock, poking her chubby finger around the assortment of nuts to better display them. "See, there are peanuts, and pecans, and nigger toes"—Katy tilted her head to one side and surveyed the hoard critically—"' 'cept there aren't many pecans, 'cause that's what Gabe likes best, and he's always eatin' 'em."

Gabe walked up in the meantime, watching silently. Clay knew Katy would not give him any of her cherished nuts, even if he asked, so he didn't. He just had to figure out a way to get them diplomatically. It did not take him long.

Katy picked up a pecan and started to put it in her mouth as Clay spoke. "Don't eat that kind."

Katy stopped, pecan poised in midair. "Why not?" she quizzed.

" 'Cause those are the bad kind, they'll make you sick," Clay answered, with bewitching innocence.

Katy, gullible as ever, looked at the offensive pecan with a critical eye and then gave her brother a look that hovered somewhere between idol worship and dazed wonder. "How'd you know?"

Clay beamed proudly. " 'Cause I can tell by lookin'; men are 'posed to know things like that."

That seemed to satisfy Katy, as she sorted all the pecans from the others, pushing them into a separate pile.

Clay stood, his hands in his pockets, and stared at the pecans. Things were going good so far. Now he had to get those pecans off that rock and into his hand, diplomatically, of course. He and Gabe discussed it, and being a religious devotee of brawn before brains, Gabe was all for grabbing them and running to the dead tree by the creek, and then eating them there. Clay vetoed that idea because he knew Katy would tell Mama. It was decided then that Clay would get the nuts and leave first and Gabe would come a few minutes later.

They walked back to the rock where the pecans lay, like a beacon, shining in a pile. Katy looked at her brothers, her button nose wrinkling with her squint as she stared into the sun. Suspicion was written on her face as she pressed her fist tighter around the remaining *good nuts*. She had been duped by these two too many times not to know when they were up to something. She clutched her fist to her chest as she listened to Clay.

"I don't suppose you'd give us some?"

Katy shook her head, clutching her hand tighter.

"You keep those, then. We'll take the bad ones." And smooth as a riverboat gambler, he gathered up the pile of pecans and walked away. The sunlight glinted on his raven tresses as he casually sauntered down the hillside, not breaking into a run until he passed the barn.

Katy looked at Gabe with a raptured expression on her face. "Wasn't that nice of Clay to eat the bad ones?"

That was when they heard the rich, rolling sound of laughter.

Looking up toward the sound, they saw a man leaning against a hackberry tree, his body bent with laughter. Gabe scrambled from the rock, leaving Katy with her pile of nuts, and headed down the same trail Clay had taken moments ago. Two hound pups came bounding out of the barn and ran yelping and baying after them as they streaked across the pasture. While her brothers were running, Katy was watching the man, studying him surreptitiously. And while Katy was studying the man, he was watching her, thinking what an adorable little girl she was. Honey-gold curls a shade darker than her mother's framed her face as she looked at him with huge gray eyes, so like his own. Unable to resist her charm, which was so like her mother's, he stepped forward. Seeing her eyes narrow, he stopped and squatted down, to appear smaller. He gave her a lopsided grin.

"Who are you?" He had trimmed his hair and shaved—she probably didn't recognize him.

Not waiting for his reply, she asked, "Are you a stranger?"

"No, I'm not a stranger, I'm your Uncle Cad's brother." He gave her time for that to soak into her little mind. "Who are you?"

"Well, you can call me Katy, but my real name is Anna Katherine Howard."

Clint winced when she said her last name. She was not a Howard, dammit, she was a Kincaid.

Katy thought for a moment. "It's all right for me to tell you my name, since you're not a stranger. Mama said we aren't 'posed to talk to strangers."

Clint smiled at her warmly. "That's right, you're not supposed to talk to strangers, but since I'm family and not a stranger, you can talk to me."

She narrowed her eyes as she studied him. "Are you the man who got mad at my Uncle Cad before dinner and made my Mama cry?" She added a warning: "You better tell the truth, 'cause my Mama said you can go to the bad place for lyin'."

"Yes, your Uncle Cad and I had a little argument, but he's my brother and brothers fight. Don't your brothers fight?"

She giggled a wonderfully childish giggle. "Oh, yes, Gabe and Clay fight a lot. 'Cept Gabe, he's the one that likes to fight the most. Clay likes to talk all the time."

"What about you and your brothers? Do you fight?"

Her eyes got big and round and she puckered her delightful

little bow mouth. "Oh, no, Gabe and I hardly ever fight, and I don't like to fight with Clay, 'cause he always talks more and gets me all messed up so I say stupid things, and then he laughs. Gabe is kinda shy and doesn't talk a lot. He likes to fight . . . mostly with Clay, though. I think it's 'cause they can do the kind of fighting that makes your nose bleed. I had a nosebleed once and I didn't like it. I cried and Mama made Gabe tell me he was sorry. Gabe doesn't like to do that, but I don't like nosebleeds either. And I don't like the hittin' kind of fighting. I always do the talking kind."

"What have you got in your hand?"

Katy held out her hand and slowly opened it, displaying five or six gummy nuts that were bonded to her hand by salt and sweat.

"May I have one?" He tentatively extended his hand.

She gave it serious contemplation for a moment, then nodded. She stepped closer and opened her hand to him. Clint reached for a nut, and when he touched her baby-soft skin a tender emotion flooded upward to lodge in his throat. He looked into her gray eyes and could not believe this tiny little creature was his own flesh and blood, nurtured and grown from a passionate seed, so wildly planted long ago. He wanted to hold her, yet he was afraid he would frighten her.

She must have sensed this, for she smiled. "I like you," she said, and she touched his cheek softly. Then she turned and ran down the hill, going past the barn, seeking her siblings.

The next morning Clint found Mourning churning butter in the kitchen. She knew by the particular cadence of the step and the click of the door that he had entered the room. Caroline, who was busy straining fresh milk through cheesecloth, heard the immediate change in the rhythm of Mourning's churning; a rhythmic tempo that had all the overtones of a South American gaucho stamping out the bolero. Without looking up, Caroline said, "Mourning, I think you passed butter a couple of measures back, you're almost to semisoft cheese."

A busy little teakettle was steaming madly on the stove and a crock of fermenting wine filled the room with a pungent, crisp smell. There were all manner of cozy little alcoves filled with pots of blooming geraniums or baskets of pinecones. Late summer roses had climbed the lattice over the bay window and hung in heavy clusters, their colors deep and rich like a purple and crimson velvet cape.

Caroline gave Clint a look that made him wonder if she had heard the erratic thudding of his heart. With a smile she slipped from the room. Clint stepped behind Mourning and paused. The churn stopped, but she did not move. He smoothly placed his arms around her, slipping his hands over her small ones, which tightly gripped the handle of the churn. "Don't freeze up so, Mourning bright. I only want to talk to you."

"I don't have anything to say to you." She could feel the sweet penetration of his body warmth, so close, it was sinking into her flesh like sharp talons. Once bitten, twice shy. She knew that touch, that glib tongue. She had been fooled once. His subtle presence was easing back into her life like tired feet sliding into old slippers: familiar and comfortable. Just when she thought she was over him, he was slipping back around her like a hangman's noose: quick, dangerous, and fatal. Fear gave her the emotional edge she needed to say coldly, "Don't think you can walk back into my life and pick up where you left off. Now, let go," she said, struggling against his grip.

"Mourning," he stammered, "I . . . dammit, you know I'm not good at this."

"I can't think of one reason why you should be. Smooth apologies usually take practice, an area in which you have no polish. But it doesn't matter anyway. As far as I'm concerned, you don't owe me anything."

"Yes, I do, but I'm not very good at apologies, regardless of the reason."

"You aren't very smart either, because I don't want you or your apology," she answered frankly.

"Regardless of what you want, I still owe . . ."

Her look, when she finally gave him one, was a rather bland, pasty expression of gracious social courtesy. "Correction. You don't owe me. Any debt you feel you raked up in my behalf was canceled when you gave me the children. That's the only thing you've ever given me that I care to keep." She turned away.

His fingers began to trace little erotic patterns along the tender flesh of her inner arm. "I know what I gave you, my love, but I'm not sure about what you took. I fear it was more than I can safely part with. I've given you my heart, Mourning. Can't I have yours in return?"

"You had it once and flung it in my face"—her voice lost its control and began to shake— "shattered and impossible to repair. You are nothing to me—an illusion stripped of its hue, nothing more. I know you, Clint Kincaid. You haven't changed. Rain may beat the leopard's skin, but it doesn't wash out the spots. Oh, you may seduce me and claim my body, but understand this: My heart is my own. I'll not risk it a second time."

He moved closer, the warm current of his breath wafting across the baby-fine curls at her nape. His voice, when he spoke, was low and caressing. "There was a time, sweet angel mine, when I would have settled for that, but no longer. I want you, Mourning Kathleen Howard. I want your body, your heart, our children . . . marriage." He leaned closer still, his lips pressing softly against the skin his breath had teased moments before. He heard her sharp intake of breath and the soft staccato of her words.

"What brought this change of heart? What happened to the man who wanted his freedom above everything?" She whirled to face him, her eyes glaring with suppressed rage. "Tell me one thing, Kincaid, just what made you realize you lost the substance by grasping at the shadow? Are you sure it's me you want? Or is it the children?"

His hands slid lightly up her arms and came to rest around the soft warmth of her throat. His thumbs traced the curving chambers of her ear, delicate and lined with pearl, like a fragile paper nautilus.

The stroke of his sure fingers and his determined perseverance made her feel like a spawning salmon swimming upstream.

"Mourning . . . I love you."

Mourning gripped the dasher to hide her trembling hands. Her voice was shaky and broken. "Fine!" she said crossly. "That's just fine! After all this time, you finally decide you love me. Don't think those three little words will wipe out five years of rejection."

"Let me make it up to you, Mourning. Just give me a chance to show you. One moment of bliss can repay innumerable hours of pain."

She slammed the dasher down inside the churn and sprang to her feet, knocking over the churn. Milk and great golden drops of butter spread across the floor. The drumfire of her heart was hitting her head with such vibrations, any thought was impossible. "Oh, yes, I'd forgotten all about that wonderful magic wand of yours, that proud poker that has left so many women awestruck. Thanks to the generosity of healthy specimens like you, all us empty-headed women can spend our days rolling and tumbling in the hayloft with rosy-fingered Aurora, not having a care in the world. That's the answer to all problems, isn't it? One little wave of that wand and all is well." She stomped to the door and jerked it open. "Why don't you take that pleasure-stick of yours and put it on public exhibition? That way you're sure to find a woman who's interested. I'm not." She moved through the door and turned to face him, her lip curled in contempt. "Sorry, but I can't think of a single thing it could possibly be used for around here, unless of course, we need it to put out a fire."

≈ 31

Primed for battle, Mourning cut Clint off at every turn. She didn't argue exactly, she just wouldn't talk, and when forced to speak, she directed any dialogue with him through a third person, usually Cad, Caroline, or Mrs. Harper. Those being unavailable, she wasn't above speaking through Romeo or Juliet. It was a successful way to let Clint know just how far down the ladder of endearment he really was. According to Clint's calculations, his present position oscillated somewhere between what lay behind the half-moons on the privy doors, and the slimy contents of the oaken buckets slopped to the hogs twice a day.

Yet he continued his crusade, despite the fact that the victories he had amassed over the past few weeks were of insufficient number, and of sufficient insignificance, to convince even the most loyal and devoted janissary that immediate withdrawal and abandonment of objective was the only recourse.

It was this conspicuous, unflagging pursuance, laced with a certain amount of hard-boiled softness on her part, that sent Mourning trotting like a standardbred to Cad. She found him leaning against the toppled-down remains of an old stone fence, moss-grown and crumbling with age. At first she thought he was watching her, but he was looking beyond, to a field of muted greens and golds where three white-tail deer bounded over a low hedge. She had an inkling that that wasn't what he was seeing in reality, but a retrospective summons from the war, a remembrance as swollen and angry as the scarred tissue on his leg.

His stiff leg was stretched out in front of him, one elbow resting on his knee, the other hand holding a blade of bluestem. She paused a moment, warming him with her smile and twinkling eyes. "Cad? Have you fallen into your rhapsodies again?" she said, jumping over the low end of the fence and trotting behind him. She began gently to massage the tense muscles along his shoulder.

"Only when you're not around, firebrat," he said with attempted lightness.

Mourning could see he was pensive and a little melancholy, a mood that had gripped him often since his return. It troubled her that Cad could be so afflicted. He was her pillar of strength, her rock of Gibraltar, her shoulder to cry on. Devil-may-care, jocular Cad, with a ready smile, a comforting word, and an everlasting air of insouciance. He was her Harlequin, her Merry Andrew, her beloved waggish friend, overflowing with joie de vivre, and like guardian angels, patron saints, and fairy godmothers, always lived in Eden—never supposed to suffer the mortal affliction of malaise.

He handed her a blade of bluestem like the one he was chewing. Popping it into her mouth, Mourning sat next to him, chatting sprightly, trying to cheer him. "It's so restful and quiet this time of day, isn't it?"

"It was until you started on your little crusade to lighten my mood." He squeezed her hand and thumped a bee that was crawling across her skirts. "Don't worry about me. I've got more bounce than a kangaroo, more lives than a cat, and more endurance than a camel. But I've been known to walk under a black cloud or two. Like you, I've always managed to survive."

The vivid twinkle in his eyes told her her wanderlust friend had returned. Tucking her arm through his, she said animatedly, "*That* is what I wanted to talk to you about."

"Kangaroos, cats, and camels?" he said in mock surprise.

"No, no. Not that. Survival."

"Yours or his?" he said, twisting her shoulders around so her back faced him.

"Mine. What are you doing?"

"Turning you around. See? Now lean against me." He leaned his back against hers and lifted his injured leg to lie upon the smooth stones. "So you're worried about your survival? He's using some pretty heavy artillery on you—you know that, don't you?"

"Yes, I know. I'm finding it harder than I imagined. Living

here, in the same house with him, seeing him with the children . . ."

"Gives him unfair advantage," he finished for her.

"Cad, do you think I should give in a little? Do you think I can trust him again? Or is he just apple-polishing me?"

Cad wasn't so sure. Before the war, Clint would have polished apples or pomegranates or even pineapples for that matter—anything to get a woman tumbling ripe. He said he loved her, that he had changed. Perhaps he had. Clint had never been so determined or so mashed over a woman, but then he had never seen a woman deny Clint anything. "I think he's changed for the better, but whether or not you should give in—I can't say, Mourning. Only you know the way you feel, what you really want. I just hope you don't end up feeling like a croquet ball before it's all over with."

"You're too late. I already feel like he's sent me sailing through more hoops than a trained tiger. He's so talented at getting what he wants. He could coax water from rocks if he set his mind to it."

Her cheerless tone sounded so dismal, Cad laughed. "You make him sound a bit like Amphion," he said pleasantly, then added, "or a snake charmer."

"Exactly," she said with a mournful sigh.

"Do you still love him?"

It was the second most oft asked question residing in her dura mater, falling right behind *why did he leave?* "I feel like I've loved him forever."

"Give in, then."

"I've already said that to myself."

"Well? What did your *self* say?"

She could hear the smile in that one. *"Self* said I had devoted too much time to building up my life again to let that roving *bed-presser* waltz back into it, leveling all my emotions with a *one, two, three . . . step, step, close."* Mourning paused, then sighed. "My pride also added a few hypothetical suppositions." She placed her chin in her palms as the shrill little cry of a bird was heard overhead.

Cad's leg had begun to pain him, but it was the first time she had really opened up and talked since Clint's return. Her pain made his take a backseat. "I'm eager to hear what sage words your pride afforded."

"*Pride* said it had been damaged enough and there was no way for Clint and me to regain the ground we had lost without her suffering humiliation." She turned to face him when she felt a cool waft of air where his back had been pressed against hers.

Cad's eyes held Mourning's with a contemplative look. "That does have a prideful ring to it." Cad rubbed his eyes as he paused in thought. Her obstinate, uncooperative little pride—that self-inflicted tendency would be her humiliation, not the splicing of enmity. *She is so uncommonly original*, he thought, *yet so typically feminine in her self-perception*. Had Clint accounted for that? The sine qua non in this impasse was a means to partner, without suffering a blow to Mourning's pride, or the subjection of Clint's masculinity to groveling emasculation. Nothing short of a cataclysmic event or divine providence could bring that off. And neither one of those was very likely to occur. Or so he thought.

"I guess the whole affair is rather hopeless," she said brokenly. "My life reads like a fairy tale about a princess turreted at the top of a glass mountain."

"So steep, climbing the vitreous incline of its glacis was nigh impossible?" Cad asked, with a tone that mocked her own glumness.

Morosely, she replied, "*So* steep, even a *charming prince* couldn't make it."

He gave a lusty laugh. "I'm afraid you've grossly underestimated our charming prince. If the mountain won't come to Mohammed, Mohammed will go to the mountain."

"Meaning?"

"Meaning, the princess could always slide down a kite string."

Cad was right. Clint was a man born to beard the most impossible quest, a proven bellwether in the war.

While they were busy discussing Clint he was in his study, holding a glass of brandy in his left hand while his right hand caressed a lock of Mourning's hair that had so casually been cut from a tree so long ago. Clint, it seemed, was contemplating Mourning with as much spirit as she was discussing him. Why had he been so willing to leave without marriage or securing a commitment from her? What had made him yearn so after his personal freedom? It had been so easy to categorize her, lumping her together with all the other liaisons he'd had, taking her time and time again with practiced ease, yet knowing within his soul he would hold himself back. What had happened to alter his desire not to commit himself to a woman?

The war. Something had happened, something that would change and alter forever his male passivity toward her. The war had done that. He had been a captain, mixing with officers and enlisted men alike. They were all the same, taking a woman with a passive sort of detached isolation in a distasteful and vulgar manner; a temporary satisfaction for an infinite longing. That was when it had begun to unfurl, this budding deep within; a grieving spirit trapped in the essence of his being, creating a desire for something beyond his brooding unfulfillment. Waxing within him was a voraciousness for something more than the placation of his libido.

The war. It had been the catalyst in his metamorphosis. It was during the war that the feeling of displacement and dislocation began to emerge. The war, and two long years spent in a rotting hole the Yankees called prison, Ft. Delaware—the Andersonville of the North. The years spent in the plain granite-and-brick hulk sitting on Pea Patch Island, midstream in the Delaware River, gave him time to think—time to remember. To that hellish place of bleak, overcrowded quarters and pitiable rations, it had come: hurtful, poignant, and burdensome. Attacking his bitter soul with a pestering tenacity.

And yet, retrospectively, he saw he had been afflicted with a farsightedness, an inability to see clearly that which was closest to him. Mourning. Sweet Mourning, with the angelic face and gilt hair, a stubborn chin, and eyes that had a tendency to cross when she encountered beetles. Mourning, a free-floating spirit, elusive as a firefly, who cleaved his head, tried to drown his pistol, and disposed of unwelcome company with the wave of a shoat's head. Wonderful, innocent, adorable Mourning. A wood sprite whose virtuous defenses were more enduring than the Chinese wall; a paroxysm of desire that haunted him for four long years.

But he had survived. Endured and survived to come back to her—to his own woman. To find what he didn't know he had until it was lost to him. He admitted now, how important it was to belong—to give, to have a permanence and purpose in his life. For the first time he saw marriage not as a castrating bondage, but as a joining—a fusing of his soul with the mate who could bring an end to the odyssey of his soul.

There was a knock at the study door. "Come on in," said Clint, tucking the lock of Mourning's hair in his pocket.

"I found that bottle of brandy," Mrs. Harper huffed. Clint surmised the huffing was due to an extra fifteen or twenty pounds she'd added to her already generous frame while he'd been away.

"Just put it on the desk."

"I knew Mr. John had a case of that stashed somewhere. Just took me longer to find it than I thought. You'll never guess where I found it."

Clint said nothing but raised his brows in question.

Mrs. Harper laughed. "In a box in the attic—under about three feet of nappies. Seems Miss Mourning had stored the children's nappies up there when they outgrew them." She stepped through the door and pulled it shut, then opened it again. "I sure hope, Mr. Clint, that you can get that gal won over. Sure would like to have those nappies back in use."

Clint laughed. "So would I, Mrs. Harper. So would I."

"You're making headway, Mr. Clint. It may not seem like it to you, but you're making headway. You just keep after her, and you'll have Miss Mourning."

Miss Mourning. She was his desire for survival, his reason for coming back, and his purpose for being here. For her, he persevered against insurmountable odds to free her from her own bondage, and unlock the door to her soul, which had been incarcerated for years. It was for this purpose that he pared with tender-hearted compassion, gradually shaving away the callus that formed over her wounded pride and broken heart.

What had taken a few short words to destroy was taking innumerable volumes to rebuild. His acidic words were forever carved in the stone he had called a heart. *Open your eyes so you will understand exactly what is happening . . . you wanted her. She's yours.*

Progress was inescapably slow, building at a snail's pace, one tiny crystallized granule at a time, each one a precious faceted stone strung upon a chain of infinite patience. She was why he persisted with languid altering pressure—tempting her with the heady opiate of desire and teasing her with the sweet fragrant promise of fulfillment. She was skeptical. She had a right to be.

It was just that morning that he had cornered her in a spare bedroom used for quilting. She was sitting upon a small stool, her feet tucked under the rungs, her dotted Swiss skirt billowing around her like the cap of a speckled mushroom. Spiraling filaments of platinum that caught and held the early-morning light surrounded a classical head, bent over the intricate pattern of a quilt, done, ironically enough, in a wedding-ring pattern.

He observed her a moment from the threshold before coming at a measured pace to stand behind her. His hand, unhurried, brushed the satin arc of a sculpted cheekbone lying beneath the velvet nap of skin. Her schoolgirl cheeks went from flush to blush, and the living heat of it penetrated his fingertips.

"Mourning . . ."

She tried to pull away, but his hold on her shoulders was firm. "Mourning," he began, "I know I'm not very good at this."

"For once I agree with you."

"Mourning . . . dammit, I love you."

Her startled response was an involuntary cry of pain as the needle pierced her finger. A scarlet droplet of blood rose from the invisible point to gleam like a blood ruby before it was pushed aside by another faceted jewel rising to the surface.

His half-closed eyes looked sleepy, and his hand gently ran along her hairline, trailing the tip of one finger. She should have bolted while her voluntary muscles were still voluntary. Grandmother Howard, she thought, is this what you meant when you said *Don't go near the water, child, if you don't know how to swim*? She could feel the gradual giving way, the sinking of her resistance in a slow-eddying pool of drowning sensation.

He dipped his fingertip into the crimson droplet upon her finger and touched it to her lip, gently spreading it like nectar before gathering another drop and touching his own lips. His palms cupped her cheeks, his fingertips touching her hair as he tipped her head back to meet his kiss.

"A blood covenant," he whispered. Lips golden and warm touched hers drowsily. "I love you. Come to me, love," he murmured. "Come to me in the colors of butter and sugar . . . gilded hair and a satin wedding-gown. Oh, love . . . help me. Help me to show you how much I care."

His knowing fingers whispered and danced across the surface of her forearm, and she could feel the blood-heat of him rising warm and suggestive against her flesh.

"Mourning-love . . . sweet, darling. Why the frown?" His

lips brushed back and forth over the ear he had just tormented and left so sensitive, his breath floating over her like wind in the willows. "Your skin is so soft, love. As soft as thistledown. Did you know that?"

The only response she was capable of was a gulp you could have heard in San Antonio. He buried his face in the warm fragrance of her neck, his hands sliding up to her breast. "I've changed, my love. I won't hurt you again, sweetheart. Give me a chance to show you."

How could two hands and one mouth wreak so much havoc? She was a confused bundle of cross purposes. She didn't want him to touch her; what was taking him so long? Clint continued to surround her with a silken net of imaginings set with smoldering jewels of promise, seducing her with the spicy warmth of his urgent kiss and filling her with beatitude.

Weakly, she said, "Stop! Don't you dare change on me now . . . not when I've already decided I don't like you."

He caught her next words with his mouth, penetrating her very thoughts. "I love you," he whispered. "Let me take you to town, today, tomorrow . . . last week. Marry me."

Marry me, marry me, what wonderful words. He was saying what she'd always hoped for. Words, words, sweet, bewitching words, words full of magic and promise. Spellbinding words, enchanting words, words with no thought of her sorrow. Inside her head his words echoed:

> Mourning, Mourning, crosspatch frown
> let me take you into town.
> On skin soft as thistledown
> she wore a satin wedding gown.

"Love, what are you thinking?" She did not have time to answer. The love magic of his fingertips was saturating her delicate body. "Mourning-love . . . I adore you. *Come lie with me and be my love . . .*"

"E-gads!" she said with a dry little croak. "Now he's hitting me with poetry!"

Now he laughed, remembering the way she had turned redder than a bloodwort and run from the room.

Mourning, sweet Mourning, so open and transparent, you

could see clear to her backbone. A delicate and fragile backbone held stiff and cattail-straight with determined resistance. Breaking down this resistance was the reason he continued with adroitness and without mercy, to flood her emotions, enticing her with loving glances, shivering whispers, and the adoration of his hands.

A childish shriek of laughter sent him to the window. Katy was running from Gabe, who was chasing her with a frog.

"Now I'm gonna make you kiss this slimy old frog and you're gonna get warts and be an ugly old hag," Gabe said with childish delight as he dangled the squirming frog inches from her impish face.

"No, I'm not. I'm not afraid of frogs. See?" Snatching the frog, she held it expertly in her hands.

Puzzled. "Why'd you run, then, if you're not afraid of frogs?"

"Gabe, sometimes you are so stupid. How could I get you to chase me if I didn't run?"

Little Katy, so like her mother, with the kind of innocent capriciousness that hit you like a swift kick in the solar plexus. Loving, gentle, spirited Katy. Always happy and bubbling like a simmering pot with a clattering lid. Warm, friendly Katy. The first to be his friend, the first to show him love, the first to call him Daddy.

Katy was always friendly. That was something positive. But on the negative side, the boys were downright hostile, especially Gabe. Gabriel Clinton, his namesake, was the one that resisted him the most. Next to his mother.

As Clint studied his daughter's face an idea came into existence, just a snowflake of subterfuge, growing to avalanche proportions by the time it was perfected. The children were the best way to reach Mourning. Katy had already come around, the boys were next.

A week later he had the opportunity to begin the monumental task of winning the friendship of his two sons.

It was a lazy Sunday afternoon. Mourning and Caroline had gone with the circuit preacher to make some calls, and Cad was greasing the axle on the wagon. Clint had just finished rebuilding a stretch of fence around a corral a skittish yearling had crashed through the day before. It was quiet.

A boisterous interruption of enthusiastic chatter and pup woofing announced the approach of three fishermen who were serious about fishing, followed by two pups who were not. Watching them disappear into a line of trees, Clint put down his hammer.

Gabe saw him first. "He's here again," he said with a sour tone that sounded surprisingly adult. Three sets of eyes drilled into him.

"Mind if I join you?" Clint's eyes drifted and lingered briefly on Katy before moving to the boys.

Gabe shrugged. "You will anyway, even if we don't want you to."

"I take that to mean you don't want me to fish with you."

"I do." Katy replied, and Gabe glowered at her.

She stuck out her tongue at her brother.

Clay offered a nonchalant "I don't care. Stay if you want . . . you don't have a pole, though."

Gabe defiantly eyed him. "I don't want you to stay," he said darkly. "I don't like you, and you are *not* my father."

"Gabe!" Katy shouted. "You better shut up or you're gonna be in *big* trouble." She moved up close to him so she could put her nose in the vicinity of his, and gave him the eye. "Mama told you to not be *odious*!" Then that adorable little girl gave his ear a big yank.

"I won't be in trouble either," Gabe said deliberately, "unless you tattle on me. *Tattletale, tattletale, sittin' on a bull's tail.*"

"I don't care. I'm not as bad as you! Mama told Grandma you were a pain in the *asafetida bag*!"

Clint's lips twitched in a smile. "My little katydid, sometime you must tell me what other charming things your mama has said."

"She said you had more crust than a cobbler!" Gabe said promptly. It was the first time Gabe had spoken to Clint in a cheerful tone.

"Boy, Mama is gonna be fu-ri-ous at you. She told you not to say anything to *him* about that. 'Sides, you'll hurt his feelings." She hugged Clint's legs, looking up at him. "I believe you're my Daddy and I like you."

Sitting pertly on his lap, Katy studied Clint's face for a long time, then tentatively put her plump arms around his neck and hugged him fiercely. It was a childish spontaneous action: compelling and powerful. He felt an uncommon closeness with this child who had compassion for him and reached out.

He held her close as he watched his two sons, desiring their love as much as Katy's. The scowl on Gabe's face told him he had his work cut out for him.

Katy saw the direction of Clint's gaze. "Mama said Gabe doesn't like you 'cause he's the one *mostess* like you . . . but I think he's the one who mostess *doesn't* like you."

Gabe whirled upon his vexatious sister with a vitriolic shout: "I'm *not* like him. You say that again and I'll make you eat this worm."

Katy squeezed Clint's neck tighter. "I'm not coming down, then." Her arms wound around her father's neck with the dint of a sumo wrestler. She had more stick than a pin.

Katy was content to fish from Clint's lap. Gabe and Clay moved several yards up the creek, just enough to snub him, yet close enough to hear what he said. Katy was a veritable chatterbox and plied him with questions. What did he and Cad do as boys? What kind of fights did they have? What did he like to eat? What happened to the big horse he rode in the war? It was the perfect opportunity to begin his winning of his children. Once that was done, only Mourning would remain. He knew the children would bring about the priceless reconciliation. He did not know the precious price that would be paid.

"You must mean Conquistador, how'd you know about him?"

"Mama said you were in the *Silver War* and fought and killed people. She said you were very brave and got shot two times and were sent to a prison. . . ."

"He didn't go to prison, saphead . . . he was a prisoner of the *Yankees,* but he escaped." Clay flashed that proud, lopsided grin that was a Kincaid legacy. "Didn't you?"

Clint mirrored the grin. "Yes, I did."

Katy spoke impatiently. "What happened to Keetador?"

Clint laughed and ruffled her hair. "In the Battle of Bull Run, he was shot out from under me and I was wounded." His eyes flicked over to the boys, whose ears were ostensibly pricked.

Clint knew what it was like to be a young boy, wearied to the point of nausea by the senseless chatter and silly nonsense women are prone to discuss, not to mention lapses when they irrevocably revert to talking about each other. The porous little minds of his sons were saturated to the gills with soapbox diction, grapevine disclosures, and hours of idle chatter. At the same time they were pathetically starved for those animated, robust, and stimulating tales of adventure that activate the mind and set a boy's thoughts adrift.

It is a strange phenomenon, like Halley's Comet, migratory birds, and gravity; what happens to a young boy beset with women. Large doses of prolonged association with the opposite sex, regardless of age, linger in a boy's consciousness like his first dose of castor oil. It is an archaic handmaiden of torture that tends to dilute reality, inspire boredom, and instigate monotony.

Clint had the sagacious wisdom to remember how nothing set a young boy's blood a-tingle or subdued his belligerent spirit like the sweet cadence of warmed-over war stories. He gave it to them. Not all at once, but a measured amount to capture their attention and hold their interest, making them return again and again, like a bear to a beehive.

It was a contrived allurement, guaranteeing their recurring interest with sketchy accounts. Like a partially clad woman—promising so much more.

"I passed out, and when I woke up, the Confederate soldiers had retreated and Conquistador was dead, lying across my legs. I couldn't move him so I was forced to lie there. The next morning a Yankee patrol found me, and after they had treated my wounds, I was sent to prison."

Clay moved closer and was now sitting on his haunches in front of Clint, but Gabe was still engrossed in his fishing. Lured into the story, Clay asked, "How'd you escape from the prison camp?"

"I jumped off a bridge." Clint watched Gabe covertly as he placed the pole on the ground and sat staring at the water, listening, but not part of the group.

"Why?" Katy asked. It was such a soft little squeak, Clint almost missed it.

Clint shifted Katy to his other leg, gently hugging her as he answered her question. "You mean, why did I jump from the bridge?"

She nodded.

"The Yankees were transporting prisoners to another camp. We were riding in open wagons across a bridge that spanned the Delaware River. When the wagon reached the center, I jumped from the wagon to the railing and dove into the water."

"Was it a long way down?" Clay asked.

Clint laughed. "A long, long way down. I thought the water might not be deep enough and I might break my fool neck."

"Did they shoot at you?" Clay fired another question.

"Yes."

"Did you get shot?" This was from Clay, the most verbal of the trio.

"Four times." The skeptical gray eyes on the bank shifted to Clint.

"Did it hurt bad?"

"Yes, katydid," said Clint. "It hurt enough to make the trip back a most unpleasant one." Gabe was staring at the water again.

After a few moments, Gabe stood. "We gotta go. I'll carry the poles. Clay, you get the fish."

"Can I ride on your horse?" asked Katy, drawing figure eights in the dirt with the side of her shoe.

"Do you think your mama would mind?"

Katy grinned up at him, "Oh, she won't care. Clay and Gabe have a pony of their own and I ride it sometimes."

"It ain't no pony," shouted Clay, running after Gabe, the fish thumping and bumping along in the dirt behind him. Clay, it seems, decided to tie the fish on the end of his pole. Good idea, bad results. Not allowing for the weight of the fish to drag down the tip of the pole, the fish were given a ride that made the frying pan a hopeful aspiration.

When they reached the barn, Katy ran into the house and Clint led Trooper to the barn. When he came out, Clay was sitting on the fence, waiting.

"Wanna help me clean the fish?"

Clint paused, looking down at the fish. After being tugged for half a mile over flora and fauna, there wasn't much in the way of skin or scales left. Cleaning half-mutilated fish might not be easy, but it had one advantage. It would be quick.

It was. After they cleaned the fish, Clay showed Clint the horse he shared with Gabe, which he steadfastly refused to call a pony. He watched intently as his father inspected the pony as thoroughly as if he were considering a purchase. When Clint nodded his approval, Clay grinned, his cowlick popping up in the breeze.

Clay turned toward the house, a pail of pink, freshly cleaned fish dangling from his hand. "Sir?" he said, and then extended his hand. "Thank you, sir."

Two down, two to go.

A week later Mourning sat on the back porch, in the late evening sun, reading *The Breaking of a Butterfly*, which was progressing rather slowly. She reread the last page three times owing to the helter-skelter pandemonium going on in the yard and still didn't know what she had read. With a sigh she flipped the book over onto her lap as the children rounded the corner of the house for what had to be the twentieth time, running as if the Yahoos were after them.

Autumn was weaving her colors into summer's fading fairness, like satin ribbons in a young maid's hair. Called to life by the deepening amber of the sinking sun were splashes of gold and purple and violet-blue and flaming scarlet. Late roses were still wreathed in heavy clusters around the tree trunks, drooping fragrance from their branches. Cannas and lilies stood tall, clustered in bunches, as if huddled together for warmth against the promise of the chill to come.

At her feet curled her two hounds, Romeo and Juliet, older, like her, with hardly a moment to call their own now that they had a young litter of pups underfoot. Romeo was asleep, chasing some smart ole coon in his dream, judging from the way he whimpered and made sweeping strokes across the floor. Juliet just lay there, the perfect picture of peaceful, with her head resting on her forepaws, her tail thumping madly from the luxurious rubbing she was receiving from Mourning's bare toes sunk deep in her abundant hide.

"Well, my love, what has set you all aquiver?" Clint said with an endearing smile she would have been tempted, under other circumstances, to save and paste in her Memory Book. "Has your little *bête noire* been harassing you again?"

She answered his question with alacrity. "The only little *black beast* that harasses me is you."

"A *bentrovato*." he said, laughing. *"Se non è vero, è bentrovato."*

"Even if it's not true, it is well-conceived. French, Latin, and *Italian* I know. It's the Spanish I'm so ignorant of."

Clint dropped his long-shanked frame into the porch swing beside her, sending it slamming backward. The force sent her feet flying up in such a hurry, poor Juliet scrambled from the porch by the shortest route available. That happened to be over the back of Romeo. Startled from the dreamy depths of howling pursuit, Romeo sat back on his haunches and let roll a baying howl that sounded like the golden trumpets of the archangel Gabriel heralding the day of judgment.

By that time the swing came flying forward, throwing her off balance. Once again it threatened to pitch her out of the waggling contraption altogether.

In the lurch, she grabbed the nearest thing to stabilize her, which in this case was Clint's thigh. His *upper* thigh to be exact, or more precisely still, his *upper, upper* thigh. It stabilized her careening body, but sent everything else hurtling with the impact of two bighorn sheep meeting head on. Realizing *where* her hand was touching, and just *what* it was touching was, to say the least, disconcerting. Jerking her hand away, she heard his low rumble of laughter.

"Are you all right?" he asked, the hint of humor still present in his voice.

"Oh, I'm just dandy," she snapped, trying to wiggle away from him. "Please stop this devilish device so I can get out."

"Love, I can't. It's taken me weeks to get this close to you." His arm, which had been resting on the back of the swing, dropped over her shoulders, dragging her against him. Once he had secured her wiggling, squirming body snugly against him, he brought his other hand against that soft little spot between her shoulder and neck. He spread his fingers, each one an instrument of torture, spreading rack and ruin across miles and miles of nerve endings. The scent of jasmine, light and airy, drifted up from her hair and he touched it with his lips.

She gasped. "Don't you need to clean your guns or something?"

"I cleaned them yesterday." His dark head dropped to her shoulder and she could feel him searching for her face, his breath subtle and warm like the brush of a fairy wing across her skin.

"Will you please stop this nonsense and let me off." Her words, she found, were about as effective as a pair of galoshes in a flood: appropriate but horribly inadequate.

"Will you stop this blasted contraption?"

"Why are you so mad?"

"I'm not mad. I'm just through swinging, that's all!" She glared at him with furious green eyes that were mindful of boiling seawater.

"Oh, I see." It was a carefully baited statement.

"What do you mean, *Oh, I see*?" She swallowed it.

"Just, Oh, I see you were through swinging, not . . ." The pause was intentional.

"Not what?" She was not even aware that she was being played like a largemouth bass that had just swallowed an artificial worm.

He smiled. "Not embarrassed because you put your hand on my secrets."

"Secrets!" she parroted. "How can anything that has been on public display for years be a secret?" The swing had slowed enough for her to torpedo out of it like a cat with a firecracker tied to its tail. She bolted across the porch and down the steps.

"Where are you off to in such a hurry?" he called after her.

"To gather eggs and then to start dinner!"

"Is there anything I can do to help?"

"Pet a mad dog," was her tart reply as she continued on her way, stomping and mumbling under her breath, the sound of his laughter provoking her to thoughts that would bar her forever from the State Missionary and Bible Society.

Mourning sent the gate back against the gatepost with a loud *thwaak!* A perky white leghorn hen had the misfortune to stumble across her path, busily clucking and following a trail of scattered grain. Without breaking stride, Mourning kicked the errant chicken. With a startled cluck the hen ran flapping and squawking, hurdling the fence like a Thoroughbred jumper, leaving a cloud of floating feathers in her wake.

Back on the porch, clear gray eyes followed the angry departure. He took a bead on her as he used to do, thinking: *That's my girl! So I do make you uncomfortable after all? That's good. I can fight that, and your anger.* It was indifference that he had feared.

The lazy heads of forget-me-nots were stirring in the breeze when Clay came running around the barn, screaming, "Daddy, Daddy, come quick. The bull's killing Gabe!"

Clint reached the bull pens first, followed by Mourning and Cad. Gabe's small body was pinned between the fence and the massive shoulder of the bull, a combination that was crushing the breath of life from his lungs.

Dropping inside the pen, Clint wedged himself between the bull and the fence, and placing his shoulders against the bull and his feet against the fence, he pushed until the bull stepped aside, tossing his head and snorting while he pawed the ground. Grabbing the boy, Clint carried him to safety.

Mourning was beside them quickly. "He's all right, Mourning," Clint said with a breathy calm to his voice. "He's just had the breath squeezed from him. He'll be back to normal in a minute." He stretched Gabe out on the grass, the small chest heaving with each gasping breath. When Gabe tried to curl his legs up in a fetal position, Clint pressed them back down. "Cad, you hold his shoulders down. He's got to stay stretched out so the air can get into his lungs."

"What happened, Clay?" Clint asked.

"Gabe was pettin' the bull and he started to climb up the fence when the bull followed him and started pushing him."

"He wanted Gabe to pet him some more," Cad said.

"Not me," Clay offered, "I like horses better."

Mourning was on her knees between Cad and Clint, her hands tense and gripped. When Gabe began to suck in large gulps of air, they released him, watching the gradual blushing color seep into his face. It was then that Mourning realized she was gripping Clint's arm. She jerked it away. He was watching her curiously. "I won't bite," he said softly.

"Except when there's a full moon," she said.

"Clint, you better take care of that arm. It's bleeding pretty bad," Cad said.

"I'll see to it in a minute." Clint placed his hand on his son's head, caressing the soft black curls as he swallowed several times to push away the tightness in his throat. "Are you all right, son?"

Gabe never took his eyes off his father. Mourning studied Clint's face intently. She saw the concern of a father for his son etched across his handsome features. She heard his love-laced voice and felt the gentle strength of reassurance in the hand that touched the small dark head.

"Yes, sir," Gabe answered softly as Clint helped him stand. Clint remained hunched down at eye level with Gabe as he studied his perfect child's face.

"Thank you, sir."

Clint grinned and tousled his hair as he corrected him. "Thank you, Daddy." Clint's heartbeat was suspended, waiting to see if he would be accepted or rejected again. He watched Gabe's eyes survey his arm, never blinking an eye. *Perhaps it won't be today*, Clint thought, *but I'll win you over. I'm sure of it.* Rising to his feet, he heard his son's words.

"Thank you, Daddy," Gabe said. He stepped into the tight circle of his father's arms.

Caroline and Mourning watched the soothing of the breach between father and son, and Mourning realized she was the only holdout.

∾ 32

It was a good day for making soap. Cool enough to heat up the huge caldrons over blazing fires in the yard, yet warm enough to prevent freezing while you did.

Soap making, like Christmas, was a family affair. Soap making, unlike Christmas, was an inevitable undertaking approached with cringing reluctance. Unfortunately there was no way to obtain soap without going through, with plugging diligence, the complete process. The children, who looked upon the whole idea of bathing with a critical eye to begin with, found the entire undertaking rather senseless. Why would *anyone* go to such ends to make something which, in turn, was used for the solitary torturous purpose of that most dreaded of all nouns in the pubescent vocabulary: cleanliness.

It was a warm, good-humored day that found Mildred the cat cleaning her calico fur with such devotion, she was sure to add an inch to the hair ball in her stomach. Behind the pigpen a badger was busy throwing up a mound at the end of its burrow, coming out at last with a round, dirt-covered nose, not unlike Katy's mudpies, which were drying on the back fence.

Caroline and Mrs. Harper were in the kitchen, processing tallow, a nearly tasteless solid that had been rendered from the fat of hogs killed last week. Clint and Cad were bringing kegs of potash from the storage shed, and stacking wood and kindling next to the fire Mourning was tending.

A contentious reenactment of the *Silver War* was going on

down by the stand of cane that grew along the creek. Clay, the hated *Yankee,* had his pockets full of Gabe's best cat's-eye marbles. Marbles Gabe traded because he wanted to be the *Rebel.* Clay said that was fine with him, he didn't want to be the loser anyway.

While they were busy slaying each other on the battlefield, Katy divided her time between her mudpies in the backyard and watching her mother mix tallow and potash together, wondering how that *nasty* mess could ever make soap, let alone get you clean.

Clint dumped a load of wood, and raised his gaze to Mourning, who was standing alone, bent over the barrel of potash, scooping up a ladleful, then sprinkling the powder across the bubbling soap. Tired, hair losing its moorings, wearing a simple dark dress and white apron that had been spotless and crisp earlier in the day, she still was lovely. Holding her in his gaze, he followed the movement of her slender arms, which reached down and, lifting a ruffled edge of her apron and using it as a pot holder, held the end of the spoon with it as she stirred the soap. She straightened, her hand going to the small of her back as she stretched to ease the stiffness. When she lifted her eyes they locked with his. It was a look like all the others he had received over the past months: unpromisingly resistant and hardened with resolve. After holding the look for a moment, she broke the contact.

He turned away, wondering why her prideful resistance forced her to remain apart from him in spite of all his endeavors. He had been so certain, so very sure, the children would bring them together, a providential occurrence. But he was wrong. There was nothing else he could do. He had made up his mind.

Come Monday, he was leaving.

"Look." Cad's voice was soft and reasoning. "It doesn't make any sense to leave. You'll never gain her confidence that way. What good will it do? Think, man. Think."

Clint dropped the load of wood he had just picked up. "Damn your persistent interference! You think I haven't been? You think I don't lie awake at night thinking and plotting? How do you think I've held up after all these months? By thinking. Thinking what might have been . . . thinking what could be if she would only let me inside that fortress she has erected." His voice suddenly became cynically amused. "But she's a tough nut to crack." He picked up the ax and delivered a stunning blow to a log, splitting it.

"Why are you making everything so difficult?" Cad asked,

coming around the woodpile to stand in front of him. "For a man who for years held a notorious record for seductive propensities, this tucking your tail between your legs like an egg-sucking dog and high-tailing it is illogically asinine. My God, stupidity is swelling like a tidal wave inside you. If you leave now, you could destroy everything."

The intense eyes hardened. "You, of all people, I expected to understand. I have done everything except hand her my liver, finely minced and desiccated, on a silver platter."

"Don't expect sympathy from me," Cad said. "You've been wallowing in self-pity for months. Are you suffering some hedonistic reversal where suffering is the sole purpose of life?"

"I'm not. I'm as close to throwing the rest of my life away in some godforsaken army post as I can possibly get. Don't harass me until I do something else I'll regret the rest of my life. Believe me," he said with self-loathing, "I'm having a hard enough time living with the first one."

"What will it solve? How will running away solve anything? Are you just going to abandon her and your children?" Cad asked, watching Clint's hands tighten on the ax before he sent it sinking into the stump, the handle quivering from the impact.

There was a short hesitation before Clint replied. "She can manage on her own."

The reply was soaked in sarcasm. "Can she? Do you really believe that? No one can stand alone. Not you, not me, not even Mourning. It's inevitable that she's going to need someone. When that time comes, when she really needs you, you aren't going to be here. What will happen then? When you're gone?"

Clint unbuttoned his shirt and threw it over a nearby post. Sweat gleamed on his naked torso. "My patience has run out. There is *nothing* that will hold me here any longer."

"That," Cad said sarcastically, "sounds suspiciously like a fool talking."

Questioning eyes studied the solitary log and narrowed suspiciously. *What is taking them so long?* Mourning wondered. She intellectualized and formed postulations regarding their obvious remiss as she added the last stick of wood to the fire. She glanced in the direction of the woodpile, wondering if they were back there working or if they had slipped off to the barn for a quick game of dominoes. A bit of feminine curiosity, as well as the more legitimate need for firewood, pressed her to see what Cad and Clint were up to. Snatching up the spoon, she gave the pot an energetic stirring before departing.

Katy flew around the corner like a fluttering autumn leaf, just in time to see Mourning stir the pot and walk away. Scampering to the bubbling caldron, she eyed the frothy brew dancing inside. With childish precision she carefully placed her assortment of mudpies on the ground, and reached for the big spoon, holding her apron like she had seen her mother do. She dipped the spoon into the simmering caldron and stirred.

Hideous screams rent the air, again and again. They were the screams of agony and fear, the screams of immature utterance, the excruciating screams of a child.

When they reached her, Katy's skirts were blazing and she was screaming hysterically, then she began to run. Clint reached her first.

In a painful blur, Mourning saw Clint overtake her, throwing them both to the ground and rolling with her in the dirt. By the time he stood with her tiny smoldering body in his arms, Cad was running out of the barn with his saddled horse. Swinging into the saddle, he shouted, "I'll go for Doc."

There wasn't much they could do for her until Doc arrived. They cut the charred remains of her clothing away and covered her with wet flannel.

When he arrived, Doc Tubbs allowed Caroline and Mrs. Harper in the room with him to assist, making Cad, Mourning, and Clint remain outside. After an eternity of listening to her painful whimpering and screams, it grew quiet. Mourning ran for the door, but Clint stopped her.

"Don't go in, love. Wait until Doc comes out."

"Don't touch me," she screamed, pounding against his chest, forgetting the nasty burns he had hidden under his shirt. "How can you be so heartless? How can you stand to listen to her like this? I want to be with her, she's my baby. Please, Clint. Please let me go in. It's so quiet. Oh, God, Katy. My little Katy. She's . . ." She couldn't go on.

"Cad?" Clint said, his look summoning Cad more than his words. By the time Cad reached them, Mourning was hiccuping with sobs. "Take her," Clint ordered. "Perhaps you can reason with her better than I."

When she felt Clint release her, she heard Cad speaking to her. "Mourning, sweet, don't take on so." His words were tiny pinging hammers in her confused head. She struggled against him until it registered that this was Cad. Her friend. She could trust him.

"He wouldn't let me go in," she sobbed. "It doesn't even bother him to hear her screaming."

"Mourning, how can you say something like that?" Clint asked with sudden harshness.

Mourning felt the vibrations of words against her cheek as Cad held her head pressed against his chest. "Don't argue with her now. Can't you see she doesn't know what she's saying? She's emotionally upset."

Mourning had a vague flashing sensation of shame cross over her, but couldn't remember what caused it. "Come with me, sweetheart." It was Cad's voice. "There is nothing you can do in there. You'd just make Doc take time away from Katy, trying to calm you."

Mourning clutched Cad's shirt-sleeves. "Why is it so quiet, Cad? Do you think she's . . ."

"No. Doc has given her something for the pain." Mourning allowed him to take her to the sofa and he sat with her, his arm around her and her head nestled against him. He placed his warm hand over her cold ones, which were nervously twisting the handkerchief Caroline had given her before Doc had called her to come into Katy's room.

The three of them waited in mute silence. Finally the door opened and Caroline came out, looking strangely calm. Mourning felt her heart lurch until Caroline gave her a half smile. "She's sleeping quietly. The burns were all on her right leg, hip, and part of her back. Her face wasn't touched. She has minor burns on her hands where she slapped at her skirts, but the others are more serious. Doc said you can come in now."

The first week passed at a snail's pace. Mourning and Clint stayed with Katy during the day and took turns sitting with her at night. When they were in the room together, it was strained and quiet between them. By the fourth day Clint tried to talk to her, but Mourning was closed to him.

Strange, she thought, sitting in the shadows of the room, looking at the dark silhouette of him sitting in a chair across from her, his head resting in his hands. His magnificently tall body was slouched over in a way that reminded her of an old carriage horse she had seen in Memphis once. An old horse that had been abused and broken.

He began to avoid her. When he could not, it seemed to Mourning that he had developed the unbelievable ability to look right through her as if she were as transparent as glass. Another strange thing began to occur. Her own mother began to see things from Clint's viewpoint more and more, making Mourning feel foolish because of the way she had treated him. Then Mrs. Harper had jumped on the wagon when Mourning went into the kitchen, drilling her with such intensity, Mourning fled from the kitchen in tears. But it was her dear friend Cad's criticism that began to make her see what she had become. She didn't like herself very much.

"I know it hurts, Miss Katy, but this has to be done," Dr. Tubbs said. "You are a brave little girl. Just think about taking deep breaths while I finish this. I'll be as quick as I can. Cry if you want to, but be still."

Mourning couldn't keep her eyes on Katy. They kept drifting across the bed to Clint. Clint, the man she had driven away. Clint, the man she loved beyond everything. Clint, the man she wanted back. But how?

"Your blisters are looking better." Dr. Tubbs kept talking to her, and Mourning knew he was taking Katy's mind off what he was doing. "Remember I told you the other day that your blisters were crying and that was where the sticky water came from?" Katy nodded weakly. "Well, they have almost stopped crying. See how they are starting to dry in places?"

He dipped his cloth into the basin filled with water and a strong-smelling liquid. He covered her burns with the saturated cloths. "That makes them feel better, doesn't it?" Her whimpers were softer now, the tears coming more slowly, as she nodded once again. "We'll leave them on for a while now. The medicine I gave you should be making you sleepy pretty soon."

Mourning and Clint followed Dr. Tubbs downstairs. "She is doing remarkably well. Burns are strange to deal with. I've seen people burned worse that survived and some burned a whole lot less that never had a chance. She's healthy and young, that's on her side. That, and her father's quick thinking. Clint, if you hadn't rolled her when you did . . . Well, it was mighty lucky for her that you were here."

Dr. Tubbs opened his bag and removed a jar. "I left the solution to soak her cloths in by her bed. Your mother has the sleeping draft. Use this ointment after you remove the wet cloths. Allow the skin to dry naturally, then cover the burned areas with this ointment. This process has to be done several times a day. If they get too dry and crack and bleed, that's not good. She will be cranky, but that's to be expected." He snapped his bag shut and walked out the door. "It is also important that the two of you get some rest."

Mourning waited until Clint shut the door. He turned, without looking at her, pausing in the threshold of the door for just a moment when she spoke. "Clint?"

"I think we should take Dr. Tubbs's advice. We're both tired. Good night."

"How two grown, reasonably sane people who love each other as much as the two of you do can be more stubborn than a block of wood is beyond me," Cad was saying to Clint over a cup of coffee early the next morning.

Clint was surprised by that remark. For his part, he had always thought Mourning more stubborn than a fence post, but *never* would he have applied that term to himself. There was little doubt in his mind that she would never, until her dying breath, give in. But that *he* would be considered stubborn was a revelation. After Cad's sudden disclosure, Clint's next question was, what do you do with a discovery after you have discovered it?

"You set about changing it," was Cad's simple answer. "You can't change someone else. Only yourself. That's where you got off the track. All this time you've been working like the very devil to change her mind, to change her way of thinking—and to my knowledge there hasn't been a man born that could change a woman's mind. I seem to remember something about people who worry about a splinter in another's eye when they have a board in their own." He gave Clint a critical look. "If what you've been doing isn't working, why are you still doing it?"

"I'll be damned if I know."

"Have you thought about trying something different?"

"I was going to leave. That was different," Clint answered, knowing his voice sounded as bewildered as he felt.

"And that didn't work either. So where do you go from here?"

Cad stood, taking his cup to the cabinet. "I wish I knew the answer. It's frustrating as hell." He reached over to where the pan of biscuits was sitting and poked one, to see if they were cool yet. Then he wrapped a couple of them up, laying them in the crown of his hat. "There doesn't seem to be much left except prayer and proverbs."

"Please . . . proverbs are Mourning's forte, not mine," Clint said, staring at the dregs in the bottom of his cup.

Cad looked as if he was doing some hard thinking. Then he said, "Then maybe you should try thinking like a woman—with your heart, not your mind." He looked a little sheepish for making a suggestion like that to his brother.

But Clint accepted it as easily as the second cup of coffee Cad poured for him. "Maybe I should. They seem to be the only ones who understand why they do the things they do."

"I can tell you one thing. If the tables were turned, Mourning would've had you wedded and bedded by now. A woman may not have much strength, but she's got strategy." Picking up his hat and poking around a little to settle the biscuits, he said, "I wish I could offer you something more substantial, but honest to God, Clint, I don't know what it would be." Combing his fingers through his hair, he leaned his head forward a little, bringing it together with his hat, then he straightened, adjusting the fit of the hat, the biscuits still inside. "I've got to go feed. I'll see you later."

Clint nodded, suddenly thinking how funny it was that although he'd seen Cad do it a million times, he'd never thought to ask him why he always put a couple of biscuits in his hat like that. He glanced up quickly, but Cad had just shut the door behind him, so he returned his stare to his coffee dregs as if he were going to find a suggestion there. A kaleidoscope of ideas whirled in his mind. There had to be some way to make Mourning see reason. There had to be. He was desperate. He would try anything, honest or dishonest, aboveboard or overboard, ruse or subterfuge . . . anything . . . If he only had Mourning's shrewd cunning. *When around foxes, play the fox. And who knew the fox better than another fox? . . . And who knew a woman better than another woman? . . . And who knew Mourning better than her mother?* No one.

* * *

Sitting in the parlor late one evening, Caroline observed how the roseate gleam of lamplight silhouetted Mourning like an alabaster rendering of the madonna—a perfection of beauty that almost transcended mortal standards. It was in quiet moments of observing her lovely daughter like this that Caroline often felt a tugging sadness that Clay, dead these many years, had not lived to see her to womanhood.

Mourning's diminutive head was bent over her needlework as it was every evening after the children were put to bed. Her fingers moved spryly as the needle repeatedly pierced the raised work panel of Andromeda and Perseus. Caroline picked up a smocked pinafore she was making for Katy, thinking Katy's improvement had enabled Mourning's natural rosy-cheeked vitality to return, and now she was blooming like a hothouse plant.

With an exaggerated yawn, Caroline stretched, then grimaced, placing her hand on her lower back. "I've been having a terrible time with my lumbago the last few days."

Mourning paused and lifted skeptical eyes. "Your lumbago?" she repeated with a tone of doubt. "Mother, when did you start having trouble with lumbago?"

"Why, it's plagued me for years, but the last two days have been the absolute worst."

Mourning was beginning to detect the faint odor of fish. Something was amiss. She knew as well as God made little green apples that Caroline had *never* had a problem with her back. "I've never heard you mention it before."

Caroline, a smile curving her full mouth, lowered her head. "There are some things vanity prevents, and lumbago is an indication of old age, which I absolutely refuse to consider."

Mourning cast her a long, speculative glance. "You're beginning to sound like you've got one foot in the grave. Surely you've got a few good years left." She lowered her needlework to her lap, her eyes on Caroline. "Mother, just what are you about? Have you been nipping the brandy again?"

Caroline cast a quick look at her daughter, met her gaze, and then immediately returned her eyes to her sewing. She made a scolding sound with her tongue. "You know what Diogenes said."

There was a gleaming look in her mother's eye that Mourning

saw repeatedly in her children whenever they were up to mischief.
"He said a lot of things."

"Well, I'm only interested in *Don't heap reproaches on old age,
seeing that we all hope to reach it.*"

"I can't see that you're looking forward to it with open relish."

"I'm not, but considering the alternative, I think I am going
to love growing old," Caroline said.

Mrs. Harper walked in. "I've just finished baking an applesauce cake for poor Mrs. Pecksniff."

"Poor Mrs. Pecksniff?" repeated Mourning. "Hmmm . . .
Pecksniff . . . Wasn't that the name of the schemer in . . . Oh,
Mother, you remember . . . the Dickens book . . . Oh, what
was the name of it?"

"Martin Chuzzlewit," Caroline offered.

"Yes, that's it. Wasn't it the same name . . . Pecksniff?"

"Something close to that, I believe," Caroline answered, giving Mrs. Harper a look.

"I've packed the cake in a basket with some jams, a smoked
ham, pickled beets, a loaf of bread, and some boiled potatoes,"
Mrs. Harper went on. "Would you take it to her when you deliver
those old clothes?"

"Who," Mourning asked with exasperation, "is Mrs. Pecksniff? I've never heard of her. Where does she live?"

"She is a poor, unfortunate soul who just moved here from
. . . Georgia, I believe. Lost her dear husband in the war, and her
with eleven youngsters."

"Eleven?" Mourning repeated, noticing how Mrs. Harper
suddenly made herself into a vapor and drifted from the room.
"How did you find out about her?"

"You remember when Brother Singletary, the new circuit
preacher, came by when Katy was ill? He told me about her. We
paid her a call one afternoon while you were resting. The poor,
poor woman is in the direst of straits, so I gathered a few meager
belongings for her. I sent word that I would pay her a visit tomorrow, but with this lumbago, I don't know . . ."

"Mother, this *lumbago* of yours wouldn't be a ploy to get me
to run this errand of mercy for you, would it?"

"You would? Oh, Mourning, you don't know what a blessing
you are to me. That would be such a burden off my shoulders. I've

simply worried myself sick, wondering how this hip of mine would stand that long ride in the wagon." Caroline stood, putting her sewing back into her sewing basket. "Now, don't you worry about a thing. I'll tell Mrs. Harper to get everything ready. You'll need to leave early, dear. Good night."

Before Mourning had a chance to say she didn't remember volunteering, Caroline limped magnificently from the room.

At six o'clock the next morning, Mourning stood in the kitchen, dressed in her rose velvet calling suit, armed to the teeth with baskets of food and clothing, along with enough blankets to keep the entire garrison at Ft. Stockton warm. "Mother, I don't think I'll need this many blankets to keep me warm. One or two will be sufficient," Mourning said as Mrs. Harper and Caroline carried two staggering stacks outside. She followed them.

"It might get colder . . . the hens aren't laying and that's a sure sign. And it is quite a nice ride to Mrs. Pecksniff's," Caroline said, limping back into the kitchen.

Quite a nice ride? Mourning repeated in her mind. When Caroline returned, Mourning was waiting. "Just how far is it?"

"Oh, not *too* far. Just to the old Bradley place."

"Mother, don't you dare slink back into that kitchen. What do you mean, the old Bradley place? That's a good day's drive from here. I won't make it back before dark."

"Of course you could, if you hurried, but Mrs. Pecksniff would be delighted to put you up for the night."

"The question isn't *would* she put me up," Mourning said sharply, "but *where* she'd put me. With eleven children I'd be lucky to find myself on the porch."

"I believe some of the children will be at the Pattersons'."

"At the Pattersons' . . ." she said. "Who are the Pattersons? I've never heard of them either." The smell of fish was getting stronger by the minute.

"Dear me! I haven't told you about the Pattersons? They're another—"

"—new family Brother Singletary introduced you to," Mourning finished.

That evening Mourning pulled up in front of the Bradley place. When she arrived, it was almost dark. Hopping down lightly, she reached for her basket when it suddenly occurred to

her that *this* house did not look lived in; even the windows were
dark.

And not only was the house not lived in, it hadn't been lived
in for quite some time. She turned up the lantern wick and looked
around. There wasn't a stick of furniture in the place. It was later,
when she rested upon a pallet in a dim corner, that she began to
think. She *knew* her mother had intentionally sent her on this wild-
goose chase, loading the wagon with enough food and blankets to
last a week, expecting her to stay overnight. The question was
why? Well, she told herself, there is nothing to be done about it
now. Sooner or later she would find out what mischief Caroline
had been about. Sooner or later.

As it turned out, it was sooner. For she had scarcely turned
out the lantern, placing a small hatchet on the floor next to her—in
case she needed to defend her person—and fallen asleep, when she
was awakened by the sound of someone walking across the front
porch. The steps were slow and steady, heavy and well placed, the
kind of steps a man would take. On her knees now, she felt around
her for the hatchet.

Just as someone on the other side of the door began to slowly
turn the handle, a thin slice of light appeared, squeezing around
the door as it opened more fully. Suddenly the door was flung
wide. He had placed the lantern on the floor behind him, throwing
long, whiplike shadows that slithered across her like writhing
snakes.

Mourning let fly with the hatchet, and scrambled to her feet.
It whizzed past the man's head, just as he ducked, whistling
through the air, end over end, to land in the darkness beyond.

It was difficult to tell just who was surprised more, Mourning
or Clint. His hand still on the door he had just opened, he directed
his stare upon Mourning, just as she was staring back at him, her
hands clapped over her mouth. Her green eyes were wide, he could
see the comingling expression of fear, apprehension, surprise, and
of course, sheer wonder. Mourning, however, her mind befuddled
with fear and fatigue, was not as nimble mentally. Eventually some
comprehension crept into her mind. All she could do was stand
there, quivering like a goose quill, looking at this dearly beloved
man, and cry like a blubbering idiot.

As she folded her trembling body against him, Clint spoke
gruffly. "I hope to God you never perfect your aim. A man would

have to have more goddamn lives than a cat to survive around you."

But when she began to cry harder, he spoke more softly, "Mourning, my darling girl, I believe it's time for us to bury the hatchet."

"I didn't know it was you," she sobbed. Clutching his sleeves, Mourning buried her wet nose in Clint's shirtfront.

Holding her close, Clint covered her head with kisses. "My love, you have the irritating but infinitely dear little habit of wetting my shirtfront whenever I'm around." Neither of them was aware of the gradual easing into old familiarities, the smooth return of that exquisitely stomach-churning magic that had always existed between them.

Suddenly conscious of the tugging feeling inside her, Mourning was reminded of the gaping chasm that lay like snarling jaws between them. Thrilled to be in his arms again, yet fearful of being forced away, she buried her head against his neck and cried harder. He kissed the side of her face, and she heard him whisper, "God, how utterly stupid we've been."

Mourning felt a liquid gush of warmth and she knew she loved and needed this man above everything. Feeling compelled to share this with him, she lifted her head to look at him, and miracle of miracles, his beautiful gray eyes were clear and shining as his mouth curved into a smile.

His warm, arousing gaze wandered over her face, to her slightly parted lips, then lower, past the wild fluttering in her throat, to the swell of softly rounded breasts. Then he searched her face, pleading urgently without saying a word. But what he said to her in that way, the words he spoke with his eyes—the agony, the regret, the despair—they all moved her, but it was the look of terror, the almost pathetic despair of loving and not being loved in return, that told her what she wanted to hear.

Too many brain waves were slamming against her skull as his head came closer. *He's going to kiss me! He's going to kiss me! After all this time, he's finally going to kiss me! Oh, joy! Oh, happiness! Oh, God! I'm so nervous! What if I've forgotten how? Don't be a sap, Mourning Kathleen.*

"Dear God, how I've missed you," he whispered hoarsely, as his mouth covered hers with a wide slanting kiss that left little doubt that she was being claimed and possessed by this incredible man. His hands were passing over her in light inquiry, forcing her close, as if he couldn't get close enough. Her own body floating, her arms traveled across the warm living muscle of his chest, feeling the pounding thud of his heart beneath his smooth cotton shirt, while his palms searched with an almost desperate urgency before dropping to fan across her buttocks and lift her against him.

His mouth left hers with trembling reluctance, and then he rested his forehead gently against hers. It was too much, this exquisite feeling of holding her once again, the taste of her mouth against his, the feel of her body, so very different when she was willing. Her eyes flew open and she saw the bold, unguarded hunger in his eyes. His voice, when he spoke, was unsteady with frustration. "Mourning, my love, my life. I came to convince you, not to seduce you."

He continued to hold her firmly against him and her hands were still splayed across the smooth muscle of his back. It was so easy to be with him like this, and so natural to move with him, from stiff fear into the rhythmic press of hips that moved one against the other. And then he pulled away.

"Well, what's it to be?" he asked. "Are you going to spend the rest of your life dancing in and out of danger and driving me insane with your infuriating logic while you pull the most damnable stunts imaginable? Or have you decided to retire from the limelight and marry me?"

She barely looked at him. He had hurt her so much, but her mind kept going back to that night after he had returned after so many years.

I loved you once. It should have been enough.

It isn't enough now. I want you.

It's too late. There are some things that can't be forgotten.

I want you to marry me.

I can't marry a man I have learned to hate so well.

I'm not your enemy, Mourning.

Oh, but you are! You are my enemy, can't you see that?

It's always been like this between us, hasn't it? We've always been at opposite ends of everything, never able to agree. Even now. Especially now, when you can't see me as anything but your enemy . . .

Because you are!

What a pit of wretchedness we've dug for ourselves. You call me your enemy . . . when I call you my love.

"Dear God, Mourning, are you going to drive me insane? Say something, for God sake! Don't keep me standing here with my tail tucked between my legs, begging."

"I don't exactly call this begging."

"Is that it? Is that what you want? Is that what you've been waiting for? To see me humbled more? To see me crawl on my belly? Damn you!" he said. "Damn you to hell!"

And then, as she stood before him, tears running down her cheeks, he dropped to his knees before her. "I'm here. On my knees and begging. Please," he said. "For the love of God!" and then his arms came around her knees and he buried his head against her legs, his shoulders shaking.

She slid down to the floor beside him, his arms still around her, and she was kissing him, across the forehead to the dip at his temple and along his jaw and across the beginning of whiskers down to his throat, feeling the wetness on his face and hers too, coming together.

She knew what he was asking of her, that he would not accept a compromise. Not this time. He had asked her to marry him, but that wasn't enough. He was asking for her surrender, her unconditional surrender, because in humbling himself before her he had surrendered himself. He had done everything he could, and now, this wonderful, beautiful man had emptied himself for her. She held him to her, seeing what she had bought with her stubborn pride, the price he had paid. Dear God! She *had* wanted him on his knees. She had thought of nothing else for years. Wanting to see him humbled, to make him pay. Stupid. Foolish. But true. *But I didn't know he would look so broken.* And she didn't know she would feel so alone. Through damp layers of twisted clothing and moist skin, she heard herself whisper, "I love you, and I'm so sorry. I don't know what else to say."

He didn't reply, but she felt his body stiffen, as if hardening against her. When she looked into his face his eyes were tightly closed, an expression of pain on his face. Then with a shattered whisper, she asked, "Is the offer still open?"

"I'll walk out of your life this minute if that's what you want. But don't patronize me, Mourning, and don't offer yourself as a sacrifice. I don't want you that way. I love you more than life. But

I won't accept half a life with you. I want it all. Or I want nothing. I want to spend the rest of my life with you, to put that well-loved look on your face each night and to wake to you, cuddled sleepy and soft against me, each morning. There is so much out there waiting for us and I want to give it all to you."

And I want it. Something deep within her cracked and a pain swelled within her chest, as if that hard shell around her heart were splitting and breaking away. "Will you kiss me now?" she asked.

"God, yes!" he said, his mouth closing over hers.

It was sometime later, as she lay in his arms drowsy and thinking how close she had come to throwing it all away, that she stirred, the memory painful and robbing her of sleep. She felt the warm brush of his breath across her face before he captured her wrists and held them against his chest. "Mourning, are you in pain?" The touch of his hand, gentle on her forehead, brought her more fully awake.

"No," she whispered. "I'm in love." There was a rectangular shaft of early-morning light shining through the door and striking the floor, and touching Clint with a silver blush. "Clint?"

"Hmmm?"

"Why are you here?"

"Isn't that obvious?"

"Humor me with the details," she said.

He told her about his talk with Cad and how he went to Caroline for her insight into feminine logic that he was so incapable of understanding. Then his hand moved to the side of her face and stroked the skin gently. "I came because I was desperate, because I couldn't stand the thought of one more day without you. I was at the end of my rope. . . . Saints preserve us, woman. I came because I love you."

Pressing closer, she began to kiss the warm strength of his neck. "Did I ever tell you," she said softly, "how I would lie in bed at night thinking about you, after you were gone?" Her face still against his neck, her every word brought the delicious touch of her lips against his earlobe with trilling little vibrations that shot straight to his heated loins. "I would think about the magic your fingertips would bring, the way they knew just where to touch me."

She felt the sudden change of his rhythmic breathing and her tongue touched the sensitive lobe of his ear, quick and light. "I wanted you to touch me, Clint, so much, my skin was alive with sensation. I found myself undoing the buttons of my gown and slipping inside to touch my breasts the way you did."

His hands moved to cup her face. "Don't," he said with a broken catch to his voice. "Sweetheart, you don't have to do this." He brushed her lips with his. "Kiss me, Mourning. Kiss me like you used to."

Her mouth opened against the gentle thrust of his tongue, like a tulip in warm sunlight. Her hand glided down his shirtfront, slipping the buttons from their binding, until she could slide her hand against the heat of his smooth, firm flesh, traveling lower to stroke the furrowed rows of his ribs.

Suddenly Clint was on his feet, lighting the lamp and carrying her, blankets and all, through the door and out to the wagon, where he deposited her. A minute later he was back, leading the horses and hitching them to the wagon. He climbed in next to her. "Don't you want to get in the back and sleep some. You haven't had much sleep these past two nights."

"Neither have you."

"I'm used to it. I haven't had a decent night's sleep since you cracked my skull in Memphis."

"That was such a long time ago, wasn't it?"

He nodded, tucking the blankets more tightly around her.

"Where are we going?"

"To Fredericksburg," he said, slapping the reins.

"Why Fredericksburg?"

"Because it's the closest."

"For what?"

"For a wedding."

"Oh." She smiled, and began to sing, terribly off key.

Lead, kind-ly Light, a-mid th' en-cir-cling gloom. Lead Thou me on; The night is dark, and I am far from home; Lead Thou me on. I loved the garish day, and, spite of fears, Pride ruled my will: re-mem-ber not past years . . .

"Kincaid, why are you kissing me now?"

"Because, my warbling magpie, it's the only way I can find to shut you up."

She smiled and tugged his head down for another kiss. "Well, then, as long as you're here . . ." Her words trailed off as Kincaid's breath moved warmly over her. "Will you take me to New Orleans for my honeymoon?" she whispered against his mouth.

"I'll take you to hell and back, if that's what you want."

"I might have known," she said crossly.

"Love, what have I done?"

"I might have known I'd get an offer like that." She heard his indrawn breath when her hand went searching. "When I was thinking of going to heaven."

He chuckled against her throat. "I'll take you to bed for that," he said as his mouth came searching. He shut her up good and proper this time.

They were married the next morning, in a small rock house that was filled with hundreds of chiming and striking clocks and smelled heavily of sauerkraut. The minister was a German immigrant who spoke broken English, but was, Clint swore to her, an ordained Lutheran minister. Exhausted, sleepy, and full of dazed wonder, Mourning kept trying to lie down upon the sofa. "No, sweetheart, it won't be long now. Just a few more words, then you can sleep. Say the words, Mourning. No, darling. Not the words to the song. *I do.* Say, *I do.*"

When the ceremony was over, the minister, a plump, ruddy-faced man with a wife who was even plumper, declared unhappily this was the first wedding he had ever been roused from a dead sleep to perform at six o'clock in the morning.

The minister's wife declared even more unhappily, this was the first wedding she had ever witnessed where the bride sang hymns and tried to go to sleep throughout.

Mourning began to sing again. Clint tried to silence her once with his hand over her mouth, but she pushed it away and chirped rather sleepily, "Kincaid, kiss my mouth shut, you wonderful man." When he looked at her with that strange look he always had just before he pounced, she giggled. Poking his shirtfront, she said, "Just pretend you're sucking the juice from an orange."

～ 34

Mourning was staring at a half-finished cup of hot chocolate, but she wasn't really seeing it, because she wasn't really looking. In fact, she was not even aware. She wasn't exactly in a daze, but rather in a state of suspension where her mind, heavy and slow with apathy, was receiving not one message transmitted to it. She was completely lost in an inert state that is rarely reached, except by dogs lying under a shady bush on a sleepy summer day, or by young boys in school who'd rather be anywhere else.

Outside, a rooster crowed and a bumbling little bumblebee was buzzing furiously, bumping and thumping against the windowpane in a repetitious frenzy, knocking himself senseless to get at a tempting display of tulips blooming in brilliant reds and yellows in a blue crockery pot on the sunny windowsill.

"Mama, Mama, Clay went outside and the mud is dry. Can we go out now?" Katy shouted as she rounded the corner and fluttered through the kitchen door like a yellow sunflower in a wind current. "Can we, please?"

"If you can stay out of the puddles, Anna Katherine . . . and tell your brothers to do the same," Mourning added, knowing mud puddles would be their first stop. Katy left the lid off the cookie jar, as she always did, and ran out the back door. Mourning heard her chiming, "We can, we can," followed by a loud splash. "Gabe! you big booby! You got my cookies all ruint!" Mourning buried her head in her arms, wondering what she was going to do with a chocolate-dipped sunflower with a fistful of *ruint* cookies.

Slowly the recuperative power of nature began to fill the void that existed between Mourning's ears. Dragging and sluggish, she felt soul-worn to the point of revulsion by that scourge of motherhood, inclement weather. It had taken her the better part of the day to reach one simple conclusion. Catastrophe hangs like the sword of Damocles when bad weather forces capricious characters to be contained for a prolonged period. She was not, however, the first to discover this phenomenon. Having no scientific background, she did not realize that the more tightly steam boilers and young children are contained, the more likely it is for an eruption to occur.

After a morning of wars and rumors of wars, where the children beat their playthings into weapons and their mother into a state of near hysteria, the rain had blessedly stopped and further toll on Mourning was blessedly avoided. After a week of rain, the children had turned their energies upon Mother Nature, who, Mourning felt, was much better equipped to deal with them.

It was while Mourning was in this somnolent state that Clint tramped into the kitchen like a Tibetan yak in nuptial plumage. Giving her a smile that would melt a furnace, he asked, "My love, what's amiss? You look like you've been wrestling wildcats."

This fatal attempt at levity was hatched from an earnest desire to cheer her up, but he knew the minute the words left his mouth, it had fallen way short of his intended mark. Mourning lifted eyes that would make a basset hound look cheerful and said morosely, *"Lay on, Macduff."*

Clint himself poured a cup of coffee and took a seat across the table from her. "Sweetheart, what is troubling you?"

She shook her head, too tired to answer, and he could see the strain of fatigue in the slump of her shoulders. To Clint, it was as if some deeper, underlying sadness had stripped her of her sparkle and strength, like petals plucked from a flower in full bloom. Anxiety began to chew at him. Was she falling away from him because of something he had done? The wedding? It ate at him, that in spite of his desire never to force Mourning again, he had used subterfuge to make her his wife. And that had bothered him, more than he would care to admit.

Whatever it was, it touched him deeply, making him want to hold her against him and fill her with love and laughter. It was as if some giant octopus had encircled him, crushing and wrapping him in an inky blackness that penetrated every corner of his being.

He studied her, noticing her skin was pale and her lips paler still. Even her beautiful green eyes had lost their clarity. There was a pensive loneliness to the way she sat with her hands curled almost lifelessly around her cup. A shaft of sunlight reflected from the glitter of stones set in her wedding band brought his mind back from where it had strayed.

She must have sensed his eyes on her and she met his gaze, giving him a lovely smile that he could see straight through. Perhaps it was her attempt to hide her feelings that caused his breath to still for a brief moment, and a slender golden thread of desire to wind itself around his heart.

A sudden drumroll of her heart and an airy light-headedness within her answered the flicker of heat she had seen in his eyes. It was almost painful to look at him, his long-shanked frame draped in the chair with casual ease, one arm stretched across the table, the other resting by his cup. There was a look of contrast to him that she found electrifying. Her gaze moved back to his face, and Clint gave her a smile she wanted to pour over pancakes. That smile hacked like a scythe through the weariness she had allowed to overshadow her cheerfulness.

"Sweetheart, can you tell me . . . is it something I've done?" The enfolding warmth of his hand came across the table seeking hers, and she gave him a smile of acceptance and gratitude. It was all the encouragement he needed. He came around the table, sliding onto the bench beside her, drawing her into his arms, pressing her head against the warm, fertile smell of his skin.

"Angel mine, what can I do to take some of this burden from you? You look as weak as pond water."

To his enjoyment she said in a woeful little voice, "If you really want to help, then next time the children want to know where babies come from, *you* explain it."

With a teasing light of sudden understanding in his eyes, he said, "Ah, a wearisome task at best. I take it you found it not to your liking?"

How could she put into words what had started out all so innocently and then turned into a nightmarish act? "It was worse than that."

"I'm sure you handled it beautifully," he said sympathetically.

He lifted his hand to tilt her face, his smooth fingers stroking her throat, his lips warm and dry on hers, and he felt the quickening of the desire that was ever present when he was with her.

"What idea did you expound upon: babies are a gift from God; sex, like dirty laundry, should be kept in a wicker basket; the great octopus theory; or everyone's favorite—I found you on the doorstep?"

She smiled faintly, but spoke crossly. "I tried to be a little more realistic than that."

"Oh, Lord, not Insert rod A into cog B and fasten down hinge C and bake until done?"

"Close," she said with a hopeless laugh. "The horrible fact is, I endured all those hideous and shameful moments when I desperately searched for the right words, drew pictures, and hoped beyond hope that what I had to say would be put to their fragile little minds in a manner that would be enlightening and yet sufficient. Then Katy had the audacity to look me in the face and say, 'But Mama, I only wanted to know where you got me. Grandma said she was borned in a house and Mrs. Harper was borned in a wagon and Mildred's kittens were borned in the barn. Where was I borned?' "

Clint's fingertip absorbed a crystal droplet that slid down her satiny cheek. "All the agony I went through giving them a multitude of colorful details and glaring facts . . ." Mourning's words became a garbled choke. Gaining control once more, she continued, "And all she wanted to know was where she was born."

Lean, hard fingers closed over her shoulders and Mourning found herself hauled into her husband's arms. His eyes held hers and searched, then silently carried her palms to his lips to press a kiss there. Returning to her shoulders, Clint began to massage her neck, sending exquisite sensations running up and down her back. *"Mmmmm."*

He kissed the soft spot just below her ear. "Feel better?"

"Ummm-hmmm. Much."

His fingers moved to the outer extremities of her shoulders and began to work the same magic there, before moving down her arms. Mourning relaxed against him. "Is there anywhere else you feel tense?"

Mourning nodded.

"Where, darling? Show me."

Mourning touched the soft skin of her throat, just above her collarbone. "Here."

Grinning, Clint whispered in muted, husky tones. "For delicate areas like this, I always recommend kisses." He lowered his head and nipped and nuzzled the soft flesh, and declared softly, "I love you, Mrs. Kincaid. Although God alone knows I fought against falling in love with a rebellious little blonde with hopelessly snarled hair and the strangest inclination to go through life like she's walking on a waxed floor."

This was the most absurd rendering of loving endearments, Mourning thought blissfully. She had received one heart-stopping declaration of love from this handsome, arrogant rogue that she loved beyond endurance—she wasn't likely to get another.

He felt her tremble. "My love, where else are you uncomfortable?"

Her fingertips brushed against his cheek as she touched her forehead. "Here."

Clint's curiosity wasn't the only thing aroused. He tightened his grip gently and felt her responsive tremors. His breath was warm and rich upon her forehead as he touched it with soft, gentled kisses, then lightly with the tip of his tongue. "Where else?" he asked softly.

Trembling fingers swept over the sprinkling of curls that lay over her small, shell-pink ear. "A little here," came a sweet, subdued voice muffled through layers of cotton shirt and leather vest. With difficulty, Clint conquered the inelegant urge to shove her back on the bench and show her what they'd both been missing for five years.

It was a painful lump that came to her throat as seasoned fingers glided down across her cheek, rubbing gently the constricted sinews of her throat. The heat from his body surrounded her, his lips fondling the delicate curl of her ear. "Where else?"

Eyes as green, intoxicating, and addictive as absinthe caressed him with a saturating heat, rolling like heated oil over coiled muscle and tightly stretched tendon. His pulse was beating thickly in his body and hammering in his ears as he watched her touch her fingertips to her lips. "Here," she whispered.

Overpowering because of the delicacy of it, a subtle message of desire dripped like a heady fluid across his body. Skimming his lips across skin as soft as a rose petal, he bent, bringing the liquid heat of his mouth down upon hers.

Warm, liquid sensations closed over her as hard lips brushed soft ones with the teasing promise of something more. Just when she was sure she was bordering on idiocy, Clint suddenly withdrew the soothing support of his arms.

"I'll check on the children," he said, and walked from the room.

She watched him go, a persistent memory of their last kiss dwelling in her mind. While it had possessed the heated intensity of the others, there had been a haunted message of promise . . . a luring quality that had not been present before. Her pulse began to pound softly when she regarded the rakish ease with which his fluid length turned from her and walked from the room.

Slow comprehension eased into her uncertain mind. Now she understood the full significance of that kiss and the invitation it carried. The choice was hers. He would not force her.

A slow, unhurried little smile tugged itself into position. So Kincaid wanted to be seduced. Remembering Goethe's words, "You must either conquer and rule or serve and lose, suffer or triumph, be the anvil or the hammer," Mourning whispered to the door he had just walked through. "You beautiful, ridiculous man, you're about to find yourself well hammered." Then she smiled happily, as she thought, *Every man can be had one way or another.* Mentally masterminding a seduction of mammoth proportions, Mourning poured herself another cup of coffee. Voltaire, she decided, knew what he was talking about when he said, "It is not enough to conquer; one must know how to seduce." Before this night was over, there would be little doubt in Clint Kincaid's mind that he had been seduced, and royally.

As Mourning dressed for bed she began to think she'd rather be kidnapped again than walk into Clint's room with him watching her, knowing what she was about. Her gown was of ice-blue satin with tiny white silk roses tied with streamers of love knots on the shoulders and again just below her breasts. A gift from Caroline, it made Mourning feel more like she was about to make her debut into society than seduction.

Mourning stood before a cheval mirror as she tied the ribbon of the robe under her chin, the three-inch ruffles of Alençon lace falling back against her wrists. Two glasses of red wine had done little to calm her jittery nerves, so she polished off three more. Armed to the teeth with every seductive trick known to woman, and all the intestinal fortitude five glasses of red Bordeaux could provide, she was ready. She marched to Clint's room thinking it might have taken five years to wed him, but she wasn't going to waste five more minutes in trying to bed him.

By the time she stepped into Clint's room, Mourning was having second thoughts. By the time she stepped up to the bed and saw her husband's desirable body outlined, with breathtaking detail, beneath a thin sheet, she was ready to spring upon him. But by the time her eyes drifted up to his eyes that were closed in sleep, she was ready to dump the entire vase of white narcissus on the nightstand over his stupid head. Asleep? How could he?

Kicking off her shoes and draping her dressing robe on a nearby chair, Mourning bounced into bed, with more vigor than necessary. Arms crossed, and leaning against the carved cherry headboard, she studied the face of her husband. His healthy tanned skin was as fragrant and fresh as tomorrow morning's biscuits, and she felt like a woman coming off a two-month fast: starving and desperate.

Clint was beautiful. Clint's body was beautiful. What she wanted to do to Clint was beautiful. There was so much about him she adored: the way he moved with all the lissome grace and flexibility of a graceful dancer; the well-honed features polished to perfection yet possessing a degree of restraint; the quick and clever wit; the seductive looks, possessive touch, addictive words. Every endearing quality he possessed—they were all working together to create a masterpiece of aesthetic value. Yet the soft play of lantern light upon his absorbing features struck with such subtle swiftness, she wondered if she would ever recover from the sheer force of it.

It is said that a person at death's door will see a reenactment of his entire life flash before him, and so it was with Mourning. Immersed in the very essence of him, she began to see in retrospect a recounting of their past. Every glaring episode, each resplendent encounter, was described to her with sudden revivification. Suffering symbolic death, she was able to forgive him and herself for every misdeed; the words of anger; the acts of foolish pride; the omissions; the humiliations; the deeds of youth and immaturity; and most of all, the foolish inclination to hurt the one you love most of all. It was a humbling experience, and in being so humbled, she emptied herself of all the hurt and bitterness. Bereft of the gnawing pain, her bruised spirit and wounded soul were pervious to the deluge of warm and rosy memories that prevailed.

She lifted her hand and allowed her finger to trail lightly along the path of a prominent blue vein that ran through the muscled bicep of his arm. "Wake up, you crazy, wonderful man," she whispered softly. Clint slept on. She let her hand drop to her lap, her fingers toying with the satin streamers of her gown. "It's a good thing," she said softly, "that we've got three children, because it looks like we won't be having any more."

She almost straightened the love knots in her ribbons when she felt the bed shake with his laughter and heard his deep voice, husky with humor.

"And what would you say, my cherished love, if I said I wanted at least five more children?"

"You're either feverish or you believe in miracles," she said woefully. He smiled a lazy, sleepy smile that made little shivers of pleasurable anticipation go trilling across her flesh. She studied his splendid gray eyes before looking away with concentrated effort. "I've given the matter much thought. Kincaid, *why* did you marry me?"

He lifted a shapely finger and stroked it lightly, masterfully, down the length of her arm. "Because I love you, my moonstruck little charmer, more than I could ever hope to show you."

Kincaid, it appeared, possessed, among other talents, a staggering flair for the understatement. *"That,"* she said with an expression that could only be described as crestfallen, "is the problem. You haven't shown me anything."

He gazed at her through eyes alive and rich with merriment. "My love, can you tell me how I've failed you? I had thought, no, I had most earnestly strived to be most thoughtful and considerate of you since our marriage. It distresses me to think I have fallen short. Can you tell me how I have disappointed you?"

She crossed her arms deliciously in front of her, having no idea what that one move was costing him in self-control. "You have been thoughtful and considerate, *too* thoughtful and considerate. We've been married for one whole week, and you haven't touched me. . . ."

There was a slight pause of consideration. Then he slowly lifted one of the ribbons on her shoulder and began to rub it with his thumb. The faint brush of his skin against hers set her heart to thumping like a nervous rabbit-foot. She frowned at him as if considering something, then said, "Kincaid, how old are you?"

His dark brows arched in surprise. "Thirty-three." Then he laughed. "My love, of all the things I expected you to discuss, my age was not among them. What exactly *does* my age have to do with anything?"

"A great deal." Her voice was prim and slightly irritated. "I've heard that when men get older they forget how . . . that they lose interest . . . Oh, stuff! Kincaid, I was wondering if you are getting too old to . . ."

Booming laughter cut her words short. His laughter, if that was any indication, was healthy and potent. "Mourning bright, my own adorable truelove, you are so innocuously frank. I hope to calm your fears, my heart's love, by assuring you I am a normal, functioning male in *every* sense of the word. I think we can safely assume I have a *few* good years left . . . at least enough to devote all my energies to making all the little faces we will ever want."

He looked at her with lazy, sensuous eyes as he let a finger trail over her cheekbone. "My darling girl, it is paramount to my eternal gratification to sustain you in a state of pampered contentment with a look of blissful ravishment upon your angel face."

Mourning wondered if he had any idea what the mere touch of his hand on her face was doing to her internal mechanism. Viscerally speaking, there was a free-for-all going on. Nothing was where it should be or doing what it was supposed to be doing. She gripped the bedcovers tightly in her hands. "Your subterfuge won't work. You can't divert me by trifling with the issue. A *normal* man does not wait a full week to make love to his bride."

He raised up on his elbow, the bulge in his arm curving and hard as the bedcovers slipped down the naked musculature of his chest. Golden light from the lantern dripped like melted butter over his bare skin to where the blanket lay low on his hips. His hand left her cheek to sift a silky curl through his fingers. "The impediment here, my love, is not a matter of insufficient desire, nor is it my dereliction of duty by nonperformance. The rub here is simply a matter of slight omission, a lack of communication . . . intercourse, if you will." He smiled softly at the rose-petal flush to her cheeks.

He studied the confused, frustrated look on her face. Poor

green-eyed creature, all this time it had been so hard to stay away from her, trying to give her time to heal and adjust to their speedy marriage, and she felt rejected. It pained him to cause her a thimbleful of pain, yet he knew he had been right. A flash of memory came to him, reminding him of his forceful nature with her before the war. That had all changed now, but how could he hope to make her understand? His only way, he had thought, was to give her time, to let her see he considered the wait a small price to pay for the happiness she brought him. How could she know, how could he put into words how the waiting had him tied in knots?

Clint was glad it had come to this, he couldn't wait another day and maintain any relationship with the rest of the family. Even good-natured Cad had informed him this morning that he was not welcome in his room another night. "The only way your ugly hide is going to set foot in my room for another night is to be carried in on a stretcher . . . out cold. Having you sleep four feet away, listening to your moaning restlessness, is keeping me awake, and I need my beauty sleep. I'm not a married man."

Clint's eyes traveled over his wife, drinking in her beautiful form washed in dusky shadows by the soft light that heightened her loveliness; the jewellike intensity of her eyes, the tiny nose, the tumble of golden hair.

Correctly reading his look and lifting a shapely leg, Mourning brushed her toes against a hairy length of bare leg peeking beneath the sheet. Beginning at his foot, she continued to his knee, then traveled back to his foot, where she nudged him with her toes. As she continued to fondle his foot with hers, she saw there was a deeper intensity to his gray eyes and his breathing was ragged, almost harsh. She continued the assault.

"Darling, I was—I have been trying to consider your wellbeing before my own." His words tumbled forth in a troubled rush.

Smiling to herself, Mourning began to trail her fingertips lightly over the generous play of sleek, flowing muscle that formed his belly. Clint's breathing, which was already unsteady, caught in his throat. He watched the sly smile tiptoe across her lovely face and he wondered if he would ever be able to fully relate to her what she meant to him, how much he loved her, and how hard, no, unbearable, it had been for him to sleep away from her for the past several nights.

Closing his eyes to gather his composure, which was scattered like leaves in a wind eddy, Clint felt the cool drape of sweet-scented hair glide across his chest like slippery silk. Underneath the attar-of-rose–scented hair, his stomach muscles contracted powerfully. "Love, I know I'm not making much sense to you . . ." The unsteady rhythm of his words faded. At great cost, he managed to finish, "But I seem to be functioning with only a small portion of my mind."

"Where's the rest of it? Lost?" Consciousness of the effect she was having upon him made her more daring.

"Mourning, my love . . ." The ragged inbreathing of her name was followed by a sharp, shuddering gasp as Mourning dispersed a riot of unsophisticated little kisses, strategically placed along the edge of sheeting that rode low on his hips. He lifted a finger to follow the line of lace across the rise and fall of her breasts. ". . . the rest . . . the rest is going insane trying to imagine what you look like under that gown and striving to the point of desperation to convince the rest of me to shut up and give you what we both want."

"Shut up, you wonderful, impossible man, because I aim to lead you as far astray as you've led me. Then I'm going to engage you in a skirmish, the likes of which you've never seen. And I might warn you, Kincaid," she said, sliding her hands beneath the sheet, "I don't take prisoners."

Cherry-red lips trailed a path of fiery kisses down the corded muscle of his thigh, and Clint said, in laborious assent, "Jesus!" As she kissed a flaming trail back across his belly and down the other powerful leg, he whispered brokenly, "I can see why you don't take prisoners, my love. After an invasion of this magnitude I'm a smoldering heap."

Sitting back on her heels, Mourning chirped happily. "By the time I've finished with you, there won't be any heap to smolder. You're living on borrowed time, Kincaid, and it won't do you a bit of good to erect any more barriers between us and then blame me."

As he watched his wife slide the satin streamers from her shoulders, the wide grin on Clint's face became an openmouthed gasp. With a hungry growl, Clint enfolded her warm body tightly in his arms, then rolled her beneath him. "My darling love, my most precious wife, there is only one erection between us now, and it is entirely your fault," he mumbled thickly.

"We women do what we have to do with what we have to do it with," she said with feigned lightness.

He grinned at her. Even his eyes were smiling. "Does that last statement mean you're about to claim your conjugal rights?"

With a seductive twist of her hips, her hand curved around the back of his head, pulling him to meet her offered kiss. Weakly she declared, "Only if you're not up to doing it yourself."

He lowered his head to kiss the top of one breast and then the other. When he heard her gasp, he felt a responsive shimmy of longing run the entire length of his body. "Rising to the occasion seems to be automatic whenever you're around." Seeing the rousing intensity in her eyes, he said huskily, "My love, my own true love, shall we see for ourselves what we've been missing these past five years?"

Clint stopped her next words with his mouth. Sensitive fingers glided across the pearly satin of her shoulder to tangle in the hair at her nape, pulling her forward to meet the thrust of his clever tongue. Whatever she was going to say flew out the window.

When he lifted the heat of his mouth from hers, he cupped her face with trembling fingers and stroked across inactive vocal cords —quivering and paralyzed to inaction. She opened love-glazed eyes that seemed to see everything in *couleur de rose,* to look into his passion-flushed face. She was lost in an impatient rapture when his talented fingers began to play across skin stretched tighter than a drumhead from the growing pressure within her. Through a shimmering veil of gauzy color, she saw the deep, smoky glitter of his eyes, heavy with passion, and shuddered deeply when the heat of his breath floated like a shower of fragrant rose petals upon her throat.

His husky laughter brushed across her face when she murmured his name weakly. "Before we go any further," she said in a soft, pleading sound that didn't sound very convincing, "I think we need to get something straight between us."

"My dearest love, that is my most treasured desire," was all he managed to say before irrepressible laughter consumed him.

A rosy radiance drifted across her delicate features and her brilliant green eyes snapped shut in persecuted frustration. "You've got me so confused, I don't know what I'm saying with all this coming at me hammer and tongues."

He tried to bury his laughter against the softness of her throat.

He stroked a long finger across her nose. "My precious love, I would like to hammer at you with more than my tongue. You have no idea how difficult it has been not to." He made a conscious effort to gain the control that was fast slipping away.

Pushing his hand away, she looked up into a face framed with sleep-tousled hair, letting her eyes rest on the slightly parted lips. "Why didn't you? What were you waiting for?"

His thumb began to brush across the fullness of her lower lip and he lost himself in the soft, liquid eyes that held him mesmerized in a swirling pool of green. "I have been waiting," he whispered hoarsely, "for some indication from you to tell me you were ready." He leaned forward and pressed a kiss against the smooth satin that shimmered along the length of her slim leg. Again she lost her train of thought as dizziness swept across her in spinning whirls. She looked at him through clover-green eyes that drugged him like an opium-induced mist.

"Love, you look at me like that much longer and I may forget all my good intentions and assert my marital rights before you're ready," he said with a hoarse whisper.

Light-headed from his tender smile and her wits sufficiently addled from the inundation of loving words, she pounded the pillow in frustration. "But that's just what I want you to do."

A spark showered in the fireplace as a gust of wind tumbled down the chimney, drawing her attention. When she looked back at him, his gaze was warm and alive, his eyes lowering to the exquisite slope of her throat, the beautiful curves of her breasts. "Don't look upon yourself as something for me to pleasure myself with. You are my wife, Mourning, my partner. You give me more than I could ever return. Whenever you desire me, my beloved, the ways you can show me are as numerous as the stars in the Milky Way. They are every bit as abundant as the ways I can show you."

His extraordinary eyes came back to hers. "It is my most cherished desire, my adorable angel, that you understand what I am saying to you, because I honestly don't think I can maintain my mental balance five more minutes. Will you come to me, love?"

Her eyes strayed back to his, meeting a subtle tempting gaze that wrapped her in a wild, energetic heat—intense to the point of being distressful. "You have been waiting for me?" she said, with a whisper of dazed confusion.

"Love, that has always been the case." There was a raw hun-

ger, fierce and possessive, glimmering in his eyes. The promise she
saw there locked her thoughts in reverie, and that fantasy led to a
riotous extravaganza.

An answer flamed within her—a swelling desire brimming
with honey and wine. She closed her eyes. "All this time," she said
disbelievingly, "the only thing that separated us was a few pitiful
words. All along, even when I thought you so far away, you have
really been so close."

A flood of relieved exuberance washed across his tense features. "As close as your fingertips."

Rolling away from him, she sat up, her legs curled beneath
her, her hands resting on her thighs. Trailing one fingernail across
his chest, she said, "I should be very angry with you. It's a painful
lesson you teach, and a hard bargain you drive as well. But tonight," she said, with a twinkle in her voice, "I'm feeling quite
benevolent."

Clint leaned back in the bed, crossing his arms behind his
head. In a soft tone he said, "You will never know, my life, how
glad I am we had this talk and you understand."

"Oh, I understand," she said, with a soft, unfocused veil
drawing over the teasing glint in her eyes. "I understand perfectly." She leaned forward, holding her body just above him, her
hands resting on each side of him. "You will find," she said wickedly, "unlike you, I find I am not the least bit reluctant to attack
you with wholehearted vigor, unmercifully, until you scream cra-
ven. Before I'm finished, I'm going to pay you back for every tiny
thing you've ever done to me. And well you deserve it too."

"I surrender," he groaned thickly. Her body pressed close, her
breasts brushed across his chest with angel-hair softness. "Oh, yes,
love . . ." Her teasing mouth hovered over the rise of his, her
breath coming into him with balmy lightness. Reflexes jerked spasmodically when her hand fluttered along the length of his long
torso, wandering downward to flick lightly across the jutting rise of
his hips. "Oh, God . . ."

A mating drive surged through him in some mystic form of
primal communication, flaming to life like kerosene thrown on an
open fire: brilliant and bursting.

"Had enough yet, you scoundrel?" she asked, with a cheerful
ring to her husky voice.

"I think you should torture me relentlessly for . . ." His

breath was frozen on the intake when she began to kiss a smoldering path across his chest. She felt the quiver of smooth flesh under her lips, and becoming more confident, she began to circle his navel.

"Enough," he said in a gasping whisper, and she suddenly found their positions reversed. He gently laid his lips on hers, his tongue touching her with sweet, probing eroticism. His thumbs stroked the hollow of her collarbone before slipping her gown from her waist to collect about the flare of her hips.

Murmuring all the delicious things he wanted to do to her, he let his hands slide the shimmering folds of her gown from her hips, then turning her against him, he removed it completely. "So long . . . so very long I've waited to have you like this, my love." The cool, silken touch of her softly feminine skin against the feverish dampness of his own brought the prickling pressure within him to dizzying demand. The steady vibration of her breath had a deep, fluttering purr and she curled against him like a soft, cuddly kitten, absorbing him into her downy warmth.

Magically gilded from the golden blush of the lamp, her high, firm breasts were rising and falling with movement so tantalizing that a trembling current of desire shot through him. "Golden," he said, his voice husky and erotic. "Everywhere, you're gilded and glittering with gold. My little golden pheasant, my goldenrod, I shudder from your golden touch."

She shivered once when his lips brushed back and forth over her breast, and his tongue stroked her before taking the aching offering into his mouth. He was fully upon her now, and she moaned low and deep in her throat, arching herself against him.

"Yes . . . yes, my golden love, come with me." His thumbs rolling across her breasts with feather strokes, he whispered, "Sweet darling, you're as soft and white as a downy dovekie. I love to touch you here . . . your breasts, they're so heavy, they fit so perfectly in my hand."

Her breath spiraled away from her, out of pace with her body, and her blood was thick as honey slushing painfully through veins ringing with sensation. He began to move over her body, his husky coaxing words offering encouragement as his mouth scattered hot, wet kisses from her lips, across her cheek to her ear, then down across the tightness of throat.

Wonderful hands and magically talented fingers were singing

across her, sweeping her into a spiraling mass of nerve endings, every molten inch of her flesh responding to him like a sea anemone fluttering against the caressing current of the sea. Cupping his hands beneath her, he pressed the searing heat of his loins against her, spreading her legs.

His mouth came hungering, dipping into her and exploring her roughly, his tongue becoming bolder and more urgent. Little garbled, incoherent cries and utterances escaped her throat, and she laced her fingers through the thickness of his hair, pulling him closer still. He buried his face against her neck, his breath hot and exhilarating. "You smell so good, love—you're as fragrant as a musk thistle. All dewy and soft and golden. You've given me gold fever, love. I burn for you, Mourning. Let me come into you."

Oh, Clint, she thought, *you are so good at this, there could never be anyone as good as you.* His gaze locked with hers in a meeting full of desire and promise. "No, my darling, my love, don't close your eyes. I want your eyes open . . . I want to see your beautiful green eyes when I come into you."

A small, aching whimper fluttered from her and he heard the words, "I love you, Clint . . . I love you, I love you . . ." And then, looking into the depths of her eyes, drowning in a surging sea of green, he slipped into her warmth and he was home.

Locked in the warmth that flushed skins radiate to each other, he held her curved against him long after their erratic breathing had subsided. "I guess," she said with an irrepressible bubble to her voice, "that you've learned your lesson."

"How's that, love?"

"Next time I tell you I'm going to attack you, I bet you'll believe me."

"Not believe, love. Hope. I will diligently and fervently hope you will always take your frustrations out upon my poor unsuspecting body. Let me be your sounding board, your whipping post."

"Spare the rod and spoil the child?"

He raised his magnificent head and cocked one delightful brow at her. "You, my adorable angel, will never have to worry about being spoiled, because I fully intend to abuse you most severely with the rod."

She locked her arms around his neck and gave him a hasty peck. "Promise."

"Promise."

"Hmmm," she said thoughtfully. "You know, we just might have those five other children after all . . . now that you've decided that you love me."

He brushed the back of his hand along the hollow of her cheek. "I've always loved you, it just took me a long time to realize it. I think I fell for you the first time we met."

"That," she said, pushing herself up on one elbow and poking him in the chest, "was only because I crowned you with an ax handle."

He grinned deliciously. "I can assure you, love, that our first meeting was staggering, and . . ." His next words were cut short when she clamped her hand over his mouth. "Hey, what's this?"

"I'm trying to shut your magnificent mouth, you wonderful, crazy man," she said cheerfully. "I have something else on my mind." He inhaled sharply as her fingers trailed across his belly and disappeared beneath the sheet.

"I love your form of distraction, Mourning, my love. What else do you—"

She lowered her lips to his and shut his mouth in a most delicious manner.

"Now what are you doing?" he asked weakly.

"Kissing your mouth shut, you absurd man."

A lopsided grin spread below eyes that gleamed devilishly. "Well, I'll be damned," mumbled Clint Kincaid with lionhearted optimism, and then again, "Well, I'll be damned," and he gave himself up to his wife's silencing kiss.

 EPILOGUE

Lives of great men all remind us
We can make our lives sublime,
And, departing, leave behind us
Footprints on the sands of time.
Longfellow, "A Psalm of Life"

And that is how it was with them, and the years were kind to Mourning and Clint, giving them five additional children, three sons and two daughters. The combined ranches of Tierra and Citadel became the fabled XXX Ranch, and the names of Cad and Clint Kincaid are recorded with those of the greatest cattle barons of the era.

It's all gone now, the era of the cowboy, along with Cad and Clint and Mourning, but their descendants are still there, riding the same pastures, splashing across Sandy Creek in a four-wheel drive.

You can still go up to Dome Rock, where children once played, and look across the tin roof of a rambling old house the Kincaid family swears was built before Santa Anna's time. And if the sun is to your back, you'll see the white picket-fence surrounding an old cemetery in a grove of hackberries. They're all there now, the old-timers, as their great-grandchildren call them. And, if you happen to talk to one of the Kincaids while you're there, he'll show you the silver spurs and leather chaps that belonged to Clinton Kincaid, and the rosewood box that he gave a young girl from Memphis, Tennessee, named Mourning Kathleen—way back, before the Civil War. If you've got time, they'll show you that the music box still plays "The Yellow Rose of Texas."

You'll be invited to sit a spell on the front porch with its gray painted floor and blue ceiling. A wrinkled old hound will creep out of the myrtle bush and curl at your feet, his tail thumping madly.

As you sip a glass of lemonade, you'll hear how you can sit on the back porch at night, when the moon is a white rind in the pale sky and the wind sifts through the oaks and hackberries, and see the silhouette of two riders on the ridge, dark against the evening sky.

Experience the Passion
and the Ecstasy

☐ **AVENGING ANGEL** by Lori Copeland
Jilted by her thieving fiancé, Wynne Elliot rides
west seeking revenge...only to wind up in the
arm's of her enemy's brother.
10374-6 $3.95

☐ **DESIRE'S MASQUERADE** by Kathryn Kramer
Passion turns to treachery in Europe's Middle
Ages as Lady Madrigal and Stephan Valentine
are lost in a web of deception and desire.
11876-X $3.95

☐ **THE WINDFLOWER** by Laura London
Kidnapped by a handsome pirate, Merry
Wilding dreams of revenge on the high seas—
until she becomes a prisoner of her own
reckless longing.   19534-9 $3.95